THE
DEVOTED

THE
DEVOTED

A LOVE STORY

JONATHAN HULL

DANCING MUSE
PRESS

Sausalito, California

Library of Congress Control Number: 2012937109

Trade paperback ISBN: 978-0-9848218-3-9

July 2012

DANCING MUSE
PRESS

Sausalito, California

Manufactured in the United States of America

Book Cover and Layout Design by ◢◢theBookDesigners
Cover images © Krkr / Shutterstock.com, mikeledray / Shutterstock.com

Grateful acknowledgement is made as follows:

Excerpt from "Fern Hill" by Dylan Thomas, from *The Poems of Dylan Thomas*,
copyright ©1945 by The Trustees for the Copyrights of Dylan Thomas.
Reprinted by permission of New Directions Publishing Corp.

Excerpt from *The Essential Rumi*, translation by Coleman Barks, HarperCollins.
Reprinted by permission of Coleman Barks.

Excerpt from *The Captain and the Enemy* by Graham Greene, Penguin Classics.
Reprinted by permission of David Higham Associates.

Also by Jonathan Hull:

LOSING JULIA
THE DISTANCE FROM NORMANDY

For the latest news, reading group guides and more, visit:
www.jonathanhull.com

TO THE MEMORY OF
MY GRANDFATHER

Samuel H. Bingham

1895 – 1976

Time held me green and dying
Though I sang in my chains like the sea.

—DYLAN THOMAS

PART ONE

The South Pacific
March 2, 1944

Dearest Rebecca,

The mail's just come. All the men are silent as they read and reread their letters, eyes running like hounds from word to word. (It's not steel that holds this ship together but hope and lust.) Some smile and laugh out loud, others roll to their sides and hide their faces. Those without mail seem to shrink a little further into themselves, thoughts traveling down roads where it's easy to get lost. Me, I just like to hold your letters right up to my lips and breathe you all the way into my lungs. (I'd gladly eat the paper if it would bring you closer.)

The truth is, I've never thought about anything so much in my life as I think about you and still I'm not even close to being done because there is always something new to think about. But if I ever do reach the end I'm going to start right back at the beginning with your smile and your voice and your skin (that one takes a while) and your hands and legs and the way your head bobs when you laugh and all the different colors in your eyes and on and on so long as it takes for this war to end. And when I think I'll go mad for wanting you (I've seen it happen and it's not a pretty thing to behold), I'll tell myself that no matter how many miles this angry world puts between us we're never really apart because I've got plenty of you and you've got plenty of me and there is no force on this earth that could ever untangle us no matter what. Promise me you'll never forget that.

Yours forever,
Jim

CHAPTER ONE

I'LL ALWAYS THINK of them as the hands of God.

What I remember most is how large and powerful they looked as they strained toward me, fingers arched as they drew closer and closer. I told myself it was only a dream. I told myself the shrieking in my limbs and the heat and the noise were a dream too until suddenly the hands found me and lifted me and carried me into the cool, sweet air. And then I remember looking back and seeing the burning station wagon and the figure of a man struggling in the flames to save my parents. I knew as I watched him that it was too late, that I was now all alone. I tried to pull myself toward the fire but my arms and legs would not move. And then I tried to cry out to the man to *please save them* but no sound would come. I could only watch the rising flames and the black smoke and pray for my mother and father to appear, until finally the pain closed my eyes and pulled me deep inside to a place of darkness and quiet.

Thirty years later I could still see those hands perfectly, reaching for me, cradling me. But I never saw a face.

I was ten that summer. We'd driven all the way from Kentucky to Wyoming to visit the Grand Tetons because someone once told my father you just had to see them and it was the kind of dream he could afford. I remember we'd been singing ever since we'd stopped for lunch, my dad howling to country songs on the radio as my mother provided backup and I sat behind them wheezing into my brand new harmonica. We'd always made a lot of noise together, putting on skits and playing charades and generally carrying on like a traveling theater troupe. (My mother was voted most likely to be a movie star when she graduated from Franklin High, only instead she fell in love with my father and became a housewife, which left plenty of reserves for our family productions.) And then I must have fallen asleep because I never saw the oncoming pickup truck swerve into our lane. There was no time for Dad to do anything but understand what was coming; maybe ask why. Still, I always think of him reaching his arm across Mom to brace her because that's what he would have done.

We collided head on.

I spent three weeks in a hospital in Sheridan, strangers hovering over me with the saddest faces I'd ever seen. I don't remember much from that time but what I do remember I've tried to forget, except for the kindness of the staff. Once I could travel my Aunt Margaret took me to live with her and her four cats in Saint Louis, where I just pretended that I was still alive until one day when I was fifteen and I noticed that I could fill my lungs all the way without wanting to cry. Aunt Margaret was the one who called them *the hands of God*, thinking it might keep my seat anchored firmly in the pew at Riverside Assembly of God Pentecostal Church every Sunday. Actually, they belonged to a Wyoming rancher who happened to be passing by when he saw the crash. His name was Mike O'Donnell.

I hadn't seen him since that day. I called him once during a college road trip, thinking I'd make a detour and say hello, but he seemed so shy that I quickly got off the phone. I understood from his voice what he meant to say, that he figured my life had been hard enough without having to carry a debt that no man could repay. Besides, he'd only done what he'd been raised to do, even if he'd burned himself pulling at my parent's trapped bodies. (The driver of the pickup truck, a thirty-five-year-old contractor with a few drinks in his system, was later found twenty feet down a ravine, neck snapped.) So instead we sent each other embarrassed cards every Christmas, his usually depicting some horse or buffalo, his rough scrawl barely legible. *With warm wishes for the holidays, Mike O'Donnell.* He always sent me a card on my birthday, too, nothing but his signature at the bottom because the *Happy Birthday* part was already printed and I'm sure he figured that about covered the bases. I didn't send him a birthday card but I did send my school picture each year, still leaving me with plenty of spare wallet-sized photos, which I hid in a drawer with the previous year's overstock. (Did other kids really have so many relatives clamoring for their photo?) I also sent him announcements of my graduation from junior high and high school and then college and even my acceptance to graduate school. I sent him an announcement about my marriage, too, but not my divorce. There wasn't a card for that kind of thing and I couldn't see writing it in a letter.

I never realized just how much his cards meant to me until shortly after my fortieth birthday when I noticed he hadn't written. I'd just returned from Saint Louis where I'd looked into nursing homes for Aunt Margaret, who'd begun to complain that my mother never called. "She always could hold a grudge," Margaret would say with a weary sigh once I stopped correcting her because each time I did the news hit her fresh. (Wasn't it enough that people died once?) "If she wants to be cheap she can call me collect. You tell her that."

"Right. I'll tell her."

"Even as a little girl she was cheap. Wouldn't let me have one single tiny drink from her lemonade stand without paying." Aunt Margaret gave a thirsty grimace, wrinkles swarming like bees over her plump and powdered face. "Little Miss Penny-pincher."

"I'll make sure she calls."

"You do that. Lately I feel like we've been losing touch." She returned to knitting the scarf I knew she'd give me for Christmas, just like the one she'd given me for my birthday as well as the Christmas before, all of them the exact same pattern of maroon and green and yellow, which she insisted went well with anything, though I had my doubts.

My flight had been delayed and then tossed by storms and by the time I got back to my fourth floor apartment in Atlanta it was nearly midnight. I emptied my mailbox, holding the contents beneath my chin as I opened the door, then dropped my bag in the front hall, took off my wet shoes and coat and headed for the kitchen where I poured myself a glass of wine, determined to wash the smell of nursing homes from my head. Then I sat at the counter finishing off a bag of stale pretzels while drinking a second glass of wine and glancing through the mail. Twelve messages flashed on the answering machine: two from Aunt Margaret asking why I never visited, six from my boss asking where the hell I was and four from Lupo Martinez, a sixteen-year-old boy I'd unofficially adopted two years earlier as a little brother, or son, or something in between. I skipped straight to Lupo's messages, smiling to myself as he sang four different renditions of "Happy Birthday," each worse than the last. *Thank you, Lupo.* Then I finished my wine, showered and fell into bed, too tired to unpack. I was nearly asleep when it hit me: Mike O'Donnell hadn't sent a card. I immediately turned the light back on and searched through the mail a second time. Nothing.

I waited three more days, hoping he'd just been late, though he'd never been late before. After the third day it took me two more days to get the nerve up to call, fearing the worst and knowing where that would take me. When I reached his wife, Alessandra, and learned that he was dying of cancer I knew right away that I had to see those hands one more time. I had to see them and touch them and somehow find the words to give thanks for the gift I was still trying to be worthy of.

The next morning I was on a plane for Sheridan, staring out the window at the rough landscape below and wondering if over the years I had somehow become my own ghost.

CHAPTER
TWO

———⁓

HE CRAWLS THE last few feet, sheltering his face from the flames. *I'm coming for you*, he yells, but she does not answer. He moves closer, stopping twice to put out the fire in his hair. *Only a little further.* His eyes burn as he tries to blink away the smoke, heat blistering his skin. *Just a few more inches.* Now the pain is so intense that he feels his body recoiling but still he forces himself forward, straining to reach her. There, he has her arm. He pulls, gently at first, then harder. *Come on, come on, come on.* Then he sees her legs pinned beneath the vehicle. He adjusts his grip and tries again, harder this time, then so hard he fears he might break her arm but there's no time left. *Please let me save her.* He lets out a cry as the flames lunge at him, sending him reeling backward. He quickly picks himself up and charges back into the smoke and fire, slamming his shoulder against the burning car over and over to free the woman but he can't move it. When he reaches her again he grabs her beneath her armpits and yanks at her, screaming and yanking with everything he has until the heat is unbearable and he feels himself letting go without wanting to because he cannot hold on any longer. He stumbles backward and drops to his knees choking, eyes slammed shut.

Three more times he tries and three more times he is hurled back until finally he can no longer rise to his feet. Then he lies on

the ground coughing and staring sideways at the flames, knowing
he has lost.

*He was asleep in the back of a truck when they hit the German mine.
He awoke in midair as the explosion tossed him into a field along the
roadside and when he picked himself up he saw men struggling from
the vehicle, bodies on fire. He'd never seen anybody die before, not right
in front of him. Their screams were the worst part, so awful that he
wanted to cover his ears from it. And then as he started to retch all over
himself the Germans began firing from the hillside. He quickly wiped
his mouth, picked up his rifle from the ground and began firing back,
terror squeezing the trigger. Three hours later he was riding in another
truck, his mouth so dry he could hardly swallow.*

He forces himself to his knees, still coughing, then slowly to his feet,
eyes following the black smoke to the burning vehicle. *My weapon.*
He frantically searches the ground, then sees the boy curled up in
the grass by the side of the road. For a moment he just stares at the
boy, chest still heaving for air as he puts the day back together: he'd
been driving behind a pickup truck when suddenly it crossed lanes,
melding on impact with an oncoming station wagon. Instincts took
the wheel as he swerved, just barely avoiding the wreckage himself,
finally braking to a stop a hundred yards down the road and then
running back as fast as he could to help.

He'd gone for the boy first, kicking out the side window and
pulling him from the wreckage just as the flames spread. He looks
at the blackened station wagon. *There were two others, a man and a
woman in the front seat. The woman had been alive but he couldn't
free her. Not in time.* He hurries over to the boy and kneels beside
him. Blood covers the child's face and soaks though his shirt and
pants and one leg is bent backwards but he's breathing. *Keep breathing.* He gently takes the boy in his arms and lifts him, then carries
him to his truck. After placing him in the cab he jumps in the driver's side and starts the engine. When he puts his hands on the steering wheel they rear back in pain. Only then does he see how badly

they are burned, skin pink and black as they ooze into his lap. He tries again to grip the wheel but each time his hands slip, leaving flesh behind. Finally he tears off his shirt and rips it in two with his teeth, wrapping each hand as best he can. He looks at the burning station wagon one more time before pulling onto the road and making for the hospital in Sheridan as fast as he can, shouting to the Lord that the boy must live.

CHAPTER THREE

IT IS SAID THAT you can't go back in life, but that's not true. You can go back all right. You can go back as many times as you like.

You just can't change anything.

I was checked in for my flight and sitting at the gate an hour early, trying to lose myself in the passing faces and thinking I wasn't the only one who hadn't slept. I took a drink of my coffee, then another, forcing my eyes wide and consoling myself with the thought of all the turning points in history that were decided in a grim fog of insomnia. After glancing through a newspaper, I leaned my head back and closed my eyes, telling myself that perhaps I slept more than I thought I did, though I always told myself that and I never believed it because the math couldn't be more straightforward. I rarely got more than six or seven hours, but anything less than five and I felt like an Etch A Sketch that had been given a violent shake, whole swaths of personality suddenly illegible. I opened my eyes and looked at my watch. Forty-five minutes until departure.

I took another sip of my coffee, then caught the eye of a middle-aged woman in mid-yawn, her makeup slightly askew. I watched as she struggled against another yawn, which rose like a foamy bubble from the sea. Hopefully the pilot had a better night. After recovering, she straightened her dark green business suit, pulled out a compact and checked herself, sighing as she tucked the compact back in her purse. I imagined her as a pretty young girl bursting with possibility, then as an old woman content in the company of all the younger selves hidden safely inside, the years stretching and compressing like a mad accordion. When she looked over at me I smiled again and she smiled too, which made me feel better and perhaps her as well.

I finished my coffee, got up and walked around the terminal, my mind running through all the reasons I shouldn't get on that plane. What good would it do either of us? Wasn't I just digging up things that were best left alone? And yet I owed it to him. I owed my life to a man I'd never met, or not that I remembered. What did he remember? That was my real reason for wanting to go, wasn't it? Not so much to thank Mike O'Donnell as to find out what he saw and remembered of that day because I'd never really had anything solid I could beat my fists upon.

I'd tried for years to recall some sensation from the crash itself: the recoiling horror of impact, the awful sound of crumpling metal—how could I not remember something so... *loud*?—and yet I couldn't. I fell asleep and the world skipped a beat. When I awoke there was only pain and heat and the high-pitched sound of my own terror. I never saw my parents' bodies or any blood or even the clothes I'd worn that day. All I remembered were the hands reaching for me and seeing the car burning and then opening my eyes in the hospital, everything gone.

After buying another coffee I returned to the gate and took a seat by the window, watching my reflection in the tinted glass as a plane taxied into one ear and out the other. I turned and looked at the groggy woman in the dark green business suit, hoping for another smile, but she'd fallen asleep, her head pitched against her shoulder like a toppled statue on Easter Island. And then as I waited for the plane to board I began to wonder if maybe everyone has a secret agony, a fissure through which the elements first begin to nibble away at the soul. Something lost. Or perhaps something never found.

Sometimes both.

I closed my eyes, immediately feeling my chin against the hot car seat in front of me, Mom and Dad singing as I blew into my harmonica louder and louder and louder.

Flight 62 is now boarding.

I'd stayed up until nearly two the night before, cautiously tiptoeing and then wading through a set of four thick childhood photo albums, each one carefully assembled by my mother with neat handwritten captions—most ending in proud bursts of exclamation points—along with restaurant napkins and matchbook covers and postcards pressed carefully between the pages. I hadn't pulled them down from my closet shelf in years, hoping that if I left them alone, they'd do the same for me. Still, I caught glimpses of their waiting contents now and then, scenes flashing from their closed covers like bursts from a sorcerer's glass ball.

I started at the very first page, leaning my face up close to examine the baby boy with curly hair and buttery cheeks all wrapped tight and full of sleepy peace. I quietly followed along as he crawled and ran and clowned his way across the pages one after another, year upon year, right up until three weeks before we packed the station wagon and headed west, bound for eternity. The last photograph shows me bouncing on our new trampoline in our backyard, summer swirling all around me. I'm in midair, my face bright with joy as I ascend. Dad stands in the background, hands at the ready. The picture is slightly blurry but I can tell that he's smiling too. I could still hear the rhythmic squeaks of the trampoline and feel the thick August air on my face as I reached for the sky. I remember thinking that I'd never touch down.

I lingered on the last page, running my fingers along the borders of the photographs. I'm not sure what I was really looking for among all those dried and yellowed days, whether I wanted to see how much power the past still held or whether I hoped that by embracing it I might somehow toughen myself for the days ahead. But by the time I placed the albums back on the shelf I realized that it wasn't just sadness that had begun to coil in my chest but fear as well. After I turned out the light I stayed awake another hour wondering what to say to the man who saved my life and was about to lose his. When I finally fell asleep I dreamed that my parents were still in Wyoming waiting for me, both standing by the roadside and calling out my name.

I changed planes in Denver for the short connection to Sheridan, knees wedged so tightly against the seat in front of me that I couldn't get to my carry-on. I tried to distract myself with a magazine but every time I looked out the window I found myself thinking of that first flight with my aunt after the accident and how I searched each cloud for Mom and Dad, hoping they might have stopped to rest on their way to heaven. Or was heaven somewhere within the clouds? Even after I watched their matching shiny black coffins being lowered into the moist soil six blocks from the small yellow house where we'd lived, I sensed they were somewhere above me, so that in those first months I got a sore neck from looking for them as I tagged along behind my aunt from open house to open house, helping her post her signs and lugging her little blue and white easels down to the street corner after she wrote in the address in chalk because my handwriting wasn't nearly neat enough. Even though I never saw them I always knew they were there, that somehow the three of us were still together because how could it be any other way? I may have lived with Aunt Margaret and her four cats in Saint Louis but in my heart I never really left home, not for years.

Once I started school in the fall I thought the hardest part of each day would be trying not to cry in front of the other children. At first I couldn't manage it and the schoolyard monitors would find me hidden in bushes and closets or hobbling as fast as my damaged limbs would take me to the ravine three blocks from school where I buried myself in leaves. But then one night as I twisted in my sheets the sadness became so unbearable that I felt something give way inside, like my soul had buckled and collapsed to the ground. I didn't cry after that. Not the next day or even the day after. From then on I knew that the hardest part of each day would no longer be in fighting back the tears. No, the hardest part would be keeping my own death a secret.

I thought Dr. Radley would uncover my secret during the six months of therapy intended to extract my grief like oil from a vast well, but he never did. He even complimented me on how well I was coping. (For some reason I found distraction in school work and my grades soared, especially in English, where I churned out page after page of molten buckshot when I wasn't submerged in the works of Dickens and Austen, C. S. Lewis and Tolkien.) "Amazing how resilient children are, surviving a thing like that," adults would whisper when I passed by. But I knew the truth: I hadn't survived. I had died inside as surely as if the fire had consumed me, too. I even visualized my heart as cold to the touch; so cold that wet skin would stick to it. But at least it didn't hurt anymore.

The best part about being dead was that it made living so much easier. I no longer cared that I'd never be any good at sports because of the injuries to my legs and shoulder that required physical therapy twice a week. (I even threw out my vast collection of baseball cards, then retrieved them in a panic hours later because Dad and I had spent entire Sundays with them spread before us like pirate treasure, taking turns contemplating their solemn mysteries.) I no longer cared what other kids said or feared the dark as I once had—I could watch the scariest movies without flinching—and I no longer felt embarrassed when Aunt Margaret showed up at school with cats coming out of her coat pockets and her bright red hair lacquered into horns that would command respect among any herd on the Serengeti. Even going to the dentist was easier because I'd endured something so much worse than anything Dr. Cavanaugh could inflict with his sharp instruments. And so I no longer cried. But I didn't smile much either.

"Hey, Ry, how come you never want to shoot anybody?" It was Bobby Kramer, making sure I didn't mind if he borrowed one of my crutches for use as a machine gun during recess. Scott Mason already had the other and was spewing hot saliva as he shot everybody in sight.

"Just don't feel like it, that's all."

Bobby gave his wiry little head a disbelieving shake before dashing for cover behind the slide. I sat on the grass and watched as gunfire erupted from every part of the playground, classmates running back and forth and falling to the ground in noisy agony. Suddenly Scott ran up and shot me right in the face.

"You can't shoot Ryan," said Cindy Biederman, jumping down from the jungle gym.

"What do you mean I can't?" said Scott, shooting me again, this time right between the eyes.

"Cut it out!" said Bobby.

"I don't mind," I said as Scott waited for me to die.

"It's not fair," said Cindy, getting between me and Scott. (She was a grade taller than either of us.)

"How come it's not?" said Scott.

"What do you think, dumbo?" said Cindy, her eyes saying the rest. "Besides, they're his machine guns."

Scott seemed uncertain.

"It's too late," I said softly, closing my eyes. I slumped to my knees, then fell sideways onto the warm grass, letting all the breath out and keeping it out as long as I could, which was a very long time.

I can still remember the day I felt the warmth return to my chest. I was fifteen and sitting in homeroom when Kimberly Jamison turned and smiled at me, and not just with her mouth but with every part of her tiny porcelain face. She'd never noticed me before and I don't believe she ever did again, but that smile changed my life just as if she'd spackled me with pixie dust. After school I hurried to my private hideaway in the woods and wept as hard as I'd ever wept before. But this time I wasn't crying from the bitter hardness of life but from the beauty of it as I understood for the first time since the accident that I could feel something besides pain.

From that day on I began to leave my parents behind, gradually freeing not just myself but them as well, or at least that's how I imagined it. By the time I headed off to the University of Kansas at Lawrence with a scholarship from a writing contest I'd won (Aunt Margaret crying herself silly as I pulled out of the driveway in a rusty Toyota Celica that would be stolen exactly two weeks later), I no longer felt quite so different from other people, except perhaps for a lingering sense of urgency because I was living for all three of us. Of all the discoveries I made in those years the most important was this: that life broke everybody eventually (it wasn't just me after all) and it was only when you found yourself wavering between the ground and your knees that things got truly interesting.

I was in my early twenties when I first glimpsed my parents in the mirror, both merging like watercolors in my features. I've got my father's height (actually, at 6'2" I'm a bit taller) and his straight nose and his ruddy skin that quickly creases with every expression so that if I live long enough I suppose I'll wear all my expressions simultaneously. From my mother I inherited my toothy smile and unruly brown hair. (It was all Dad could do to keep from fondling Mom's hair and messing it up when she first came downstairs for a party, her shiny locks falling like streamers around her freckled shoulders.) I've also got her green eyes, which were a shade lighter than most green eyes, like a shallow northern lake with a white sandy bottom on a sunny day. It wasn't just the color that made them striking but the way they always seemed to be brimming with the things that can't be said. Lately I've noticed the same fullness gathering in my own eyes.

I no longer hear my parents' voices as I once did but I still think about them a lot, especially on those days when the rest of the world seems somehow muted and I wonder if time is linear after all. What bothers me most isn't that I lost them but that I never really knew them; I didn't have time. Instead I've tried to assemble them from what pieces I possess, imagining them this way and that, leaving blank the parts I cannot fathom.

Of some things I am certain. I know my father always regretted never going to college where he'd hoped to become an architect, instead taking over the family machine shop at the age of twenty-two after his father had a stroke and his mother began a slow and vocal death by heartbreak. I know my mother was a gifted actress and dancer with a deep sense of social justice, always trying to organize neighbors for various causes because how could anybody get a good night's sleep with things the way they were in the world? And I know that of all the dreams they shared I was one of the few that came true.

But the most important thing I know about my parents is that they loved each other with a strength and reverence so invincible and true that the rest of creation seems a sort of agonizing prelude. In a letter written from the South Pacific where he was an anti-aircraft gunner on a destroyer during the war, my father wrote my mother that sometimes the whole crazy world seemed to him like one big shipwreck and maybe the only hope was to find something that floats and hold on like hell. *There's not a day that goes by out here that I don't thank God I've got you to hold on to.* She wrote him back that she was holding on just as tight.

That's the way I'll always think of them, even in those last awful moments: both clinging to each other with every bit of their strength. Sometimes I wonder whether they made it all the way to God's eternal shore or if it's victory enough to slip under with a fierce and almighty love sounding out your last breaths.

One day I hope to find out.

I try to visit their graves once a year, usually in the fall when the tall maple tree that shades their narrow plot ignites with color. The first time I ever visited on my own I brought along a harmonica, thinking we'd need some music to liven things up. But I didn't have the heart to play it so instead I just left it behind on the grass in front of their single headstone. Now I bring a harmonica every year, always leaving it behind and smiling at the thought of the neighborhood children puzzling over the mysterious offering.

After so many years it's no longer sadness I feel as I stare at their names locked in stone so much as a sort of speechless wonder, time howling through me like a sacred wind. I've even come to look forward to my visits, thankful for the aching freedom and determination that floods my limbs as all the unimportant things fall away. By the time I say goodbye and head back down the gravel path my very soul burns with the certainty that the only way to die is with love clenched in both fists like precious gems.

I like to think that's exactly how they went.

CHAPTER
FOUR

The moment I heard my first love story
I started looking for you, not knowing
how blind that was.

Lovers don't finally meet somewhere.
They're in each other all along.

– Rumi

IT WAS A two-hour drive from the airport in Sheridan to the O'Donnells' ranch. I pulled off the road twice just to sit on the hood and let my thoughts catch up, always wondering: was this where it happened? (A part of me felt certain I could somehow divine the spot by sheer intuition.) I pulled over again when I saw the house up ahead, stranded as though by some ancient flood along a barren stretch of dirt road where the flat prairie gave way to foothills that rose in folds to meet a long sweep of burly, pine-covered mountains. The first thing that struck me was the raw emptiness of the place, no neighbors for miles and nothing but cavernous sky pressing down. The road itself ran in a perfectly straight line north to south, bordered on both sides by endless strands of rusty barbed wire adorned with clumps of windblown sagebrush. In the rearview mirror I could see a cloud of dust trailing behind me like a weary parade float.

As soon as I parked in the rutted gravel driveway I caught the scent of horses coming from the nearby barn, which was sun-bleached gray and listing precariously. An old red tractor sat rusting on the balding lawn while the house itself had the weathered look of an old snake trying to shed its last skin, the white paint curling and all the wood settled at various angles. Apparently the O'Donnells had fallen onto lean times, or maybe times were always lean in a place like this. I immediately regretted not booking a hotel.

I'd fully intended to, not wanting to get in the way and knowing I'd need plenty of time to myself. But Mike's wife Alessandra—who to my surprise spoke with an Italian accent—had insisted there weren't any hotels nearby and besides, she wouldn't hear of me staying anywhere but in their guestroom. "So it's settled," she'd said before I could think of a response. At least I'd held her to two nights. (She'd suggested a week, promising to make a wrangler out of me.) I decided to leave my bag in the car, figuring that if the O'Donnells proved to be unbearably strange I'd make some excuse about a crisis at work and beeline it for the airport.

I was still trying to find the buzzer when the door opened.

"What a beautiful sight," said the woman who answered, clasping her hands in front of her heart before enveloping me in a long hug. Tall and statuesque with Mediterranean features, she had long gray hair pulled back into a tight ponytail, striking brown eyes and a warm, open face that still contained the unmistakable contours of youthful beauty, even great beauty.

"I hope this isn't a bad time. I can come back if—"

"It's a perfect time." The tenderness in her voice made me like her immediately.

She hugged me again. "I always told Mike you'd grow into quite a handsome young man someday," she said, her eyes studying me so closely that I felt myself blush. She started to reach for my face, then caught herself. "I hope my directions were okay?"

"Perfect. Straight shot, just like you said."

She took my hands in both of hers. "I'm so delighted you're here."

"I want to say how sorry I am." I felt my insides rising to my face.

"You're just what he needs." She gave my arm a tug. "Come on in, he's been waiting all day to see you."

She led me up the narrow stairs, which creaked loudly, and to the first door on the left, where she paused. "He's not doing well," she whispered, sadness bunching at the corners of her eyes. "He falls asleep a lot and he gets confused."

"Maybe you want to see if he's awake." I noticed my palms were damp.

"Alessandra, is that you?" The voice from the bedroom was frail and dry.

"He's awake," she said with a wink. She started for the door and then turned back to me. "He's been a little nervous about seeing you."

"That makes two of us."

She gave my shoulder a gentle squeeze, then opened the door and let me enter first.

Mike O'Donnell sat propped up against two pillows, his sunken chest and thin arms lost in a freshly pressed red plaid shirt with pearl buttons. I could see from his frame that he'd been a large man, not exactly handsome but powerfully built, with an honest face and square, reassuring features. I looked for some vestige of the strength that once carried me to safety but saw only death in his clouded eyes and gray complexion, the tone broken by purple splotches that spread like ivy across his cheeks. A large green oxygen cylinder rested on the floor beside him and a thin tube fed into his nostrils, which glistened red. A walker and cane stood in the corner while the bed stand was covered with at least a dozen pill bottles as well as a jar of Vaseline, a box of tissues and a neat stack of folded washcloths.

As I approached the bed he made an attempt to get up.

"Now you stay right there," said Alessandra, easing him back into the pillow.

Mike slowly offered his hand.

It looked so much worse than I had expected that for a moment all I could do was stare at it. The tips of two fingers were missing while the thumb lacked any place for a nail. Everywhere the skin was discolored so that I wasn't immediately sure if it was real skin or some sort of synthetic glove. The other hand looked even worse, the fingers all shrunk and crouched tightly together. Meanwhile, a series of large gray scars ran all the way up both his forearms as if they'd been dipped in dirty wax. *And all these years I never even bothered to visit him.*

I took his hand in mine and squeezed it gently.

"You're a lot bigger than I remember," he said.

"I guess I am," I said, still staring down at his hand and fighting the tightness in my throat. Finally I forced myself to look away, my eyes catching the silver lip of a bedpan tucked beneath the bed.

"I'll get started with dinner," said Alessandra. Mike watched her leave.

I stood by the bedside trying to remember all the things I wanted to say. From a painting above the headboard a lone buffalo stared mournfully back at me, either oblivious or resigned to the wagon train silhouetted on the ridge behind him.

"Hope the trip wasn't too much trouble," said Mike.

"No trouble at all." I looked back at his hands, wanting for some reason to touch the scars. Was the skin softer or harder? Was there any sensation left? How does a man endure that kind of pain when it's voluntary, when all he had to do was to stand back from the flames like anybody else would have?

Mike looked toward the window. "Smell that?"

"What?"

"Storm's coming. Be here in a few hours. We need the rain."

I followed his gaze, watching the branches of a large tree groan back and forth. From downstairs I heard the faint strains of opera music seeping through the worn floorboards, two voices wrapping around each other as they climbed.

"You must be hungry," he said.

"I'm fine, but thanks."

"You need anything you just ask. But don't let her fuss too much over you." He tried to smile. "You know how fussy women can be."

I nodded.

"My father used to say that they all fuss but I think some are fussier than others."

"Guess there are worse things than being fussed over."

"Guess there are."

I looked over at the rocking chair near the dresser but decided to remain standing. "I really don't even know where to begin," I said.

His face tensed. "No need to."

"But there is."

He began to cough, spasms coursing through his body. I waited anxiously until he finished, then poured him a glass of water from the pitcher by his bed and helped him bring it to his lips.

"Thank you," he said, his forehead moistening from the effort. I noticed him fighting to keep his eyes open.

"I meant to make this trip years ago but somehow I just never got around to it."

He didn't respond.

"The truth is, I think I was afraid."

"It's a hell of a thing you went through," he said, his voice dropping to a hoarse whisper.

"It's a hell of a thing you did."

"Wish I could have done more." He eyes stared off somewhere I couldn't follow. Was he back there searching for life in the flames? Was there only time to save one of us?

"I just want you to know that I've never for a moment forgotten what you did that day."

A pained look came across his face.

"Are you all right?" I asked.

He nodded.

"Are you sure?"

He nodded again. Then he blinked a few times and sunk back into the pillow with a series of shallow breaths. Within seconds his eyes were closed. I stood watching for a full minute, leaning forward to make sure he was breathing, then quietly backed out of the room, my heart pounding like a ten-year-old boy's.

CHAPTER
FIVE

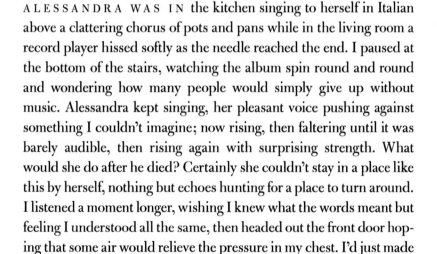

ALESSANDRA WAS IN the kitchen singing to herself in Italian above a clattering chorus of pots and pans while in the living room a record player hissed softly as the needle reached the end. I paused at the bottom of the stairs, watching the album spin round and round and wondering how many people would simply give up without music. Alessandra kept singing, her pleasant voice pushing against something I couldn't imagine; now rising, then faltering until it was barely audible, then rising again with surprising strength. What would she do after he died? Certainly she couldn't stay in a place like this by herself, nothing but echoes hunting for a place to turn around. I listened a moment longer, wishing I knew what the words meant but feeling I understood all the same, then headed out the front door hoping that some air would relieve the pressure in my chest. I'd just made it to the far side of the barn when I felt all the grief inside of me rise up with such force that I had to lean against a wooden rail and close my eyes. I took a series of deep breaths, letting the musky air fill me.

"Hey, are you okay?"

I looked up to see an attractive woman in jeans, cowboy boots and a frayed denim work shirt standing just a few feet away and staring at me. I quickly stood up straight, feeling myself blush. "I didn't know anyone was out here."

"Sorry, I didn't mean to intrude." She started to back away, hesitated, then stepped forward and offered her hand, which was remarkably dirty, like a farmer's. "I'm Shannon."

I cleared my throat. "Ryan Brooks."

"Yes, I know who you are." She looked so pleased that for a moment I wondered if she thought I was someone I wasn't. How long had she been watching me?

"You must be his daughter." I recalled Alessandra mentioning something about a daughter on the phone.

"That's me." She brushed off her jeans. "Or at least, this is the messy version of me." She had dirt everywhere: on her knees and thighs and the front of her shirt and the tops of her boots and even a smudge on her left cheek. I thought of my first wife, Carol, and how she didn't like camping because it was too dirty. After our divorce I tried to find a bad picture of her but I couldn't. She always looked perfect.

"Guess I got a little overwhelmed there for a minute." I quickly cleared my throat again.

"I don't blame you," she said. "It must be… a lot." She gave the front of her pants another few whacks with her palm, raising a small cloud of dust. Then she started to back away. "You probably want to be alone."

"No, I'm fine. Really." As I tried to hold her gaze I found myself wondering whether, if I got close enough, she'd smell more like woman or horse. "I'm sorry about your dad."

"Me, too." Her face filled with sadness, which made it hard for me to look at her. (Whenever Aunt Margaret cried, which was rather frequently, I had to leave the room because I couldn't stand to see so far inside of her.) "We're a real pair, huh?" she said, wiping her eyes.

"Maybe I should go unpack my things." I turned toward the house.

"No, just give me a second." She wiped her eyes again, leaving dirty smudges, then gave her cheeks a quick pat. "I've been kind of a wreck lately. My dad and I are really close and, well, my mom and I *aren't*, so…" She gave her shoulders a twist. "I've kind of been going crazy—and spending a lot of time in the barn." She held up her dirty hands. "But don't mind me, you've got enough to deal with."

"I'm not minding you."

We both stood looking at each other, then away, then back at each other. By the time we looked away again I'd decided she was about the most interesting thing I'd ever seen.

The shyness in her face reminded me of her father and yet her looks all came from her mother. She had an oval face, an olive-colored complexion and large dark eyes that sprang from beneath long, thick eyebrows. Her black hair was cut short and arranged haphazardly, as if she'd been wearing a hat, while the only jewelry she wore was a pair of simple silver hoop earrings. And a wedding ring. I guessed she was in her mid-thirties, although she had the loose posture of someone younger. Or did people in the country carry themselves differently?

"I remember you," she said, her eyes drawing into a squint as she leaned closer. Even her hair was coated with a fine layer of dirt.

"You do?"

"In the hospital. We'd visit Dad every day when he was recovering from his burns and one afternoon Mom took me to the fourth floor to see you. You were sleeping so…" A look of embarrassment came over her face.

"What?"

"It's nothing."

"Tell me."

"So I sat and watched you."

"Sounds exciting."

"It was more than that." Her face came alive. "I wanted to sit there all day and night until you were better but Mom wouldn't let me. And then I wanted to take you home with us—I think the whole hospital wanted to—but Mom said you had a home to go to. I must have sat there for hours looking at you and hoping you'd wake up. I felt so… so bad for you. Sometimes at night I'd cry myself to sleep just thinking about you."

"Sometimes I cried myself to sleep thinking about me."

We both laughed.

"It must have been hard seeing my dad," she said, her expression changing again, eyebrows drawing together. I decided she was one of those people who live right in their face, moods and thoughts passing like fast-moving clouds.

"It was a long time ago."

"Mom used to say a prayer for you every night during grace.... I'm not saying it made any difference but it's what she did."

"You never know."

"Guess not." She kept staring at me so intently that I wondered if she was searching for lingering signs of damage. "She always wanted to invite you to visit—I did too—but Dad wouldn't hear of it. He figured it would just upset you."

"I'm glad I finally made it."

"So am I." She smiled, then we both turned to the sound of Alessandra's voice drifting from the kitchen window as she hit a high note.

"Your mother seems to be holding up pretty well," I said.

"Florence Nightingale." Shannon rolled her eyes as her mother hit another high note. "I've been here for the last month trying to help out—I live in San Francisco. The problem is, she doesn't need any help. Never did."

Alessandra's voice rose a little higher before trailing off. Shannon started toward the barn. "Come on, I'll show you around."

The barn smelled sharp and damp, while above in the darkness something flapped its wings in alarm. "Meet Renegade and Rita." She gestured toward two horses peering out from their stalls, then walked over to the nearest one and rubbed it just above its nose. "Dad stopped riding months ago because of his health and Mom's not getting around like she used to. Our neighbor's son makes sure they get exercised." She walked over to the other horse and patted its neck.

I gingerly offered Renegade my palm, then quickly pulled it away when he curled his lips into a snarl, exposing enormous teeth.

"He won't bite."

"It's a good thing." I watched as she took a brush off a hook and began to work it through Rita's mane, her movements tender and easy.

"Dad inherited the ranch right after the war but he was too banged up to run the place properly. He sold most of the land and all of the cattle and went to school on the GI Bill to become a geologist. He was on the road a lot, working sites, sleeping out of his truck." She paused. "I used to miss him so much."

I looked over at three worn saddles that rested on rough horizontal wooden posts. Above them ropes and bridles hung from a series of hooks while another wall was covered with ribbons in an assortment of faded blues and reds and golds. "It must have been wonderful growing up in a place like this."

She looked up at the ribbons, as if surprised they were still there. "Sometimes it was great and sometimes I felt like the only child on the planet. I spent a lot of time with my puppets. I told a therapist once that I was raised by puppets, but he didn't laugh."

"I thought the world was run by cats."

"Cats?"

"My aunt had a lot of cats. Very peculiar cats."

"Well, at least you didn't have to trick-or-treat at your own house."

"You're kidding?"

"It was that or walk five miles for a piece of candy. Mom made me count to one hundred before I could ring the bell again and each time she opened the door she acted surprised and made a great fuss over my costume as she dropped another piece of candy into my bag."

She returned the brush to its hook and walked up close to me. "Pathetic, huh?"

"Actually, yes." I fought an urge to wipe a smudge of dirt from her cheek.

"On the other hand, I did get to choose the candy."

"No small consolation."

She nodded as she pulled out a cigarette from her shirt pocket. No, a joint, which surprised me even more. With the other hand she pulled a red Bic lighter from her jeans and lit the joint, taking a deep hit before offering it to me.

"No thanks."

"You're sure?"

"I'm sure."

She looked down at the joint pinched between her fingers. "I only get high when I come home. Then I really want to get high." She took another hit, exhaling contentedly. Or maybe not so contentedly. "The funny thing is, I don't even like being high except when I'm here. I just get confused."

"And how do you get when you're here?"

She looked down at the joint again. "I get so I feel like I'm somewhere else." She took one more hit, then stubbed the joint out against the wall and placed it back in her shirt pocket. "Come on," she said, heading out the door.

I followed her past the corral and down to a small creek that ran between a narrow band of birch trees just beginning to bloom.

"Dad was nervous about seeing you again," she said when we reached the creek. The sound of the water reminded me of a stream near our house in Kentucky where I spent hours fashioning little boats from leaves before sending them off on their fateful voyages.

"Probably not as nervous as I was."

"How did he react?"

"I think he was tired. I might have caught him at a bad time."

She tucked her fingers into the back pockets of her jeans. "I probably shouldn't say this but the truth is, he didn't really want you to come." Then she added quickly, "Not because he didn't want to see you. He's kept every Christmas card you ever sent him. I found them once, in a little bundle beneath his socks. And when you sent him your high school graduation picture he couldn't even speak all evening he was so proud. But I think he figured that coming here would just be one more thing to make you sad and that you'd had enough sadness for one life."

"I had to see him again."

She nodded. "I know. At least, I think I do." She sat on a rock by the water's edge. "I also think he needed to see you again too."

I debated whether to sit next to her but decided to remain standing. It wasn't a large rock. "I had so many things I wanted to say to him but then when I saw his hands..."

Shannon reached up and took my arm, squeezing me slightly before letting go.

"I didn't realize he'd been burned so badly," I said.

"He got some fuel on his hands. That's what the doctors said."

I looked over at the house. "I don't think I would have done what he did. I'd like to believe that I would have but I'm not so sure."

"You never know." She gave her head a shake, dust flying. "But I don't think I would have either."

I walked to the edge of the creek and bent down, testing the water with my fingers. It was much colder than I had expected.

She watched me. "I thought you'd look different."

"You mean, crippled?"

"I didn't mean to imply—"

"No offense taken."

"It's just that you looked so... *broken*."

"I never did make varsity." In fact, I spent as much of my remaining boyhood as possible on my bike because it was the only way I could taste the freedom of speed. (Darkness always seemed to me to be something that had to be outrun.) I still retained a slight limp despite years of physical therapy.

"Mom said it was a miracle that you weren't burned. She's a big believer in miracles."

"Your dad was the miracle."

"Did he say anything about the accident?"

"We didn't really talk about it."

"He never has." She looked up at the sky, her eyes following a lone hawk that soared overhead in a broad descending circle before disappearing. I found myself watching the movement in Shannon's throat as she swallowed. "A few weeks after the accident the fire department gave him an honorary plaque but I never saw it again."

"Maybe it's been enough to live with those scars."

"That's what I used to think." She stopped herself. "I don't mean to bring all this up. God, I must be stoned. Sorry." She gave her forehead a gentle whack with her palm. "Here we've only known each other a few minutes and—"

"No, it's okay. Go on."

She hesitated.

"Please."

She gave me a long look before continuing. "It took me years to realize this but I think he's always felt guilty for not being able to save your parents, that if only he'd gotten there sooner or tried a little harder..."

"Nobody could have saved them," I said firmly, trying to concentrate on a large bug skittering across the water. In the hospital I'd overheard a sheriff describe the wreckage, saying in a voice not quite low enough that no betting man would expect to find life in such a fiery hell.

"I know that. I'm just not sure he does. You don't know Dad."

I looked up at the second floor window of Mike's room, regret rising in my chest. *I never should have come. What could I offer the O'Donnells but the memory of a day that everyone would rather forget?*

"I meant to cheer you up but I don't think I've done a very good job," she said.

"It's been thirty years."

She nodded slowly but I sensed she knew there were other ways to measure time.

I tried to change the subject. "So, your mother's from Italy?"

"She was a war bride. Can you imagine coming to a place like this?"

"Actually, no. Do you go back to Italy much?"

"Never. Dad hates to travel and after my grandmother died my mother had no reason to go back—her sisters live in Florida and her brother Marcello was killed in a car accident in 1952. Besides, I think it's too painful for her. She lost a lot of family in the war. She won't even talk about it." Shannon ran her hand up and down her forearm, smoothing a trace of fine black hair. "If it wasn't for the weather I'm not sure what we'd talk about."

We sat in silence, both staring at the water. Now and then she looked over at me in a way that surprised me. Was she still trying to connect me with that wretched boy in the hospital bed? What was it like for a little girl to witness something like that, seeing that sometimes a child's worst nightmare really did come true?

"I keep telling myself that at least he's going first," she said. "He was always the tough one on the outside—just like a big ol' bear—but Mom's stronger on the inside. She can handle it. Actually, I think she could handle anything. Not Dad. He would have followed her right into the grave."

"I can't imagine losing a partner after so many years."

She picked up a twig and tossed it in the water, watching it drift away. "Sometimes I think they lost each other a long time ago." I waited for her to say more but instead she rose to her feet. "I should go check on him. Dinner's usually at seven." She started to walk away, then turned back to me and smiled, her whole dirty face joining in. "It's really good to see you again." Then she walked quickly toward the house. I watched her the whole way.

CHAPTER
SIX

*Please send me your last pair of shoes, worn out with
dancing as you mentioned in your letter, so that I might
have something to press against my heart.*

– Johann Wolfgang von Goethe

ON MY SIXTEENTH birthday Aunt Margaret cooked me my
favorite dinner of chicken enchiladas and gazpacho soup followed
by double chocolate cake, all served with great fanfare in her small
green dining room, then sat me down on the couch in the living
room and told me to close my eyes. When I opened them two large
wrapped boxes sat on the coffee table before me.

"These belong to you, not me," she said, large thick tears blotch-
ing her heavy makeup as she stood beside me. "I thought it was best
to wait a few years. I hope I did the right thing."

"What are they?"

"It's your parents' papers. There are letters, too." She wiped her
eyes with the backs of her hands. "I thought you should have them."

I stared at the boxes.

"You don't have to open them now," she said. "But if you want to…"

"I'd rather take them to my room. But thank you."

She leaned over and gave me a big red kiss on the cheek. "Happy birthday, Ryan."

As soon as I closed my bedroom door I sat in the middle of my bed and carefully unpacked the contents. The first box contained tax returns, their marriage license, insurance documents and files from my father's business. Near the bottom of the second box, beneath more tax returns and legal documents, I found a neatly tied bundle of letters. They were organized chronologically, beginning shortly after they began dating (actually, just hours after their first date) and continuing until my father came home from the war. I began with the first letter, written by my father when he was seventeen.

September 12, 1942

Dear Rebecca,

I don't know if I'll have the courage to give you this letter but I surely must write it or I shall never sleep again. What a nervous fool I must have seemed tonight, never finding the right words for all that I wanted to say—and the truth is I wanted to say everything. And now I've started this letter a dozen times and I still don't know where to begin except to tell you that the ceiling of my bedroom is on fire with a thousand stars and as I sit here at my desk I can feel warm sand between my toes and hear the sound of waves casting their ceaseless prayers upon the shore, which is something for a guy who's never been anywhere near the ocean.

Yours, no matter how foolishly,
Jim Brooks

From another small light blue envelope I pulled out my mother's response:

September 14, 1942

Dear Jim,
    I've never seen so many stars in all my life.
Yours truly,
Rebecca

I stayed up until three in the morning reading through their letters and when I was done I realized that I'd been wrong in thinking of their lives as unfinished because they'd completed the most important part of the journey long ago. As I turned out the light I wondered whether someday I, too, would find somebody I could hold on to and never let go of. And then in the darkness I told myself that I had to because surely the only thing harder than to live alone would be to die alone.

The very next morning I put aside the story I was working on—I was always writing something, piling up words like a bricklayer racing a storm—and started a new one, this time about a sailor during the war and the girl he left behind.

I never did finish it. I couldn't.

CHAPTER
SEVEN

———

THE THREE OF us ate dinner in the kitchen at a round white table that overlooked open scrub land where a dozen cows grazed, though on what I couldn't imagine. The clouds had a bruised, distended look and as soon as we sat down rain began to stream against the small window panes. Alessandra did most of the talking, telling stories about Mike while I tried not to stare at Shannon, who looked back at me frequently. Now and then I distracted myself by studying the appliances, which were so dated that had I been stoned, I would have sworn I'd been dropped into a diorama of farm life in the 1950s. As the room darkened I began to wonder whether so much open space drew people closer together, maybe even too close.

"He's usually better in the morning," said Alessandra, who'd already gotten up twice to check on Mike.

"Mom, you haven't even touched your food," said Shannon. I'd felt a vague tension between her and her mother all evening, both negotiating obstacles I couldn't see.

"I just can't stand thinking of him alone up there."

"I'll go check on him," said Shannon.

"You don't have to check on him. I just checked on him."

Another round of silence, broken only by the loud hum of the refrigerator.

"The dinner's delicious," I said.

"Mom's a great cook," said Shannon. The redness in her eyes made me wonder if she'd been smoking more pot or crying or both.

"Not like my mother," said Alessandra with a knowing shake of her head.

"Thank god I never had to cook for her," said Shannon.

Alessandra turned to me. "She's being modest. Her father is crazy about her cooking."

"He'd eat kibble if you fed it to him," said Shannon, looking at me. "And then he'd tell you that it was the best damn kibble he'd ever had."

"He's always been appreciative," said Alessandra, dabbing her lower lip with her napkin. "I just keep thinking how lucky I've been all these years."

"Mom, *please*."

"What is it, Sweetheart?"

"How can you..." She stopped herself, then suddenly rose from her chair. "I'm sorry. I'm tired. I need to go to bed."

Alessandra looked flustered. "But what about dessert?"

"I'm not hungry." Shannon placed her dishes in the sink. When she reached the door she turned back and looked at me, her eyes lingering just briefly. "Goodnight." Then she hurried out of the room.

Alessandra and I sat in silence as we listened to Shannon's footsteps on the stairs, followed by a door closing.

"You'll have to forgive her," Alessandra said. "These last few weeks have just torn her apart."

"It's a difficult time for everybody." I looked out the window where a lone porch light cast a yellow beam of rain.

"She's always been her father's girl. Sometimes I think they can read each other's thoughts." She toyed nervously with her napkin. "But for some reason we've never seen eye to eye and I've never understood why." Her accent had grown stronger and I wondered if that happened when she was upset. I looked down at her hands, which were lightly freckled, her long thin fingers unadorned except for a simple wedding band. "I don't mean to rattle on. Are you cold? Spring seems to be dragging its feet this year. I thought we might make a fire if you wouldn't mind bringing some wood in. The dry logs are in the shed next to the barn. Mike's slicker should be by the back door."

It took me a pack of matches and most of the Sunday *Casper Star-Tribune* to finally get a fire going. "The wood must be damp," she said politely as she returned from Mike's room carrying an untouched tray of food. After pouring two glasses of brandy she handed one to me and then curled up in a rust-colored overstuffed chair with her feet folded to one side. I took a sip of the brandy, then sat down across from her and stared at the flames as they gradually filled the soot-covered hearth, which was made of large gray stones. The room itself was decorated in an odd mix of Western art—mostly inexpensive-looking oil paintings and a few small bronze sculptures—and Italian pottery.

"I know this trip must be hard for you," she said.

"I should have come a long time ago. I just hope my being here is okay. Mike seemed kind of uncomfortable today and the last thing I want to do is to be a burden."

"Nonsense," she said. "It's just a little hard for him being seen the way he is, that's all. He's always been so independent."

Upstairs a door opened, followed by footsteps, followed by another door closing, then water running. Alessandra gazed toward the ceiling, then clasped one hand on top of the other and cinched them close to her stomach, summoning her composure. The more I looked at her the more I realized just how pretty she must have been in her youth, her face like a once proud estate whose owners could no longer afford the upkeep. Was the decline of age that much harder when begun from such a great height?

"Here I've gone and forgotten all about my dessert," she said, putting down her glass and rising from her chair. "I made a special pie just for tonight." She stopped and looked at me. "Unless you're too full?"

"To be honest, I'm—"

"Never mind, I'm stuffed too." She gave her stomach a pat and sat back down. "Besides, I'd much rather sit here and drink my brandy." She gave me a smile that told me she meant it. "We'll have it tomorrow."

I took a large swallow of my drink, enjoying the soft burn in my throat and chest, then stared into a bright orange cavern of embers, remembering the small fireplace in my parents' house and the white mantle covered with photographs, nearly all of them of me. I noticed that Alessandra kept looking at me.

"Your daughter looks just like you," I said as I examined a photograph of Shannon displayed on a table by the couch. She was standing beside a horse and holding up a ribbon. I guessed she was about sixteen, all the beauty in her features just breaking through.

"She's got her father's smile. He's always had a wonderful smile." Alessandra got up and took a picture from a buffet table, handing it to me. Mike was sitting on a fence post with a shovel by his side, his work gloves in one hand and a smile starting across his broad cheeks. His shirt was damp with sweat and his hardy face set in the concentrated expression of a man about to lift a heavy object—and knowing he's got the strength for it.

"You're right, he has a great smile," I said, shocked by how different he looked with all the life still in him.

"He'd just finished building the new corral. He put up all the fences himself. Every one of them." She looked at the photo for a moment before putting it back. "He's always taken such joy in his work, even the simplest thing." She sat back down by the fire. "I know he'd love to hear about your work. You should have seen his face when he learned you were going to be an architect."

I started to tell her that I'd dropped out of graduate school after the first semester, realizing my heart wasn't into it, but she looked so pleased that I just nodded. Besides, there was no pretty way to summarize the years that followed, when I traveled relentlessly in search of a peace that outran me, taking what jobs I could along the way, then tried to quell my demons with painkillers, an addiction I finally quit on my twenty-five birthday because I could no longer bear to dishonor the memory of my parents and the courage of the man who saved me.

"I miss his smile," she said, her voice changing as she tucked her hands between her thighs. "But you know what the hardest part is?" I waited for her to continue. "He's ready but he won't let go because he knows he can't die without hurting the people he loves and that's just not in his nature."

She sat perfectly still, her face bathed in the orange glow of the fire, which made her look younger. Moments later a low growl of thunder shook the house, nearly causing me to spill my drink.

"We get the most wonderful storms," she said. "I hope it won't keep you up all night."

"We had our share back in Kentucky when I was a kid. Our dog used to hide in my closet."

Another rumble crowded the room.

"When I was a little girl in Italy my father used to crawl into bed with me and make up wonderful stories about the great big creatures who were making such a racket. I felt so safe and happy with him beside me that I used to pray that the storm would never end."

"What part of Italy are you from?"

"A village in the Apennines northwest of Florence." She smiled to herself. "I never knew how beautiful it was until I left."

"What's it called?"

"San Gianello. No one's ever heard of it, at least not tourists. But it's quite lovely. It's perched on the slope of a wide mountain surrounded by woods and meadows and farmland, mostly grapes, olives, wheat. What we lacked in size and sophistication we made up for in our fierce pride. According to tradition the village was begun back in the time of Tiberius and three miracles are said to have occurred on the site of our church, though exactly what sort of miracles remains hotly disputed."

"What did people do for a living?"

"The men were mostly peasant farmers—*contadini*—but by the way they carried themselves you would have thought they were all bishops if not cardinals. The more prosperous families were landowners or shopkeepers, though beginning in the early 1930s more and more men took the bus early each morning to work in a canning factory that had been built to the south. We had electricity when the power plant down the valley was working but no running water; charcoal was used for cooking and heat. Each year groups of men would pack up supplies—mostly wine—and disappear into the forests for two to three weeks at a time to collect and slowly burn enormous piles of wood, which they kept covered with dirt to deprive the fire of oxygen, causing the wood to turn to charcoal. Their return, blackened from head to toe, was always a source for celebration and I can remember listening with awe to their stories of the ogres and dwarves that dwelled in the deep forest."

She stopped and took a drink from her brandy. Outside a series of flashes pounded against the sky.

"Not much ever happened in our village. I suppose that was part of its charm, though as a child I used to dream about living in a big, loud city like Rome or Paris. When something did happen it usually took place in either our small church, first built in the 1400s and in need of repair ever since, despite annual efforts to raise money (which instead always went to the *festa della Madonna*, when a great shrine was erected and the main road carpeted with flowers), or the piazza, which was bordered by several shops and two fiercely competitive cafés, Umberto's and Aldo's, or the *campo* just below the village, where we played sports. For one brief period in the summer of 1938 there was also a great deal of activity in an empty lot just behind the school where the men had built a *bocce* court after months of painstaking deliberation. But when three fights broke out in the course of a single week over accusations of cheating, resulting in several disfigured noses, the women threatened to withhold food until the *bocce* court was dismantled."

She stopped again but from her expression I sensed that she wanted to continue. Did anyone ever listen to her stories? Whom did she have to talk to all those years when Mike was on the road?

"Tell me about your family," I said.

"There were originally seven of us but my baby sister Maria died when she was two, leaving me, my twin sisters and my three older brothers. Fortunately we didn't have to work in the fields—except during the grape harvest, when almost everybody worked—because my father was a mechanic, and not just an ordinary mechanic but one of the best in all of Italy. I can still see him at the basin washing the motor oil from his hands before dinner. When I was young I used to stare at his hands, fascinated by how black and powerful and exotic they looked, like panthers. He repaired cars mostly but he could fix anything. Nothing made him happier than to bring some broken heap coughing back to life. I think he considered himself more of a doctor than a mechanic. He even talked to his patients, whispering encouragement to their engines and undersides, which drove my mother crazy.

"'Have you been drinking, Antonio?' she'd say.

"'Shh. Can't you see you're interrupting?' he'd respond as he gently caressed a fender.

"His garage was right next to the house and he let us children visit any time we wanted so long as we were careful. I don't think my mother ever set foot in there, not after the day she tried to clean it up when Papa was away. She kept the house spotless but Papa always said that neatness was a sign of religious anxiety—and he for one didn't have any. Anyway, she was always after him to tidy up the garage and so finally she took it upon herself, thinking she'd surprise him. I'll never forget the look on his face. It took him weeks to get things back the way he liked them: piles of engine parts and scrap metal everywhere, tools lying about like they'd been dropped from the sky. But he knew exactly where everything was. I sometimes suspected that the whole purpose was to keep Mama out."

Alessandra got up and prodded the fire with a brass poker. When she sat back down I noticed that she was trying not to laugh.

"What is it?" I asked.

"I was just thinking about this race the children had every year in our village. We rode in these little wooden cars assembled from whatever we could find." She shook her head in amusement. "I'd forgotten all about it."

"Tell me more."

"Oh, it was quite an event. The course began at the top of the village in front of the church and continued down through the piazza before finishing near the small lake where we swam. Of course, with my father's help we always won. You should have seen the cars he built. They were the envy of every child in the village. I'll never forget the first year I got to steer. The thrill of flying through the piazza and past all the houses with the wind in my eyes and everybody cheering!"

She took a drink of her brandy, then held the glass against her chin as she stared at the fire. "Father ran the garage while my mother ran the house. She took enormous pride in it, always making sure there were fresh flowers from her garden in every room and insisting on a new coat of paint every other spring. She inherited the house from her father, who built it at the turn of the century to keep himself busy after my grandmother died in childbirth. *The House that Grief Built*: that's what neighbors called it." She put her glass down. "I don't mean to do all the talking."

"No, please. I'd love to hear more."

She hesitated, a look of momentary confusion on her face.

"You were talking about your house."

"Oh, yes. Well, despite its name it was a lovely home. A row of tall cypress trees sheltered us from the road while on three sides we were surrounded by ancient olive groves where I spent a great deal of my childhood, feeling as if the wise old trees were attentive listeners to my most private thoughts. Whenever the weather was nice, and even sometimes when it wasn't, we ate outside in a courtyard beneath a trellis of wisteria and surrounded by mother's flowers and her prized tomato garden. She grew the most delicious tomatoes, timing down to the very hour when they were ready to pick. I can still remember Papa sneaking one or two straight from the vine when Mama wasn't looking, the juices dribbling down his chin and shirt so that he was always caught and swiftly reprimanded.

"'Two more days and they would have been *perfect*,' she'd moan.

"'But they *were* perfect, my dear. Besides, I couldn't help myself. You know how I get around your tomatoes.' He'd begin to chase her until she fled into the house.

"The courtyard was bordered by a low stone wall with a small wooden gate in the middle, which Papa built after I wandered off for several hours one afternoon shortly after I learned to walk. (Apparently I traveled some distance.) The roots of a large Ficus tree pushed up the paving stones this way and that while bougainvillea grew up along the side of the house, which was salmon-colored with deep-set windows and a terra-cotta roof. (Grief built to last.) From the courtyard we had a sweeping view of the valley and Papa used to say that it was the best view in all of Italy, which meant of course that no better view could be had anywhere in the world. He spent hours sitting in one of the big wooden chairs he'd built himself, a glass of red wine in one hand and a cigar in the other as he looked out over the valley and murmured contentedly.

"'What are you looking at, Papa?' I'd ask, sitting in his lap and secretly savoring his cigar smoke, which I enjoyed (probably because my mother hated it).

"'Why, paradise, of course,' he'd say, wrapping his arms around me.

"I was the third youngest—my twin sisters Claudia and Carlotta were eight years younger—and I always liked to think I was his favorite, at least when I was small. I had a special little hideaway up in the rafters of the garage and I used to sit up there for hours after school watching him work. I decorated the walls with artwork—I loved to draw—and I had a special bed for my doll as well as a secret supply of *caramella*—sweets. Papa built a railing so I couldn't tumble out and there was a small window from which I could see the road and the valley spread out below. I felt just like a princess up in my tower. I can still remember listening to the rain drum against the roof just above my head and feeling so safe and snug as I watched my father work and listened to him tell stories about when he was a boy and the world was full of magical creatures that would entertain him when no one else was about.

"'But weren't you scared?' I asked when he described the night an enormous bat snatched him from his bed and carried him out the window to play on the treetops with elves and fairies.

"'I was having too much fun to be scared!' he replied.

"My mother worried because I didn't play with the other children but I think my father enjoyed my company because he was just as shy and quiet as I was. 'The world is full of too many talkers, eh, Mouse?' he'd say, looking up at me in my perch high above him. 'Everybody talking themselves blue in the face with nothing to say. But when *we* talk people listen, and you know why they listen?' He wagged an oil-blackened finger up at me. 'Because they know we must really have something to say.'

"I never tired of watching him work. He treated each automobile that came into his shop like a beautiful bride, running his hands lovingly over every part. 'A good mechanic always trusts his hands more than his eyes,' he'd say, sliding underneath a vehicle until I could only see his feet. I think my mother was jealous of his work but I was enormously proud to be the daughter of such an obvious genius. After all, people came from all over just so that he could fix their cars as well as generators and pumps and motorcycles and bicycles and all sorts of things. Sometimes I'd fall asleep watching him and I can remember waking up in his arms as he carried me to the house. 'Look what I've found,' he'd tell my mother. 'A sleepy little mouse up in the rafters.'

"One of the things I liked most about the garage was that it was far away from the kitchen. In San Gianello, as in the rest of Italy, life seemed to revolve largely around the subject of food, which meant that a woman could spend the better part of her useful life either cooking or cleaning. As best I could tell, the entire village leapfrogged in unison from one meal to the next, while the conversation among grownups centered on either the characteristics of the current meal, especially texture, or the anticipated glories of the upcoming meal. The work required to produce this almost continuous succession of triumphs was, to my young mind, appalling, especially being the oldest daughter. It often seemed to me that I did little but help Mama prepare meals and clean up after them. To her horror, I had no talent for either task. And worse, I wasn't much interested in food at all.

"'Do you want to be a spinster like your Aunt Camellia?' Mama asked, nearly crossing herself at the thought as she attacked a greasy pot.

"'I wouldn't mind, so long as I don't have to cook and clean all the time.'

"'What am I going to do with you?'

"'You could banish me from the kitchen.'

"She shook her head with a long groan, then smiled and hugged me before handing me a dishtowel to wipe down the dinner table.

"'When I'm finished with you you'll be the second-best cook in San Gianello,' she said, her voice trailing off as she hurried to check on the twins, who were screaming at each other upstairs."

Alessandra paused as the living room windows flickered. "But soon my mother had more important things to worry about."

"You mean the war?"

She nodded, then rose to her feet as a loud rumble squeezed the air. "I should go check on Mike. Sometimes these storms wake him."

"Do you want me to check on him?" I'd been wanting to be in his presence again.

"I'd better go myself. He gets so confused some nights that I'm afraid he might look at you and..." She didn't finish.

I helped her close the grates of the fireplace and turn off the lights, then followed her up the stairs. When we reached the door to Mike's room she turned and kissed me firmly on each cheek.

"*Buona notte*," she whispered.

"*Buona notte*," I said.

CHAPTER
EIGHT

THE CEILING OF my small room sloped so sharply that I had to duck down as I approached the small brass bed, which was covered with a bright yellow quilt. I sat for several minutes and watched the lightning out the window, smiling at the immense beauty despite a sense of unease. I thought of the view from my childhood bedroom, which overlooked the tidy sutures between half a dozen backyards. Sometimes when I couldn't sleep I used to pull a chair up to the window and keep silent vigil, whispering *goodnight* each time another house darkened and ordering up the sweetest of dreams with the plastic wand I had received from a magician my parents hired for my seventh birthday.

I got up and quietly unpacked my things, then slowly inspected the room. No matter how lightly I stepped, the worn floorboards howled beneath my feet as I tiptoed around looking first at the artwork on the walls—lots of cowboys and big sky— then the framed photographs that covered the small dresser. I picked up a picture of Shannon and her father, arms wrapped around each other and horses in the background. I thought of her in her bed in the next room, wondering if she was still awake or whether she'd learned to sleep through such storms. (And how did she look when she was asleep?)

After brushing my teeth in the narrow bathroom at the end of the hall I stripped down to my underwear and crawled into bed, struggling to loosen the tightly made sheets until I could stick a foot out. Almost immediately a loud crack of thunder caused me to jolt. *Christ.* I turned to my side and stared out the window, watching as great jagged thrusts of light pierced the nearby foothills. I counted the seconds after the next flash lit up the barn, bracing for the thunder. At least nature had not been entirely usurped by man. Maybe that explained the charm of country dwellers: they retained a certain modesty that only nature can sufficiently bestow.

I closed my eyes, fighting off a sudden sense of sadness. Ever since I was a child it was always the same sensation: a sudden hollowness in the chest as if one had been submerged in very cold water, not quite life-threatening but close enough to produce a sort of small death nonetheless. I rolled to my back, watching the flashes of light against my eyelids as I remembered how as a boy I would lie awake and pray that God would somehow cough my parents back up like Jonas from the whale. But he never did.

I opened one eye and looked at the clock by my bed, then watched the red minutes lumber past like empty rail cars. Even as a child I'd felt time's slippery absurdity, stealthy as a pickpocket working a drunken crowd. How many times did my parents imagine their future when it wasn't their future at all? What would they have changed if they knew? What should I change because I don't know? *And isn't that the most important question of all?*

After they died I struggled for months to comprehend how all that tangible, noisy, loving presence could simply vanish. I spent hours at the library after school gazing at illustrations of heaven, squeezing my eyes shut in concentration as I tried to visualize some workable scenario. I wasn't convinced that such a place really existed, but I felt better knowing that if it did, then that's exactly where they would be. One night when I couldn't sleep because my head was so full of things I needed to tell them I sat at my desk and pulled out a sheet of lined paper and wrote them a long letter, the pencil tight and sticky in my trembling fingers, then another the next night and another the night after that until I had dozens of letters stuffed beneath my mattress because I didn't know what else to do with them.

And then I started writing stories, just a few pages at first and then longer ones as I tried to coax my parents back to life. I don't think three people ever had as many adventures as we did in my stories, sparring with pirates on one page and outwitting the darkest shades of evil on the next. I loved the freedom of being able to make things the way I wanted them to be rather than the way they were. Sometimes I was a superhero who pulled my parents from the fire with seconds to spare and other times I rerouted us to Disneyland. Yet I had difficulty composing happy endings that felt believable, and occasionally I had to stop midstory when I sensed something terrible was about to happen and I wasn't sure I could prevent it. Every week I wrote another story, not just about my parents but about kids at school and my teachers and Dr. Radley's nervous tics and even Aunt Margaret's psychotic cats. But the more I wrote, the more I became aware of a swelling chasm between the world as it was and the way I longed for it to be. Gradually I understood that a person could get lost in such a place if he wasn't careful.

My mother always said that her sister didn't have a maternal bone in her considerable body and she was right. But Aunt Margaret did her very best imitation of a mom even if it was mostly guesswork fortified by a nightly gin and tonic. (I once caught her reading a manual on parenting carefully hidden behind her soap opera magazine.) When she was hospitalized that first winter with a respiratory infection I thought she would die too, which made me want to bang my fists against the world all over again. *You can't have her!* Twice I rode my bike to church to pray for her and twice I had a vision of God as a sniper picking us off one by one. And damned if he wasn't the best shot there ever was.

Aunt Margaret soon recovered but I never did. As far as my young mind could tell, we were all tiptoeing across an enormous trapdoor that might be sprung at any moment, hurling us into the abyss. Night after night as I wrapped myself in my sheets I wondered where the trapdoor led and when it would spring open next. Nobody made it all the way across, not even movie stars or Olympic athletes or the richest people in the world. Some just made it farther than others, or traveled in greater comfort. Was that the point, to see how far you could go before the ground gave way? *Whoosh.*

Another large crack of thunder shook the house, the sound rolling through the floor and walls while the wind pried at the window. I sat up and turned the light on, then pulled a book from my bag and tried to read. After ten minutes I turned the light off again and tried once more to sleep, this time with the pillow over my head. Within seconds another burst of thunder sent my whole body into contraction. *To hell with it.* I turned the light on again, pulled on my pants and shirt and quietly opened the bedroom door, deciding to wait out the worst of the storm downstairs by the fire.

I'd just entered the darkened living room when I saw Shannon sitting on the couch, dressed only in a long white T-shirt that came partway down her thighs.

"Hi," she whispered, crossing and re-crossing her arms over her chest. Her face was just barely lit by the orange glow of the embers and I couldn't tell if she was embarrassed.

"Oh, hi. I hope I didn't startle you. I couldn't sleep."

"Neither could I."

I remained standing.

"Might as well join me," she said, sliding over to one end of the couch. I noticed a half empty wine glass on the table beside her.

I hesitated, then took a seat, trying to ignore her bare legs.

"Is this your run-of-the-mill Wyoming storm or are we in the End of Days here?" I said as another thunderclap shook the house.

She smiled, still covering her chest with her arms. "This is nothing."

"That's a relief."

"How about some wine?"

"Great idea." I went into the kitchen and poured myself a large glass from the open bottle on the counter, deciding that the brandy had already been blasted from my system. When I returned Shannon was adding more wood to the fire. Almost immediately all the tones changed from orange to yellow and I could see her face clearly.

"Sorry about tonight," she said, sitting down again and trying to cover herself with her shirt. "I shouldn't have gotten started with Mom. You'd think after all these years I'd do better around her but sometimes I think I just get worse."

"You're both under a great deal of strain."

"We're both crazy is the problem." She took a drink from her wine. "Did you and your aunt fight a lot?"

"I think we felt too sorry for each other to fight." It was true. At first we were like two strangers stuck in an elevator, polite but increasingly anxious for rescue. Only gradually did we come to love each other; a protective, unquestioning sort of love that made up for our impossible differences.

Shannon kept looking at me, then drew her knees into her chest and pulled her T-shirt down over them, wrapping her arms around her legs. "Mom says you're a big shot architect?"

"Actually, I'm not an architect. I thought that's what I wanted to be but it turned out it was what my father wanted to be, only he had his hands full running the machine shop started by my grandfather. I work for an ad agency." I took a long drink of my wine. "Pays the bills."

"I thought you were going to be a writer," she said. "I thought you were going to write books."

"What gave you that idea?"

"You did."

"I did?"

"In a Christmas card. You must have been about twelve. I still remember what you wrote: *Merry Christmas and Happy New Year from your friend Ryan. P.S. I got a story published in the school paper and I'm going to be a writer when I grow up.*"

I smiled self-consciously. "Things change." I took another drink, deciding not to mention two unfinished manuscripts I'd abandoned years ago. "I teach a writing course on the side at a local youth center. Two nights a week, nothing fancy. We worked on a literacy campaign at the agency and I started doing some tutoring, which lead to the class, though I don't remember exactly how. If you're wondering why teenage dropouts would be interested in creative writing the answer is free pizza. And basketball privileges."

"I bet you're a wonderful teacher."

"Not on the days I want to jump out the window. It's kind of a rowdy crowd. Touchy, too. But now and then something amazing happens." I looked out the window as a flash blanched the trees and the barn. "Hopefully it helps."

"Them or you?"

Her question took me back. "Them." I finished off my wine, then sat back in my seat to get some distance from her. "So what do you do in San Francisco?"

"I'm a veterinary assistant. I used to be in management consulting but I got tired of throwing up Monday mornings. I do better with animals than people."

We listened to the storm and the fire, one shouting and the other whispering. *Three things will always calm your soul*, my father used to say whenever we roasted marshmallows by Dobson's Lake: *a campfire, the night sky and the sea*. I liked to think that if he had lived he would have mentioned other things as well.

"I thought you were married," Shannon said, looking at my hand.

"I was."

"Oh."

I thought back to the day I gave my ring away to a homeless woman who lived in the park across from my apartment. I assumed she'd pawn it but instead she placed it on her finger—actually her thumb—and kept it there, batting her eyes at me every time I passed by. To my horror, I soon realized that she actually believed we were married, or at least betrothed. I never told Carol but I was tempted once or twice. I don't imagine she would have seen the humor in it.

"Any kids?"

"No kids."

"That's good—I mean if you think it's good. Though to tell the truth I always imagined you with lots of kids—after what you'd been through and all."

"In this case it's good." But she was right: every time I visited my parents' graves I promised myself that if I had children I'd have at least two because no one should have to bury their parents alone.

"I hope you don't mind my saying that."

"I don't mind."

"So what happened?"

It began to occur to me that she might ask just about anything. "It was probably all the things that didn't happen," I said finally. I'd never found a good way to put it without sounding dismissive or sour.

"Like what?"

Before I could think of how to respond she stopped me, her small palms braking in the air. "Forget it. It's none of my business. I think I'm still stoned."

I stared at the fire, the day suddenly condensing into a weight I wasn't sure I could carry much longer. "So what about you?"

"We've been married five years. But no kids—or not my own. I have a stepdaughter, Melissa. She's twelve and about the cutest thing you've ever seen. Brian has joint custody so I'm sort of a half mom. I was terrible at first but I've gotten better. I just adore her." She hooked her hair behind her ears. "Brian went home last week. He's not too good at this kind of thing."

The room went white, followed almost instantly by thunder that seemed to rise from the ground.

"We lost a tree once to lightning," I said. "I was about five but I still remember the sound. My mother was terrified but not my father. He would have stood in the yard to watch a lightning storm if my mother had let him."

She picked up her wine and took a drink, then spun the glass slowly in her hand. "Do you have a lot of memories of your parents?"

I shrugged. "Some. To tell the truth, I'm no longer sure which ones are real and which ones I made up."

"I wonder the same thing." She fixed her eyes on the fire. As I studied her profile I thought of how much she looked like her mother, all the years peeled away. Was that how Alessandra felt when she looked at her daughter, as if she were staring back at herself?

After a few minutes Shannon turned to me. "How did you do it?"

"Do what?"

"Survive? I keep trying to think about how I'm going to deal with Dad's death but you were just a boy…"

"I didn't have a lot of choice."

She turned back to the fire. "Sometimes I feel like my fingers are being pried from the one thing I've always been able to hold on to."

"You find other things, eventually."

"What did you find?"

I didn't respond.

"I'd like to know."

"Well… there are plenty of things I'm grateful for."

"But something's missing?"

"Something's always missing, isn't it?"

"I'm starting to think so." She drank from her wine. "My mother's always found comfort in prayer—she even keeps a picture of the Pope on her dresser—but I'm not like that at all."

"So what *are* you like?"

She looked surprised by the question. "How did we get into this conversation?"

"I have no idea."

"Well I guess I'm…" She seemed suddenly embarrassed. "I'm tired, that's what I am." She put her glass down and stood up. "I'd better go to bed." She started toward the stairs, arms crossed over her chest. Outside the flashes were almost continuous now. "You'll be okay?"

"So long as I'm not struck dead."

"Think of it as a show," she said.

"Right. Front row seats."

She smiled briefly. "Goodnight then."

"Goodnight."

CHAPTER
NINE

April 29, 1944

Dear Jim,

It's nearly two in the morning but I couldn't sleep with all the thoughts and fears fluttering inside of me so I got up and read through every single one of your letters, thinking it would help. But it didn't help at all and now I miss you so much I don't even know what to do with myself except write you another letter, knowing my words will find their way to you even if I can't.

At least I've got Hank with me. I promise to give him back when you return but it won't be easy. Even my mom's warmed up to him and she's been afraid of dogs since she was five and got bit. I wish you could see him right now all curled up in a tight little brown ball beside me. (How anything can shed so much hair without going completely bald is beyond me.) I know you told me not to let him sleep on the bed but I just couldn't help it because he looked so lonely on the floor. Besides, we both need the company. Tomorrow I'm going to take him down to the river for a swim and then we're both going to visit Steve Jeiter, who came home from the hospital yesterday. Everybody pitched in to build a ramp up to his front door and there's going to be a party for him on Saturday. I know I'm going to cry but I'll try my best to hide it.

Remember how you always liked to take my hands in yours and look at them? I'm afraid you'd hardly recognize them now they're such a mess from helping Mom all week with the scrap metal drive. Dad says she could talk a person out of their teeth just to get to the fillings. (I happen to know that he's hidden a few items from her and he's not the only one.) I think she'd launch another drive next week if she thought there was a single spare coffee pot left in the county. Somewhere out there is a tank or bomber that ought to have her name on it.

Everything is so quiet right now that I can hear a train all the way in Linton hauling its lonely freight to God only knows where. Outside my window the moon is watching me and I wonder if it's watching you, too. It's nice to think we might both be looking at the same thing, even though it makes me miss you even more.

Sometimes at night if I try real hard I can almost feel your arms around me. And then I imagine your skin against mine and the roughness of your face and then your breath in my ear until I can hardly think straight with my heart pounding so. And then when I tell myself that you're halfway around the world I want to fly like a bird to you but I can't. I can't seem to do anything but ache.

Hank's just woken up and started poking his nose at this letter so I think he sends his love too. (Those are Hank's drool marks on the left.) My eyes are too tired to write any more so I'm going to turn off the light again and imagine your arms around me. Please squeeze me as hard as you can.

Love,
Your Rebecca

CHAPTER TEN

SOMETIMES I THINK we're born with all our love in us, that first cry of life like the bursting of a cork. Then it's a matter of making sure, *absolutely sure*, that we give it all away before we die. But there are some kinds of love that you can't give to just anybody, which is why some people die with a lot of love still trapped inside of them like screaming passengers on a sinking ship.

Of all the things I fear, that is what I fear most.

So does Lupo, who's become the closest thing I have to kin besides Aunt Margaret. He doesn't know he fears it but he does. I can see it in his eyes. I think it's one of the reasons we understand each other so well.

I first met Lupo two years earlier when he dropped in on one of my classes at the center. He only attended once. "Writing is *not* my thing," he huffed, handing in his assignment at the end of class. Instead of an essay he'd covered every inch of the page with doodles.

"Just what exactly is this?" I said.

"It's a picture of an essay. *And*, it's a limited edition so you might want to hold on to it. I even signed it."

"Very thoughtful."

"Thanks." He peeled out the door.

Lupo never came to class again but I saw him at the center

frequently playing ping-pong and pool and basketball, especially when there was any food around. And then one evening after class I caught him trying without success to remove the stereo from my car parked two blocks away. I had a distinct size advantage—he was only fourteen at the time and barely weighed 120—and I quickly pinned him to the ground.

"Ah man, I didn't know it was your car," he said, squirming beneath me.

"What difference does it make?"

"It makes *all* the difference."

I called the police and had him arrested, thinking he needed a good scare. But when I went to press charges and learned that his father was serving twelve years for armed robbery and his mother had recently died of breast cancer (Lupo lives with an older brother who runs a towing service) I began to ask more questions. When he broke down in tears near the end of our first meeting I saw enough of myself to think that maybe I could help. We've spent almost every Sunday together since and Lupo is pulling a B- average at school. In his own guileless way, he's one of the most charming people I know.

He was wary at first, his insides clenched like a fist. Sometimes when I took him out for a pizza we'd just sit there in silence, both of us staring at the last piece and pretending we didn't want it. But then I discovered that he loved movies and that the good ones had a way of softening him so that afterward he'd want to talk. Pretty soon we were covering more ground than either of us expected. When he learned how my parents died I think he decided I was the first person in his life he could trust.

"So how come your marriage didn't work?" he asked as we sat on the floor propped up against my couch after watching *Cinema Paradiso*. (When I noticed he had to squint to read the subtitles I had him fitted for contacts. He was so excited that for the next month he read every road sign and billboard out loud the moment it came into view until finally I told him I couldn't take it anymore. *"Twenty-five when school children are present!"* he'd holler, slapping his thighs in delight.)

"We thought two halves could make a whole, only it doesn't work that way."

"How does it work?"

"I think it's more like a journey that you both need to make on your own two feet." I was making this up on the fly. In truth, I'd come to believe that two wholes were often reduced to a bewildered half. There were even times when I wished I'd never read my parents' letters because they only reminded me of what I couldn't find, and was tired of looking for.

"If I met the right woman I'd carry her."

"I'm sure you would, Lancelot."

"Why are you always calling me that?"

"You're a romantic." And he was: half the fights he got in (and inevitably lost) were over girls and he could hardly make it from one end of the mall to the other without going into multiple states of rapture. The first time I brought him to my office he was so taken with the receptionist that he developed a tic in the left side of his long, lovelorn face.

"I'm a romantic without a girlfriend, which is pretty much like being a big time celebrity without any fans."

"Kind of awkward."

"Extremely awkward." He chomped down on his thumbnail. "I *really* need a girlfriend."

"Give it time."

"Time is the worst part."

"Time is the essential part, at least if you want to long fully and properly."

"I don't wanna long at all."

"Dude, we're humans. Longing is one of the things we do best. It may even be our cosmological assignment. If it's helpful, think of Earth as a sort of gospel choir for the rest of the universe."

"It's not helpful and you're not being funny."

"You think I'm kidding? Name one person you know who's not aching for something they can't quite get their hands on—and I'm not just talking about a date."

Lupo grew silent, thoughts tunneling across his face like anxious gophers. Gradually his large mouth opened wide as his head swung side to side. "That is *soooo depressing.*"

"The trick is to long with *style.*"

"The trick is to get a girlfriend." He finished off the last piece of pizza, cheese dripping down his chin. "So how come I've never met any of your girlfriends?"

"If I find someone special you'll be the first to know."

"How long have you been divorced?"

I rolled my eyes. "A long time. Now can we—"

"Who dumped who?"

"Nobody *dumped* anybody."

"You got dumped, didn't you?"

"*No.* We just made a mistake, that's all. It was very mutual."

"Yeah, right. Want to know what I think?"

"Nope."

"I think she probably got tired of waiting for you to say what's on your mind."

"What the hell is that supposed to mean?"

"What it means is that you've got to loosen up a bit."

"*Oh, please.*"

"Someone's got to tell you. For example, I look at you, I can't even tell whether you're enjoying the movie or not." He gestured toward the TV, the silver bracelet on his wrist jangling. "You ever consider going into the Secret Service? 'Cause you'd be *per*fect. You could be my bodyguard." He laughed to himself.

"Thank you for your insights."

"What are friends for?"

"Beats me."

"Now with me, see, I put it all on the table. And I do this little thing with my eyes—make 'em all twinkly, only there's more to it than that so don't even try it—to give the girls a taste of what's in store." He bugged his eyes out and gave a big smile.

"No wonder they're pounding down your door."

"I don't hear your doorbell ringing. How come you got nothing better to do than hang out with me every weekend?"

"I'm starting to wonder that myself."

"I think you need to get laid."

"Enough."

"How long has it been?"

"None of your damn business."

"I bet it's been a *long* time. All you ever do is work."

"I've got seven projects going right now, okay? Actually, you make eight. I'm *very* busy."

"Okay, okay." He raised his palms in the air, then went to the refrigerator and served himself a huge bowl of ice cream. *"Busy busy busy,"* he muttered, making a face at me. After he finished eating he insisted on replaying the last fifteen minutes of *Cinema Paradiso.*

"Man, that's a killer," he said at the end, wiping his small eyes. Lupo was so sensitive that at times he resembled a man walking barefoot over gravel. He scavenged the empty pizza box for crumbs. "So you think there's like, one person out there for you?"

"Maybe a baker's dozen."

"How you supposed to ever find them?"

"I'll defer to the poets on that one."

"I'm pretty certain there's only one woman for me."

"What makes you think that?"

"I can feel it inside me, like a voice."

"A woman's voice?"

"Of course it's a woman's voice. And I'm pretty certain that wherever she is, she can feel it too."

"That must be comforting."

"More like torture." He scoured the pizza box one last time.

"Well, good luck finding her."

"Thanks, I have a feeling I'm gonna need it." He started biting on his thumbnail again. "Mind if I get myself some more ice cream?"

I should have known from his tattoos that Lupo was in a gang but I didn't, not until he got in trouble again for shoplifting. I asked the court to give me three months.

My first plan was to have him move in with me for a semester but his brother Jorge wouldn't hear of it, afraid of losing control over one of the few people he could order around. So instead I drove Lupo to and from school every day for six weeks, hoping that if he could avoid the treacherous commute through his neighborhood long enough he could fade safely into the background. The day I didn't drive him he got his nose broken two blocks from his house.

"It doesn't matter," he said the next time I saw him.

"What do you mean it doesn't matter? How about you let me talk to these idiots?"

"Ah man, they'd kill you. I mean, you're big and all but you're like, so *white*."

Finally I came up with a solution.

"You're going to tell them you found Jesus," I explained as I tried to teach him how to play tennis one Sunday. I figured it was time to make good use of all the years I logged within the humid confines of the Riverside Assembly of God Pentecostal Church, Aunt Margaret sweating beneficently at my side.

"*What?*"

"They're going to keep beating you up if they think you're suddenly too good for them so we need an entirely different strategy. We need something from *above*."

His eyes rolled up. "Above?"

"They can't beat up a kid who found Jesus. Their mothers would wring their necks. They'll want nothing to do with you."

"You're crazy."

I reached into my gym bag and pulled out three fake gold crosses on heavy chains. "You're going to wear these. Just between home and school."

Lupo's eyes mushroomed out of his face. "What have you been smoking?"

"Just try it. Tell them you've been saved and that Jesus is walking with you. Start talking about their souls."

"They don't have souls."

"That's why it'll make them nervous. Just give it a try."

"No way."

"Come on, we'll practice." I put down my racquet and gave him my best born-again imitation, which I used to practice in my room each Sunday after church until one day when Aunt Margaret found me on the carpet speaking in tongues and threatened to beat the devil out of me with a broom. (A week earlier she'd confiscated a Ouija board I'd bought at a garage sale and was using to try to contact my parents. The only word I'd successfully spelled with my eyes closed was *cat.*)

"You're scaring me," he said, backing away. By the time I demonstrated a laying on of hands he was rolling on the court in laughter.

After two more beatings Lupo put on the crosses.

"It worked!" he said, all smiles the next time I saw him. "I felt just like a skunk!"

"How about a lion of Christ?"

"No, definitely more like a skunk."

Four months later I took Lupo to have his gang tattoos removed, leaving only the heart on his scrawny left bicep that said simply: *Mom.*

Once Lupo stopped hanging out on the street he spent most of his time in his room wishing he was somebody else. The only things that seemed to interest him were girls and cars, neither of which he could get his hands on. Sometimes I felt like he was going under and I couldn't get a good enough grip on him to pull, not until the day we were driving down I-75 and he pointed up at a graffiti-covered overpass and announced, "I did that."

I quickly looked up, catching just a glimpse of brightly painted concrete. *"That?"*

"Yeah."

"You're bullshitting."

"How come you get to swear and I don't?"

"I'm older. How the hell did you get up there?"

"I had a rope. I kinda hung over the side. I'm not saying it was ideal."

"Jesus, Lupo." I took the first exit.

"Where are you going?"

"I'm turning around so I can take another look."

"Really? It's not that good. I can do better."

I slowed as we approached the overpass again. Brilliant swirls rolled above us like surging waves, each one interlocked with the next. "It's amazing."

"Thanks." He beamed.

"How did you learn to do it?"

"Just practice. My mom used to paint. I've been thinking we need a painting class at the center."

"So where else have you practiced?"

"You don't even want to know."

I smiled despite myself and he smiled too. "How would you like to make money painting?"

"It's not even legal."

"Not graffiti, you knucklehead. I'm talking about houses. You know: walls, ceilings."

He made a face. "Walls and ceilings? Like, all one color?"

"Like, *yes*."

"What's the point of that?"

"Money."

Once school ended I got him a summer job working for a contractor I knew and for his birthday I bought him a box of paints and an easel, promising to keep him supplied with materials so long as he kept his grades up. A week later I got home from work to find a large oil painting of my parents hanging above the sofa in the living room, their poses identical to an old photo I kept by my bed. Only this time I was between them. A note attached to it said, "This is why I like to paint."

Lupo was the only person I told about my trip to Wyoming. I wasn't going to tell him but I knew he'd find out. Keeping a secret from him was like visiting a kennel with a pocketful of treats.

He called me the night before I left.

"You gotta take a picture of his hands."

"No, Lupo."

"How am I ever gonna see what they look like?"

"You're not."

"You sure you don't need me to come with you? School's kinda slow right now."

"I think I can manage."

"I don't know, seeing those hands might really fuck with your head."

"You don't swear with me, remember?"

"Oh yeah. Sorry. So what are you going to do when you see him?"

"I don't know."

"Shit, I'd give anything to be there."

I closed my eyes and rubbed my temples.

"I did it again, didn't I? Sorry, I'm just kinda wired at the moment."

"You haven't been partying have you?"

"No partying. I'm a skunk of Jesus, remember?"

"So what's up? Wait, let me guess: you finally asked Jasmine out?" Two months earlier Lupo had ridden his bike all the way across the city to my apartment to tell me that he'd found his true love. "It's her!" he said breathlessly, grabbing me by the shirt. Jasmine worked at the 7-Eleven near where he lived and each day he stopped in for a Slurpee hoping she'd realize that he was the one she'd been looking for. So far he'd put on eight pounds and she still hadn't looked up but he figured it was just a matter of perseverance.

"She did something with her hair," he said.

"So?"

"So, it's perfect."

"I'm happy for both of you."

"I'm not saying it wasn't perfect before, but now it's *totally* perfect."

"She's a very pretty girl."

"Pretty? Lots of girls are pretty. She's like... can I swear?"

"Try to work around it."

"She's like..."

"You can do it."

"You know what I'm saying. And see, that's what I need to talk about because the situation is *totally out of control.*"

"You've been buying a Slurpee from this girl every day for two months and now that she's done something with her hair—okay, perfected her already perfect hair—the situation is careening out of control?"

"*Exactly.* And the worst part is, I can't stop thinking about her going out with some... can I swear?"

"*No.* Now listen, you have got to ask her out."

"I told you, I can't."

"What's worse, being rejected or watching some other guy—"

"Don't say it."

"Sweep her off her feet?"

"Ah man, you said it." His voice twisted like a corkscrew.

"Well, which is it?"

He groaned. "I need another choice."

"Have you ever heard of Emerson? Ralph Waldo Emerson?"

"Maybe, maybe not, but anybody who is a Ralph *and* a Waldo could probably use a big ol' cross."

"Here's a little advice from one of his essays: 'Never mind the ridicule, never mind the defeat: up again, old heart!' Now I have to finish packing. We can talk when I get back."

"You sure I can't go with you?"

"Positive."

"I'm here for you if you need me. You can even pull me out of class if you want to, that is, unless my ridiculous old heart is on the floor, in which case you can just mop my sorry ass up when you get back."

"Thank you, Lupo. And remember: only one Slurpee a day."

"Right. And you give those hands of God a high-five for me."

"I'll try."

CHAPTER
ELEVEN

"RYAN? RYAN, ARE you awake?"

I opened my eyes and focused on a series of hand-painted horse-shoes that hung in a row above the dresser.

"I hate to disturb you but it's such a lovely day." It was Alessandra, her cheerful voice pressed right up against the closed bedroom door.

I looked at my watch: almost eight. "Be out in a minute." I threw back the sheets, sat up on the edge of the bed and rubbed my temples, wondering if other people awaken as if tossed from a speeding train. I thought of Shannon and how nice she looked by the light of the fire, then of Mike in his bed just down the hall fighting for every breath, which made me feel guilty for thinking about his married daughter.

"You like pancakes, don't you? I make 'em large or extra large."

"Sounds great." I gave my head a shake and stood up.

"Extra large then."

I quickly dressed, threw some water on my face and hurried downstairs, where opera music filled the living room. I paused, enjoying the scratch and pop of the record player, which re-minded me of the parties my mother used to throw, everybody putting on silly hats and prancing around the room when the liquor got flowing.

"Coffee?" asked Alessandra as she placed a plateful of Frisbee-sized pancakes on the kitchen table.

"Thanks." I stifled a yawn.

"I hope the bed wasn't uncomfortable?"

"No, it was great."

She poured me a cup, then took a seat across from me and smiled. Once again I was struck by how attractive she was, her youthful beauty replaced by something just as interesting.

"Is Shannon up?"

"She left early to run some errands in Sheridan. She's always been an early bird just like her father."

I tried to hide my disappointment.

"There are plenty more pancakes," she said, eyeing the stack on my plate. "Or I can make up an omelet if you prefer…"

"This is just great, thank you."

She watched me eat, her fingers laced together on the table and her back straight. With each bite I took she nodded in satisfaction. "I thought maybe you and Mike could have some time together this morning. He's alert now."

"As long as he's up for it. I don't want to tire him out."

"You're the best medicine he could have." She got up and took a red-checkered dish towel from a wooden rack, then began to wipe down the counter. "He can be shy. Sometimes you have to push a little bit." She made a gesture with her hand.

"Got it."

Mike was propped up in bed watching a documentary about penguins on the small TV in the corner when I knocked. "Mind if I bother you?"

"Come on in." He searched his lap for the remote until I found it for him and helped him turn off the TV.

"Sleep all right?" he asked, not looking directly at me.

"Yes, fine. How about you?"

"Seems to be the only thing left I'm any good at. Never slept past five for forty years and now I'm like an old sheepdog." He reached for a glass on the bed stand and took a drink of water, spilling some on his shirt. His brow creased in concentration as he put the glass back down. "Hope you got a good fill of breakfast."

"Delicious, thanks." I hesitated by the foot of the bed, then pulled up a chair. "Are you in a lot of pain?"

"Could be worse." He folded his hands on his lap. His breathing was so shallow that I found it difficult to listen to.

"Let me know if there's anything I can do," I said, feeling stupid as I said it.

He waved me off, then refolded his hands. I looked across the bed at a large black and white photograph of three smiling young soldiers, arms draped around each other as they leaned toward the camera. "That's you in the middle, isn't it?" I said.

"If you can believe it." Mike turned toward the photo. "And that's Rick Allers on the left and Ben Wallerstein on the right. Both crazy as coyotes but damn good soldiers. If that truck hadn't pulled up right behind us you'd see the Roman Coliseum in the background."

"Are you still in touch with them?"

"They never came home."

"I'm sorry." I stared at the faces in the photo. "My father was in the service. The navy. I always wish I knew more."

Mike didn't respond.

"I'd be interested to hear about your experiences—that is, if you don't mind me asking?"

"It was a very long time ago."

"But it doesn't feel that way, does it?"

For the first time he looked straight at me.

"What I mean is… I would think sometimes it would seem like it wasn't very long ago at all."

"You're right about that," he said.

"What year did you join?"

He struggled to sit up. "I was drafted right out of high school in '42. I didn't think twice about it. It's just what you did."

"Did you go to boot camp here in Wyoming?"

"Texas. Hot as Hades. We didn't even have real rifles at first because there weren't enough of them to go around. Hell, some of the boys were shooting Germans before they'd had much chance to shoot targets. Figure that. 'Course, being from Wyoming I knew a thing or two about guns."

"And then you were shipped to Italy?"

"Clark's Fifth Army. I was just a mortar man but a damn good one if I may say so."

"I don't really know anything about the Italian part of the war."

"Not many people do." He glanced over at the photograph on the wall. "We landed at Anzio just south of Rome in January of '44. Kesselring's troops put up a hell of a fight and it wasn't until May that we broke out of the beachhead. We marched into Rome two days before D-day. Of course, Normandy got all the attention. Still does." He fiddled with the oxygen tube beneath his nose, then looked back at the photo. "In the fall of '44 the retreating German Army dug in behind a series of defensive positions in the mountains north of Florence. The Gothic Line stretched from the Adriatic to the Mediterranean. Behind that the Germans built the Winter Line. Lots of fortifications, tank traps, mines, booby traps—the Germans had a knack for that sort of thing. We had a hell of a time. But don't get me wrong, I was one of the lucky ones."

He stared down at the green oxygen tank. "I meant to send you a birthday card," he said.

"Don't worry about it."

"Forty is a good age. I suppose most of them are good except for mine."

I looked down at his hands, wanting to hold them. "I thought I died in the accident. When you pulled me from the fire I thought... this may sound strange but I thought I was dead. I thought you were... well, I don't know what I thought but I can never thank you enough for what you did."

"I tried my damnedest to save your parents."

"I know that."

"Maybe if I'd gotten to them a few seconds sooner." I noticed that his fists were clenched.

"You couldn't have done more. Nobody could have."

He was breathing fast now, sweat melting down the sides of his face.

"Are you okay?"

"Just tired, that's all." He turned toward the window, the light catching all the lines that crisscrossed his face without any defining pattern, like time had taken a bullwhip to him.

I hesitated, then backed slowly out of the room. "I'll be downstairs if you need anything."

He didn't respond.

"How'd it go?" said Alessandra, who was in the living room watering the plants that crowded every corner.

"Fine, I guess. He got tired."

"I'll just go and check on him."

"Actually, he seemed to want to be alone. But maybe you should anyway."

She started toward the stairs, then stopped. "No, when he wants to be alone he means *alone.* Took me years to learn that but I finally did."

"What do the doctors say?"

She paused. "That he's living on nothing but willpower."

"I had no right to ask."

"Of course you did. You're practically family." She gave my arm a squeeze, then crouched over a small amaryllis and probed the soil with her fingers. Moments later a vehicle careened into the driveway.

"She rides horses the same way," sighed Alessandra, putting down her watering can.

Shannon burst through the door.

"I didn't expect you back so soon, Sweetie," said Alessandra. "Did you forget something?"

"I was halfway to Sheridan and I got this terrible feeling. Is he—"

"He's resting."

She looked at me, then quickly looked away. "I'll go check on him." She loped up the stairs.

Alessandra watched her with a sigh. "She's always flown by intuition. Even as a young girl she'd get these premonitions. Luckily they were usually wrong or the world would be nothing but cinders by now. Is it 'cinders' or 'sanders'?"

"Cinders."

When Shannon returned she looked relieved. "He's sleeping." Then she gave me a quick smile, shyness drawing her features together. I tried to think of something to say but all my thoughts seemed suddenly so complicated that I just smiled back.

"No use all of us sitting around here all day," said Alessandra, looking back and forth between us. "Why don't the two of you go for a ride? Lord knows the horses could use the exercise."

Shannon blushed. "I really think I should stay with Dad."

"You can't just watch him sleep."

"I like to watch him sleep."

Alessandra looked disappointed. "But just for a few—"

"*Mom.*"

After an awkward silence Alessandra turned to me. "Well, I suppose there's no reason I couldn't take you."

"I'm really not much of a rider and—"

"Oh, go on," said Shannon. "You can't come all the way to Wyoming without getting on a horse."

"Sure I can."

"No you can't." Shannon put her hands on her hips, chin up.

"It's settled," said Alessandra. "I'll go change and meet you by the barn in twenty minutes." She turned back to Shannon. "You're sure you'll be all right?"

"I think I can handle things, Mom."

Alessandra already had Rita and Renegade saddled and tied to a rail when I arrived, feeling slightly self-conscious in an old pair of Tony Lamas I'd packed, relics of a brief and not very convincing Western phase in college.

"Couldn't ask for better weather," she said with a big smile. She was dressed in jeans, boots and an orange shirt and wore leather riding gloves.

"I don't want you to feel like you have to entertain me."

"Nonsense. You're entertaining *me*."

I made a quick approximation of how far a horse could kick, doubled the distance for good measure and then drew an imaginary line in the dirt, making sure to stay on the far side of it. "I should warn you that I haven't been on a horse since my fifth birthday and that was at a petting zoo."

"It's a little bit of common sense and a lot of sitting." She untied the larger horse. "You'll ride Renegade." She ran her hand along Renegade's shiny auburn flank.

"Friendly name."

"He's Mike's horse. Gentle as a mouse."

"Can't say he looks very mousy."

She lifted a stirrup and adjusted the cinch. "Now, to mount up you face the back of the horse like this with your left hand on the horn holding the reins, then place your left foot in the stirrup and swing up like this." She demonstrated, looking surprisingly nimble for her age.

After two tries I managed to get up. Renegade snorted and stomped. "I'm not sure he likes me."

"Give him time. The important thing is to let him know who's boss."

"Oh, he knows all right."

She adjusted the stirrups, then handed me the reins. "You want to hold them in your left hand like this." She showed me.

"But that's my shooting hand." She gave me a funny look as I raised my index finger and cocked my thumb. "Never mind."

"To go left, move your hand over like this, and same thing on the right. Just a tap of your heels will get him going."

"I'm more interested in the braking mechanism."

"A firm pull on the reins. If he gets testy give him a couple of sharp jerks."

"Testy?"

"You'll be fine." She untied her horse and mounted, her swift movements displaying the physical assurance of someone who has spent a great deal of time outdoors. "Ready?" Before I could answer she turned and headed off. Renegade stomped, snorted, then grudgingly followed. I made sure my heels got nowhere near his flanks.

We went at a walk for the first hour, following a fence line before joining a trail that wound gradually up through rocky, pine-covered hills. Once I felt that Renegade and I had come to terms—Renegade would lead and I would make as little fuss as possible—I began to enjoy myself. Maybe I'm a country boy after all, I thought, as I watched Renegade's enormous head bob up and down. I tried to imagine Lupo on a horse but found it almost impossible to put one on top of the other. I promised myself to look into riding stables around Atlanta as soon as I got home.

When the trail widened Alessandra drew alongside me. "Perhaps Shannon can take you out tomorrow. She's a wonderful rider. Mike stuck her in the saddle when she was four and that was the last we saw of her. She won all sorts of awards in school: barrel racing, pole bending, you name it. I used to get so nervous watching her that Mike would make me wait in the car." Alessandra smiled apologetically. "But I'm afraid you're stuck with me today."

"You're a great guide." I wondered if she'd sensed my disappointment.

"I'm an old, arthritic guide. The truth is, I haven't been riding as much lately." She leaned forward and patted her horse along its neck. "Of course, things could be worse. You could have Brian as your guide."

"Shannon's husband?"

"He thinks he's John Wayne but he doesn't understand animals. Or women. He tries to manhandle them both when it's all in the nuances. Is that how you pronounce it, *nuance*?"

"Yes, *nuance*."

"I always thought she'd end up with someone more like her father." Alessandra seemed to be speaking to herself. "Brian means well but he just doesn't see what she needs. And she needs a lot. She always has. The truth is, I wish she'd just leave him—they're always fighting about one thing or another—but she's lost all her confidence. And she adores his daughter Melissa." She sighed. "God knows, she doesn't want my advice."

I wanted to ask more—a lot more—but decided not to. Instead I braced myself as a squirrel darted across the path. Fortunately, Renegade didn't have squirrel issues. "I can see why you love it out here," I said as we entered a meadow filled with small yellow flowers.

"I didn't at first. Not when I was younger. But you get so used to all the elbowroom that you can't hardly breathe anywhere else. Mike can't even go into Sheridan without feeling crowded." She laughed to herself. "He took me to New York once years ago for our anniversary—this was before Shannon was born and I'd begged him to go—but after two days he was as jumpy as a jaybird. Poor thing, I practically had to drag him out of the hotel each morning. 'By god, it's like being caught in a cattle drive,' he'd say as we walked down Fifth Avenue."

"I think I need to get out in the countryside a little more myself." I gripped the saddle horn as we crossed over a large log.

"No better medicine." She ducked under a large branch. "But I don't suppose an architect would find much work around here."

"Actually, I work at an ad agency."

"Oh. Well, that must be fun."

"Not really. I'm thinking about a career change. I've been teaching a writing class at a youth center and I really enjoy it, except for the occasional brawls."

"*Brawls?*" She struggled with the word.

"It's kind of a rough crowd. But you should read some of the stories they write. And then there's some you really don't want to read. Either way, I figure it's good for them."

"Some words seem to spend their lives looking for paper to rest on," she said.

"You sound like a writer yourself."

"Not a *real* writer." She paused. "But I do enjoy the feel of a good pen in my fingers. When I first moved here I used to write every night after Mike fell asleep. I didn't know what else to do with all the things inside of me and it was a way for me to practice my English. Some nights I could hardly turn off the light because there were always more words wanting to be set free."

"Did you ever show your work to anybody?"

"Oh goodness no," she said. "The words weren't meant for reading. They just needed a place to go. And then for some reason I stopped. I guess there seemed no point to it. But lately... well, it's given me something to do when I can't sleep." She pulled out in front of me. "Here's a nice open stretch. Shall we go a little faster?" Before I could respond she was off.

Trotting was about as much fun as riding a large jackhammer, but once we broke into a slow gallop I gradually found a sense of rhythm and before long fear gave way to a childlike sense of enjoyment.

"See, it's not so hard," she said as we slowed to a walk.

"I knew I was a natural at something."

We stopped at a stream to let the horses drink, then walked for another hour until we reached a high ridgeline. I turned in the saddle and looked down at the valley spread out far below, surprised by how far we'd traveled. Above us a single cloud, plump and creamy, inched across the ocean blue sky. "Shouldn't we be heading back?"

She looked at her watch. "I'm afraid I completely lost track of the time." She turned her horse and this time let me lead.

Renegade walked faster now. His neck was damp and the air strong with the smell of horse sweat mingled with leather and the scent of the surrounding pine trees, which produced a surprisingly pleasant aroma. I thought of Mike sitting in the same saddle and what it must have been like when he went for his very last ride. Then I thought of Shannon, a fleeting sense of hope rippling through me, followed quickly by unease because it had been years since I felt a deep sense of wanting.

I was twenty-eight when Carol and I married and thirty-two when I realized we were both moving in opposite directions, two duelers counting off the paces but too afraid to turn around and be done with it. Or maybe she was moving and I wasn't, which made her move even faster. I later understood that she married me for the man I might become while I married her to leave behind the man I was, which gave us at least one thing in common. Unfortunately, neither of us got our wish.

"You don't really have both feet in the game, do you?" said our marriage therapist, leaning forward in his chair during one of our private sessions.

"Which game would that be?"

"Your life."

I let his words wander the airless, book-lined room before slipping through the open blinds. "So where are you suggesting the other foot is, exactly?"

He took off his glasses, placed one end in his mouth and gave it a loud suck, then put them back on again, a process he would repeat several times before the fifty minutes were up. "I think it's kind of in midair somewhere, waiting for a safe place to set down."

"Sounds tiring."

"It does, doesn't it?"

The day Carol and I agreed to divorce I got on my bicycle and rode for seventy miles. And then when I couldn't ride anymore I got a hotel room and pretended to sleep and the next morning I go up and rode all the way back to the temporary apartment I'd moved into three weeks earlier.

But I never cried.

I turned in the saddle to look out over the valley below. "What a—" Suddenly Renegade reared. I tried to grab the horn but missed as my head snapped back, then forward, then back again.

"Hold on!" shouted Alessandra, bringing her horse close and leaning over to try to catch the reins. "Renegade, easy boy!"

He reared again, then sprung forward. I felt myself hurtling through the air just before I struck the hard ground.

"Are you all right?" Alessandra crouched over me.

I struggled to catch my breath. "I'm still deciding. What happened?"

"Something must have spooked him. Snake, maybe. I'm afraid you've got a nasty little cut." She took out a handkerchief and gently patted away the blood that trickled down from my forehead just above my left eye. "Fortunately it doesn't look too deep. Does anything else hurt?"

I wiggled my legs and slowly shook my head. "More a general sense of humiliation," I said. "But I'll live."

Alessandra suddenly stood, an anxious look on her face.

"What is it?"

"The horses."

I looked around but didn't see them.

"I should have known better. It's been months since I've ridden Rita and Renegade's not used to strangers." Alessandra started down the trail calling their names. When she returned her face was drawn. "I'm afraid they're back in the barn by now."

"I think I've had enough riding for today anyway," I said, holding the handkerchief to my forehead and waiting for the bleeding to stop.

"I should have tied up Rita. I don't know what I was thinking. Mike never would have let this happen." For a moment she looked so upset that I thought she might cry but she quickly steadied herself. "We'll have to walk."

"Frankly, I'd just as soon walk anyway."

"It's probably ten miles—downhill at least. But your leg?"

"It's just a limp. I don't even notice it. But what about you?"

"My knees aren't what they used to be, but I can manage. I just hate thinking of Shannon alone at the house with her father. If something were to happen…" I could see the urgency on her face.

I refolded the handkerchief and gently patted my forehead again. Despite a steady throb the bleeding had already slowed. Then I rose to my feet and dusted myself off. "I'm ready when you are."

She looked at me closely, as if assessing whether I could really manage. Then she turned and headed down the trail at a surprisingly fast clip.

We walked in silence at first. She kept a few paces ahead, slowing to let me catch up before she accelerated again. I sensed that she was anxious to get some distance behind us before wasting any breath on conversation.

"Am I going too fast?" she asked, slowing once again.

"No, not at all," I said, now sweating. I thought of Shannon, imagining her reaction when the riderless horses returned to the barn.

A few minutes later Alessandra began to sing in Italian under her breath.

"You have a nice voice," I said.

She stopped, bringing her hand to the small of her neck in embarrassment. "You'll have to forgive me. I'm so used to being alone."

"On the contrary, I was enjoying it."

As I followed her down a steep bend in the fire road I tried to imagine her as a young war bride reinventing her life in the American West. "I guess you don't get a lot of opportunity around here to use your Italian?"

"I dream in Italian. That's enough."

"When did you move to Wyoming?"

"Right after the war. I was quite a novelty back then."

"That must have been a real adjustment."

"I was young."

"I'm not sure I could handle it—I mean, living in a place this rural."

"Sure you could."

"But doesn't it ever get kind of…" I couldn't think of a way to finish.

"Lonely?"

"Yes."

"It doesn't get lonely in Atlanta?"

I smiled. "Well, yes. I just thought you might get a little isolated."

"I guess I'm used to it." She looked down at her watch. "Shannon will be furious with me. So will Mike. I can just hear him now: *Well, hasn't Alessandra made a fine mess of things.*"

"Maybe he'll have a good laugh."

"You're his *guest*." She hopped across a narrow stream.

"I consider this an adventure. I needed an adventure."

She gave me a doubtful look.

We walked in silence for another half hour, then sat against a large tree to rest, both of us swatting away the flies. The air was still and the sky sagged like a crowded hammock, clouds jostling for space.

"Shannon said her father never talks about the day he saved my life," I said.

"He keeps most thoughts to himself," Alessandra said. "It's just his nature. We've made it through entire winters with hand signals. It used to drive me crazy when we first married but I've gotten used to it. If there is one thing age has taught me it's that you can get used to just about anything." She wiped the sweat from her forehead with her sleeve. "The important thing is he's got a good heart. And you won't find a harder worker or a better father." She smiled to herself as she drew her knees up to her chest. "You should have seen his face the first time he held Shannon, those big leathery hands of his cradling her little head like he was holding a Fabergé egg. Sometimes he'd just sit in her room watching her sleep, always worrying about her kicking off her blankets and putting his ear to her mouth to make sure she was breathing. The day she left for college was the worst day of his life. I can still remember him standing out front after she drove off, like he was going to wait right there until she came back for the holidays. She'd always been the life of the house, filling it with all her noise. And then suddenly it was so *quiet*."

As I watched her expression change I found myself wondering what was worse: the things that had happened to her or the things that hadn't. I tried to change the topic. "Mike told me a little bit about taking part in the liberation of Rome during the war. He's had an amazing life."

"He was a good soldier. And of course, we Italians were so grateful. All the Americans were very kind to us."

"To be honest, I've never really quite understood what happened in Italy."

"It was a confusing time."

"When did Italy switch sides?"

"Mussolini was arrested on the orders of the king in the summer of 1943 after it was obvious even to the fools around *Il Duce* that he'd led Italy to disaster. Two months later the government declared an armistice with the Allies. Hitler wasn't too pleased and soon

Mussolini was freed as German troops took control of Northern Italy. Even families were torn by politics. It's a period most Italians would rather forget." She rose to her feet.

"You must have gone through a lot."

"We all did." She ran her hands distractedly over her hair, pulling her ponytail tight.

"What was it like in San Gianello during the war?"

Her face tensed.

"I didn't mean to pry."

She started to walk again. "I wouldn't even know where to begin."

"We don't have to talk about it."

"No, I don't mind, it's just that…" She stopped.

"Are you okay?"

Her expression wavered as she crossed her arms. "For years I've tried to leave my childhood behind because the war ruined it. It ruined it for millions of people. But then last night when I tried to sleep I couldn't because I felt so many things, things I hadn't let myself feel in a very long time." Her face filled with something I couldn't quite understand as she briefly closed her eyes and took a deep breath. "And then I realized…" She paused. "I realized that one of the things I'd left behind all these years was myself."

I waited for her to continue but instead she stared off at the valley below. Then she reached out and touched my cheek lightly with her fingertips before she turned and continued down the trail. As I tried to keep up I found myself trailing behind a pretty young Italian girl with the world just about to crash down upon her.

CHAPTER TWELVE

I WAS IN the rafters drawing pictures the first time I heard Papa and my oldest brother Marcello arguing about politics. We never talked about politics at the dinner table—it wasn't allowed—and as I peered down at them from my perch (they must have thought I was in the house) I was shocked to hear that my father didn't like Mussolini. Worse than that, he actually seemed to hate our leader! How could any Italian hate *Il Duce*, whose face had stared down at me from the classroom wall since I was a child? And besides, Marcello had told me that Mussolini had given Italy back its pride.

"When did we lose our pride?" I asked him as he rode me to school on the handlebars of his bicycle one day. "Long before you were born," he said.

I didn't dare move as I listened to them shout back and forth. Marcello was explaining why he wanted to join the Fascist militia— he spent all his free time hanging around the *fascio*, which was a kind of political clubhouse just off the piazza—but Papa wouldn't hear of it. "You are young and foolish," he said. "Please, just this once, listen to me and trust that I know better."

"The world's changing, Papa. You can't stop it."

"You have no idea how dangerous ideas can be, do you?"

"At least we have ideas."

"No, you have only empty slogans and silly songs and fancy costumes."

"We have armies." Marcello stood erect, chin up. For the first time I noticed that he was slightly taller than Papa, which surprised me. He'd also inherited Papa's broad shoulders and large hands, as well as his thick curly hair and strong Roman nose. All the local girls thought him the most handsome young man in our village and were only too happy to come and play at my house after school, which improved my status considerably.

"So it's war that you want, is it?"

"We're willing to fight for what we believe in, if that's what you are asking."

"You just may get your wish."

"What I want is your blessing."

"A father cannot bless his son's wish to die."

I'd never heard my father speak like that before and I'd never heard anybody talk back to my father, especially not one of his children. When they left I remained in the rafters, wrapping myself in the yellow blanket Mama had made for me and staring out the window at the green valley below, feeling more confused than I ever had before. If one of them was right, that meant that the other was wrong. Certainly Papa wasn't wrong because he was never wrong. Mama liked to joke that he knew the answers to questions people hadn't even thought to ask. And surely he knew a great deal more about Mussolini—and politics—than Marcello. Yet that meant that my oldest brother was wrong, along with a great many other Italians. It also seemed to mean that Marcello might somehow die.

They argued more and more after that, raising their voices even at dinner despite Mama's threats to put them both on rations of bread and water. Renaldo, my second oldest brother, who was good at sports but always getting into trouble, sided with Marcello while Stephano, who was frail and shy but extremely smart, sided with Papa. I began to hate Mussolini for ruining my happiness, even though I feared that hating *Il Duce* might be a mortal sin. You have to understand that we'd been brought up to revere *Il*

Duce as part savior, part Father Christmas, as ridiculous as that now sounds. Even in the smaller villages there were Fascist organizations for all ages and it could be dangerous not to join. As a child I'd belonged to *Figlie della Lupa*—Daughters of the Wolf— and when I turned eight I had to join the young girls group called *Piccole Italiane*—Little Italians—even taking an oath to spill my blood if necessary for the Fascist revolution. So you see, the idea that *Il Duce* might actually be a jackass, to use my father's word, was quite unsettling to me.

Finally I asked my mother. "Do you think Mussolini is a jackass?"

She nearly dropped her paring knife. "Alessandra, how dare you talk like that?"

"But do you?"

"I think someone's been putting words into your mouth, that's what I think."

"I need to know."

"And I need you to learn to speak like a young lady."

"Do you think he's a bad person?"

She seemed to hesitate. "It's complicated."

"But why?"

"Because politics are always complicated, especially for one so young. Now run out to the garden and get me some basil." She pinched my cheek and returned to peeling a large pile of boiled potatoes.

Alessandra stopped walking, looking suddenly embarrassed. "I don't know why I'm boring you with all this."

"I'm not bored in the least. And I was just beginning to forget that we have miles to go."

She looked uncertain.

"Please go on."

"Are you sure? It's so long ago and—"

"I'm sure."

She hesitated briefly, then scrunched her eyebrows together as she continued walking. "Now I've forgotten where I was."

"You'd just asked your mother if she thought Mussolini was a jackass."

"Ah, yes."

From then on it seemed that politics was just about all that anybody talked about, or maybe I was just getting old enough to notice. Everywhere I went it was *Il Duce* this and *Il Duce* that. Even the barn never felt quite as safe again. I'll never forget the look on my father's face when Marcello came home in his uniform strutting about like a matador and talking about the new Italy. Papa didn't even touch his dinner that night and afterward he sat in the courtyard for hours despite the chill. Obviously he preferred the old Italy, though I had no idea what the difference was.

I wept when Marcello left home, but in a way I was relieved, too, hoping that now things could go back to the way they were. But they didn't, not for long. Military service was mandatory, no matter how many rosaries my mother said, and gradually *Il Duce* took away all of my brothers, willing or not.

Renaldo was the next to go. Of the three boys I always thought he was my father's favorite, not only because he showed some interest in taking over the garage one day but because you could hardly look at Renaldo without feeling better about things. He wasn't nearly as handsome as Marcello—his eyes were a bit too far apart and he had Mother's small chin—but with his animal-like serenity it was widely agreed that he was the happiest soul in our village, his face permanently sweetened with the kind of smile that makes you smile back, even if you're in a terrible mood. "Either he knows something we don't or he's in for a big surprise one day," Papa would say affectionately as Renaldo skipped off to school in the morning, bursting into song before he even made it through the gate. He wasn't eager to join the army, not like Marcello, who would have slept in his uniform if it didn't wrinkle. But he didn't complain either, because he never complained about anything except for being hungry all the time no matter how much Mama fed him. (That was his one fear about the army—that there wouldn't be enough to eat.)

"But aren't you scared?" I asked him as he tucked me into bed one evening.

"Why should I be scared?"

"Because you might get shot."

"Shot?" He pretended to duck, then let out a laugh. "I'll just have to shoot first." That was Renaldo, carefree as our dog, Romeo. (His real name was Titian but Papa nicknamed him Romeo in honor of his exceptional ardor. Besides, I think Papa loved hearing my mother call out for Romeo. "Right here, dear," he'd say, emerging from the garage with a sweep of his arms.) Anyway, the only thing Renaldo really took seriously besides food was girls. I guess you could say that he and Romeo had a great deal in common. He fell madly in love at least once a week, welling up in the middle of dinner at the mere mention of his latest beloved's name, and he once nearly got jailed after being caught trying to peek through Luchina Garmandi's bedroom window. "You keep an eye on her for me until I get back, all right?" he'd said with a wink.

"But what if she falls in love with someone else?"

He drew his face close to mine, his expression so grave that I sank back in my pillow. "Then you must find out who he is and cut his throat!" He drew his hand across his neck in one swift motion.

The night before he left, Renaldo and his two best friends got terribly drunk, waking half the village as they sang in the streets. He didn't get home until two, still singing as he stumbled through the door. Papa and Stephano had to carry him into bed and the next morning we just barely got him to the train station on time. He looked and smelled so awful that the twins held their noses and Stephano joked that the army wouldn't want him. Yet even with his head aching he was as excited as a school boy, as if the army were just another one of life's great amusements. I still remember that big goofy smile of his as he waved to me, his other arm wrapped tightly around the large basket of food Mama and I had prepared for him. No one said a word during dinner that night or even asked for seconds of Mama's delicious *frittata di zucchine*. As soon as he finished, Papa returned to the garage, working until well after midnight.

That was in 1940. Two months later Mussolini declared war on France and Britain. I can remember Papa sitting by the radio, which he'd built himself, and shaking his head in disgust. "It's a disaster," he moaned. "A complete and utter disaster." I was afraid for Marcello and Renaldo, wondering if they were already under fire, but to be honest I was secretly excited, too. After all, war meant change and I was desperate for any sort of change in San Gianello, where life seemed so predictable that I couldn't tell one day from the next except by my mother's moods. Only nothing happened. For months and months I waited for the world to come rushing up the winding road that climbed from the valley, but the only change in our village was that more and more of the young men left, which meant that life became less exciting than ever.

I didn't see my first German soldier until 1942. I was fifteen then and Papa made me and the twins, who were seven, hide in a special crawlspace he'd built beneath the floorboards of the small pantry off the kitchen. You would have thought the devil himself was coming from the way Papa acted. He'd fought the Austrians on the Piave in the Great War and he'd always hated the Germans. "Hurry, girls!" he said, rushing us into the house and pulling up the floorboards.

"But there are spiders down here!" the twins cried.

"Hurry!"

I never saw a German that day. I figured it was the only chance I might ever get—so little happened in San Gianello—and I was furious. But then the very next day as I was walking home from school an entire column of German soldiers marched right down our main road. I'd never seen anything so exciting in my life. I wasn't about to hide, not without Papa there to chase me. Anyway, no one else was hiding. The soldiers smiled and waved and all the children waved and I remember feeling relieved that we were on the side of such handsome and strong looking men. What did I know? That's when I began to wonder whether perhaps it was my father who was mistaken. After all, even my teacher spoke highly of our German brethren. Why should I hate them for what happened in the past? I even began to feel sorry for Papa, who spent more and more time alone in his garage, often not returning to the house until late at night. When he buried Mama's jewelry and the silver beneath the chicken coop one afternoon I feared he might be going crazy.

It was months until I saw another German up close. Occasionally from our courtyard we could watch a convoy pass on the road that wound along the bottom of the valley, but the war still seemed far away and very confusing to me, with names of places that I could hardly pronounce. Then in the fall of 1942 Stephano went into the army, leaving me alone with the twins. I'd been dreading his departure for months. We'd always been close and I felt like he was the only one besides my father who really understood me. Marcello and Renaldo were both loud and outgoing but Stephano was a thinker, everything simmering just beneath the surface. Thin, soft spoken and sensitive, he had decided from the age of about five that he wanted to be a doctor, which was highly ambitious in our village, where few could afford to send their children to a university. He studied hard at school and read so many books—Papa was always trying to keep him adequately supplied—that Mama feared he'd go blind. I loved to sit next to him and look at his books with their drawings of skeletons and hearts and lungs and brains, listening as he patiently explained how each part functioned.

"Don't you think it's just a little bit gross?" I would ask as he traced his fingertip along a colored illustration of the intestinal tract.

"On the contrary, I think it's beautiful." From the tone of his voice you'd have thought we were standing before Ghiberti's baptistery doors.

"Could you really cut someone open?"

"Of course I could."

"Could you cut me open?"

He reached over and pinched my earlobe. "Only if I had to."

Whenever any of us were sick he insisted on overseeing our care, doting over us like we were at death's door. He said it was good practice and besides, he had a much better bedside manner than Dr. Cardoni, who always seemed slightly disappointed with any case not requiring last rites. I can remember Stephano placing his hand gently on my forehead when I was burning with fever, his face full of concern. I knew then that he'd make a wonderful doctor if he didn't go blind first reading all those books.

"It doesn't seem fair making you go kill people when you know so much about fixing them," I said as I sat in his room watching him pack.

"No it doesn't, does it?"

"At least maybe you'll get to see some real guts."

"Yes, maybe I will." He carefully folded his overcoat and placed it in his bag, then set two medical books on top.

"Promise me you'll be careful with your fingers."

"My fingers?"

"Who ever heard of a doctor without all of his fingers?"

The house seemed terribly empty after that, even with the girls always running around screaming and breaking things. When I wasn't chasing them or washing dishes I kept myself busy helping Papa with his paperwork and working in my Aunt Lucia's bakery. Each night I tried to write at least one of my brothers and whenever a letter arrived Papa would prop it up in the center of the dinner table and insist on waiting until after desert was served before I would open the envelope with great fanfare and read the letter out loud in my best voice. Marcello's letters were short and serious with lots of grammatical errors—he'd never been a good student—while Renaldo's were funny and even a bit spicy and Stephano's went on for pages describing places he'd been and things he'd seen and how there was never enough to read. When no mail arrived Papa would have me read the previous letters again, nodding eagerly as though hearing each sentence for the first time.

With the boys gone, Papa and I grew closer than ever. "It's just you and me and the little possums, eh, Mouse?" he'd say as I sat in his garage trying to help organize his accounts, which he kept piled in a large box because he had no patience for paperwork. (Mouse was his favorite of dozens of names he had for me; he had nicknames for everything, including his tools.)

At least he had his work to keep him busy. Mama was as restless as a cow that needed milking. She began to go to church more often and redoubled her efforts to track down and expel every speck of dust from the house, beginning before breakfast and sometimes not finishing until after I was in bed. It drove Papa crazy. "Perhaps, my sweet buttercup, we should simply seal up the house and sleep in the orchard," he said, tiptoeing past her one morning as she furiously scrubbed the wooden floor.

"Don't tempt me," she replied, grimacing as she worked the brush back and forth.

"Now now, be reasonable. Why don't you take a little break before you rub the skin off your lovely little hands?"

"I won't live in a pigsty."

"Pigsty? The Virgin Mary wasn't this immaculate."

"Don't you talk like that in this house."

"And don't you bring that brush anywhere near my garage," he said as he hurried out the door.

She often talked while she cleaned, sometimes to the germs and sometimes to God. It took me awhile to realize that the germs represented the devil, but once I did I understood her perfectly. She was a commando in the army of God, and if she kept that house clean enough her boys just might one day return home.

She kept her side of the bargain all right, cleaning with the fury of an avenging angel so that I dared not put my fork down during dinner for fear she would snatch it up and wash it.

But God had other plans.

The last letter we got from Renaldo was in the fall of 1942. He was with the Alpini Division of the Italian Eighth Army on the Don River front, deep inside Russia. We knew other parents whose sons were with the Alpini and none of them had heard any news either. Then gradually rumors spread of a disaster. I'd never felt such sadness before, the kind that makes you wonder if the world is so reasonable after all. I said a prayer for him every night, sometimes burrowing my nose into his favorite sweater, which still smelled of his laughter.

I even dreamed about him, but the dreams never ended well. *I'm so hungry, Alessandra*, he would say, standing just out of reach. *I'll bring you food*, I'd promise. *As much as you can eat. Just please tell me where you are.* And his reply was always the same: *I don't know where I am. I'm hungry and I don't know where I am.*

"Maybe they've been taken prisoner," I overheard Mama say one night as she and my father sat in the living room, where she liked to spend the evening sewing and repairing our clothes, at least when she wasn't cleaning.

"The Russians don't take prisoners," said Papa.

And so we waited.

Everything changed in the spring of 1943 with the surrender of the Italian and German armies in Tunis and the Allied landings in Sicily that July. When the King ordered Mussolini arrested Papa was overjoyed! Despite a nationwide curfew Papa threw a party that lasted until one in the morning with musicians and dancing in the courtyard. Our hopes swelled as Italian soldiers began to trickle home, many walking for weeks after deserting their units. Any day I expected to see Marcello and Stephano coming up the road, and then maybe Papa would smile again and Mama would stop cleaning and life would be happy once more. Meanwhile I said prayers for Renaldo every night and some for my parents, too.

If only prayers were enough.

Soon there were reports that German divisions were pouring across the Brenner Pass. Would Italy remain in the Axis or would it switch sides and fight its former ally? Everyone in the village seemed to have at least three opinions, except for Papa, who never wavered in his hatred of all things German. When Badoglio finally announced the Armistice with the Allies in September we celebrated again. The war was over, at least for Italy, which never had its heart in it in the first place. Now it was simply a matter of waiting for the Allies to drive the Germans off Italian soil. But any hopes we had that Italy might sit out the war safely on the sidelines ended almost immediately as Hitler seized control of Rome and all the major northern cities and ports, disarming most of the Italian army in a matter of days. "Why aren't we putting up a fight?" said Papa, pounding his fist furiously on the table.

I'll never forget Papa's reaction the day we heard news of Mussolini's rescue by German paratroopers from the mountaintop hotel where he was being held. He turned so red I thought he'd explode. "Idiots!" When Mussolini announced over Radio Munich the creation of another Fascist state—at least in the parts of Italy controlled by the Germans—Papa threw a glass at the radio, which was as angry as I'd ever seen him. Italian soldiers were ordered to appear for duty or face arrest and before long we began to hear terrible stories of atrocities by the Germans. It was so confusing for a young girl: Fascists and Royalists and Communists, all trying to kill each other. All I knew was that Italians had begun to fight Italians and that Germans were now very dangerous. When Marcello wrote to say that he had joined Mussolini's new army Papa tore the letter from my hands and ripped it to pieces. We hadn't heard from Stephano in weeks and there were so many different rumors that I couldn't sleep at night for fear of my own dreams.

"My father says that soon the Americans will drop from the sky and kill all the Germans," said Pietro Bruscanini, walking me home from school one day even though I asked him not to because if Pietro had his way he'd walk me everywhere. He first asked me to marry him when he was ten (and I was only eight) but as we grew older he became more and more shy around me until sometimes he'd simply stutter and flee. I didn't mind him—he had a sweet face and a funny laugh—but I wasn't especially fond of him either. Like all the Bruscaninis he was very short, acutely self-conscious and prone to tripping as well as the hiccups, which only added to his general sense of discomfort. But somehow he'd worked up the courage to talk to me as we walked from school. (He stayed slightly behind me because boys and girls our age were not to walk together.) "He says nothing can stop the Americans because they have all the money in the world."

"Let's hope your father is right."

"I'll be joining the army soon myself."

"You're too short."

"I'll grow. You wait and see." He hiccupped. "Can I walk you home tomorrow?"

"I didn't even say you could walk me home today."

"But it's not so bad, is it?"

"It's not so good, either." I couldn't afford to give Pietro any encouragement.

He stopped as we neared my house, knowing my mother would chase him off with a broom if she saw him. "Alessandra…" His face began to sweat and his toes turned slightly inward.

I stopped and turned back to him. "What is it?"

"You're the most beautiful girl in the whole world."

"Pietro—"

"It's true."

"You've never even been out of San Gianello."

"But I know it's true." Another hiccup. "And don't worry, whatever happens I'll always protect you. Even if Hitler himself comes here I, Pietro Bruscanini, will protect you." He drew himself up to his full height, which wasn't very high at all, and then slammed his fist so hard into his chest that I could see him struggling not to cough.

"I have to go."

He smiled, bouncing on the balls of his tiny feet. "This is the happiest day of my life so far."

"Go home, Pietro."

"Thank you, Alessandra of San Gianello. Thank you for allowing me the honor of walking you home." Then he let out a yelp before turning and running off, nearly falling on his face twice.

From that day on I found myself looking up at the sky now and then, imagining it filled with American paratroopers. But they didn't appear. And then in the late summer of 1943 the German Army arrived on our doorstep.

At first we thought they were just passing through, but soon so many trucks arrived, mostly at night, that we quickly realized they had other intentions. Within days a large supply depot took shape in the woods below our village, carefully camouflaged to avoid detection by Allied planes, which appeared in the skies more and more frequently. Papa was distraught, knowing he couldn't keep me hidden for long. "You must never look them in the eye," he told me, cupping my face in his large hands. "Do you understand?"

"Yes, Papa."

Everybody was nervous at first and many stayed indoors, expecting the worst. Even on a normal day San Gianello was quiet, deathly so in the midday sun when everybody lolled in the shade and only the stray cats dared slink across the narrow dusty lanes. In the first days after the Germans arrived the village seemed uninhabited, every shade and shutter drawn closed and not a sound except for the dogs and roosters and the few remaining mules that hadn't been taken by the army. Would they steal all our valuables and molest the women? Would the men be taken away? Who would protect us?

Two Jewish families from Pisa that had been living in a barn on the north side of the village for the last three months fled in the middle of the night, while all the local men of military age—Italy was full of deserters—either disappeared into the forests or remained out of sight to avoid being conscripted or even shot. And yet otherwise nothing happened, at least nothing dramatic. Gradually people began to venture outdoors until before long some of the older girls even began to flirt with the more handsome soldiers. (And a few of them were quite handsome indeed.) I was careful to keep my distance despite my curiosity and Mama would make us cross the street if we had to walk past a German, but for the most part they seemed well behaved, if a bit full of themselves. Needless to say their presence greatly emboldened our local Fascists, who gathered at Umberto's Café each day—always the same table, as each political faction had its own seating area, though exceptions were made in the interests of card games—and patiently explained to anyone who would listen how the Allies would yet be beaten because the Western powers were rotten to the core.

"It all gets down to discipline," insisted Ottavio Pierino, who, along with Aniello Bonaccio, was among the village's most militant Fascists. "We have it, they don't. It's as simple as that." He folded his arms smugly across his chest and leaned back in his chair.

"Discipline?" said Carlo Manucci from a nearby table. "Is that why you're so fat?"

Pierino patted his enormous stomach with pride. "No, that, my dear friend, is Fiorella's cooking. You should be so lucky."

"Too much Weinerschnitzel isn't good for you," said Manucci.

"We'll see who goes hungry," said Bonaccio, whose nose still swung left from one of the *bocce* court brawls back in 1938. According to Papa, Bonaccio was making a small fortune on the black market reselling German supplies.

The German base was only about two miles from our house, though you couldn't see it unless you were nearly upon it. Sometimes at night we could hear convoys arriving, their headlights off, and in the morning small groups of troops would jog past our house, singing songs as they went. Father visibly winced every time they ran noisily past but I found it secretly thrilling, even if I disliked them, because at least now I could hear the great irresistible throb of the world right from my own bedroom. Only a few Italians were granted papers to enter the base, while curious children were shooed away by guards stationed behind sandbags along the perimeter, their positions camouflaged with netting. As best we could tell there were about four hundred soldiers in all, though the numbers seemed to change frequently as more came and went. Those allowed inside reported seeing row upon row of gray crates and even several antiaircraft guns and there always seemed to be a great deal of commotion, which kept everybody in a state of anxiety trying to guess what the Germans would do next. Occasionally a tank would rumble by, causing all the dogs to bark furiously and creating much excitement among the children—as well as enough dust to keep Mama busy for a week—but most of the vehicles seemed to be supply trucks, as well as a few ambulances.

"It's only a matter of time before the Allies discover the base and once they do we'll be added to their bombing list just like Genoa and Arezzo and Pisa," said Emilio Bagiani, talking to Papa one evening as they sat in the courtyard playing cards. Bagiani was a tailor despite the fact that his own clothes seemed worthy of a much larger man, which couldn't have been good for business.

He lived down the road and dropped by almost daily to talk Papa into a game of cards, though not always successfully because Papa could only take so much of Bagiani, who spoke with a wheeze and never shut up, even when he ate. He considered himself San Gianello's unofficial historian and liked nothing better than to demonstrate his ability to recite the names of entire generations of San Gianelloans going back to the Middle Ages.

"You'd rather the Germans weren't bombed?" Papa said.

"I'd rather we weren't bombed."

"I'll take my risks," said Papa.

The Germans performed random searches and frequently checked identity papers—"the only thing a German enjoys more is getting drunk," growled Papa, after we were stopped on our way back from Uncle Giancarlo's woodshop—and yet we knew of only two people who had been arrested, both young men of military age who'd made the mistake of attempting to travel by daylight. The greatest annoyance for many of the older men was the fact that the Germans took all the shady seats at Umberto's and Aldo's, seats that had been jealously reserved for decades. "You'd think the Germans had stolen their dog bones," laughed Papa, who had no time for sitting around gossiping.

The Germans also took over the small lake where we used to swim, using it to bathe themselves in the nude, which was a subject of much whispered conversation. (Some of the braver girls even took to spying on them from the woods.) They also added enormous pressure to our local food supply, which was already dwindling each month because of the war. Stocks of grain were now hidden behind false walls, while cured meats were buried in every yard and gardens were plucked clean of fruits and vegetables before they could fully ripen to prevent the Germans from taking everything. But for the most part we were all relieved because our new neighbors weren't nearly the monsters we had feared, which only encouraged Fascists like Pierino and Bonaccio to tout the cultured glories of Teutonic civilization.

And then one day a truck full of Germans pulled up to our house just as we were finishing lunch. Mama was in tears as they trampled through each room, turning over mattresses and throwing open drawers and, worst of all, tracking dirt everywhere. Papa held tightly to the twins while I stayed next to Mama, wishing she would stop mumbling prayers.

When they finished, a young and rather nervous-looking soldier approached my father. "You are a mechanic?" he asked in fluent Italian with a strong German accent. He was more polite than the others and appeared quite uncomfortable addressing my father.

Papa nodded.

"You have a fine workshop."

Papa didn't respond.

The soldier cleared his throat, rocking forward on the balls of his feet. "I've been instructed to inform you that the commander will be requiring your assistance—at least for several weeks."

"Assistance?"

"Your skills. We have many vehicles in need of repair and many of our mechanics have been… what I mean is…" he blushed, "… you see, we don't have enough mechanics."

Papa said nothing. The soldier looked over at me but I avoided his eye.

"Then you will provide this assistance?"

Papa hesitated. "Do I have a choice?"

The soldier blushed again. "It is better that you agree."

Finally Papa nodded his head slowly.

"So you agree?"

"I'll do what's best for my family."

"Good." The soldier looked at me again, his eyes a mixture of misery and embarrassment, then turned and walked away. We remained standing by our front door until the Germans drove off. Just before we went back inside I noticed Pietro up in a tree across the street. I pretended not to see him.

From then on Papa hardly had a free moment as each day the Germans brought him battered and broken-down trucks and cars and motorcycles, insisting the work be done immediately. Mama was terrified that he'd refuse to obey or somehow get himself into trouble but he kept quiet, though I could see that inside he was burning with rage.

One night I overheard them talking in the kitchen.

"I know you, Antonio, and I know what goes on in that head of yours. But if you are thinking you can sabotage the German Army you will get us all killed, do you understand? We have the children to worry about."

"I'll do my job and you do yours, eh?"

"Antonio—"

"Goodnight, my sweet bride."

I tried to keep a close eye on him, at least when I wasn't at the bakery or watching the twins. I dreaded every moment that the Germans were within earshot, afraid he wouldn't be able to control himself any longer. And yet secretly I hoped that somehow he really was waging his own little mechanical war against the Germans because now I hated them too, or at least what they stood for. Occasionally I thought I caught a certain look of devious satisfaction in his face as he crawled out from beneath a German motor car, but he never said a word to me, not even a wink.

Each day I prayed that the Germans would pack up and leave, but the base only seemed to get bigger until I feared that Papa would be worked to death. Meanwhile Mama was forced to become more and more creative with her recipes. San Gianello had always grown most of its own food, but between the Germans and our own Italian government—which demanded that every farmer turn over a large percentage of his crop—there was less and less to go around. Papa reminded us that we were much better off than those in the cities, whose ration cards were increasingly useless. He and Mama were both generous with others in San Gianello who had less than we did. Much of the trade in our village was still handled by barter and because of Papa's work he had a storage room in the garage full of items from canned goods and swaths of fabric to several pieces of furniture and even a few remaining bars of soap—nearly impossible to come by—as well as a long list of services owed him by local craftsmen. Gradually, he and Mama transferred these goods and debts to others so they could be exchanged for food, never expecting to be repaid despite face-saving promises that everything would be settled properly after the war.

One day a German staff car carrying the local commander drove up to the garage. The vehicle was billowing smoke and when the driver got out I immediately recognized him as the young soldier who'd spoken to my father when our house was searched. He was tall and rather good-looking, but in a more delicate fashion than Herr Hitler might have preferred, with long, thin limbs, sandy brown hair and shy, thoughtful eyes set deep beneath big eyelashes. I guessed he was about eighteen, not much older, and he was obviously quite intimidated by the officer, who looked as though he was used to intimidating people. I tried to avoid looking at him, especially with Papa in the room, but despite myself I couldn't help feeling sorry for the young soldier as he translated the officer's orders, seeing how hard he was trying to be polite. The vehicle had to be repaired immediately, even though Papa had three other vehicles to fix by morning.

Mama was out with the twins so Papa had me serve them water and a small portion of *panzonella* (hardened bread and onions soaked in olive oil) in the courtyard while he worked, telling me in a hushed voice to remain indoors once I'd finished. The officer—whose name was Henecker and who was surprisingly short, with a fat, sweaty face—made himself quite at home, putting his feet on the table and smoking one cigarette after another while the young soldier remained standing. I tried to stay out of sight, though I couldn't resist peeking out the window now and then. The truth is, it was exciting to have a real German officer sitting in our courtyard, even if I was afraid for Papa. And something about the young soldier fascinated me. He seemed so painfully self-conscious, his dark blue eyes full of torment. And the way he looked at me, as if he knew all sorts of things about me. So I kept peeking through the curtains, watching as he walked around Mama's garden smelling her hibiscus and hydrangeas and agapanthus and examining her tomatoes. Who could blame a seventeen-year-old girl for being curious?

Two hours later Papa came to the courtyard and announced that the car was ready. I hurried out and followed them to the driveway in front of the garage, hoping the young German might say something, or that I might at least feel his eyes on me once more. But just as we approached the car Papa let out a shout. There was Romeo with one leg in the air as he urinated happily against the front tire.

"Romeo, no!"

But Romeo was not to be interrupted.

"I'm terribly sorry," said Papa, pulling out the rag he kept in his back pocket and hurrying toward the car. The young soldier began to translate Papa's apology, but was immediately interrupted by the officer. I had no idea what the officer was saying but the reaction on the young soldier's face frightened me. He seemed to hesitate, his face turning dark red. The officer spoke again, this time louder.

"Alessandra, go to the house immediately," said Papa.

"But I—"

"Now!"

The young soldier looked at me helplessly, still hesitating. Then without warning the officer reached out and slapped him across the face, repeating his command in an angry hiss of German words.

I had begun to back away when I saw the soldier reach for the pistol he carried in a brown holster at his waist. That's when I understood. I started toward Romeo, who sat wagging his tail, but Papa grabbed me and nearly carried me toward the house. We'd just reached the front door when I heard the shot, followed immediately by another. Moments later I heard the car drive off.

That was the first time I ever saw my father cry. He didn't make any noise but the tears splashed down his big, dirty face, tracing paths through the grime and gathering in his moustache. Romeo was as much a part of the garage as the tools, always hovering at Papa's side and diligently sniffing each new vehicle that came into the shop. I think he considered himself Papa's assistant, if not his supervisor. And now he was gone.

Papa made me wait in the house while he wrapped Romeo in a blanket and carried him inside, not saying a word as he placed him gently on the couch. That evening at dusk we held a funeral service out by the orchard, all of us dressed in black and swapping stories of Romeo's many noble feats. Pietro attended too, appearing from nowhere, his head bowed low. For a moment I thought my mother would chase him away but then I saw her smile because any boy who would show up in clean clothes for the funeral of a dog couldn't be all that bad. When I finally met his eyes I knew that he had seen what had happened.

After we got home Papa sat up late at the kitchen table drinking wine and running his hands helplessly through his thick gray hair, his face swollen with grief.

"Come to bed, Antonio," said Mama. "Come and get some rest."

"I'm not tired."

"Well I am and if you don't get to bed then I won't. Please, enough of this awful day."

At last from my bedroom I heard his heavy footsteps across the wooden floor. The next morning when I awoke he was already at work in the garage.

And then two days later the young German soldier returned. Papa was out trying to find parts and I was alone in the garage doing paperwork when I heard a motorcycle approach. When it pulled up outside the garage I jumped up and quickly hid in the storeroom as we'd planned because the only ones who had vehicles in those days were the Germans, who had taken everything. There was a light knock on the garage door, followed by a louder knock. I remained perfectly still. Would they break the door down? Then a voice called out in Italian. "Please, I must speak with you."

I knew it was him. I told myself to count to a hundred but I only got to twenty before I pushed opened the storeroom door and began to tiptoe across the garage toward the entrance.

"I must speak with you please, just for a moment."

I never should have opened the door. God knows, Papa would

have killed me. But I was seventeen and fearless. Besides, I wanted to give this heartless killer of innocent pets a piece of my mind.

He looked surprised when he saw me. "I must speak with your father."

"He's busy."

"I'll wait."

"He's very busy."

The soldier seemed to hesitate. "Then I'll speak with you."

"I'm busy too."

"I've come to apologize." He looked distraught, the skin tight around his narrow mouth.

"You shoot helpless animals as well as people, is that it?" I said without thinking. That was not the way to talk to Germans if you didn't want to be deported.

"I had no choice."

I began to close the door. "You're not welcome here."

"Please."

"Please what?"

"I am so sorry."

"Sorry?"

"It was an order. What could I do?"

"Disobey."

"And be shot?"

"Better you." I began to close the door.

"Wait." He reached into the saddlebags of his motorcycle and pulled out several packages. "I've brought you some things." He held them out. "Jam, sugar, even real coffee."

I tried to hide my amazement. "You think you can just buy us off like that?"

He stopped, his hands full. "No, I just... I wanted to do something."

"Then you can leave and never come back here again."

Pain swept across his face as he stood there motionless. I meant to turn and shut the door but hesitated.

"I'm not what you think," he said.

"You have no idea what I think."

"Yes, I can see it in your eyes. But you're wrong." He stepped forward. "My name is Johann."

"I don't care about your name."

"I am from Hamburg."

"Please go."

"You are familiar with what happened to Hamburg?"

"I've asked you to leave."

His eyes shifted out of focus as he continued to speak. "My sisters would have been asleep when the bombers came."

"Why are you telling me this?"

"My father would have carried Anna into the cellar. He always carried her. She was so light, like a doll. I can still see her plump little face and her curly blond hair. The Silkworm, that's what we called her, spinning such lovely hair. Mariel would have insisted on walking, always so proud and dignified, telling Anna not to be scared because only babies were scared of loud noises and certainly the Silkworm was no baby. Yes, they would have all been in the cellar. Mother would have wrapped Anna and Mariel in blankets and my father would have told stories. He told such wonderful stories, his voice rising and falling with the action, then dropping to a whisper as the tension became unbearable until the girls squealed with agony. Perhaps my sisters had begun to fall asleep, or maybe my father spoke louder and louder to drown out the sound of the bombers. Mother might even have begun to sing if Anna had started to cry. They always felt better when she sang. But then the firestorm started."

"Please go."

"It must have become so hot down in the cellar. And the smoke. Father would have tried to seal the single ventilation shaft and the cellar door, but soon it must have become difficult to breathe. As the girls coughed and cried they would have clung to Mother while Father tried to think what to do. What choice was there but to flee? Yet where could they go when the world above them was on fire, when even the handle of the cellar door had become too hot to touch?"

"Stop."

"Soon the heat would have begun to blister the girls' skin. Their screams must have filled the cellar as Mother tried to shield them. And then there was the wind, roaring overhead like a wild animal until everything began to collapse. You see, the heat created such a wind that it sucked the air from people's lungs. And the bodies—"

"Stop!"

He stood staring at me, his face trembling and wet with sweat. "I am sorry I shot your dog. I am sorry for all of us." Then he turned, mounted his motorcycle and drove off.

CHAPTER
THIRTEEN

"WE MADE IT," said Alessandra, stopping at the edge of the trees to look down at the house in the distance. The back of her shirt was drenched with sweat.

"I was kind of hoping we had a ways to go," I said, trying to ignore an almost nauseous thirst. "What happened next?"

"I've been talking too much already."

"No really, I'd like to know more."

She seemed embarrassed. "They gave my father more and more work while there was less and less to eat. But somehow we managed. Thank God the Allies finally came."

"What happened to that German—Johann?"

"He was eventually sent to the front. They all were. And then one day the front swept right past us and it was over—at least for us." She began walking again. "But enough of my stories. I believe someone is waiting for us."

"God, I've been worried sick," said Shannon, running out the front door to meet us. "The horses came back hours ago."

"I fell," I said sheepishly.

"How's he's doing?" asked Alessandra, hurrying to the house.

"He keeps asking where you two are. I was running out of

excuses." She turned to me, her hand starting toward the cut on my forehead. "Are you okay?"

"Just a scratch."

"The sheriff's got two men out looking for you. I would have gone too but I didn't want to leave Dad."

"Well then, we'd better make some calls," said Alessandra, already at the front door. She paused to turn back to me. "I don't suppose I can interest you in an iced tea?"

"Name your price," I said as I followed her with Shannon by my side.

I took a long shower, my mind sifting through Alessandra's story, then dwelling on her daughter, then back to Alessandra again with the forlorn German soldier standing at her door and armies closing in. *What a family.* After I dried off I stood in front of the bathroom mirror and examined the cut, which looked much smaller clean than dirty. No need for stitches. Probably wouldn't even scar. I held up several different-sized bandages that Alessandra had given me before settling on the smallest one I could manage. As soon as I was dressed I knocked gently on Mike's door.

"What the hell happened to you?" he said as I entered. He was propped up in the same position, arms limp at his sides and his skin a slightly yellowish hue, green veins protruding near his temples. I noticed a faintly sour smell like bad milk despite the fresh flowers on the dresser.

"Bumped into something. It's nothing."

"She got lost, didn't she? She's never had much of a sense of direction. I figured you were in Montana by now."

"It was quite a ride. Beautiful countryside."

Mike made several attempts to clear the phlegm from his throat. "Renegade's a fine animal, isn't he?"

"Just like driving a sports car."

He suddenly winced, then let out a small groan.

"Can I get you anything? Some water maybe?"

"Just having a bad day, that's all." I watched him struggle again to clear his throat, hating my helplessness.

"You never told me if you had any kids," he asked when he recovered.

"No kids. Actually, I'm divorced."

"Oh."

"Just one of those things."

He nodded. "Well, still time yet."

"Right."

He turned to look out the window where the darkening sky gave way to a silver moon peeking over the horizon like a bashful child. "I always hoped to have grandkids before I died. Not that I'm complaining. Don't imagine there is a luckier father on this green earth." He winced again, the pain visible as it shuddered through him.

"You sure I can't get you anything?"

"Maybe some water."

I quickly poured him a glass and helped him with it, offering him a tissue to wipe his chin.

"Alessandra said you're leaving tomorrow?"

"Gotta get back to work." I half hoped he'd ask me to stay longer but knew he wouldn't.

"You were good to come."

I nodded, stuffing my hands in my pockets. As I thought of all the things I might say to him I realized that what I really wanted to tell him was that I loved him, and not just for saving my life but for showing me how to live it because it's only when we put others first, even strangers, that we touch greatness. I started to say something and then stopped myself, thinking he was in too much pain to hear anything I might say. Maybe tomorrow. "You should rest," I said at last, hoping he wouldn't look at my eyes. Then I gave his shoulder a gentle squeeze before walking out, anger rising in me that even the best among us are granted no mercy.

I was sitting on the edge of my bed trying to gather myself when there was a knock on the door.

"Hi," said Shannon, her face rounding with a shy smile.

"Feeling better?"

"Cleaner, but I won't be on the rodeo circuit anytime soon."

"You've just got to get back in the saddle."

"Not a chance."

She remained in the doorway, her expression flickering like a loose bulb. "I was wondering if maybe I could take you into town and buy you dinner? Mom's tired—I told her she's not allowed in the kitchen tonight—and I wouldn't mind getting out of here for a while."

"Only if I can buy you dinner."

"We can fight over it."

"Deal."

Ten minutes later we were in Mike's white pickup barreling down the dirt road, the radio tuned to a country station, volume loud. I was surprised by how nervous I felt, every thought closing the small space between us.

"Thanks for getting Mom home safely."

"She got *me* home," I said.

"I think she has a crush on you."

"She's adorable." We were both yelling over the radio.

"Yes, everyone seems to think so."

I watched the headlights roam the darkness like a submersible prowling for ocean wrecks. "She has some amazing stories about her past."

Shannon looked over at me. "She really does like you."

"Why do you say that?"

"Because she hardly ever talks about Italy and the war."

"She must have told you some stories?"

"We don't talk much about ourselves in this family. It's unbecoming."

"How exactly did your parents meet?"

"He was wounded near her village. She helped care for him and they fell in love. After the war he arranged for her to come to America."

She turned sharply at an intersection and I watched as the headlights panned across a field of sagebrush, then a lone tree, then two cows that stared back dumbly. After another twenty minutes I saw the neon lights of a bar in the distance. Harley's Tavern.

"I hope they make a good cosmopolitan," I said as we pulled into the parking lot.

"You're kidding?"

"Yes."

"Thank god."

Inside, a dense band of smoke clung to the ceiling and the floor was littered with peanut shells. Four men sat at the bar hunched over their drinks like vultures over carrion while three couples sat at tables. I counted four baseball caps and two cowboy hats. As soon as we entered I noticed a momentary lull in the noise level, heads turning. Immediately several smiles greeted Shannon.

"Hi, Angel," said the heavyset bartender, leaning over the bar. "Damn sorry about your dad."

"Thanks, Harley." Shannon said several hellos, then we ordered two beers and sat at a small table in the corner. When I caught myself staring I quickly shifted my attention to the mounted animals and rusty trinkets that covered the walls. "Great atmosphere," I said.

"It's the only atmosphere around here."

The waitress brought us menus.

"Any recommendations?" I asked.

"The bison burger is excellent."

"A bison burger it is."

When the food arrived she hardly touched her salad.

"You're not hungry?" I asked.

"I had a big lunch. How's the bison?"

"Very... *Western*."

"You don't like it."

"It's okay." I stared down at the massive patty on my plate. "Just seems like kind of an inglorious end for such a noble beast."

"That's why I never order it," she said with a smile.

After the plates were cleared she got up and walked over to the jukebox, loading in two dollars and then flipping slowly through the selections. I watched her, then watched all the other men in the bar turn and watch her. When she returned she leaned forward on her elbows, chin propped up in her hands. "I was thinking about what you asked me last night."

"What did I ask you?"

"You asked me what I was really like but I didn't answer. So then I was thinking about it and I realized that I'm not sure what I'm really like." She took a quick swig of her beer, then spread her small cocktail napkin with her fingers before folding it into tiny squares. I noticed that her nails were trimmed short. "I know what I used to be like and I know what I want to be like, but right now... I'm not so sure."

"You're going through a difficult time."

"It's not just Dad. It's me." She began to rearrange the sugar packets on the table. "Do you ever feel like you can see your life from one end to the other and it scares you to death?"

"I think a lot of people get that feeling."

"Even you?"

"Sometimes."

She studied me closely. "I wouldn't have guessed it." She put the sugar packets back in the holder, then moved around the salt and the pepper shakers along with the ketchup and mustard as if setting up for chess. When she finished her beer she signaled for the check. "Do you mind if we go?"

"Already?" I gestured toward the jukebox. "We haven't even heard your songs."

"Not home. I want to take you somewhere."

"I'm not getting on a horse."

"I promise you won't have to."

Half an hour later we were parked at the end of a dirt road near the top of a ridge. "This is where I used to come when I ran away from home," she said, turning off the engine. The cab felt so small and quiet that I had to tell myself not to move. Below in the distance I could see a single pair of headlights slicing through the night.

"You ran away from home a lot?"

"Didn't everybody?"

"It never occurred to me."

"I'm sorry, I didn't mean it like that."

"I know you didn't."

We got out of the pickup and sat side by side on a small rise. The air was dense with the rhythmic chirping of crickets while above, thousands of stars swayed like drunken concertgoers.

"It's beautiful," I said, wondering what my parents would think if they were watching. Sometimes I still felt them looking down, their expressions holding all my mistakes. There were days when I could feel myself thinking, *Don't look now. Just give me time.*

"The night sky used to make me lonely but it doesn't anymore," Shannon said, craning her neck.

"That's progress."

She made a face, then looked up again, eyes squinting. "It's hard to look at all those stars without feeling kind of silly and small, don't you think?"

"We are silly and small."

She laughed. "When I was a little girl I used to crawl onto the roof at night and lie on my back and talk to the stars."

"Did they ever talk back?"

"Once."

"Really?"

"You don't believe me?"

"It's just unusual. So what did they say?"

"I can't tell you."

"Maybe when you know me better."

"Maybe." She kept looking at me. "Have you ever heard things you didn't expect to hear?"

"I guess I have."

"Some people don't take the time to listen, which is a shame because you miss some really interesting things." She tilted her head back. Somewhere to our left a small animal rooted cautiously through the leaves. "Do you want to know what I think when I look at the stars?"

"What?"

"You can't laugh."

"Promise."

"I think something vast and wonderful shattered into millions of pieces a long time ago, like a death only much bigger and worse. I think we're trying to mend something terrible that happened."

"Long way to go," I said.

"I think about that, too." A faint smile crossed her face as she turned back to me.

And then I kissed her. I hadn't intended to. In fact, I'd distinctly intended not to. But then it suddenly seemed like the one thing in my life I really needed to do.

"Wow," she whispered when I pulled back. She touched her fingers to her lips without looking at me.

"Sorry. I had no right—"

"You don't have to be sorry."

"Actually, I'm not *really* sorry." I reached over and kissed her again, this time harder. When I pulled back she looked right at me, not saying anything, then we both looked up at the stars, or pretended to.

"Part of me really wanted you to do that and part of me really didn't," she said finally.

"Which part's bigger?"

"I don't know." She leaned her head against my shoulder. "Can we just sit here for a few minutes?"

"We can sit here for hours." I stared at the sky, which seemed to be drawing nearer, a candlelight vigil marching straight toward us. *She's married.*

"I was afraid I was going to like you," she said.

"We can just stop. It's a bad idea for a lot of reasons."

"I don't think I want to stop," she said.

I kissed her again. This time her arms came around me until we were like two people trying to switch places. I couldn't remember the last time I felt such certainty inside of me, everything moving in a single direction. *I'm alive.*

"I always knew I'd see you again," she said, rubbing her face against mine.

"Really?"

"Oh, yes. I just didn't think it would take so long."

"My fault."

"Actually, it's my fault too. I was in Atlanta once and I was going to call you but you were married and it seemed kind of strange so I didn't."

"Guess our timing is off."

"Way off," she whispered. Above us the minutes pushed one by one against the stars, time heaving with all its might.

"Do you want to know the reason why I started going up on the roof at night?" she said. "I wanted a place to cry where nobody could hear me."

"Why were you crying?"

"I don't really know. I just felt so sad. That must sound pathetic to you. What did I have to be sad about compared to what you went through? But the thing is, I wasn't sad for myself. I was sad for *everybody*."

As I looked at her I began to wonder what had happened to her. Or was it just the ingredients that went into her? "That's an awfully big burden."

"Mom took me to a doctor once but it didn't help. Sometimes I still feel like climbing on the roof."

When she looked up at me I kissed her again. As I felt her lips and face against mine, our breaths running together, I found myself wanting to say things that surprised me.

"If it wasn't for Dad I could stay out here all night," she said, her face still close.

I looked at my watch. "We should probably go." I started to get up, a muddy sense of guilt stirring inside.

"No, a few more minutes." She took my hand and pulled me back down. Then we sat in silence, arms around each other. For some reason I thought of my parents and how difficult all those months apart during the war must have been, not knowing if they'd ever see each other again. What was it like when he stepped off that troop train and saw her waiting there for him? Was there anything finer in the world?

"I think I've secretly been waiting a long time for something like this to happen to my life," she said. "But now that it has I'm not sure what to do."

"That depends on what you want."

"It depends on a lot of things, but right now I'm too tired to think about any of them." She burrowed closer against me.

"We don't have to think about anything right now," I said, pressing my lips against her hair.

"The truth is, sometimes I wish Dad would just die because I don't know how much longer I can take this."

"Maybe you should go home for a few days and rest."

"No, he needs me here. It's my mother I can't seem to deal with. She's always so...."

"What?"

"So noble and tireless and perfect. Have you ever seen anyone so chipper in your entire life?"

"Why are you so hard on her?"

"Is that what you think?"

"Just an observation."

"Let me ask you a question: do you believe you can tell when someone loves somebody? Do you think you can see it in their face?"

"I suppose I do."

"Take a close look at my mother's face some time."

"I don't understand."

Shannon leaned back on her arms, legs out straight. "When I was growing up I always knew there was something wrong between my parents. Sometimes it felt like they'd both suffocated in that house years ago and I was raised by their ghosts. And then one day as we were sitting at the table during dinner I realized what it was: my mother didn't love my father. It was there right in her face like a shadow. I always knew he adored her. Even after all these years he's never stopped looking at her. He used to say to me, 'The problem with your mother is that she's Italian. Or course, that's also why she's so beautiful.' And she's always been the perfect wife: kind, dutiful, she never even disagrees with him. But she doesn't love him.

She likes him and she respects him, but she doesn't *love* him."

"How can you be so sure?"

"Every year she receives a letter from Italy; sometimes more than one but always at least one letter. Dad and I assumed they were from her relatives and we knew not to pry because anything having to do with Italy was in all likelihood bad news. I actually used to wonder why so many Americans were so eager to visit Italy when I'd always imagined it as a place of unspeakable tragedies. And then one day when I was fifteen I found one of the letters after she'd opened it. It took me awhile but I got out our Italian dictionary—Mom tried to teach me Italian but I never really took to it—and I translated it."

"And?"

"It was a love letter. A really beautiful love letter."

"Who wrote it?"

"It was unsigned, which is strange unless your lover happens to be married."

"How do you know she loved whoever wrote the letters?"

"Because of the way she would change after a letter arrived, floating off somewhere far away. And because it explains so many things about her."

"Do you think they ever saw each other?"

"She hasn't traveled in years but when I was younger she used to go to Florida occasionally to visit her sisters. That's the only possibility I can think of."

"Did you confront her?"

"I kept waiting until I had more proof, and then eventually it didn't seem to matter anymore. But Dad knew. Maybe he didn't know the details but he knew her heart wasn't his. Sometimes I think he's always known that."

Shannon sat up and buttoned her leather coat, pulling the collar tight. "When I left for college I thought maybe they'd get divorced— I'm really the only thing they have in common. I knew Dad would never leave. Where would he go? But I thought that maybe one day Mom would gather all her strength and make a break for it. But she never did." Shannon stretched out on her back, eyes wide as they roamed the glittering sky. "Sometimes I wish she'd left. Maybe that's a terrible thing to say—it would have just killed Dad—but anything would have been better than all the silence. She pretends she likes living here, that all she ever wanted was to look after Dad and sur-round herself with fresh air—have you heard her *fresh air* speech?—but I never believed her. I mean, imagine a young girl dreaming of America and winding up here?"

"They must have had some good times."

"Apparently I missed them."

"Did they fight much?"

"They're both much too polite to fight. That's part of the problem."

"And you never asked her about the letters?"

"Once, when I was older. She was furious and insisted they were harmless. She claimed they were from an old friend."

"Why didn't you believe her?"

"Because only lovers write letters like that. And because Mom's always been secretive about her past. And now that Dad's dying it makes me hate her." Shannon wiped her eyes with her sleeve. "No, I don't hate her. But I hate what she's done to my father."

When we got back to the house it was nearly eleven. "I didn't mean to ruin our evening," she said.

"You didn't ruin it."

"I don't want you to leave tomorrow."

"You might change your mind about that."

"No I won't. I promise I won't."

"Let's wait and see."

"But you'll think about it?"

"I'll think a lot about it."

I held her in my arms, both of us just breathing, then we quietly entered the house and said goodnight at the top of the stairs.

CHAPTER
FOURTEEN

Tuesday evening

Dear Mom and Dad,

It's me again. I finished all my homework and I don't feel much like reading anymore so I thought I'd say hi before I go to sleep. Sorry about the chocolate stain but I was eating an ice cream bar only I wasn't eating it fast enough because it's about 200 degrees in my room right now and today's practically a cold spell compared to yesterday. I've got a fan but it makes an awful sound like a propeller coming right at you and it gives me airplane dreams and I don't mean good ones. Frankly, I've had about all the airplane dreams I can take.

I can hear Aunt Margaret's TV blasting in her bedroom but I bet she's asleep because it's nearly 11:00 and she hardly ever makes it past 10:30, especially when her asthma is acting up. When I finish this I'll sneak in and remove her glasses and shut the TV off like I always do, though if you want to know the truth I sometimes sit on the floor and watch a bit first if it's any good. (I can't always hear what's going on because she snores so loud.) Please don't be mad at her. She just runs out of steam, that's all. I wish the cats would run out of steam once in a while but they never do. You won't hear a bird chirp for miles around here because they are all dead. It's a good thing I'm not a bird.

Guess what? Dr. Sanders says my leg is getting much better and that I won't need crutches for more than a few months if I keep following Susan's orders. She's the therapist. (I won't tell you what I think of her but let's just say she could use a bath.) Other than that it was mostly a boring sweaty day except that at PE I got to be the ref which was pretty fun even though I'd rather be playing. I tried my best to be fair but if you were watching then you can decide for yourself.

Well, I hope you had a good day in heaven or where ever you are. I bet it's more fun than where I am, especially if you don't have to deal with mentally disturbed cats. (Did I tell you that Sweet Pea has started sleeping behind the toilet and guards it like a dragon hoarding a den full of jewels?) I never should have let them take Maxwell away even if he is happy living with the Raymonds. He would have taught these cats a lesson (right before he ate'em).

Guess I'll go turn off Aunt Margaret's TV now. I just wish I was more tired because there is nothing I hate more than lying in the dark sweating and listening to that fan and feeling like I'm in the middle of a runway and nobody can see me. Besides airplanes I've been dreaming a lot about our house. Last night I dreamed we were all playing baseball in the living room—don't worry, Mom, I only broke two lamps, ha ha. I hope I don't have that dream again either because it's too confusing in the morning. The truth is, I wish I didn't have any dreams.

Goodnight Mom and goodnight Dad.

Love,

Ryan

XOXOXOXOXOXOXOX

P.S. Don't worry about me because I'm fine.

P.P.S. I <u>really</u> miss you.

CHAPTER FIFTEEN

The human heart has hidden treasures,
In secret kept, in silence sealed.
– Charlotte Brontë

I WOKE EARLY the next morning, turning toward the window to watch the sunlight bleed down from the distant mountains and across the yellow plains. Then I rolled onto my back as I thought of Shannon just down the hall, her olive skin warm with sleep, then of Mike clinging to each shrinking moment and Alessandra dreaming in Italian (about a secret lover?) and Aunt Margaret dining with her cats and how I would have to find homes for them when I put her in a nursing facility. And then I thought of my mother and father and how strange it was that people seemed to keep changing even after they died. I closed my eyes briefly, trying to follow the orange shadows that swam lazily from side to side, then stared at the ceiling and wondered if there are moments when it's possible to feel every sensation at once, life thundering like the Super Chief right through your chest. And maybe that's the very best we can hope for, not happiness or safety but a sort of wordless awe, time spread before us like the Grand Canyon and we're dangling from the rim.

I looked out the window again as I went over my decision one more time: I couldn't stay, not when everything about what I wanted was wrong, no matter what else I tried to tell myself. And I'd tried most of the night to tell myself there was a way even though I knew there wasn't. Not that I could live with.

I had to leave.

Alessandra was already awake when I got downstairs. We drank coffee together on the porch, both hushed by the beauty of the changing light, then I helped her feed the horses, surprised by her strength as she dug into a bale of hay with a pitchfork. The air smelled sweet with dawn and I enjoyed the rhythmic sound of the horses' jaws working the hay. When we got back to the house Shannon was in the kitchen making breakfast, her face still pressed with sleep. I could hardly look at her.

"Good morning," she said, searching for my eyes.

"Good morning." I wanted to say more but I couldn't with Alessandra in the room so instead I helped set the table, then concentrated on my food even though I wasn't hungry.

"You're not still planning on leaving today are you?" asked Alessandra.

Shannon looked at me, waiting.

"My flight's at eight," I said, not looking up. "I'm connecting with a redeye out of Denver."

"Couldn't you stay just one more day?" asked Alessandra. "It means so much to Mike having you here."

"Please don't, Mom," said Shannon softly.

"I'm just being selfish, that's all," said Alessandra.

"I really have to get back to work."

"I can't bear to see you leave so soon," said Alessandra. "You've only just gotten here and there is so much to talk about."

"He wants to leave," said Shannon, staring at me.

"I *have* to leave," I said.

"Well, I tried," said Alessandra, pouring more coffee. "But you have all day to change your mind."

After breakfast Shannon and her mother went upstairs to give Mike a sponge bath while I cleaned the kitchen and then busied myself looking through Alessandra's records, which were mostly opera, with a few musicals and some early Sinatra. Once Mike was dressed I went up to see him but he was already asleep again, his chin sinking into his fresh plaid shirt. I started to leave, then changed my mind and took a seat in the chair by the bed, thinking I'd at least get to spend some time with him. Twice he opened his eyes and looked at me, squinting as if trying to focus, but each time he slipped back under like a whale sounding. Before I left I placed my hand gently on his, my fingertips lightly exploring his scars, then carefully drew up his sheets and tucked them around his shoulders.

I ran into Shannon on the stairs. "Maybe we can go for a walk?" I said when she tried to pass me.

"You don't have to explain anything."

"Yes, I do."

We followed the creek that curled down through the foothills. I'd been waiting all morning to talk to her but now that we were alone together I couldn't think of what to say so instead I took her hand in mine and kept on walking, my thoughts running far ahead. When we reached a meadow circled by trees she stopped, letting go of my hand and slipping hers into her pockets.

"I knew you'd leave," she said.

"It's better for everybody."

"Not for me."

"Maybe not for me either but it's what I have to do. I want to apologize for making things more difficult than they already are. I wasn't thinking."

"Well I have been thinking and what I realized is that last night was about the nicest night I can remember."

"You're married."

Her face tensed as she looked away. "I don't feel married. I haven't felt married in a long time."

"Do you love him?"

She hesitated. "I care about him. And I know he loves me. He tries. In his own stubborn way he really tries." She laughed nervously, her weight shifting from side to side. "Mom can hardly stand him. I think it's one of the things I like best about him."

"You didn't answer my question."

"I'm not sure I've ever really loved anybody but my father."

"You can't live like that."

"It's how I've always lived."

I looked across the meadow and then at the trees and the sky, not knowing which way to go.

"I'm sorry for being the way I am," she said.

"It's nothing to be sorry about." I brushed my hand along her cheek, wondering which one of us had more secrets buried inside.

"I want to change," she said. "I really want to try. I don't know what that means or where it's going to lead but I want to try. Please don't leave."

"This isn't right."

"Neither is the way I'm going to feel if you leave." She was close to tears.

I tried to think clearly. "What about your father? I wouldn't want to do anything to upset him."

"Don't worry, I wouldn't let you." She stared at me but I couldn't look back at her. "What is it?" she said. "Tell me."

I knew what I intended to say. I intended to say that I wasn't raised to fall for another man's wife and that I'd be waiting if the time came but right now the best thing for both of us was for me to get in my car and head for the airport. But I didn't say it. Instead I took her by the shoulders and kissed her, nearly lifting her into the air with the force of all my wanting.

"That was a really great kiss," she said when I let go.

"There's more."

"I hope so." We kissed again, both of us trying to fill ourselves with as much as we could take. Then we dropped to the grass and she rested in my arms with her head on my chest. "Do you want to know what I thought when I first saw you again?" she said. "I thought you were too late. But maybe it's not too late. Maybe it doesn't have to be."

"This is going to be a lot harder for you than for me."

"Nothing could be harder than waking up every morning feeling like you made a mistake you can't ever change."

"Why have you stayed with him?"

"I forgot I had a choice."

We kissed again, both pressing against each other. It felt so good holding her in my arms that I had to make sure not to squeeze her too tight. It wasn't just my heart that wanted her but every part of myself, my limbs and my skin and all my thoughts straining like a trapped miner who glimpses daylight.

"This means you're not leaving, doesn't it? Not today?"

"I'm not leaving," I said. "I'm not sure I ever was."

We lay side by side in the grass, wind and sky blowing over us.

"I feel so different inside," she said. "Like my chest is full of birds."

After a moment I began to laugh to myself.

"What is it?" she said.

"I was just wondering how I'm going to explain this to a friend of mine. His name is Lupo Martinez. I met him at the youth center and he's kind of like family. I'd describe him for you but it can't be done with words. You'll just have to meet him sometime."

"I look forward to it." She rolled back toward me, her face right up to mine. For several minutes we just stared at each other, smiles and possibilities passing back and forth.

"I'd want you to know everything about me," she said.

"I'd want to know everything."

"And you'd have to tell me everything too."

"I could try."

"There's a lot you might not like about me," she said.

"I wouldn't be so sure."

"I'm moody and I need to be alone a lot and I think too much about everything."

"Sounds like we'll get along just fine."

"And I used to have a problem eating—kind of a serious problem—but I don't as much anymore."

"Okay."

"And I've never felt the way I want to feel with a man. What I mean is, I think there's more but I don't really know."

"We'll work on that one. Anything else?"

"I think that's enough for now." She kissed me, then we rested in each other's arms. She was quiet for several minutes, her breaths slowing. I began to wonder if she'd fallen asleep when she said, "How long do you think it would take?"

"For what?"

"For us to tell each other everything?"

"I can't remember everything."

"I mean the important things."

"I don't know. A while, I guess."

"Maybe we should go slow, like eating something really sweet," she said.

"Yes, maybe that's better."

She rolled on top of me and then I flipped her over and rolled on top of her, kissing every part of her face as she ran her hands under my shirt and up and down my back.

"I'm still scared," she said, her body arching toward me.

"Me, too," I murmured, my lips pressed against her skin. I don't think she heard me.

.

CHAPTER
SIXTEEN

THERE IS AN instant when she knows, legs bracing with all the power in her, eyes looking for some last possibility, heart bellowing. *No no no...*

The two vehicles collide.

When Rebecca was seven years old she fell down the stairs. She remembered losing hold of the banister, then hitting the first stair, then the second, but as she kept falling there was no sensation at all, just colors dancing all around her. When she opened her eyes her father was looking down at her, eyes full of fear as he scooped her into his arms. Was she dying? Was she already dead? And then her head began to hurt and she knew she was alive. But for just a moment she understood how easy, how quick and effortless, it could be to die. She clung to her father with all her strength.

I can't move.

The first time Jim kissed her she knew that she had just kissed the man she would marry. She was so certain of it that she couldn't look at him without imagining their features and tones blending this way and that, which made all the seasons run through her cheeks whenever he stared at her. At night in her bed she would lie awake and think of his hands searching her and then she would wonder how the weight of his body would feel pressed upon her and what it would be like to wake up every morning with your whole life right beside you. Sometimes she would pretend that he was in bed next to her and she would talk to him and listen to all the things on his mind and then they would weave themselves together and float through the night like castaways on a raft. And no matter how many times she thought about it, she really couldn't believe that life could be so perfect and lovely, even for her.

She reached across the sheets. Jim? Where are you, Jim?

She wants to cry but she cannot. Everything is covered with a white silence so sweet and thick she can taste it on her lips. And then she sees all the shadows circling the rim of her soul, waiting.

Hello, Rebecca.

Then the pain starts, so sudden and complete that she feels her heart trying to stop. Or has it? No, she is alive. But which way back to life? Are my eyes open or closed?

And then she sees light and there is a man staring at her. His mouth is moving, shouting, but she cannot hear. He reaches for her and grabs her by the arm and pulls but she does not feel his touch. What does he want with me?

She remembers the day Jim returned from the war. She rose early that morning, then quickly dressed and took Hank for a walk all the way to the river and back, thinking the exercise would calm her. Then she showered and sat for an hour before the mirror putting on her makeup and fixing her hair, a new hope rising with each stroke of her brush.

She'd picked out her dress the night before, ironing it and then draping it on the chair by the window. But now she changes her mind and returns to her closet and tries on five other dresses before finally settling on a blue cotton cinched-waist dress she made from a magazine pattern the previous winter. Halfway down the stairs she stops and hurries back to her room, carefully removing her grand-mother's pearl necklace from the small Chinese box on her dresser and clasping it around her neck.

She arrives at the station nearly two hours early, pacing up and down the length of the platform and then sitting on a bench with her knees tight together. She thinks of the things she wants to say and especially the things she wants to keep from saying, at least today. And then she tells herself that when he steps off the train she must be grateful for the man who has come home and not look too hard for the boy who went away.

She checks her watch, then opens her purse and pulls out the last letter he wrote her, reading it twice. Then she takes out a handkerchief and pats down her face, wishing she'd worn the green dress instead. She runs her fingers along the pearls around her neck, hesitates, then quickly unclasps the necklace and places it in her purse. After checking her watch again and adjusting her dress she reminds herself not to talk too fast or ask too many questions. But most of all she tells herself not to cry because once she starts she is afraid she might never stop.

And then when she can no longer bear the waiting another minute she hears a sound and soon the ground begins to shake. One last time she adjusts her dress and her hair and then she stands and takes a place among the crowd swelling along the platform. When she sees the engine rounding the last curve she closes her eyes and whispers *thank you* and then when she opens them again all the fear inside of her turns to laughter.

I want to live.

The first time she ever saw Jim cry it was the afternoon their son was born. And then for days after that she noticed tears in his eyes as he sat in the rocking chair in the living room of their small apartment holding Ryan high in his arms, as if still trying to convince himself that such a thing was possible. In the beginning she thought it was the wonder of life washing over him but then one morning as she watched him without being seen she understood that he was crying not just for the child who was born but for all those who never would be. And then she knew that the brightest moments of their lives would always be like that, each milestone leaving the men he had loved and lost further and further behind in a place of unspeakable darkness and pain.

She opens her eyes and sees the man again, his arms outstretched as he pulls at her. Who is he and why is he here? She tries to turn her head but she cannot. And then she remembers the pickup truck in the other lane and suddenly it swerves and her arm starts up to protect her face but it's too late because everything is rolling. *No, it's not time. Not for us. Not for my son.*

Somebody please help us!

She grips the man's hands, fighting to free her legs but she can't and there are flames rising all around her and snapping at her face and hair, everything afire.

Jim!

Ryan!

She must live.

She must she must.

The man pulls harder and she kicks her legs and tries to buck against all the burning metal and she hears his voice telling her she can make it *please keep trying* and she wants to tell him that his shirt is on fire but she can't move her lips because they are no longer hers.

Where is Ryan? Where is my son?

She hears a voice. Is it Jim? No, it's the stranger's voice shouting at her over the roar of the fire. She listens to his words, wondering who he is and where he came from. And then when the hands slip from hers and all the pain becomes sleep she knows it is time to die.

CHAPTER
SEVENTEEN

WE SPENT THE rest of the morning by the corral, first cleaning out the stalls and then brushing down Rita and Renegade. Shannon and Alessandra insisted on teaching me how to groom and saddle a horse, the two of them laughing at my attempts to get a bit into Rita's mouth, and then Alessandra and I sat on a rail watching and clapping as Shannon lead Rita through a series of tight turns around three barrels, sprinting between them. We ate lunch at a picnic table in the shade of a large oak tree behind the house and then Shannon drove into town to buy groceries while I helped Alessandra repair a leaky faucet and take down the storm windows.

"Mike has always taken care of everything," she said apologetically, bracing the bottom of a rickety ladder as I inched my way to the top. "You name it and he can fix it."

"I'm glad to help," I said, struggling to dislodge a window and trying not to look down. I'd hated heights ever since my first—and last— tree house collapsed during opening ceremonies when I was eight, nearly sending my mother into shock (but leaving me only with bruises).

Mike was more alert in the afternoon and I spent an hour in his room, the two of us talking mostly about the war in Italy when we talked at all. Between his bouts of pain and his natural shyness it was difficult to reach him and every time I tried to bring up the accident, searching for details, he seemed to withdraw completely. Only gradually did I realize that he wasn't just trying to shield me from what happened that day but that he was trying to shield himself, too, because his memories were far more vivid than mine.

When I got downstairs Shannon and her mother were in the living room folding laundry.

"I can do this, Mom," Shannon said.

"I really don't mind doing it myself," said Alessandra.

"I *want* to do the laundry, okay? Can you just let me do this one thing?"

"Of course you can if you want." Alessandra blushed as she put down a shirt. "I'll just be in the kitchen then."

"So when do I get a turn?" I said.

They both looked at me in surprise, then laughed. "You don't get a turn," said Shannon, rolling a pair of socks and throwing them at me as I fled to the front porch.

Just after four Mike's doctor stopped by, taking time for a glass of iced tea after he finished his examination.

"So there's really no change?" said Shannon, toying nervously with her hair, which always seemed slightly unkempt, like a sailor's.

"Nothing significant. My main concern is pain management," said the doctor.

"He never complains," said Alessandra.

"That doesn't mean he isn't in pain," said Shannon, rising from her wicker chair and folding her narrow arms tightly across her chest.

"I know that, dear, I'm just explaining that he doesn't complain."

"I'm making sure we're doing everything we can," said the doctor.

"But it's not enough, is it?" said Shannon, her dark eyes already holding the answer.

"Sweetheart—"

"I don't think it's ever enough," said the doctor.

We ate dinner on our laps in Mike's room, the three of us trying to ignore the changes in his face whenever the pain hit him. Alessandra served her lemon meringue pie and Shannon fed bites to her father, much of it ending up on his chin. Every few minutes she reached out and stroked his hand or shoulder and several times I noticed her fighting to keep a smile on her lips.

"We talked Ryan into staying longer," she said. "Isn't that great?"

Mike looked surprised. *He knows*, I thought, feeling uncomfortable. It was there on our faces for anyone to see; the way we kept looking at each other like we shared the finest secret in the world. And yet, how could he know?

"Just don't let them put you to work," he said.

"I'm afraid we already have," said Alessandra.

After Alessandra went downstairs to clean up, Shannon began to read out loud from Wallace Stegner's *Angle of Repose*, her voice and gestures full of animation. I could see that Mike enjoyed it, his expression opening wide like a child's during story time. Or maybe it was just the chance to stare at his daughter and hear her voice. Did the dying find themselves trying to stockpile sights and sounds like a bear fattening for winter?

When she finished a chapter I took a turn, self-conscious at first but glad to be able to do something. When Shannon went to take a bath I decided to keep on reading, at least until he fell asleep.

"Should I go on?" I asked when I finished the next chapter.

"Maybe that's enough."

I put the book down, not wanting to leave yet. Mike adjusted the oxygen tube, glancing down at the large green cylinder by his bed as if making sure it was still there, then folded his hands on his chest. He seemed unusually alert.

"I need to know more about the accident," I said, thinking I might not get another chance.

He didn't respond.

"I need to know more about what happened that day. Maybe my asking sounds awful but I believe you saw or heard something and I need to know what it was."

There was a light knock on the door and Alessandra peered in. "Mind if I interrupt?"

Mike looked relieved as she sat on the edge of the bed and placed four pills in his palm, helping him bring a glass of water to his lips. When he finished she took a damp towel and tenderly wiped down his face, then picked up a bottle of lotion from the bedside table, poured some into her palm, rubbed her palms together and ran them slowly up and down Mike's arms.

"Thank you," he said in a soft voice, his eyes gazing at her like she were a beautiful mountain he no longer had the strength to climb.

Then she pulled back the covers, unbuttoned his shirt and rubbed more lotion on his chest. I noticed a large gray scar just below his right shoulder and wondered if it was from the war.

"Are you cold?" she asked.

"I can't tell anymore."

"I'll get you another blanket." She walked over to the closet and pulled down a red blanket, which she unfolded and spread over the bed.

"Better?" she asked.

"Better."

As she stroked her hand through his hair he drew toward her touch like a magnet, gratitude loosening his rough features. Maybe in the end that was what mattered most in marriage: having one person who just won't quit.

She leaned down and kissed him lightly on the forehead. "I'll leave you two be. Holler if you need anything." She gave me a wink as she closed the door behind her.

"You should have seen her when she was younger," he said, his eyes lingering on the door. "By golly, never seen anything so pretty in my life. We couldn't go to a square dance without the men going quiet and the women getting all out of sorts."

"She's still pretty."

"She is, isn't she?" He shook his head as if after so many years he still couldn't quite believe his good fortune. "Truth is, I never did figure how she ended up with a fella like me, nothing but a country boy."

"I wouldn't overthink it."

He didn't seem to hear me. "When she agreed to marry me I thought she was just pulling my leg. She could have had *anybody*."

"Ah, come on."

"Honest truth. I only asked her because I figured I couldn't live with myself if I hadn't at least tried. We hardly even knew each other. She barely spoke English. But with all the men buzzing around her I knew I'd have to move fast." He went silent for a moment before continuing. "So one day I just gathered the words in my mouth and let them sit there until there was nothing to do but spit them out. I'd even memorized my lines in Italian. When I finished she just sat there looking at me with those big brown eyes of hers for so long that I figured she hadn't understood a word I'd said. Then I figured she'd understood exactly what I'd said only she didn't have the words to tell me to crawl back in my hole. I was just about to excuse myself when she says, *yes*. Just like that. *Yes*." His eyes moistened. "From that day on I swore to myself that I'd make her the happiest girl in the world. Didn't have much to offer except this house and my two hands, but I tried. I tried every day the best way I knew how." His eyes squeezed shut.

"Are you okay?"

"I tried but I failed. I don't know why I failed but I did."

"Don't be silly," I said, sensing he was going somewhere I didn't belong. "She's a lucky woman. You just need some rest."

I started to get up from my chair when suddenly he reached out and grabbed my hand, his strength surprising me. "That's why I was there that day. That's why I was able to get to you in time."

I slowly sat back down. "I don't understand."

It took him several moments to continue. "When I heard you were coming I found myself praying for the first time since the war, and do you know what I prayed for? I prayed that I would die before you got here." He paused, the stillness of the room broken only by his breathing. "But I can't seem to die, not with the truth still in me." He released my hand and stared straight at the ceiling, his voice now cracking. "It's not me I care about. Never has been. It's Shannon." He turned to me. "She's all I've got."

"What are you trying to tell me?"

When he spoke again he kept his eyes fixed on the ceiling. Sweat ran down his face. "I knew something wasn't right as soon as I brought Alessandra home. She was just like a fragile plant that won't take to the soil. At first I told myself she just needed to make some friends, improve her English, get used to things. Then I told myself it was the trouble we were having trying to conceive a child." He paused. "After Shannon was born she seemed happier—at least it kept her busy—but then she started getting that look again. I tried to pretend that it was not being able to have another child, that it would pass. And eventually, as the years somehow piled up on us, I just got tired of thinking about it."

"What does this have to do with the accident?"

He pulled at the bed sheets nervously before continuing. "Every Thursday for years Alessandra went into Sheridan for services. She's always been devout and the bigger the church the better. So one day I find myself in Sheridan and I think, *it's Thursday and Alessandra ought to be coming out of church about now*. Only there's no sign of Alessandra or her car. So finally I get the nerve to go inside and talk to the Father and he says he only sees her about once a month or so and how is she?"

Mike paused, gathering his strength. "That night at dinner I asked how the service was and you know what she says? She says it was wonderful. I didn't say anything more because what's to say when you don't have any proof, when the whole idea is... *unbearable*." He paused again. "The next Thursday I tried to follow her into Sheridan but I lost her. I was so nervous about being seen. Wasn't until two weeks later that I managed to follow her all the way." He wiped his lips with the back of his hand. "She parked by a restaurant, place called Milly's, and went in like she was in a big hurry. I thought of going in after her but I couldn't because my limbs wouldn't do anything but sit there. So that's what I did."

Mike began to cough so hard that his thin legs flopped up and down under the sheets. When he recovered he spit into a tissue, then balled it up and let it fall from his fist. "If only I'd set her free years ago. But how could I? How could I let her go?"

I waited.

"Must have been two hours before she came out. She was with someone. A fella." He wiped his lips again. "I didn't think life could get any worse than watching them hug each other goodbye. But I was wrong. Never been so wrong in my life."

He took a series of long breaths before continuing. "I couldn't face Alessandra, not yet, so instead I followed the man as he pulled out of the parking lot, not knowing why or what I planned to do. I followed him for an hour feeling all the anger running like a pack of wolves through my veins. And then just before the road rises and turns east I decided to pass him because I can't stand even the sight of his license plate. I was just drawing alongside him when I caught his eye. And do you know what he did? He smiled at me. Big ol' smile like the day just couldn't get any better. That's when I gave the steering wheel a little jerk, just to scare him. That's all I meant to do, to scare him." Mike turned his face toward the far wall. "He must have overcorrected."

I stared at him, acid rising up in my throat. "What are you saying?"

"He's the one. Todd Skillman. It was his pickup."

"No."

"He lost control and swerved into your lane." Mike turned back to me. "I killed your parents. I killed all of them. I'm responsible. That's why I was there." He gulped for air as panic rimmed his eyes.

I sat in disbelief, wanting to get up and leave the room but unable to move.

"I tried to save your parents but I couldn't. No matter how many times I tried I couldn't. And then I was going to tell the police but how could I let them take me from my daughter when she needed me, when she was the only thing right in this whole forsaken world?"

"No one ever learned the truth?" My voice shook.

"There were no witnesses. No survivors except... you. When the autopsy found that Skillman had been drinking—he must have had a few at the restaurant—the police had their case. They made me a hero. Even you made me a hero."

"But what about Alessandra?"

"She never knew I saw her at the restaurant. She never knew I'd followed her to Sheridan. And then after what happened... how could I tell her?"

"She never admitted to knowing Skillman?"

"Not one word. Maybe she thought God was punishing her." He looked straight at me. "But you were a miracle. She thinks the grace of God put me on the road that day. She thinks I performed a miracle by saving you."

I started to stand up, then sat down again, afraid I might get sick.

"I'm sorry," he whispered, tears rolling down his cheeks as his mouth opened and closed. "God almighty I'm sorry."

I sat staring at him for a minute, maybe more, my eyes dropping to his hands, then forced myself to my feet and walked blindly from the room.

CHAPTER
EIGHTEEN

I DIDN'T BOTHER to turn down the sheets. Instead I stretched out on my back in the darkness fully clothed, my limbs too heavy to move. I tried to close my eyes but I couldn't, not for more than a few moments before they sprung open. Finally I gave up and turned my head toward the window, watching the pale light of the moon lap against the barn.

I don't know how much time had passed when I heard a light knock on the door. When I didn't answer the handle turned, first one direction, then the other, but I had locked it.

"Ryan? Ryan, are you awake?" It was Shannon. After a minute she knocked again and whispered my name louder.

"I need to be alone."

"Is everything all right?"

"I just need to be alone."

"Something's wrong, isn't it?"

I didn't answer.

"Do you want to talk?"

"I can't talk right now."

"Okay," she whispered. "If you want to talk later just knock on my door. You can knock anytime." There was a long pause. "Well, goodnight."

"Goodnight."

After another minute I heard her walk away.

CHAPTER
NINETEEN

⌒

I REMEMBER WHEN I first opened my eyes in the hospital. There was a woman sitting in a chair reading, her gray hair in a bun. She was dressed all in white and I thought she must be an angel, which at least meant that I'd made it to heaven despite stealing three dollars from my UNICEF box in third grade. And then I saw strange-looking animals lined up along a window sill, all of them staring at me. Did animals go to heaven too?

I couldn't find my body at first. Instead all I could do was move my eyes and they could only stay open for a few seconds before closing. When I opened them again the angel was staring at me, her face right up close.

But where were my parents? Were they in heaven too or were they still alive on earth? If they were alive I'd have to wait for them. How many years would that be? Forty? Fifty? But no, they couldn't be alive because I saw the station wagon in flames. They must have died. We all died.

Maybe they're resting too.

I closed my eyes again and thought of my mitt at home and my bat and bike and my baseball cards and posters and the eighteen dollars still left in my piggy bank, which made me miss some things about living. But at least I wouldn't have to go back to school. There was something to be said for that. Did they have sports in heaven?

Pizza? Hopefully it wasn't all vegetables. Mom would know. She's probably met everybody by now. I wonder if Dad feels bad about the car? At least he won't have to go to work anymore. I smiled to myself, thinking of all the time we'd have together. Heaven's supposed to be wonderful, isn't it?

So I'll just wait here until they find me. I'm sure they're looking for me. I'm sure they must be looking very hard...

Mom? Dad?

Mom?

When I awoke again I knew.

CHAPTER
TWENTY

AS SOON AS the first light crept across the plains and up the foothills I rose and packed, then wrote a brief note for Alessandra thanking her for her hospitality. As I tiptoed past Mike's closed door I hesitated, fighting the impulse to look at him one last time, even to shake him hard and tell him it can't be true because I wouldn't let it be; then I continued as quietly as I could down the stairs. I was almost to my car when a voice called out from an upstairs window. It was Shannon.

"Where are you going?"

I stopped, keeping my eyes on the car, then continued walking.

"Wait!" She disappeared from the window. Moments later she rushed barefoot out the front door holding the top of her yellow pajamas together with one hand. "What's wrong? What are you doing?"

"I shouldn't be here. I never should have come."

"But why not? What are you talking about?"

"It's too hard on your father... and it's too hard on me."

"He talked about the accident, didn't he?"

I didn't respond.

"He saw something horrible, didn't he? I always knew he did."

"I can't talk about it. Please tell your mother I had to leave. Give her my thanks for everything."

Her eyes filled. "But you can't leave."

"I have to."

"No you don't. And I'm not going to let you." She grabbed my bag and pulled it from my hand. "I'm about to lose my father and I'm not going to lose you."

"Shannon—"

"Don't you see that the accident has ruined enough of your life? It's time to let it go. That's what your parents would want."

"You don't understand."

"You're right, maybe I don't. But I understand that I'm falling for you. I understand that when you kiss me I feel something I didn't know I was capable of feeling." She rose to her toes and pressed her palms against my cheeks. "Please don't go yet. *Please.*"

"I have to. I'm sorry." I picked up my suitcase and turned and walked to my car. She didn't move as I drove away.

PART TWO

CHAPTER ONE

*They are always saying God loves us. If that's love I'd
rather have a bit of kindness.*
– Graham Greene

I SPENT FOUR days in Atlanta, most of it at the office where I
worked late each evening, not wanting to leave time for anything
else but sleep. Then on Friday I flew to Saint Louis and made ar-
rangements for Aunt Margaret to be put into the Meadow Lane Care
Facility, the brightest of the five nursing homes I'd visited. (She'd always liked a lot of light.) The woman I'd hired to keep an eye on her
helped me pack her things while she sat on the back porch playing
with Sasha, Snowball, Sammy and Sugar—all uncanny reincarna-
tions of the cats I'd grown up with.

"Are we going on a trip?" she asked as I led her to my car. She'd
insisted on wearing a large-brimmed red hat and matching pumps
that made her wobbly gait even more precarious.

"Yes, you might say."

"How *wonderful!*" She clasped her hands together, then turned
and looked at her luggage in the back seat. "I hope I packed enough."

"I think you've got just about everything."

She adjusted her dress and then sat up straight and took a deep breath, patting herself on the chest. "Goodness, it's been so long since I've traveled that I've got butterflies."

"Me, too."

When we pulled into the parking lot of Meadow Lane I sat with the car running.

"Are we there already?" she asked.

"We are."

She lifted the brim of her hat and peered out the window. "They look French," she said, watching three elderly people shuffle by. "Are they French-speaking? I used to speak a little French but it's been years." She let out a nervous giggle. "If I'd known I would have pulled out my old French primer—I still have it somewhere." Then she waved out the window. *"Bonjour!"*

"They're Americans. They all speak English."

"Oh." She stared out the window. "Well, I suppose that makes things easier. Shall we see if our rooms are ready?" She gave me a big smile, her hands perched on the gold buckle of her red patent leather purse.

"This is not a hotel, Aunt Margaret."

She looked confused.

"Do you remember how I explained to you that I'd found a really nice place where you could live and where there were lots of nice people to help take care of you and lots of fun activities every day? They even have dance classes and movie night and lots of games and—"

"But I have a home."

"You need more help."

"Nora is helpful."

"You need more help than that. And you'll have lots of company here. You know how you enjoy good company."

She stared out the window again, hands going limp in her lap. "This is all my sister's doing isn't it?"

"No. *No.* She's dead. Rebecca's been dead for thirty years. That's why she doesn't call."

Aunt Margaret turned and looked at me in horror, then confusion.

"I'm sorry. I'm really sorry."

She stared down at her purse, tears furrowing through her makeup. "What's wrong with me?"

"You forget things, that's all. But you won't have to worry about that here. You won't have to worry about anything."

She looked out the window again as a man with a walker inched past, his head barely cresting his shoulder blades.

"Are they expecting me?"

"Yes, they are. They're very nice people. I looked at a lot of places and this really seemed like the best. They even have a grand piano and a library full of books."

"It must be expensive. I don't want to be expensive."

"Don't worry about that."

She looked back at her luggage, as if fitting the various clues together. "How will my friends know where I've gone?"

"I'll tell them. I'll take care of the house and everything else so there's nothing you have to worry about."

She pressed her palm against her cheek. "I'm a burden, aren't I? I never wanted to be a burden."

"You're not a burden. This is just best. It really is a nice place. There are lots of windows. I made sure they had lots of windows."

"You'll visit me?"

"Of course I will. And I'll take great care of the cats."

"You mean…" She couldn't finish.

"I'm afraid they are not allowed."

She sat perfectly still, fear rippling beneath her powdered cheeks.

"We can do this another day," I said finally, putting the car into gear. "We can take our time with this."

She reached over and put her hand on mine. "Today is good enough." Then she checked herself in the mirror, bracelets rattling as she applied lipstick to the general vicinity of her mouth. "Well, no point in keeping them waiting."

I spent the afternoon getting her settled in, trying my best to smile and promising to return in the morning before my flight. When I left she was sitting in the day room explaining to two other residents her secret to a successful open house. (Two squirts of Chanel

No. 5 in every bedroom and rolled oatmeal simmering on the stove.)

"*Au revoir,*" she said, giving me a wink.

"*Au revoir,*" I said, hurrying to my car.

I was so happy that the cats survived the flight to Atlanta that I accidentally let them out of their cage in baggage claim, nearly causing an airport shutdown as they each took off in a different direction. Once I finally got back to my apartment I locked the cats in the bathroom, then dropped onto the couch and examined the scratches on my arms. I was on my second beer when I noticed eight phone messages on the machine.

"Hi, it's Shannon." Pause. "I'm not sure what happened but I really miss you and I—"

I quickly skipped to the next message.

"It's me again." This time her voice sounded smaller. "I promise I won't call you anymore but that doesn't mean I'm going to stop thinking about you or waiting for you to call or hoping that you're thinking about me. Whatever you're going through I want you to know—"

I skipped forward again.

The next six messages were all from Lupo, who never called just once. The first three gave differing versions of why he bombed an algebra test while the last three were devoted mostly to Jasmine's near infinite charms. "You want to know the truth? It's not even fun to look at her anymore," he said. "In fact, it's probably the worst part of my day, like I'm going to vaporize right there in 7-Eleven. You ever seen those movies where the guys just vaporize? Yeah, that's what I'm talking about. I am telling you, this girl is *hot*."

After listening to his messages I opened another beer and stretched out on the couch, anger building in me as I went over all the reasons I couldn't call Shannon. There was no way to go back, not without hurting people.

The truth was impossible.

I quickly unpacked, fed the cats, then returned to the kitchen and listened to Shannon's messages straight through, feeling her voice on my skin.

"Please call me and tell me you're okay. I know Dad must have told you something about the accident, about what he saw and how terrible it was. He's been so quiet since you left. He was right in not wanting you to visit. I didn't think he was but he was and now everything's... everything's awful." Her voice dropped to a whisper. "I miss you so much. I miss you and I'm worried about you and most of all I want to feel your arms around me again. Please call me, at least just to tell me that you're all right and that you miss me, too. We don't have to talk about anything else if you don't want to. We don't ever have to talk about it. So *please* call."

And the last message: "I told Brian I'm leaving him. Not just because of you but because it's something I've needed to do for a long time. But I'm not sure I can change my life without you. I'm not sure I have the courage." Then she hung up.

I slammed my fist down on the counter wishing I could grab Mike O'Donnell and tell him I hated him for killing my parents and then lying all those years and now forcing me to lose one more thing. But I couldn't hate him, not when every time I thought of him all I saw was a broken and dying old man who'd lost his own life years ago. I walked back into the living room and sat down on the couch, then got up again and circled the apartment, finally stopping in the bedroom where I sat on the windowsill and looked out the window at the cars below, my knees drawn into my chest. Who else was there to blame? An unfaithful housewife? Her lover? Aunt Margaret's fickle God?

I spent an hour at my desk paying bills and catching up with some work, then checked on the cats again before calling Lupo.

"Is he dead?" he asked.

"Not last I saw him."

"What did his hands look like?"

"Scarred. They looked scarred."

"No kidding. You got a picture, didn't you?"

"No, Lupo, I didn't get a picture."

"You don't sound so good."

"It's been a long day." From the bathroom I heard something fall.

"So what happened?"

"I don't want to go into it right now. How did the mural competition go?" At my prodding Lupo had entered a competition to paint the side of the community center in his neighborhood.

"I didn't do it."

"What?"

"They said you couldn't do anything political."

"So?"

"So, that's censorship."

"Ah, Christ, Lupo. How are you ever going to get anywhere if you don't take risks?"

"Where exactly are you trying to get me?"

"You really want to know? College. You could study art. You have a lot of talent."

"I'm not the college type. I'm not even the high school type."

"That's what we're working on."

"That's what *you're* working on. I'm working on Jasmine."

"Do you have any idea what it took to get you into that competition?"

"Now you're mad at me. How come everybody's always chewing on my ass?"

"Forget it. Listen, what are you doing this weekend?"

"Nothing, same as last weekend."

"Want to take a drive?"

"I'm your man. Where are we going?"

"Kentucky."

CHAPTER TWO

―――

I'M NOT SURE why I needed to visit my parents' graves but I did. Maybe I thought I could leave the truth with them. Or maybe I just wanted to see if it would feel different to look at their names and know what really happened that day and why. Or maybe I just couldn't think of any other place to go.

We made the six-hour drive straight through, Lupo complaining most of the time because of the cats.

"Didn't you know I hate cats?" he said as Sammy curled in his lap and Snowball nibbled on the laces of his red sneakers. Sugar and Sasha were sleeping in the back seat. "I'm telling you, cats are not my thing. I wouldn't even let Catwoman sit in my lap and she's hot."

"These are my aunt's cats, okay? They're family."

"Family?"

"Yes, *family.*"

He shook his head in disgust. "Well, I am clearly not a family man."

Somewhere between Atlanta and Louisville I told him everything that had happened in Wyoming. I hadn't planned to but then I found myself needing to talk about it because not talking was getting too difficult. Besides, Lupo had always been a good listener even if he was short on meaningful advice.

"That is *sooo* fucked up," he said when I finished. "You could charge him with murder."

"It was an accident, Lupo," I said, surprised by the firmness in my voice.

"If you say so." He tried to shoo Snowball away from his feet. "What are you going to do?"

"Nothing."

"That's it? You're just going to walk away from the whole thing?"

"It's better for everybody."

"But what about this girl? I've known you for two years and I've never heard you talk about any of your dates like that. She's hot for you and you are *extremely* hot for her."

"I can't tell her the truth. It would devastate her."

"So, lie."

"I can't do that either."

He thought for a moment. "Jeez, you're fucked."

"I knew you'd clarify things for me."

"You gotta admit, the situation deserves a swear word." He picked up Sammy and placed him in the backseat. As soon as he turned back around Sammy leaped into his lap again.

"He likes you," I said.

"He's possessed. Haven't you noticed that all these cats are possessed? And that's what got me thinking that maybe if we took them to one of those animal shelters—"

"No."

"You wanna get scratched to death, fine by me," he said, crossing his arms across his chest. Sammy purred contentedly in his lap.

"So why are we going to Kentucky?"

"I feel like it, that's why. I can show you where I grew up. It'll be fun."

"We're going to visit your parents' graves, aren't we?"

"We can stop there, too."

"I hate going to my mom's grave. All she's got is this little tiny stone in the ground and there's nothing around but lots of other tiny little stones. It's like, there's dead people and then there's poor dead people." He turned and looked out the window. Moments later Sasha woke up and jumped onto his shoulder and began licking his nose. "Ah, no, man, not my damn face."

We spent the afternoon driving by my old house and school and the park where I played Little League, then ate at a diner my father and I used to stop at on our way home from a game. For dessert we swung by a 7-Eleven where Lupo had a Slurpee in Jasmine's honor, then I drove across town to the cemetery, reaching it just before dusk. I asked for a few minutes alone.

"Do what you gotta do," said Lupo respectfully. He took off the large gold cross from around his neck and offered it to me. "You want to borrow this?"

"I think I'll be okay, but thanks."

"Anytime." He sat on the hood of the car tending to the scratches that ran up his arms while I walked down the stone path and headed for my parents' plot.

I thought maybe I'd say something but I didn't. Instead I just stood there, then knelt, then stood again. And then as I cleaned the dirt from their headstone with the tail of my shirt I realized why I'd come: I needed their help.

I'm lost.

I'm lost and I don't know which way to go.

I closed my eyes, straining for their voices. Yet all I heard were more questions rising up inside of me. Or maybe it was all just one question: *Wasn't love enough?* Yes, that was it.

Wasn't love enough?

"So that's them?" said Lupo, joining me.

"That's them."

He let out a low whistle and tucked in his shirt, chin down and narrow shoulders back. "If you start crying I'm gonna start crying."

"I won't start."

"I don't care if you start, I'm just stating the facts."

"I know, Lupo." He could barely get through a martial arts

movie without a sniffle. When we rented *Field of Dreams* he got so distraught that he refused to go to school the next day because "people are gonna think I stuck my face in a beehive."

"Maybe you should go ahead and start because if I cry first that's gonna seem strange," he said, welling up.

"How about I don't look at you and you don't look at me?"

"Good idea," he said, shuffling one way, then the other. "But there's one thing."

"Yes?"

"I was just thinking a little poetry might be in order."

"Poetry? You've got a poem to share?"

"Not my own poem. It's by some dead guy named John Donne. We read it in school and I memorized it. You know how you're always quoting this and that? Well, I figured I could use a quote or two—especially on the whole female front—and this one seemed like it would come in real handy someday."

"I can't wait."

"Okay, here goes." His voice began to crack. "Ready?"

"Ready."

He took a deep breath. "'The day breaks not, it is my heart.'" He barely squeaked out the last word as he turned his face away.

"Lupo, that's beautiful. Thank you."

He wiped his eyes with his T-shirt. "Doesn't make you feel a whole lot better but I like how it clarifies the situation, everything busting all at once. I've been saving it in case things go south with Jasmine but looking at all these headstones, well, it just felt right."

We both stood slapping at mosquitoes for several minutes, then I reached into my pocket and pulled out a harmonica, placing it on top of the headstone. "Ready?" I said, turning to go.

He wiped his eyes again. "You're just going to leave it there?"

"Yep."

"What for?"

"It's just this thing I do, okay?"

"Okay." He walked over to the headstone. "Mind if I try it before we leave?"

"Why not?"

Lupo picked up the harmonica, studied it for a moment and then began to blow into it. He spent several minutes struggling for a melody, eyes closed and shoulders rocking back and forth.

"You want it?" I said after he'd placed it back on the headstone.

"I thought you were going to leave it?"

"I don't have to leave it."

He looked down at the harmonica.

"You have it. It'll get more use that way."

"But it's like this thing you do."

"Maybe I don't need to do it anymore. Now let's go."

Lupo sat up late that night in our hotel room playing the harmonica, then played it most of the way back to Atlanta. The cats never once ventured near him.

CHAPTER
THREE

I WAS JUST getting home from work four days later when I heard the phone ring. Alessandra's voice came over the answering machine.

"Ryan? It's Alessandra. I'm sorry to bother you but I need to talk to you." Pause. "It's Mike." I closed my eyes, bracing. "His condition has changed and the doctors… they don't think he'll make it through the weekend. The reason I'm calling is that he wants to talk to you. In person. I wasn't going to call you but he says it's important. It's about your parents." A longer pause. "If you don't call back I'll understand… but I hope you do call. We all do."

I waited twenty-four hours, glad for a deadline at work that kept me busy. Each time I looked at the phone I told myself that I wouldn't go back, that I couldn't stand to see Mike again or listen to his apologies or look at Alessandra knowing that if only she'd been faithful my parents might be alive. Most of all I told myself that I couldn't bear to look at Shannon knowing she was one more thing I'd lost before I even had a chance to understand what I'd found. And yet Mike had one more secret left.

The following morning I dropped the cats off at Lupo's place and hurried for the airport, time draining from every clock. Just before boarding I called my boss and asked for two more days off, promising to work through the weekend when I returned.

He told me I was fired.

CHAPTER
FOUR

Hold me but safe again within the bond
Of one immortal look.
– Robert Browning

SOMETIMES HE CANNOT sleep from the sorrow of the world and sometimes from the beauty of it. Tonight he just wants to hold the moments in his hands, enjoying their heft and workmanship before they vanish.

He sits in a chair in the corner of the hotel room, the moonlight dripping beneath the drawn curtains. His wife and son are asleep in the king bed, both slowly sailing for the middle, breaths long and deep as they row through the night. Outside, the world is still and lovely.

Today they drove 300 miles, pulling over twice to read the tombstones of pioneers who died on the Oregon Trail and then examining the ruts still visible in the sandstone from the wheels of the wagon trains. For lunch they had a picnic at Independence Rock, where they marveled at the names of pioneers carved hopefully into stone. And then after climbing to the top they'd looked out over the plains towards Devil's Gate, all three of them blinking at the strangeness of time.

"Do you suppose they found what they were looking for?" asked Ryan, standing beside him.

"I suppose some of them did."

"I bet they were scared."

"I bet they were too."

They laughed their way through dinner, taking turns making up lyrics for an ongoing song about three Kentuckians on the road west. Back in their hotel room they'd played cards for hours, Rebecca and Ryan taking turns winning because Jim couldn't concentrate on his hand.

Once his wife and son had fallen to sleep he'd gotten out of bed and walked outside to feel the night air and stare at the moon, an ancient smile rising in his heart as he understood how a single well-lived day could unlock years. Then he returned to the room and took a seat in the chair in the corner, letting all his thoughts pass by like a brightly colored caravan laden with goods.

He thought of the day he met Rebecca and how he still couldn't look at her without picking out a place to plant a kiss. The years had begun to settle on her face and yet still she looked beautiful, always finding a smile just when he needed it, which was surely more than she imagined when she married him. And when he slipped too long into silence she soon came after him because she had too much pride and fight to let the weariness of life weigh too heavily upon either of them.

Then he thought of his son and all the things he wished for him. Over the years he'd begun to wonder if such wishes were like Christmas ornaments passed from one generation to the next; a few broken, a few more added, each glittering with hope and remembrance. He smiled to himself in the darkness, imagining the boy as a grown man making wishes on the sleeping souls of his own children, each heart a courier bearing a message decipherable only by God.

He rose and pulled the covers up on his wife and son, pausing to watch the flickering of their eyelids. Then he quietly poured himself a drink from a bottle of bourbon on the dresser and returned to his chair, the glass resting on the table beside him. He drank slowly, letting each swallow loosen up a different part inside of him. Closing his eyes he thought of his work and all the days ahead that were full before he'd even had a chance to plan them, which got him thinking about the ways in which his life was far different from what he had imagined. It wasn't disappointment he felt so much as the pang of hearing a summons now and then that you couldn't answer because life was like that. He'd come to believe that everybody has three lives all mixed up inside: the one in front of us, the one we dream of and finally the one we fear. The thing was to try and keep them straight.

He sat quietly in the chair for another hour, hands on his knees and eyes open as he watched the moonlight drift across the bed, sheets rising and falling in unison. With each breath he felt the goodness of life washing through him, and yet he could never shake the presence of those left behind, young hopes forever trapped in time's bloody amber. *Look what you're missing.* And there wasn't a single day when he didn't feel the shame of what mankind had destroyed. After the war he told himself that he'd been spared because of the part he was to play in the world. But gradually he came to understand that his part was too small to make any difference, just a man with a job and a wife and a son, every day coming about as fast as he could catch it. Closing his eyes he saw the Japanese planes diving, skies full of hate, then the horror and pain. And always, the sadness, which waited for him like a tireless dog by the door.

But there was beauty, too. More beauty than he could ever understand.

He kissed his wife and son goodnight, then slipped into bed, closed his eyes and swam after them.

CHAPTER FIVE

SHANNON WAS WAITING when I got off the plane in Sheridan. The moment I saw her face I knew that her father hadn't told her the truth. I'd made the decision that I wouldn't either—not ever—because what good would it do but cause more pain? And yet I wasn't sure I could keep it a secret either, not when she looked right into me.

"I've missed you so much," she said, running up to me and nearly jumping into my arms.

"I missed you, too," I said, kissing her all over her face and wondering how I'd had the strength to leave her.

"Why didn't you call me?"

"I wanted to. I just... I needed time to think."

We stood holding each other for several minutes, neither speaking, then walked arm in arm to the parking lot. We were halfway to the house when Shannon suddenly accelerated.

"What are you doing?" I asked.

"It's Dad." She began to cry.

"What's wrong?"

"I think he's dead."

Alessandra was sitting on the front step when we got there, eyes bloodshot and the end of her dress bunched in her fists.

"This time you were right," she said as Shannon jumped from the pickup and ran toward her.

"No!" cried Shannon.

"It was time for him to leave us," said Alessandra, rising and taking Shannon in her arms. "He didn't want to leave us but it was time."

Shannon burst into tears and ran into the house.

Alessandra watched her go, then walked up to me and took both my hands in hers. "Before he died Mike became feverish. I couldn't make out everything he said—words were just tumbling from him—but toward the end he spoke to you... as if you were there in the room." She paused. "Your mother knew you were alive. She knew you survived the accident. Mike was able to talk to her before she died and she knew you'd been saved." She squeezed my hands in hers. "That's what he wanted to tell you. Your mother knew you'd been saved."

CHAPTER
SIX

WE WAITED NEARLY five hours before calling the coroner. First Alessandra and Shannon sat together with Mike's body, both women crying and hugging each other as Alessandra worked round and round a rosary of white beads decorated with a small silver cross and Shannon talked herself back and forth between grief and anger, her words gathering in helpless piles. Then they took turns, Alessandra quiet and barely moving as she sat for an hour beside her husband, her hand resting on his; Shannon weeping and telling him over and over what a wonderful father he'd been and how she'd miss him more than anything in the world.

I stayed downstairs most of the time, trying to keep out of the way and feeling Mike's secret digging into my sides. I'd given up trying to hate him for what he'd done because I couldn't, not when I could see that the accident had claimed his life too, killing him one day at a time until there was nothing left of him but remorse. And it was an accident, even if he was to blame. With time I'd find a place inside to bury his memory, a place where only forgiveness endures.

When it came my turn to say goodbye I nervously approached Mike's bed and looked down at his empty face wondering if he really was at peace or whether some things followed you forever. *God almighty I'm sorry.* I reached out and gently placed my hand on his forehead, fighting the urge to recoil at the coldness. I tried to put together some kind of prayer but nothing came to mind, nothing except questions that had no answers. Instead I just stared at his gnarled hands, which were crossed over his stomach on top of the sheets. Slowly I placed one, then both of my hands on his.

"You know he loved you, don't you?" said Shannon, appearing in the doorway, her eyes puffy.

"I know." I tried to imagine telling her the truth. No, I never could.

She entered the room and stood beside me, her fingertips resting on the top of the bedspread. "I'm sorry it was so hard for you two to see each other again but still I'm glad you did." She ran her palm along her father's arm. "When I was a little girl he used to try to keep his hands from me, thinking they'd gross me out. But I loved his hands more than anything because they reminded me that my Dad was something special." She started to say more when Alessandra walked in.

"The coroner's on his way."

"I could have called," said Shannon.

"I'm perfectly capable," said Alessandra, joining us by the bedside. She began to tuck the bedcover under Mike's chin when she stopped herself. "He's not dressed properly," she said.

"They'll dress him at the funeral home," said Shannon.

"I think we should dress him. Why should we let some stranger do it?"

Shannon looked down at her father. "You're right."

"I'll get some warm washcloths and tidy him up first."

"But what are we going to dress him in?"

Alessandra walked over to the closet. "That's easy. We'll just imagine he's planning on taking Renegade for a long and beautiful ride."

Shannon smiled as she wiped her eyes with the back of her hand. "I'll get his boots. And his gloves, too. He'd never go riding without his gloves."

I started for the door.

"We could use your help," said Alessandra.

"I—"

"Please?"

I looked over at Shannon, who nodded with a hopeful smile. "I'd be glad to."

"Thank you." Alessandra pulled back the bed sheets. "Now if you'll help me take off his shirt I'll see if I can't get him cleaned up a bit."

Forty minutes later Mike O'Donnell was dressed and waiting for his last ride as the coroner pulled up to the house.

CHAPTER
SEVEN

———

THE FUNERAL WAS as concise and Spartan as the brown shoe-box-shaped church located just across from an auto parts store and backing up to a cow pasture. No one cried, not audibly, and I figured that Wyoming was probably not the kind of place where people got noisy with their grief. Several dozen people sat scattered among the first four pews, many dressed as if for a cattle auction. I hadn't planned on being one of them. Twice over the previous three days I'd booked a flight back to Atlanta, feeling I couldn't hide the truth from Shannon another minute, not with her eyes all over me. But I couldn't leave because I was in love with her.

The service began precisely at three, tinny music seeping down from the musty white rafters. After the minister reminded us of just how far we'd fallen, Shannon got up to speak, her hands firmly gripping both sides of the lectern as she began. She looked so pretty and sad in her plain black dress that I found myself looking now and then at the hymnal shelved in the pew in front of me just to slow everything down.

"I want to start by thanking you all for being here, and to say how much it means to me and Mom." She shifted side to side, her eyes nervously scanning the ceiling before settling back on the audience. "I had a whole speech planned for today—those of you who know me were probably expecting a PowerPoint presentation—but last night I realized that everything I really want to say I want to say to Dad... and I can't." She took a deep breath. "So I tore up my speech and decided to keep it simple because if there's one thing Dad always insisted on, it was keeping things simple." Another deep breath, chin dropping to her chest. "As most of you know, Dad wasn't a man of a lot of words. Some days he wasn't a man of any words." Scattered laughter. "You see, the thing about Dad was that he preferred to do most of his talking with those big green eyes of his." Murmurs of agreement. "When I was growing up I always knew how much he loved me just by looking at him. And you could look into his eyes and see how much he loved Mom, too." She looked over at Alessandra, who sat perfectly erect, hands crossed in her lap. "So maybe he didn't say it much—the truth is I wished he'd said a lot more about a lot of things—but at least you always knew just where you stood with him. And so I guess what I really want to say is that the thing I'm going to miss most is being able to look into Dad's eyes and see all that big wordless love right there for the taking."

From the church we drove to a nearby cemetery for the burial, wind throwing the loose soil into our eyes, then back to the house for a small reception. I kept to the corners, not wanting to explain my presence but sensing from the curious looks that everybody knew exactly who I was.

By eight the last guest had left and we began to clean up.

"That was nice, don't you think?" said Alessandra, running her palms down the sides of her dress, which looked noticeably dated.

"Very nice," I said as I stood at the counter drying a stack of plates.

Shannon didn't say anything as she emptied the punch bowl into the sink and began to wash it.

"I think Mike would have been pleased," said Alessandra, taking the dry plates from me and placing them on a shelf.

"He would have spiked the punch," said Shannon, finally smiling.

"Yes, you know I believe he would have," said Alessandra, smiling back. I noticed that she carried her grief differently than her daughter, not concentrated so entirely in her eyes but spread throughout her body so that her movements seemed slower and more hesitant. Shannon, on the other hand, did everything faster, as though motion alone could keep the pain at bay.

"I'm exhausted," said Alessandra after the last dish was put away. "If you two don't mind I think I'll head up." She'd gone to bed early every night since Mike died.

"But I thought we could sit and talk—or just sit if you want," said Shannon, her voice earnest.

"I'm too tired, Sweetheart."

"If you're going to your room to pray, maybe we could do that together."

Alessandra smiled gently. "I'm not praying."

"Then what are you doing? Because I know you're not sleeping. I see your light on for hours."

"I'm... I'm thinking, that's all."

The phone rang but nobody moved. Brian had been calling three times a day and sometimes more. Shannon looked at me, then back at her mom. "I could come up with you," she said after the phone stopped ringing. "We could even bunk together."

"Oh no, you stay down here." Alessandra gave Shannon a hug.

"It's all right to cry, Mom."

"I know it is," Alessandra whispered. Then she gave me a quick hug before she turned and headed upstairs.

Shannon watched her go, then wiped her nose. "Everything's private. Even mourning."

"Maybe it's the only way she can deal with it."

"Well, I personally am going to have a big fat glass of wine." She headed for the refrigerator.

"That makes two of us."

After I made a fire we sat side by side on the couch, Shannon curled up with her cheek against my chest. I pressed my face into her scalp, breathing her in.

"Does it get easier?" she asked in a small voice.

"No, not really."

"I didn't think so." She laughed through her tears, then took my hand in hers. Her skin felt hot. "I don't know what I'd do if I didn't have you. You've been so wonderful through all of this." She kissed the side of my face before resting her head against my chest again. "You know what I keep thinking? I keep thinking that you're like this gift that Dad gave me. Maybe it's not fate but it feels that way to me."

I didn't say anything.

"I don't know what to do about Mom. I've asked her to come to San Francisco with me but she won't hear of it."

"You have to give her time."

"Everything takes a lot of time, doesn't it?"

"Sometimes years," I said.

She curled up closer, her knees pulled in tight. "I have a favor to ask you."

"Anything."

"Mom's going to look at headstones tomorrow—I can't believe I'm saying this—and I need to meet with the lawyers about Dad's will, and so I was wondering if you could go with her?"

"Maybe she'd rather be alone."

"No, I know she'd like the company—especially your company." Shannon turned and kissed me again. "Now I have one more favor to ask you: I want you to hold me all night."

CHAPTER
EIGHT

ONCE WE WERE in her bed she fell asleep almost immediately, her breath warm and moist against the side of my face. As I held her I wondered if just a few absolutely perfect moments can make the final difference between contentment and despair. Are the very best parts of life always so fleeting and fragile, so that our divinity can only be glimpsed, never attained? Is happiness no more than a brief absence of longing?

I pressed my lips gently against her forehead, then propped myself up on my elbow and strained to make out her features in the grainy darkness. I watched her long into the night, time waiting just this once. *So this is it*, I thought to myself, smiling at the silent enormity of love. Then I kissed her lightly on the cheek and rested my head on the pillow beside her, in no hurry to sleep.

CHAPTER
NINE

CAL WINFREY'S MONUMENTS and Memorials sat between an Easy Pay gas station and the Stirrup bar. Before entering the cinderblock building we had to pass through a small courtyard crowded with headstones and benches and little statues, which reminded me of a neighbor back in Kentucky who liked to hide in the bushes during Halloween and scare the bejesus out of little kids.

"Maybe I should just do this over the phone," said Alessandra, pausing at the door. She'd been nervous all morning, fidgeting with her hair and drumming her fingers on the steering wheel as she drove.

"We might as well take a look," I said.

Her eyes moved quickly over the monuments. "Mike wouldn't want anything too gaudy."

"No, not gaudy," I said.

She seemed to waver, then pushed herself forward, the effort visible on her face.

As soon as we entered, a loud bell chimed and a nearly spherically shaped man hoisted himself from a chair behind a metal desk in the corner. After turning down the volume on a portable radio that sat on top of a tall gray filing cabinet, he took one more bite from a sandwich on his desk, stashed it in a drawer, rubbed his hands on his brown polyester pants and began to waddle our way.

"Name's Cal." He gave a quick adjustment to the big turquoise slider on his bolo tie.

"Alessandra."

"Ryan."

Cal nodded respectfully as he shook hands, then tucked his large thumbs into his belt. "You're at the right place," he said. "May not be anybody's favorite place but it's the *right* place."

"Good to know," I said.

"Well then, I assume you're here on behalf of a loved one? I only ask because these days more and more people like to prepare for their own final *RE*-pose. Gives them a sense of *control*."

"A loved one," I said when Alessandra didn't respond.

"My deepest sympathies." Cal's bushy eyebrows dropped a good inch as he shook his head at the hardness of life.

"To tell you the truth, I don't know where to start," said Alessandra, clasping her hands together.

"Why, of course not. That's why I'm here," said Cal. "With all the choices available it's easy to become overwhelmed—as if you don't have enough to deal with already." He cinched up his belt buckle, which immediately slid back down beneath his belly. "Let me try to keep it simple, give you some options, then we can *narrow* things down." He swept his hand around the showroom. "First off, we've got your monuments, your markers and your benches." He walked over to a dark gray monument and gave it a good slap. "In your granite uprights—what folks would call a headstone—we've got your star blue, pink pearl, paradise black, Dakota mahogany, you name it. Then of course there's polished and unpolished, or we can just polish the sides. Plenty of options there."

"What about something... *plain*?" said Alessandra.

"Plain? Why certainly. Take this straight upright here." He rubbed his hand on the top of another monument, this one reddish in color. "Simple yet elegant. Or perhaps you prefer another style, maybe oval or concave or serpentine—my personal favorite—or convex or tapered? And of course we can do a matching base." He ran his fingers along the words etched in a shiny black monument, which read: *John T. Smith,* though *YOUR NAME HERE* would have been funnier. "Then there's your lettering, which is where it all comes together. You've got your v-sunk in polish, your v-sunk in frosted panel—like that one over there—or we could always go for a polished square raised?"

Alessandra began to back away.

"Or maybe you'd prefer a memorial bench?" He began walking toward a row of benches. "Always nice to be able to take a load off when you visit. Gives grief a certain *practicality*."

"Thank you for your time," said Alessandra, now halfway to the door.

"Or maybe you're more interested in a marker, inexpensive but dignified?" He gestured toward half a dozen markers displayed on the floor, one section devoted to pets. "We've got granite, bronze, flat bronze on granite, slant granite. Or maybe you'd prefer something beveled?"

"Thank you for your assistance," said Alessandra.

"Did I mention that we specialize in NeverFade memorial photos so that every time you visit your loved one you can—"

Alessandra was out the door with me right behind her.

"I can't do that," she said, her voice shaking. "Not right now I can't."

"There's no hurry," I said, putting my hand on her shoulder.

When we got back into the car Alessandra sat with the key in the ignition.

"I miss his snoring," she said. "For years I couldn't stand it, especially if he'd had a few drinks. I used to feel like I was sleeping out by an African watering hole. And now I miss it."

I nodded, not knowing what to say.

After a moment she turned to me, her face changing. "Toward the end—the last hours—Mike became feverish. I couldn't reach him wherever he was but then, after I thought I'd lost him, he began to speak. He couldn't at first but he kept trying. He was so determined."

I kept my eyes focused straight ahead.

"And then I realized that he was speaking to you, as if you were there in the room, as if he could see you." Her fingertips searched nervously for her collar. "That's when he said that your mother knew you'd been saved, that he'd been able to speak to her and tell her that you were okay and that you were going to live." She hesitated again. "But there's more. I've tried to make sense of it, going over the words again and again and thinking I must have misunderstood him or that he'd been confused..."

"What else did he say?"

She turned to me. "He kept mentioning the name of the driver... in the accident."

"Skillman."

"Yes. He wanted, well, this makes no sense, but he asked... he *begged* you to clear Skillman's name. I don't know why I'm even telling you this. Poor Mike didn't know what he was saying. He was delirious. But I felt I had to tell you. He was thinking of you, that's the important thing. He always thought the world of you."

"Mike knew," I said, unable to hold back any longer.

"What are you talking about?"

"He knew about you and Skillman. Before he died he told me the truth."

"What truth? What are you saying?"

"For god's sake, Mike saw you and Skillman at the restaurant that day. That's why he followed Skillman. That's why he was there at the accident."

She tilted her head sideways in confusion. Then her expression went solid as she fell back in her seat, her hand rising to her mouth.

"It's over," I said, feeling more sorry for her than I expected. "None of it matters now."

When Alessandra could speak again she turned her whole body toward me. "Tell me everything Mike said to you."

"He looked for you one day at the church—he happened to be in Sheridan—and when you weren't there, when he found out that you hadn't been going to church every Thursday, he decided to follow you the next time you went into town. That's when he saw you and Skillman together—at the restaurant. And then he trailed Skillman because... because I don't think he knew what else to do.

"He only meant to scare him. I believe that. I believe it was all a mistake. But Skillman lost control of his truck. Maybe if Skillman hadn't been drinking it would have been different, but it was Mike who caused the accident. That's why he was there that day. That's why he was able to get to me in time."

She sat motionless, then slowed crossed herself. Finally she spoke in a whisper: "Skillman wasn't my lover."

"Then what the hell was he?" I asked. "I need to know the truth. I need to know what happened that day and why everything in this family is such a goddamn mystery."

She turned to me, eyes glazed. "Yes, I did lie to my husband. Not in the beginning. For the first few months I did go to services every Thursday because I didn't know where else to go. Because I needed to get as close to the possibility of hope as I could. And because... because some days I could no longer hear the sound of my own heart."

She fidgeted with her collar again. "During the war there were things that happened, things that I can't..." She paused, searching for her voice. "What I'm trying to say is that I left parts of myself behind. I left behind parts so big that I didn't know how to be a wife and mother without them." She wiped her eyes with the backs of her hands. "And then one day at church I saw a notice for volunteers at the Veterans Hospital. I would have told Mike but he never wanted me to work, especially not around all those men, even if half of them were in wheelchairs. So yes, I lied to my husband because finally I'd found a way to believe in myself again. I'd found a way to *do something*."

"That's where you met Skillman?"

"Todd was a counselor and helped coordinate the volunteers. He'd been wounded twice in Korea, then ended up on the streets before finding his way back. He made his livelihood as a building contractor, but he put his heart and plenty of his own money into helping veterans. All the patients loved him because they knew he understood them.

"I'll never forget my first day. He had me sit in on one of his sessions with the patients and as I listened to the men tell their stories, as I felt the compassion and quiet strength in that room, I just...

well, it changed me. From that moment on I wanted to help out at the hospital every free moment that I could. So that's what I did on Thursdays; I pushed wheelchairs and sat at bedsides and tried my best to brighten up a few lives.

"The day of the accident there was a luncheon for Todd given by the board of the hospital. He'd won a grant to help fund an outreach program and we were all so excited for him." She steadied herself before continuing. "There were speeches and toasts and he must have had a drink or two but I didn't... I didn't think anything of it. I've wished a thousand times that I could reach through the years and take those keys from him."

"Mike saw you in Skillman's arms—in the parking lot."

She brought her fists to her forehead. "I gave him a hug goodbye. That's all it was. Just a hug."

"But what about Mike? Didn't you wonder why he was right there at the accident?"

"I thought it was a miracle. I thought it was... God."

I knew she was telling the truth.

We sat in silence, words falling around us like hot embers. I wanted to ask more about that day and all the unspoken hours that followed. And I wanted to ask what happened during the war, to trace the lineage of her sorrow back to a time when her heart was once whole. Most of all I wanted to tell her that Mike loved her even if he died believing she'd betrayed him. But I didn't know how.

"Shannon never needs to know," I said finally. "I'll never tell her."

"You're wrong. She must know."

"But why?"

"Because she's in love with you and if she doesn't learn the truth now she'll learn it later and if you wait she may never forgive you for hiding it from her."

"I couldn't tell her," I said, trying to imagine the horror of her father's secret sinking in to Shannon's eyes.

"I'll tell her. I've made my mistakes but I am her mother."

"She may not accept the truth. She may not be ready for it."

"The truth is the only thing left to hold on to." Alessandra started the car.

I looked back at Winfrey's Monuments and noticed Cal standing at the window watching us, a sandwich in one hand. As we pulled away he began to wave. I found myself waving too.

CHAPTER
TEN

I WATCHED THE conversation from the window of the bedroom where Mike died. They were standing outside by the tractor, Shannon motionless while Alessandra reached out now and then to caress her daughter's cheek or shoulder. I saw the moment the truth hit, the way Shannon stepped back, then turned, then stepped forward again to fight back with words because the truth had to be wrong. *Not Mike O'Donnell. Not my father.*

When Shannon turned for the barn Alessandra started to follow, then stopped, looking for a moment as if she might fall to her knees. Minutes later Shannon emerged on Renegade, horse and rider passing swiftly through the gate before surging forward on the trail that ran along the creek and through the foothills to the mountains, the sun easing wearily down behind them. I watched them until I couldn't see them anymore, then sat on the edge of Mike's bed and stared into the framed face of the young GI, his arms draped proudly around his two buddies. But it wasn't his eyes or boyish smile that held me. It was the smoothness of his large, strong hands.

Shannon didn't return until nearly eleven. Alessandra and I were waiting up in the kitchen, each taking turns at the window.

"Are you sure we shouldn't send someone out looking for her?" I asked.

"No, she'll be back," said Alessandra, folding a pile of dish towels. "Besides, you'd never find her."

As soon as the front door opened I started to get up but Alessandra put her hand on my shoulder to stop me. We listened as Shannon hurried up the stairs and into her room.

"She needs time," said Alessandra, her face drawn tight.

Once I was in bed I knew I wouldn't sleep. It was only silence I wanted, a pure snowy silence gathering in great drifts upon me. But somehow I must have dozed off because when I opened my eyes I noticed Shannon standing in the darkness, the door closed behind her.

"I went into Dad's room to kiss him goodnight," she said. "Isn't that silly?"

"No, it's not silly," I said, sitting up.

"Then I looked at all his stuff waiting for him and I didn't have the heart to tell his shirts and his old boots and his hats that he wasn't coming back."

"No need to tell them yet."

She started toward the bed and then stopped. "Ever since I was a little girl he told me that one day I'd fly away to see the world for myself and that I could do anything I wanted because I was as good as anybody and better than most. But I think he always hoped that eventually I'd come back. I'd come back and he'd build a house for me right next door and help with the grandchildren. But I couldn't come back." She began to cry. "It's true, isn't it?"

"Yes, it is."

She slumped down on the bed beside me. "I hate it. I hate all of it."

I put my arm around her and she turned and pressed her wet face into my shoulder.

"I've lost both of you," she said.

"No you haven't."

She stood up again, backing away slowly. "My father killed your parents."

"It was an accident. Everything just went horribly wrong."

"I was so proud of him for saving your life. Mom was so proud of him too. When I was younger I thought it might be the one thing that could make her love him, make her understand how lucky she was to be married to such a man."

"He did save my life."

"How can you say that?"

"Because it's true. And you're not going to lose me, too." I walked up to her and took her hands in mine.

"But how could I ever look at you without thinking of what my father did? How could I ever make love to you without remembering you in the hospital and how even the nurses cried when they left your room? How could I even... *kiss you?*"

"This is how," I said, taking her by the shoulders and kissing her hard on the lips.

Her arms started around my waist, then went limp. "No, I can't." She backed away until she reached the door. "I really can't. I'm sorry. I'm sorry for everything that's happened." She quickly turned and walked out, closing the door behind her.

CHAPTER
ELEVEN

The South Pacific
October 5, 1944

Dear Rebecca,

    I watched a young midshipman die of his burns yesterday. All night I asked myself how this world could ever make amends for something like that but I knew in my heart that it couldn't even come close. You could bring that poor boy back a king in his next life and he'd tell you that what he endured wasn't worth a hundred castles. And he's not coming back a king. He's not even coming back a hog farmer's son from Mississippi.

    I know this life is more questions than answers but sometimes I can't help thinking that the world was born with a streak of meanness in it and we've been paying mightily ever since. It's surely not the courage to endure that we lack. I've seen that first hand. I only wish we had the wisdom to match our courage because one without the other is an awful thing.

    I don't mean to scare you with my darkness. It'll pass because it always has, especially when I think of you. (I have beside me the picture I took of you by the river on our last day together, a smile just rising in your eyes, and I can tell you it would fetch a handsome sum around here.) But there are moments when I feel so angry at the things I have seen that I wonder how I'm going to stand another day of it. And yet all my questions and prayers just seem to slip silently into the infinite blueness of these waters just like the canvas-wrapped body of that boy from Mississippi.

We buried two others at sea this week. The first time I ever saw it done I decided there was no lonelier place on God's earth for a person to end up. But I've given it a lot of thought over these landless months and I'm starting to wonder if I was wrong to think of heaven as somewhere beyond the stars when it just might be hiding beneath these tireless waves. I imagine it's a peaceful place, full of beauty and splendor. Sometimes at night when my thoughts won't settle I like to think of all the watery life flowing beneath the hull of this metal beast, oblivious to our foolishness. I picture enormous schools of brightly colored fish and great forests of coral and sharks and whales and dolphins and turtles and all sorts of strange sea creatures. And then I imagine vast stretches of silvery nothingness, the silence so complete and eternal that just thinking about it stirs a speechless reverence inside of me. I don't suppose it's the kind of heaven that boy from Mississippi had in mind, but I hope it'll do.

Please give my love to your parents and tell everybody I'm doing fine. Now I think I'm just going to lie here and look at your picture and imagine what it's going to be like to kiss that pretty face of yours again.

Love,
Jim

CHAPTER
TWELVE

You think of me, and I will think of you.
– St. Catherine of Sienna

THE NEXT MORNING Alessandra was sitting alone in the living room, opera playing on the turntable. "Puccini's *Turandot*," she said, picking up the album cover that sat in her lap, its edges worn. Her eyes were sleepless and I noticed for the first time that her hands trembled slightly. "Leinsdorf is the conductor. I think it's the best version."

"It's very moving."

Neither of us spoke until the aria ended. Then Alessandra got up and took the record off the turntable, carefully sliding it back into its cover. When she finished putting the album away she stood up straight and hooked her fingers together, elbows wide, as if trying to pull her hands apart.

"She caught an early flight back to San Francisco."

"Did she say anything before she left?" I asked.

"No, she didn't."

I skipped breakfast. Instead I followed the trail that ran along the creek, stopping now and then to listen to the water scurry over the rocks. I'd never felt so many thoughts before, all of them crowded in my head like seasick passengers. I thought of Mike with his secret eating away at him all those years and of Todd Skillman fighting with the steering wheel. I thought of my mother with just enough life left in her to see her son carried to safety by a stranger and of Alessandra with no hope but the grace of angels to tell her husband that Skillman was not her lover. Then I thought of Lupo waiting on the one true love that might save him (if only she'd look at him) and Aunt Margaret wishing her sister wasn't too cheap to call and Shannon searching for a man as good as her father only even he was broken inside.

Are we fools to even try for happiness, time and death chewing hungrily at every lifeline? Is that where everything goes wrong because the real choice isn't between joy and despair but rather between a sort of numb retreat and the fearsome sensation of standing our ground?

And yet what hope is there if even the strongest hearts can lose their way?

When I got back to the house Alessandra was upstairs sorting Mike's clothes into neat piles on his bed. "I never met a man who cared less about what he wore," she said, folding a pair of jeans. She held up a shirt and stared at it, her head tilting to one side. Then she set it on top of a pile to her left, gathered up the pile and placed it in a laundry basket. "I thought I'd give everything one more good wash before taking it to the Salvation Army."

"I'll carry it," I said, taking the basket from her and following her downstairs to the laundry room. While she prepared the wash I used the phone in the kitchen to book a flight home that afternoon. After I packed my things I placed my bags on the porch and then walked out to the barn to see the horses one last time before meeting Alessandra at her car.

"Ready?" she said, trying to smile.

"I don't like leaving you alone."

"No need to worry about me." She started the engine. "Besides, I'm used to it."

Once we pulled out of the driveway and headed down the narrow dirt road I turned to look back at the house but it was already cloaked by the dust rising behind us. And yet still I could see it rising out of nowhere, the wood frame slightly bent by the wind, or maybe something stronger. I knew I'd always be able to see it, even when I didn't want to. And I knew with equal certainty that I'd always be able to see Shannon's face, too.

I looked over at Alessandra, who sat forward with her hands high on the wheel. What was left to hold on to when every expectation of happiness was gone? Would she live by sheer habit or was there something else that kept people going, something that only comes into view when everything else has been torn away?

After several miles we turned onto a paved road and headed north, the sudden quiet of the wheels making my thoughts feel louder. As we passed the cemetery Alessandra crossed herself.

"I'd like to stop," I said.

She looked surprised.

"Just for a few minutes. We have time."

She slowed, then made a U-turn and pulled into the small parking lot. "It's me you should blame," she said in a quiet voice as she turned off the engine.

"I don't need to blame anybody."

I kept slightly behind her as we approached Mike's freshly dug grave. A strong wind sent waves rolling across the grass and a rabbit stood off in one corner watching, ears alert. Above, pale lean clouds hurried past like stragglers and all the colors of the day seemed slightly faded.

"For some reason I keep thinking he's young again," she said, kneeling down. Then she smiled to herself. "He was so strong and straightforward and polite. So *American*. Even though I'd never met any Americans he was just what I thought they'd be like."

"How long did you know each other before you got engaged?"

"Only a few weeks. That must sound crazy to you."

"It was a different time."

"Yes, that it was."

"Did you fall in love immediately?"

She placed her hand on top of the copper brown soil, pressing into the earth. "I never fell in love."

So Shannon was right. Was Alessandra in love with another man all these years? Was that why she looked so guilty because if it wasn't Skillman it was someone else and Mike knew it; he knew she'd been unfaithful?

Alessandra continued without looking at me. "When he asked me to marry him I really believed I could make him happy, that with time I could learn to love him. How hard could it be to love a man who was kind and hardworking and honest? But I couldn't, not the way a wife should love her husband. I tried for years but I just... couldn't." She paused. "He was a good, strong, simple man. But you see, I didn't want a simple man. I wanted a man whose heart was on fire."

"Why did you marry him?"

"Because he loved me. And because... because I didn't know any better." She looked up at me. "I don't want you to think I feel sorry for myself because I don't." She smiled, her eyebrows struggling to lift the sorrow from her eyes. "My father once said that people waste half their lives licking their wounds and the other half talking about them. He was right." She slowly rose to her feet. "You don't want to miss your plane."

We said goodbye at the airport, a dry wind flapping against our collars as we stood outside the small terminal.

"What will you do now?" I asked.

"The only thing I can do: I'll clear Todd Skillman's name."

"Do you want my help?"

"No, I want you to go and live your life while it's still ahead of you." She gave me a hug and kissed me firmly on both cheeks. I started to walk away when she stopped me. "Wait." She reached into the backseat of the car and pulled out a thick manila envelope. "I have something to give you." She held the envelope out.

"What is it?"

She shrugged nervously. "It's the rest of my story. It's where everything went wrong." She stared down at the envelope in her hands. "I'd forgotten how much it helps to put words on paper where they can breathe. So that's what I did because I thought... I thought that if Shannon understood me, if she knew what happened and why I made the choices I did..." She paused, her face looking for strength. "You see I thought that if I retraced my steps, that maybe I could find a place to start again. And so I wrote down everything I could remember because I don't know what else to do." Her eyes were filled with tears as she pushed the envelope into my hands.

"But why are you giving this to me?"

"Because my mistakes cost you very dearly. You have a right to know why I made them. And because Shannon is going to need help with this. I'd help her but she won't take any help from me. Not right now. Not for a long time." Alessandra reached out and put her hand lightly on my cheek. "So I need you to help her."

"But she's gone. I won't see her again."

"Oh, but you must. It's the one good thing left." She kissed me again. "Her address is on the last page. Please tell her that I love her more than anything in the world. Make sure you tell her that." And then she got into her car and drove away.

CHAPTER
THIRTEEN

SHE STARTED AT the beginning, her words tightly spaced on the unlined pages of the salmon-colored clothbound journal as she described the village of San Gianello and her brothers and sisters and the small girl in her perch in the garage watching her father work and listening to his magical stories. And then one day the German Army came and Romeo was shot and the frightened young soldier appeared to apologize, his eyes lingering long after he left. The next several pages were missing, torn from the binding. And then the story started up again, the words filling page after page as they hurried forward.

At first she seemed to be addressing her daughter, words gathered to rouse the past for the benefit of the future. But gradually I felt another, larger presence. By the time I finished I realized that she'd made the journey endless times; that the paving stones between her past and present were worn smooth with her silent footfalls.

I waited until my plane was in the air before opening the cover and turning to the first page, pausing every few minutes to look out the window at the mute landscape below. By the time I had landed in Denver for my connection to Atlanta I had made my decision: I wasn't going home. Not yet. Instead I rebooked myself on the 10:00 P.M. flight to San Francisco, then sat in an airport bar reading and drinking and stopping now and then to pace up and down the concourse trying to burn the energy from my limbs.

PART THREE

CHAPTER
ONE

Italia! O Italia! thou who hast
The fatal gift of beauty.
– Lord Byron

I NEVER TOLD Papa that the young German soldier who had shot Romeo had come to apologize. What could I say? That I'd disobeyed him and opened the door to a handsome young man who seemed genuinely sorry? But I couldn't stop thinking about what had happened. Even in my dreams I found myself listening to Johann as he told his terrible story, wishing I could somehow remove the pain from his eyes. I'd never seen such eyes before, so blue and sincere that you could see right away that he meant what he said. I even started to feel bad for the way I'd treated him. And yet he was a German who'd shot our dog.

I saw him again three days later. I was walking home from the bakery when he passed by on his motorcycle. He slowed down but I wouldn't look at him. I even made a point of averting my face because I didn't know what else to do. And then the next morning there was a box by the garage door. A very noisy box.

"What have we here?" said Papa, gently lifting the lid and picking up a small brown puppy.

I knew immediately it was from Johann but I didn't dare tell Papa. He would never accept a gift from the Germans and I wanted him to keep the dog. He'd been so sad since Romeo was killed, spending what little free time he had sitting alone in the courtyard, all the joy drained from his features.

"Maybe Mr. Bagiani left it for you," I suggested.

"He hates dogs."

"Or one of your customers? It could be any of dozens of people." It was true, my father was well loved and had done many favors over the years.

He lifted the puppy into the air and eyed it closely. A broad smile spread over his face. "She's cute, eh, Mouse?"

"She's adorable."

"We shall call her Juliet." From that day on they were inseparable.

I saw Johann again two days later in our small piazza, which was built around an old well that had been sealed long ago and replaced by a small fountain that was always dry because no one could agree on who was in charge of assuring an adequate water supply. He was trying to calm down Dr. Cardoni, who was complaining bitterly that German soldiers on patrol during the nightly curfew had made a habit of relieving themselves in his wife's flowerbed. I feared that Johann would get angry—what could he care about Mrs. Cardoni's flowerbed when his own family had been burned alive?—but he was apologetic, offering to see what he could do. When he saw me I tried to look away but I couldn't, not immediately. For the first time I saw a smile come across his face, which made me smile too even though I hadn't intended to smile. I hurried quickly past him and into Pardino's Grocery, pretending to be busy and trying to ignore the sudden warmth in my chest.

I'd never felt that way before, happy and anxious and confused and guilty all at once. It was the first time I realized that certain feelings have their own destiny, regardless of whether they are right or wrong or even manageable. After that all I cared about was how soon it would be until I could see him again, even if it was just a glimpse so that I could discover whether the delicious warmth would again surge through my limbs.

But why was I so attracted to him? He was interesting to look at, tall and even somewhat exotic with his burning eyes and slightly haunted features, as though he'd survived a great many childhood illnesses. But he wasn't exactly handsome, not like Marcello, who made all the girls giggle. There was something boyish about the way he carried himself, his long arms dangling loosely at his sides. You could see right away that he was intelligent, his eyes taking everything in as they swept back and forth, and yet he seemed uncertain of himself, with the preoccupied look of a person in great turmoil. No matter how I counted, and I began to count frequently, there were a great many more reasons not to like him than to like him. And yet whenever I saw him I felt laughter tickling my heart.

Fortunately I got to see him almost every day, passing by on the road or in the piazza because he was constantly needed to translate as tensions flared between Germans and Italians. At first I consciously tried not to like him, reminding myself over and over that he'd shot Romeo. (And how could anyone with a heart have pulled the trigger?) But it was useless, especially seeing how his face would turn crimson when he had to explain each new set of regulations, which were posted almost weekly on flyers that would suddenly appear on walls and trees throughout the village. The truth is he really wasn't like a soldier at all. Certainly not a German soldier, most of whom seemed to take everything terribly seriously. He even had a habit of talking with his hands when he was excited or telling a story. (In a single day I watched him accidentally send two glasses flying as he sat talking at Umberto's, which was just across the piazza from the bakery.)

As the weeks went by everyone in our village came to like him; everyone, that is, except for my father. *The-German-with-the-heart-of-an-Italian*, that's what people called him. From the bakery I could often see him through the window as I worked, trying hard not to stare as I watched him mediate some dispute or play *Briscola* or *Tressette* with the older men or just sit by himself by the fountain lost in thought. Sometimes he looked so sad that I longed to sit beside him and comfort him, but then his face would come to life again and he looked as if there was nowhere else in the world he would rather be. No matter how he looked I couldn't take my eyes from him.

"Feel free to give me a hand," said Aunt Lucia, catching me daydreaming.

I quickly returned to cleaning the baking sheets as my aunt noisily mixed her closely guarded recipe for *crostata di frutta di stagione*, shortcake with fresh fruit, which she would bake that afternoon in honor of Father Gregorio's birthday.

In the beginning we rarely spoke to one another. I was relieved, at least partly, because I wouldn't have had the faintest idea what to say to him. Whenever he stopped by the bakery he addressed himself to Aunt Lucia, always so polite that she was soon feeding him free samples of *pan d'oro* and *michetta* as he asked her the names for various items, carefully practicing his pronunciation, which was excellent. He took great interest in everything Italian, always asking about the meaning and usage of different words and why we did things the way we did and especially how we produced such delicious meals despite the rationing. He became quite popular with the village children, too, learning all their names and performing sleight-of-hand tricks when school let out, pulling candies out of ears and noses and making coins disappear.

"He can't be German," said Aunt Lucia, joining me to watch him out the window as he pantomimed for the children, always paying special attention to little Alfonso Vittorini, who had Down's Syndrome. Yet even his laughter had a slightly desperate edge and the more I saw him the more I began to wonder whether he was immersing himself in our lives to escape the memories of his own.

Before long almost everyone in San Gianello had a reason to be thankful for our Italian-hearted German. Not only had he managed to stop the nightly patrols from relieving themselves in Mrs. Cardoni's garden and to get the curfew shortened by one hour on Saturdays but he had even somehow secured the necessary travel papers for Celia Magreno to visit her ailing brother in Bologna. When he turned up Alberto Biano's confiscated violin it was widely agreed that he had to be at least a quarter Italian, and maybe more.

And yet there were limits to what he could do, especially around Henecker, whose presence caused Johann to shrink into his skin like an abused dog. One day three German soldiers beat Marco Selvini right in the piazza at noon. I don't know why they attacked him, except that Selvini, a big, fat man who owned the butcher shop, was notoriously incapable of hiding his contempt of anyone or anything he didn't approve of. Several of us stood by watching, ashamed of our helplessness. Johann was there too, standing right behind Henecker, who liked to spend his afternoons sitting out at Umberto's—always at the best table—drinking red wine and ordering people about.

Johann's face was stricken but he didn't move. Nobody did, not even when Selvini was on the ground being kicked mercilessly. I remember closing my eyes and praying for Selvini, but also for Johann, too, hoping he wouldn't do anything stupid. That's when I realized for the first time how much I cared for him, though I didn't understand why.

The next day as I was walking home past the small roadside shrine that marked the spot where eight-year-old Larissa Brunelli was struck by a car—our village was full of *Madonninas* in their glass-covered displays, which meant that it took Mama hours to walk anywhere—Johann appeared on his motorcycle.

"Can I give you a ride?" he said, slowing beside me.

"Of course not," I said without stopping. Imagine me being seen on the back of a German motorcycle!

"I'm sorry about what happened yesterday."

"You're sorry about a lot of things."

"Yes, I am." I was afraid he would leave but he continued beside me. "Is he okay?"

"He'll live, if that's what you want to know."

"Not all the men are like that."

"I should hope not."

"But you must be very careful."

"Do they beat women, too?"

"I only warn you because you are very beautiful, and beauty is always in danger." And then he rode off.

Papa always told me I was beautiful but I never really believed it, even though I felt the eyes of the village boys on me more and more as I got older. (Especially Pietro, whom Mama continued to chase from the olive grove where he liked to stand and watch my window when he wasn't raiding Mrs. Cardoni's flower garden for the bouquets he'd set along my path.) Did Johann really find me beautiful or was that what he said to all the Italian women he met? And what does a man who finds a woman beautiful really feel inside? Yet he was warning me. Was I in danger? From what? I turned and checked the road behind me, quickening my pace.

When I didn't see him again for several days I began to worry. Had something happened to him? Had he been sent to the front? I felt terribly lonely, losing patience with the twins as they trailed me around the house begging me to play. Twice Papa caught me staring dumbly out the window as I sat in the garage going through his accounts.

"Where are you today, Mouse?" he said, giving me a look that made me feel like he could see each thought as it passed through my head.

"I'm just tired, that's all."

He sat down on the edge of my chair and put his arm around me. "When I was your age my thoughts were so restless they'd run three laps around the world before breakfast."

"Were they nice thoughts?"

He let out a deep laugh. "Nice thoughts don't require so much exercise. I used to think of them as hunger pangs, only they were in my head where I couldn't feed them—at least not with anything but more thoughts, which just made them hungrier."

"So how did you get rid of them?"

"I married your mother."

I couldn't suppress a smile. "And they went away?"

He pursed his lips and tugged at his large chin, his eyes swiveling up toward the ceiling. "Actually, no. But I learned to outthink them."

"How can you outthink your thoughts?"

"By thinking with this." He pointed to his heart with a wink, then got up and went back to work.

A week later I was working alone in the bakery when Johann suddenly appeared. I tried to hide the joy from my face as he entered.

"I need your help," he said quickly, keeping his eye on the window.

His tone frightened me. "What can I do?"

"Henecker has ordered the confiscation of all bicycles."

"You're too late. Ours were taken away yesterday. Do you have any idea how long it took me to save up for my bicycle? And my father—"

"Listen to me. I'm having trouble with Mr. Tuchini. You must help."

"Everybody has trouble with Tuchini." Tuchini was old and stubborn and lived alone in a small, dark house on the edge of town.

"He won't cooperate and the deadline is midnight. You must talk to him."

"You should be ashamed for stealing the bicycle of an old man whose legs can hardly carry him."

"It's not me."

"It never is, is it?" I wasn't about to let him off easily, even if he did have the sweetest eyes I'd ever seen.

"Henecker is not to be fooled with. You have no idea what he is capable of."

"I have some idea."

"Please."

"Tuchini is not easily intimidated."

"You must try."

Johann stood waiting as I busied myself wiping down the pastry board. Finally I shrugged. "Okay, I'll talk to him."

"By midnight."

I nodded. "But I can't promise anything."

"Thank you." He began to leave.

"What if he refuses?"

"You must make sure he doesn't."

As soon as I left work I hurried to Tuchini's house, which was built into the side of a hill near an abandoned quarry and was said to be haunted by ghosts, especially Tuchini's deceased wife, Frederica, who allegedly poisoned herself with her notorious *polpette in salsa crema*—meatballs—which could be smelled as far as the churchyard. I was one of the few people who could reason with Tuchini—he said that my long hair reminded him of a beloved sister who died many years ago—but no matter how much I begged and pleaded with him he refused, insisting that if he gave the Germans his bicycle today they'd come back for his shirt tomorrow. "I'm too old to be afraid," he said, easing himself into a rocking chair and rubbing his swollen knees. "And believe me, if I survived forty years of Frederica's cooking—God have mercy on her soul—I can handle anything the Germans can dish out."

Finally I decided to lie. "If you don't cooperate they intend to punish the rest of us."

He sat forward in his chair. "Who told you this?"

"The German commander is eager to make an impression. Everybody knows it. He's just looking for an excuse. In fact, I'm sure he'd be delighted if you refused to cooperate."

"An impression, eh?" Tuchini sat rubbing his knees for several minutes, his large juicy face more purple than usual (a condition also attributed to Frederica's cooking).

"Please. I'll take it to them myself."

He growled a few times and stomped his feet. "Oh, hell, it's around back," he said finally, waving his hand through the air. "But if they so much as scratch it…"

"I'll tell them to be careful," I said, hurrying around the house. As I rode off on his rickety old bicycle I felt for the first time that just maybe I had made a small difference in the war.

Three days later Johann stopped me on the road to warn me that Henecker was planning to confiscate all remaining livestock during Sunday Mass. At first I didn't know what to do. If I told too many people someone would surely tell the Germans, because you could never really be sure who was and wasn't a secret Fascist, or at least trying to play all sides. Yet I had to tell somebody. Finally I left an anonymous message for Father Gregorio, certain that he would know what to do.

Our priest had arrived shortly after the death of Father Tomasso twelve years earlier. For the first few years he was so shy that only those in the front pew could hear the service, or at least fragments of it. Without the benefit of any verbal cues there was a great deal of confusion about when to sit and when to stand, and after it was over there was even some debate about whether Mass had actually taken place.

"How can God hear him if we can't?" Aunt Lucia would complain, straining forward in her pew like all the others.

Tall, thin and nervous-looking, he turned so red every time he faced the audience that many feared he would expire right there on the altar.

"If he dies during the service we'll all be cursed," groaned Margerita Bagiani. "We'd have to build a new church."

"Where would we get the money to build a new church?" said Aunt Lucia, throwing her hands into the air.

But gradually Father Gregorio grew into his skin and his congregation became endeared with his red-faced determination to overcome his shyness. Over the years he'd even become the object of secret affection by many of the older women, who took an almost parental pride in his progress. By the time the Germans arrived on our doorstep, Father Gregorio was a force to be reckoned with.

The day after he got my warning Father Gregorio paid visits to dozens of villagers—especially those who punctually attended Mass or suffered hardships—advising them to slaughter their chickens and goats and pigs or hide them in the forest, leaving a token chicken or two for the Germans to find. That Sunday as I sat in church listening to him give the homily in an unusually loud voice I felt so close to God that I could almost feel the divine heat of his glorious presence on my face.

And that's how it began. I never said anything to my family of course, and Johann and I were careful not to be seen talking. But soon we were co-conspirators trying to prevent bloodshed between Germans and Italians, which would have been all Italian blood. I'll never know why he took such risks—whether it was for me or to compensate for his part in the war or because it was just in his nature, but he never complained. His position as a messenger, translator and driver allowed him to move freely and he enjoyed a great deal of access to people and information and sometimes even medical supplies, which I would leave on a doorstep, feeling like a guardian angel. When he explained to me that a powerful uncle in Berlin had helped him avoid duty on the Russian front his face darkened with shame.

"You should feel fortunate," I said.

"My family is dead. My neighbors are dead. Many of my friends are dead. Many more will die. How can I feel fortunate?"

I didn't have an answer.

CHAPTER TWO

TWO WEEKS AFTER the Germans scoured the village for livestock I saw Johann walking alone by the ruins of the twelfth century watch tower that sat on a rise above the church. After circling around the cemetery so no one would see me I hurried to him, my lungs filling with a question I'd been waiting to ask but hadn't dared to.

"My brother Renaldo, he was with the Italian Eighth Army… in Russia. We haven't heard from him in almost a year. I thought maybe you could find out something? Any news at all…"

Johann shook his head. "I can't help you."

"But why not? You have connections."

"Because no one comes home from Russia. Not Italians, not Germans."

"It can't be true."

He put his hand lightly on my arm. "I'm sorry."

I cried all the way home.

He began to stop by the bakery almost every morning, lingering over the small display of *focaccia*, *ciabatta*, *pane casareccio* and *biscotti* and always complimenting Aunt Lucia until she was light on her large feet. We were both careful not to pay any attention to each other and we didn't dare talk, not unless we were alone. Of course, we were hardly ever alone. Soon it became unbearable, stealing little glances and feeling a million thoughts clustered on the tip of my tongue and seeing from his eyes that he needed to speak to me. How could he warn me of Henecker's plans if we couldn't talk?

Finally I couldn't stand it anymore. I waited three days until I saw him alone on the road south of our house near the German encampment, this time on a bicycle because the Germans were low on fuel.

"*Buon giorgno*, Alessandra," he said loudly, his face opening into a huge smile that almost made me forget what I wanted to say. He circled me once on his bicycle, then jumped off and gave a small bow.

"We can't talk here," I whispered, not even looking at him in case we were being watched.

"But we must talk," he said.

We both turned at the sound of an approaching vehicle. "I know a place," I said, speaking quickly. "At the far end of the olive grove behind our house there's a large oak tree—just where the woods begin. I'll be there tomorrow at four." Then I hurried off.

He was waiting when I arrived. The moment I saw him emerge from behind the oak tree I felt my heart pirouette in my chest.

"I didn't think you'd really come," he said, walking up so close to me that for a moment I thought he might kiss me.

"Why wouldn't I?"

"A lot of reasons." He rubbed his palms nervously against the sides of his uniform like a boy at his first dance. "I mean, to be alone with a German soldier…"

I felt my cheeks grow hot. "You've risked your life for us. Of course I trust you. Now follow me." I walked quickly through the woods and up the hillside, feeling the perspiration gather on my neck.

"Where are we going?" he asked, keeping close behind.

"You'll have to wait and see."

"But your feet?"

I'd gotten into the habit of going barefoot except when I worked at the bakery or went to church. I'd long since grown out of my shoes and shoe leather was impossible to come by. Most villagers either kept repairing what they had or wore *zoccoli*—wooden clogs—but

I couldn't stand anything I couldn't run in. Anyway, I preferred to feel my feet against the ground and wouldn't have worn shoes even if I had ones that fit, despite my mother's protests.

"You just worry about keeping up with me," I said.

The entrance to the cave was hidden among a cluster of boulders strewn against a wooded hillside and overgrown with roots and vines. If I hadn't stopped him Johann would have walked right past it, just as I had hoped.

"This way," I said, leading him between two large rocks and then on to the small ledge.

When he saw the opening his eyes grew wide. "No one would ever find you here," he said excitedly, scrambling up the last few feet.

"You must never tell anyone."

"My word of honor."

He followed me through the narrow entrance, ducking until the cave opened into a chamber nearly eight feet high and fifteen feet across at the widest point.

"How far back does it go?" he asked, peering into the darkness.

"About thirty feet, but you have to crawl toward the end." I remembered how as a child I would squeeze myself as far back as I could go, determined to find the source of the mysterious breeze that rose from somewhere within the mountain.

"We used to play here as children. No one knows about it except my brothers." Again my cheeks grew warm. "Anyway, I thought that if we needed to meet... I mean if there was anything I could do..."

He smiled. "Yes, it's perfect."

I felt self-conscious as he looked at me and yet wonderful, too. "I should probably go now," I said, taking a step toward the entrance.

"But can't we stay for just a little while?"

"Well, I suppose if you want."

He spent several minutes exploring the cave, pausing to run his fingers along the damp rock where my brothers and I had carved our names years earlier. Then we sat together just outside the entrance on the outcropping, both looking out at the valley far below. I tried to think of something to say but he seemed preoccupied so I remained silent, my breath quickened by a sense of intimacy I'd never felt before.

"This is what I'd want," he said when he finally spoke.

"What is?"

"I was just thinking that if things were different, that if…" His voice trailed off.

"That if what?"

"That if things were different, I'd want this: the stillness, the view stretching for miles, the colors of the sky, the sweetness of the air, and you right here with me. It's perfect, don't you think?"

"Well, it's… it's rather nice, yes." I began to toy nervously with my hair, a habit Mama had tried to break me of for years. "I've been meaning to thank you for all you've done. You probably saved Tuchini's life and if you hadn't warned us about the livestock—"

"There's no need to thank me."

"But there is. You could be shot for such things."

He turned toward me. "So could you." At first I thought he was joking but I could see from his expression that he wasn't.

"But it's my village," I said, trying to sound brave. When he didn't respond I tried to change the subject. "Where did you get the puppy?"

I saw the muscles along his jaw line contract. "Her owners were deported." He paused, seeming uncomfortable. "She was so frightened. I couldn't just leave her. I thought that if I found her a new home, that at least that would be something… something good."

"She's adorable."

"I'm sorry she wasn't quite housebroken."

"Not as sorry as my mother." I smiled.

He was quiet for several minutes. "Your father hates me. I can see it in his eyes."

"Don't take it personally. He hates all Germans—and Austrians, too."

"Such good company." He tried to smile but he couldn't sustain it, not for more than a fleeting moment when two opposing forces seemed to struggle for control of his features. I resisted the urge to reach out and touch him. What would happen if I did? But of course I couldn't. Being alone with him was daring enough. (I cringed at the thought of what Mama would say if she found out.) But I wanted to touch him. I wanted to reach out and run my hands over his face more than I'd wanted to do anything in my life. I'd never felt so drawn to another person before, like a heavy object that once dislodged begins to roll downhill faster and faster and cannot be stopped.

"Why are you helping us?" I asked.

"Why not?"

"Because you're German. And because there's no reason for you to."

"You're wrong, there are a great many reasons."

"But to go against one's own country..."

"It's not my country I'm against."

"But aren't you afraid?"

"Sometimes."

I looked at him closely. "I think your parents must have been wonderful people."

"Why do you say that?"

"Because you're so different from the others. People even joke that you must be Italian."

"I'm not so different."

"But none of the other Germans—"

"You don't understand," he interrupted. "They are good men, most of them. I grew up with them. I know them. I know their families."

"But—"

"Do you know what they want? To survive. That's all. Who can be blamed for wanting to survive?"

"And don't you want to survive?"

He hesitated.

"Answer me."

"Not at any cost."

"What cost is too high?"

"That's the question, isn't it?"

"Would it make a difference if I told you that I want you to survive?"

"You've already made a difference." His hand started toward me, then stopped.

I tried to concentrate on a robin that landed on a nearby rock, head tilted to one side as if eavesdropping. "You must hate the people who killed your family."

"No, but I hate that it was so easy."

A sudden wind swept up the valley and rolled across the treetops, swirling through the cave with a long groan. Johann started to say something and then stopped himself. When I looked over at him he seemed completely different, his teeth clenched and his face bathed in sweat as though suddenly gripped by a fever.

"Are you all right?" I felt scared now.

He looked down at his hands, which were shaking.

"Johann, talk to me."

"It happens sometimes," he said, speaking in a stammer.

"What happens?"

"I can't describe it." He got up, keeping his face turned away. "We should go. I'll walk you to the edge of the woods."

"I want to know what's wrong?"

But he couldn't talk. Or he wouldn't. Instead I followed him as he walked quickly through the woods until we reached the edge of the olive grove where he said a brief goodbye before hurrying off in the direction of the German encampment.

CHAPTER
THREE

"DID UNCLE ROBERTO really kill himself?" I asked Papa that evening as we sat in the courtyard after dinner. Uncle Roberto had suffered shell shock in the Great War and never recovered. Even fifteen years after his mysterious death he was only mentioned in whispers, usually only around religious holidays.

"Who said he killed himself?"

"You did."

"I did?"

"Renaldo overheard you talking to Mama."

"What big ears my children have."

"Is it true?"

"Your uncle died in 1918. What was left of him after the war wasn't my brother at all."

"What happened to him?"

Papa leaned back in his chair, his hands resting on his thighs. Above us several bats crisscrossed hungrily through the inky sky. "How can a simple mechanic find the words for things that even Dante's quill could not possibly describe?"

"You mean shell shock? Is that what happened to him?"

"And other things, too."

"What kinds of other things?"

Papa began to raise his hands, then let them fall back on his thighs. "Someday when you are older you will learn that the very best and the very worst things in life touch a place in our hearts that words cannot reach."

"Did he really kill himself?"

"He finished what the war started." Then Papa rose from his chair and walked slowly into the house.

The next afternoon there was a soccer game on the *campo* between the Germans and an Italian team comprised of boys who were too young for the army and men who were too old. Of course the Germans won—22 to 0—but we all enjoyed ourselves immensely because it was a rare opportunity to boo the Germans without fear of deportation. Even Papa attended, cheering so loudly for the Italians that I worried about his heart. I spent most of the game watching Johann, who was off to one side on his hands and knees giving rides on his back to the smaller children, especially Alfonso Vittorini, who couldn't keep his hands off Johann, constantly hugging him and following him around like a little duckling.

The game had just finished when two British fighters suddenly appeared, swooping down with the sun at their backs so that at first we couldn't tell whose planes they were. But the Germans knew right away and scattered like mad, knocking over villagers as they ran for cover. As Papa and I hurried for the nearby shelter of the trees I saw Johann pick up Alfonso and carry him off the field. Less than a minute later the planes reappeared, their engines howling as they skimmed just over the now empty *campo*. This time several of the German soldiers who'd managed to get to their weapons fired into the sky, which terrified the rest of us even more as we were all mixed in together, pressed against the ground.

"Do you want to get us all killed?' Papa yelled at the Germans as he tried to shield me with his body. I saw Pietro on the ground nearby, his wide eyes fixed on me, and for a moment I feared that he would pile on top of Papa in an attempt to further protect me.

Then I saw Alfonso emerge from the woods and run wildly across the *campo*, screaming and pulling at his hair as he went.

Johann dashed out after him just as the planes came roaring down again. As the Germans began firing the planes dropped so low that we could see the pilots and the insignia on the shiny silver wings and fuselages. Johann reached Alfonso just as the first plane came overhead, its shadow streaking across the ground. In a single motion he hoisted the child into the air and ran for the cover of a stone wall.

They are both going to die, I thought, trying to push myself up from beneath Papa, who held me to the ground with his weight. But the planes didn't fire. Not that day. Within seconds they had vanished over the horizon, leaving us all frozen on the ground until slowly we began to emerge from our hiding places, all eyes on the sky above as we hurried home.

The next morning we awoke to find that the Germans had placed an antiaircraft gun in the woods beside the *campo*.

There were no more soccer games.

I met Johann at the cave a week later so that he could give me a vial of drops for twelve-year-old Luigi Marzano's eyes, which were both so infected that Dr. Cardoni feared he would go blind. Johann looked better and though I wanted to ask him why he'd become so upset the other day I didn't, afraid I might upset him again. From then on we tried to meet every four or five days, which was as often as I could get away without Papa becoming suspicious. Fortunately, my parents were used to me wandering off in the woods at all hours of the day. For years they'd tried to keep me safely corralled like every other good Italian daughter, insisting I be accompanied by one of my brothers whenever I bounded off on one of my adventures. But I was headstrong and always restless, exhausting just about everybody who tried to keep up with me on my endless expeditions through the olive groves and vineyards and into the surrounding hills. Finally they gave in and I was allowed almost as much freedom as my brothers, at least until the Germans arrived. Then my parents tried once more to keep me within sight but it was impossible because now there were no brothers left to escort me while Mama was busy with the twins and Papa with his work.

Sometimes Johann and I met for a few minutes so that he could warn me when Henecker was preparing a new round of searches. Other times we sat and talked for an hour or more. Maybe I should have been afraid to be alone with him but I wasn't. If you'd met him, if you saw the kindness in his face, you'd understand. Anyway, it was the only safe place for us to talk and Johann was desperate for conversation. I was too, but more than anything I just wanted to be around him. I couldn't even explain to myself why.

In the beginning he talked a great deal about his little sisters. He wanted me to know everything about them, about the games they played and their favorite dolls and how Mariel loved to dance and Anna liked to sleep under his bed when he was home.

"Not in it?"

"She figured any monsters would fill up on me and by the time they found her they'd be too full to eat any more."

"Smart girl."

"She was very smart," he said, unable to look at me.

I don't think he'd been able to share his grief before, certainly not with a woman, and when his eyes filled with tears I thought it was the saddest thing I'd ever seen. But it made me feel stronger, too, seeing that I could help carry someone else's pain. Gradually he told me about his childhood and his parents and his dream of being a tour guide in Italy.

"So that's why you speak such good Italian."

"We had an elderly neighbor who was half Italian. Mr. Luzzatto. As a child I was always pointing to things and asking for the word in *Italiano*, much to his delight, so eventually he convinced my mother that he should give me formal lessons. In return, she agreed to teach him how to play the piano—she'd studied since she was a young girl. I couldn't wait to go to his house every day after school. He made the language come alive with stories of Italian history, telling me about the emperors and the Medicis and the Doges and about the wars between the great city-states of Venice and Genoa and Florence and Siena. But then when I was thirteen he was taken away in the middle of the night."

"Why?"

"He was also part Jewish." Johann worked his jaw back and forth, the muscles flickering just beneath his skin. "We waited and waited for him to return, but he never did."

"What happened to him?"

"We never found out. Of course there were rumors…"

"Well, he must have been a very good teacher."

"Yes, he was, and a talented piano student as well. After he was gone I studied Italian in school but it wasn't the same."

"Why are you so interested in Italy?"

"Before the war my parents took me to Venice. They didn't have much money but it was a dream of my mother's and so Father saved up until one evening at dinner when he pulled an envelope from his pocket and placed it in front of my mother, a big smile on his face. She just sat there staring at it until tears rolled down her cheeks, not even opening it at first because she knew what it was and she wanted to treasure every moment. I'd never seen my father look so proud before, sitting high in his seat and keeping his eyes on Mother. Three weeks later we boarded a train for Venice.

"I'll never forget coming down the Grand Canal that first time. It was as if I'd walked right into the pages of one of the books my mother loved to read." He closed his eyes briefly and I could see the memory of happiness tugging at the corners of his mouth. "I knew right away that I'd have to go back."

"I've never been."

"But you must!" He slapped his thighs with excitement. "We'll go together, after the war. I'll show you everything."

I raised my eyebrows. "We?"

"You'll need a guide."

But in his heart I don't think he ever expected to see Venice again. Even if he survived the war he said that Germans would never be welcomed back to Italy. And he didn't see how anybody could survive what it would take to destroy Nazi Germany.

"The retreat will be terrible," he said one afternoon after passing me a small bag of sugar, which I made sure found its way to

Maria Gribella, who had lost her husband and had three small children who were always sick.

"Retreat? But it could be years before—"

"The day will come," he said. "And when it does everyone will be in danger."

"Why must it be terrible?"

"Because the men will have nothing to lose, and men with nothing to lose aren't always men at all."

"What will you do?"

"I'll retreat too. What choice do I have?"

Sometimes when we arranged to meet at the cave he wouldn't show up because Henecker needed him and as I waited nervously I would fear that I'd never see him again. And then the next day he'd appear with that wonderful smile on his face and I was the happiest girl in Italy.

I'd never met anybody so interesting before—and so interested in me. He seemed to know a great deal about history and art and politics, even reciting by heart passages of things he'd read, particularly Blake and Schopenhauer. As I listened to him I sensed for the first time the enormous possibilities of the world beyond San Gianello. So much for a young girl to learn and see and think about! And then I would look at the insignia on his uniform and want to cry as I reminded myself that he was a *tedesco*—a German soldier.

"I want to know every single thing about you," he said one morning as we walked along a narrow stream that ran through a steep ravine not far from the cave. The air smelled of damp wood and the trees were full of birds that dashed from branch to branch as they sang.

"There's not much to tell."

"Of course there is. If you could have anything in the world, what would it be?"

"I'd want my brothers back."

"Yes, I'm sorry." He was quiet for several minutes, his shoulder sometimes brushing mine so that I wondered if he might take my hand.

"You can ask me more if you want," I said, balancing on a rock as we crossed the stream.

"I don't really know how to ask the important questions."

"What questions are those?"

He shrugged.

"Tell me."

"What I really want to know is what you're thinking right now and what it feels like to be you and whether the world looks to you anything like it looks to me, but you see there is no way to ask such things."

"I could tell you what I'm thinking."

He waited for me to continue.

"What I'm thinking is how much I'll miss you when you have to leave."

"Then I won't leave."

"You won't have a choice."

"I'll desert."

"You'd be shot."

"I may be shot anyway."

"Don't say that." I sat down on a large rock beside the stream. "Maybe I should ask the questions."

He spread his hands wide. "Anything."

I thought for a moment. "What was your mother like?"

He sat beside me. "She was very... what is the word?... *regal*. I think when she was younger she must have had her choice in men, which always made me wonder why she chose my father, except that she loved his laugh and his blue eyes. She was tall with sharp green eyes and long blond hair that she always wore in the latest styles. Her family had once been quite wealthy until her father lost everything in some sort of land speculation when she was young, later drinking himself to death. I'm not sure she ever really recovered from the loss but she tried never to let it show, dressing as well as she could afford and carrying herself as though she didn't have a care in the world.

"She was much more refined than my father, who was always a bit in awe of her. She liked to read and to dance and she loved music.

At night when her work was done she would sit at the piano that once belonged to her father—it was one of the few belongings that hadn't been sold off. I remember she had the most beautiful hands with long, slender fingers and she wore lots of rings. Sometimes as I watched her fingers sweep across the keys and her shoulders sway side to side she looked so far away that I worried she wouldn't come back. But I loved how the music filled our small house, seeping under my bedroom door at night like a heavenly light. If I was in bed I would try to put a story to each song, imagining great clashes of armies or the death of a princess. Yet there was always something in every melody that made me feel sad. Was she sad too? Or was sorrow built into every musical instrument like salt in a tear? And then one evening when I was older I suddenly understood: my mother was like a lonely bird singing in her cage."

"But what about your father?"

"He was always so busy with work—he was a floor manager at a munitions factory—or down at the beer hall. I don't think he really understood women, and certainly not my mother with all her mysterious layers, though he loved her enormously. Deep inside I think he always felt inferior to her, never able to offer what she needed. You could see in her eyes that some part of her had wandered off, that the life she had wasn't enough. From then on when I listened to her play I felt like I'd broken a secret code, that I finally understood not just my mother but music itself. You see, it was the only way for her to tell the truth."

"But not all songs are sad?"

"No, but the best ones are."

"You don't really believe that? Why can't a song just be entertaining?"

"Lots of songs are entertaining, but great music isn't meant to entertain, it's meant to tell the truth, and the truth is always bittersweet."

He never ran out of questions. He wanted to know everything about my family and the different types of Italian bread and what I thought of Roosevelt and Churchill and how often I washed my hair—he talked a great deal about my hair, insisting it was an entirely unique shade of black—and whether I'd read such-and-such a book, which of course I hadn't. When I talked he just sat there staring at me with a great big smile on his face and sometimes I felt guilty for thinking that maybe the war wasn't such a hardship after all. I'd never felt so beautiful before, not a little girl anymore but a young woman who could lift a man out of his grief. Some days I felt almost weightless as I ran through the olive groves and then the woods to meet him.

It was three weeks before he kissed me, though we came close many times. I used to lie awake at night imagining what his lips would feel like against mine and praying that God couldn't read my thoughts. Imagine praying that God won't hear your prayers? I knew that he wanted to kiss me. He was so polite but I could see it in his eyes, which ran over my skin like a velvet glove, making me feel all prickly inside. I even wondered if he was falling in love with me.

I can still feel that kiss and how perfect the world felt, just for a moment, sunlight pouring through every crevice. I never realized how perfect everything could feel.

It was the day the Allied planes returned. We were used to the sight of bombers flying high in the sky on their way to Germany. There seemed to be more each month until they passed overhead like great flocks of migrating birds. But these were fighters, and this time they came to fight. I was out in the herb garden pulling weeds with Mama when three planes dropped out of the sky, diving down almost to the treetops. Papa came racing from the garage and we grabbed the girls and ran to the house, barely reaching the door before we heard explosions less than a mile away.

"This calls for a celebration!" said Papa, looking happier than I'd seen him in years as we all crouched under the kitchen table.

The sound of gunfire and explosions continued for several minutes as the planes returned again and again, rattling the windows. By the time it was quiet I could hardly breathe from fear.

"Well, that should give them something to think about for a few days," said Papa as we crawled out from beneath the table. I ran up-stairs and looked out the window. Black smoke rose from the main road where three German transports had been caught out in the open.

Johann.

I ran back downstairs and started out the door but Papa stopped me. "Where do you think you're going?"

"People are hurt. We must help."

"They are *Germans*."

"What does it matter?" I tried to pull away but he tightened his grip.

"It's too dangerous."

"Please let go." But he held me firmly until I stopped resisting. Then I ran to my room and buried my face in my pillow, praying that Johann was unhurt.

The Germans quickly closed off the road. From my window I could see them running about and pulling bodies from the wreck-age. I stayed at the window most of the afternoon, watching the smoke grow thinner as it rose into the hard blue sky. I didn't touch my dinner. As soon as I finished helping clean the kitchen I told Mama that I had work to do at the bakery and hurried out before she could stop me. I ran all the way to the cave, thinking Johann would be there if he was still alive. After crossing through the olive grove I entered the woods where the hill began to climb through thick forests of oak and pine. Then I turned off the narrow path and scrambled up a rocky slope to a point where the cave's entrance was hidden by several large boulders.

"Johann?" I whispered in the growing darkness, which seemed to thicken as the air cooled, nature slowing to a standstill.

Silence.

I sat down on a rock, remembering the first time Marcello showed me the cave and how I struggled not to cry when he swore me to secrecy by pricking my finger and mixing my blood with his during my initiation ceremony. Renaldo and Stephano let me know that it took several rounds of voting before they agreed to allow a girl into their secret society. (Membership, they assured me, carried all sorts of yet undisclosed privileges.) I was so honored! "It's only because you're not a normal girl," they said solemnly as they smoked their cigarettes and told me how the cave was once used by Visigoths to hide the bones of Roman children whose blood had been drained and offered to the evil spirits, who were always thirsty and still lurked in the far recesses of the cave. I peered into the darkness, scooting closer to Marcello as I thanked God for not making me normal.

We met in the cave almost every week, telling stories and sinful jokes and putting on elaborate skits—Marcello and Renaldo took turns playing emperor while Stephano and I were invariably fed to the lions. I never felt so happy as when I was in the cave with my brothers listening to their stories and watching the shadows play off the walls when we made a fire. But gradually Marcello lost interest—after all, there weren't any other girls in our society—and then Renaldo stop going and finally it was just me and Stephano. Eventually even he tired of our games and I would sit in the cave by myself and imagine that I was a princess who'd been kidnapped by a dragon and awaited rescue. Would I wait forever?

The day before Stephano went off to the army he asked me if I wanted to hike up to the cave with him—our first visit together in years.

"I'll pack a lunch basket," I said, hurrying to the kitchen.

We spent all afternoon there, laughing at the games we used to play and tracing our fingers along the walls where we'd carved our names. It made me terribly sad, sitting on that ledge beside him and knowing that I was about to be left behind, which seemed the harder part of any goodbye. Was that what life would be, a series of goodbyes until each one was final?

"Things could get difficult for you and the family," he said after we'd eaten the sandwiches I'd made. A copper haze hung over the valley and the air smelled of pinecones.

"I can handle it."

He looked at me and smiled. "I know you can. But you'll have to look after the rest of them."

"We'll be fine."

He lowered his voice. "You could always bring the family here—if things become dangerous."

"What could be so dangerous?" The tone in his voice scared me.

He shrugged. "I'm just saying."

"You forgot. I'm sworn to secrecy."

"I'm giving you official permission."

"Can you imagine Mama sleeping in a cave? She can hardly sleep in the house with all the germs."

He laughed, but then his narrow face grew serious again. "I'm not saying you'll ever need to. But just in case."

And so as I waited for Johann I told myself that Stephano would forgive me, that perhaps when the war ended they might even become friends someday. After all, they really weren't so different without their uniforms. Or was Johann dead? I waited on the ledge another hour, calling his name as loud as I dared and then just crying at the bitter cruelty of everything. Above, a narrow caravan of clouds crossed slowly in front of the crescent moon.

"Johann?" I called out once more in the darkness.

"Alessandra?" His voice came from below on the footpath. I quickly apologized to God as I hurried down to meet him.

And that's when he kissed me, nearly lifting me into the air as he pressed his lips hard against mine until I felt for the first time what it was like to dissolve the borders of my own skin.

I'll never forget that first taste of his lips, of *him*, and how I'd never tasted anything so delicious and exotic and soothing in all of my life. I'll never forget anything about that night: the damp, almost sweet air, heavy with autumn; the hooting of the old owl that had lived in a nearby tree for as long as I could remember, disappearing now and then on his mysterious errands, his majestic wings slicing through the moonlight; and especially the sky, which seemed crowded with more stars than I'd ever seen before, each one vying for our attention. From our perch on the ledge it seemed like the whole great magnificent world was spread out below us, though you couldn't see any lights because of the blackout regulations.

And I felt as if all of it, everything as far as I could see, had been patiently waiting for this night.

I'd never imagined that my heart could contain so many layers and textures. It wasn't just happiness I felt but sorrow, too, because now I sensed for the first time what a desperate thing happiness was—wanting and needing things that would never last long enough, things that would one day be torn from my grasp no matter how hard I tried to hold on. (And I would hold on with all my strength.) It wasn't until he held me and kissed me and ran his hands over me that I realized just how lonely I'd been, trapped within the depths of myself. *So this is what it's like to be set free*, I thought, feeling his arms surround me as though I were the most precious thing in the world. And isn't that what everybody really longs for, to escape from the imprisonment of their own skin? Isn't that what some people wait their whole lives for, desperately tapping out messages on the four walls of their souls, praying for reply? And now this young German soldier had answered me. *I'm not alone anymore.* I lifted my feet into the air until I hung in Johann's arms like a silken coat on a hook. Is this what my parents felt when they first held each other? Did the whole point of being born become so suddenly clear that they wanted to weep from the sheer mad joy of being alive? And then what happens? Does anything else in life ever come close? Or is it the memory of that feeling that sustains people through their lives, even as it torments them?

CHAPTER
FOUR

AFTER THAT EVERYTHING inside of me had a desperate, hungry edge to it. My brothers were gone and now I feared losing Johann, too. Meanwhile the Germans kept bringing Papa more work, sometimes threatening him if he didn't finish on time, and each week there was less food, while more and more Italians were being arrested and deported, usually for no discernable reason at all. Johann said that Germany's situation was becoming increasingly desperate but that Kesselring would fight to the finish in Italy.

"Thank God you're not at the front," I said as we sat just inside the entrance of the cave during our first meeting in over two weeks. It had rained for four days and a dark gray fog clung to the hillsides.

"Henecker would like nothing better but he's afraid of my uncle."

"Your uncle must be very frightening indeed."

"He knows people." Johann stretched out on his back in the dirt, eyes staring upward. "Good old Uncle Heinrich. Ever since I was a boy he's taken a special interest in me—he never had a son of his own—but I'm afraid I've been quite a disappointment to him." He smiled to himself. "I can still hear him talking to my father. 'That boy of yours is too soft,' he'd say as they sat in the living room in their brute clouds of smoke, playing chess with the world. That's what they all told me—my father, the army, even my friends: 'You are too soft, Johann.' Yes, I told myself, if hard is what you are then I am soft. Infinitely, irrevocably soft.

"My father tried his best to harden me—he was always afraid of his brother." Johann shook his head slowly. "Poor man, I don't think he really had any idea how to go about it. Each morning before school he would make me do exercises and on my eighth birthday he sat me down and explained that I was now too old to cry anymore, which made me want to cry oceans on the spot. 'The world crushes the weak under its feet,' he would say, driving his fist into his palm in imitation of his brother.

"'I don't want to be crushed, Father,' I'd whimper, my voice breaking like a girl's.

"'Then you must be strong!'

"But I wasn't strong, not like other boys. I wasn't good at sports and I had frequent nightmares that sent me howling into my parents' bedroom. After school I liked nothing more than to sit in a corner and read. My mother was the only one who seemed to understand that I had other possibilities within me, if only given the chance.

"'You're too hard on him,' she told my father as I listened from the top of the stairs. 'All he wants is a kind word from you.'

"'I fear I'm not hard enough.'

"'He's not like you, and he's certainly not like your brother. But he's your son.'

"'Don't you see that he'll be taken by the army soon and made to fight until only a few are left standing? Don't you know what happens to boys who are too soft?' His deep voice grew hoarse with urgency. 'Don't you see that only the hardest will survive?'

"But he was wrong. The hardest were often the first to die." Johann closed his eyes momentarily as the rain drew a glistening sheet over the entrance of the cave. I waited for him to continue.

"My friends Günter and Dieter got me through combat training, sharing their food, pushing me forward, even carrying me on their backs when I could no longer walk.

"'Johann, you must toughen up,' they pleaded. But I was too tired to answer, always tired, so that even my thoughts seemed to drag along the ground as we marched. And one night as I sat on the roof of our barracks in a thunderstorm preparing to shoot myself because only death spoke of freedom, it was Dieter who saved me.

"'So, you're going to give Henecker the pleasure of spitting on your grave,' he said above the wind, climbing up beside me, his uniform drenched. Henecker hated anything soft. He wanted *steel*.

"I wiped the tears from my eyes, still holding my pistol in my lap. 'I'm not like you, Dieter.'

"'You're not like anybody. That's your gift, Johann. Now put that away,' he placed his hand on my pistol. 'You'll have plenty of other chances to die.'

"And he was right.

"I never died all at once. Not like the others. Instead I died in little pieces, one at a time until my soul was littered with fresh mounds of earth. I think it's easier to die all at once."

"Don't talk like that," I said, wishing he would stop.

"It's true. Henecker enjoyed seeing me die slowly. He *delighted* in it. But you see, one thing troubled him." Johann paused. "He knew my hands were clean." He sat up and looked down at his hands, turning them slowly side to side. "Even when we ambushed partisans I made sure to aim too high or too low. He couldn't prove it but he knew it and he hated me for it. Who was I to keep my soul unsullied? But then one day we captured an Italian boy carrying two stolen German grenades and Henecker had his solution. A perfect, *foolproof* solution."

"I don't want to hear this."

"But you must." Johann wiped the sweat on his forehead with his sleeve. "Someone said he was sixteen but anyone could see he was younger. He was short with stringy black hair that fell in front of his eyes and a small face still round with youth. I could hear his rapid breathing as he was led across the yard and made to stand against a stone wall, hands bound in front but eyes uncovered. I tried not to look at him but I couldn't help myself. And when his eyes caught mine I felt his terror reach out and grab at me so that I had to turn away.

"Henecker conducted an inspection of our weapons, then the order was given to assemble. When I hesitated Dieter gripped my arm and pulled me along. 'Don't be a fool, Johann,' he whispered.

"'I can't do it,' I said.

"'You must.'

"'But I cannot.'

"'Then you'll be next.'

"'I don't care anymore.'

"I wanted to cry. I wanted to crawl into my bed at home and weep a million tears until the whole vicious world drowned in my raging sorrow.

"Henecker stood to the side, hands clasped behind his back, eyes fixed on me.

"'Johann, listen to me,' whispered Dieter. 'Henecker will put you against the wall and then I will have to shoot you and you know I can't do that. Then they will shoot me. Do you want us all to die?'

"'Attention!'

"I moved numbly into position beside Dieter. The boy looked at me, his face breaking apart as he struggled not to cry. *Why are you staring at me? It's not my fault, don't you see? I am only a piece of flotsam carried along in a terrible flood that will destroy us all.* And still he stared.

"'Ready!'

"My hands shook with agony; hands that were soft little virgins amongst whores. So I'd miss again. A bit too far to the left or to the right. Yes, at least I could do that.

"The boy was weeping now, his face contorted like a young child's. Yes, a child. Anyone could see that. *Please stop looking at me.* But still the boy stared, his eyes desperately searching for my soul because men with souls would never do such a thing, not to a child.

Or has God already come for men's souls and forgotten to take mine?

"'Aim!'

"Sweat and tears stung my eyes as I stared down the sight of my rifle at the boy's heart, then shifted just to the left of his shoulder.

What if others were to miss? What if the boy didn't die in the first volley? Better that he dies quickly, mercifully. *Why must he keep staring at me?* But how can I shoot an unarmed boy? Impossible. I fought back a dry heave, wanting to throw down my rifle and tear off my helmet and run until I found the edge of the world, where I would cast myself off into sweet blind oblivion.

"*'Fire!'*

"I closed my eyes and squeezed the trigger."

After Johann finished talking he slumped against the side of the cave and wrapped his arms around his knees as if to hold himself together. I put my hand gently on his head, which was damp. "It's over," I said. "There is nothing you could have done."

"There was only one bullet," he whispered, slowly raising his head.

"I don't understand."

"I had the only bullet. Henecker made sure I had the only live weapon." Johann pulled his knees tighter against his chest, his limbs now trembling. "I meant to aim off to the left, but I... you see I couldn't bear the thought of the boy suffering and so in those last seconds I went back and forth, back and forth... just a few inches, that's all it is. A few inches. Henecker had me cornered either way. If I missed, I would join the boy in front of the firing squad, and if I didn't miss..."

"The boy... did he die quickly?"

"Not quickly enough."

CHAPTER
FIVE

I WAS ALONE in the bakery the next morning stacking kindling for the wood-fired oven when Henecker walked in. He didn't seem to notice me at first—he was busy leaning over our display, which held only a few loafs of bread because like everything else flour was rationed—but after pulling off a piece of *pane alle olive* and stuffing it into his mouth he began to stare at me.

"What is your name?" he asked, still chewing and speaking such awful Italian that I could barely understand him.

I debated whether to make up a name but feared he might already know the answer. "Alessandra."

"Alessandra?" He smiled, looking me up and down, then said something that I couldn't understand. He seemed to think a moment, then asked in Italian, "Your age?"

Again I thought of lying. But what would be better, to be older or younger? I finally told him the truth. "Seventeen."

He nodded slowly, then suddenly reached out and touched my hair just behind my ear, running his fingertips gently down until they reached my shoulder, where he hesitated briefly before withdrawing his hand. I froze, fighting the urge to scream.

"Seventeen," he said softly. Then he smiled, tipped his head slightly and turned and left.

I didn't dare say anything to Johann, fearful of what he might do. I was already afraid that he was taking too many risks, foiling several of Henecker's searches for hidden stocks of food and weapons and most of all Jews and deserters. We never knew where Henecker got his information, though many in our village were willing to point fingers and spread rumors, poisoning San Gianello with fear and distrust.

"You must be more careful," I said to Johann after he handed me three tins of meat from Henecker's personal locker. San Gianello continued to fill with refugee children from cities like Genoa and Arezzo, which were subject to Allied bombing, and many were malnourished.

"I'm the last person Henecker will suspect. And do you know why he trusts me? Because he considers me far too much of a coward not to be trusted."

That evening after dinner Papa asked me to come out to the courtyard.

"Sit down," he said, patting the bench next to him.

Immediately I knew that someone had seen Johann and me talking.

Papa sat in silence for a few moments before he began, his large hands resting on his knees and his face turned to look out over the valley where the hilltops were bathed in the white glow of the rising full moon, as though dusted by snow. "When I was eighteen the Austrians overran our position. Twelve of us were ordered to surrender or be shot. We only had a few seconds to make our decision. Which way, God? Which way toward life and our families and our homes? Some wanted to fight, most preferred to surrender. We agreed to surrender." He drew a breath. "Moments after we tossed our weapons out of reach the Austrians opened fire. We ran in terror, wondering how God could choose to side with the enemy. Somehow I made it. Others did not."

When he finished he sat staring at me, his soft brown eyes filling with so much sadness that I couldn't look at him.

"Why are you telling me this?"

"Because the only thing worse than an Austrian is a German."
He leaned toward me. "Do you understand what I'm saying?"

I nodded.

"Tell me about your friend."

"What friend?"

"I'm not a fool, Alessandra."

I pulled at my hair nervously. "I've only spoken with him a few
times. He's very helpful around the village—ask anybody. He's really very nice and he loves Italy and—"

"He's German."

"He's different."

"Different?" Papa scowled.

"He has no choice in who he is, he just tries to help. If it wasn't
for him—"

"Listen to me, Alessandra. Everybody has a choice, do you understand me?"

"Not if you are born a German."

"He wasn't born in that uniform."

"What alternative does he have?"

"Don't you realize that the mountains are full of Italian boys
who have deserted because they refuse to fight for something they
don't believe in?"

I couldn't think how to respond.

"I'm asking you to stay away from him." He leaned over and put
his hand on my shoulder. *"Please."*

But I couldn't. Even when I was in Johann's arms I wanted to draw
closer, as though he was another, deeper cave I could hide inside.
We didn't make love—I felt I owed God, and especially Papa, at least
that—but we spent every moment we could huddled together on a
gray German Army blanket spread out on the earthen floor of our
secret hideaway. Even in my dreams I'd never fully realized the possibilities of touch—that you could submerge yourself in another just
like slipping into a steaming bath. As he ran his lips and hands over
me I felt as if I'd been turned inside out, my entire soul glistening

on the surface of my skin where he could reach it. Yet the more I touched him the more lonely I felt inside, knowing that each caress and kiss and hug was only a brief escape from the solitude that engulfed me the moment we were apart. At night in my bed as I prayed for his safety I began to understand that loneliness would always be the worst thing, that it was like a disease that nibbled away at the edges of every moment and day and lifetime. It explained everything: why Papa surrounded himself with his tools—each given a special name to keep him company—and why Mama prayed and cleaned and why all the great Italian artists I'd studied in school spent their lives trying to carve and chisel their visions into the finest marble or fling themselves onto canvas or upon the walls and ceilings of churches and palaces. It was the dread—the absolute horror—of being trapped forever within themselves.

At least I had my family. But Johann had nothing to hold on to, nothing except for me. Before we met I think he'd given up, like a man lost in a blizzard who finally lies down in the snow and willfully succumbs. Sometimes when we held each other he would begin to shake uncontrollably, his grief burning like a fever that wouldn't break. But gradually he would come back to life and then it seemed that our happiness would be our revenge against the world for all its bitterness.

"Tell me more about Venice," I asked him one afternoon, trying to turn his thoughts from the war. We lay side by side on the gray blanket just inside the cave, our legs intertwined.

A smile came over his face, which always changed his look completely. "I think it must be the saddest city in the world, and yet that's the beauty of it—a lovely and haunted and doomed beauty." He softly stroked my cheek.

"Because it's sinking?"

"Because everything is sinking."

"You make it sound depressing."

"Oh, not at all. I've never felt so peaceful in my life."

"Maybe you really are Italian—even Venetian!"

"One day I'll take you. You'll see." He took my hand in his and laced his fingers through mine. "When I stepped off the *vaporetto* with my family I had goose bumps all over me, and do you know why? Because I saw that here was a place that expressed exactly how it really feels to be alive; a city where glory and decay were locked in eternal battle."

I watched the excitement in his dense blue eyes, imagining how pristine they must have looked before the war, untouched by loss. "I remember one day we went to look at the Basilica of Santa Maria Gloriosa—the Frari, as it's known. I was standing before the famous wooden choir listening to a guide bring it to life when suddenly I felt the presence of everybody who had ever been in that church, their spirits pressed around me and a thousand prayers rising through the damp stale air."

"So that's why you want to be a tour guide?"

"Yes, don't you see? And I'll learn everything there is to learn about Venice and Florence and Rome and Siena…"

"You'll be very busy."

"Do you know why people will pay money and travel around the world just to stand in the hot sun among old ruins? Because we can walk through history and feel immortal. No matter how great the horrors, we are always spared. Not even the worst epidemics or cataclysms can touch us. And we have the one thing that even the mightiest kings would drop down to their knees and beg for: we have life." He leaned over and kissed me, tugging gently on my lips with his.

"You said you felt all those ghosts in the church in Venice, but what about God? Did you feel him?"

"No, but I felt his absence."

"And how did his absence feel?"

"The way it always feels: terrifying."

"But if you prayed?"

"I'm finished with praying."

"You can't blame God for all the bad in the world."

"He must bear some responsibility if he wishes to exist."

"But everything is so hopeless without God."

"I find it easier."

"How could you?"

"Because it's enough that humanity allows such evil, but what hope is there if all that has happened is ordained?" I noticed his hands had begun to shake. "At least people can be changed... educated... held accountable. But if we are just... *playthings*..." He began to raise his hands, then dropped them by his side.

"Then what do you believe in?"

"I believe in the sound of your voice. I believe in your lips and your eyes and your skin and the way you play with your hair." He kissed me again.

"You're being silly."

"Not at all. And I believe in things that are gone, too: Mr. Luzzatto and my sisters and my mother and father..."

"But you don't believe there is a reason for things?"

"How could I?"

"Because... there has to be."

"I can't think of any reasons I could ever accept, not for the things that have happened."

"Then our lives really have no meaning. Is that what you're saying?"

"No, I think our lives are full of meaning. It's not the meaning that I have trouble with."

"What is it, then?"

"It's the... *madness*," he whispered, the coloring draining from his face. Then he turned over onto his back.

"Do you love me?" I blurted out, not meaning to. "You don't have to answer," I added quickly. "I don't even know why I asked."

"You're the only thing left that I love."

I propped myself up on my elbow so that I could see his face. "Do you mean that?"

"I love you completely."

I tried to ignore a tear coming down my cheek. "Is it anything like you thought it would be?"

Suddenly he laughed. "Actually, no. To be honest it's nothing at all like I thought it would be."

Then I laughed too, overcome by the absurdity of everything, the two of us perched on one end of a seesaw while the world seemed to crowd on the other. "No, I guess it isn't."

He rolled on top of me and kissed me for several minutes, then lay on his side facing me. "It doesn't scare you?"

"No... well... maybe a little. But it's wonderful. It's really... *wonderful.*"

He placed his palms gently on either side of my face and drew them down along my cheeks, then cupped my jaw in his hands and tilted my head up toward his. "I love you I love you I love you," he said. I closed my eyes, feeling his words wash over me like a sweet rain. Then he reached his arms around me and pulled me against him, kissing the top of my head and then running his lips down the bridge of my nose toward my lips.

"All I ever think about is you," I said, feeling short of breath. "Sometimes it's more than I can even stand."

He pulled back to look at me, squinting in the sun that now streamed into the cave as it dropped toward the horizon. He was so handsome that I wanted to kiss him from his chin to his forehead and then back and forth across his cheeks until my mouth was dry.

"Could your father ever accept me?" he asked.

"I know he'd like you if he had the chance. He really would."

"I don't blame him for what he feels."

"He's just been through a lot. But with time..."

Johann sat up. "I'd wait. I'd wait years if I had to." He brushed a strand of hair from my face. "I just want to know one thing: do you believe we'll have a chance?"

"Of course I do," I said. "And more than just a—"

He put his finger to my lips. "No, don't say any more. I only need to know that it's possible, that's all. I only need a *possibility.*"

But then just as he leaned forward to kiss me again I saw all the hope slip from his eyes.

CHAPTER
SIX

———

I'D NEVER FELT so confused before. When I was younger I assumed that love was full of answers. But it wasn't, it was a hundred impossible questions welling up inside of me night and day.

Mama noticed the change in me. She sensed that some young man had caught my eye, but assumed, rather wishfully, that it was Mario Venetti, whose father owned the second largest house in San Gianello.

"You're glowing like a hot coal," she said one afternoon, touching her palm to my cheek after I'd finished tutoring the twins in math. (Schools throughout Italy had been closed because of the war.) I turned away in embarrassment.

"It's not Pietro..."

"Mama, please."

"But it's a boy all right. A mother can tell." She patted my cheek again. "I see how they look at you. Believe it or not they used to look at me that way once too." She gave her dress a quick tug at the hips. "I wasn't much older than you when I first met your father. You've never seen such a handsome young man. And to think that he was interested in me!" She fanned her face. "I never said so many rosaries in my life." Then she smiled, the first smile I could recall since Renaldo had gone missing. (She'd taken to wearing black and had gained a great deal of weight.)

"Did it ever scare you?"

"What?"

"Being in love?"

"It still scares me. What would I do if something happened to your father? Just ask yourself that." She turned and headed off to the kitchen, which was filled with the aroma of boiling chestnuts. "And he wonders why I worry so much."

Four days later we were having dinner when there was a light rap on the door. Papa cautiously opened it and let out a gasp. Stephano was standing in the doorway, his uniform filthy but a smile rising from his small face. We swarmed around him, nearly knocking him over as we covered him with kisses. Then Papa hoisted him up in the air and spun him around before passing him to Mama, who squeezed his face between her palms until he looked like a fish as she covered him with more kisses.

Everybody was crying. Even the twins cried until they were nearly inconsolable and Stephano had to gather them in his lap and explain to them that some tears sprung from happy places and that those were the most precious tears of all. I cried almost as hard as the twins, seeing in our joy how unhappy we'd been. But what made me cry the most was the look on Papa's face, his eyes shining like a man who'd suddenly been spared from the gallows.

"How long is your leave?" Papa asked as we finally sat Stephano down at the table and filled a plate with food.

"Forever."

"I don't understand?"

"I've deserted. I'm through." Papa didn't flinch but I saw Mama raise her hand to her mouth. We all knew what happened to deserters.

"A dozen of us from my unit ran off. We had no choice. The Germans are going to lose and they want us to die with them." He ate so fast I thought he might get sick. When his plate was empty Mama quickly refilled it. "They treat us like livestock. No, worse than livestock. And thousands have been deported. I've seen with my own eyes trains full of Italian soldiers being taken to Germany. And do you know what happens to them? They are worked like slaves and when they can't work anymore they are killed."

There was a long silence broken only by the sound of Stephano's fork scrapping against the plate as he finished off a second helping of Mama's tortellini, which could take several days to digest.

"You can't stay here," said Papa. "The Germans are just up the road."

"I had more trouble slipping past Pietro," said Stephano with a smile. "I see he still hasn't given up his vigil."

"His parents should be ashamed," scowled Mama.

"He's a harmless boy," said Papa. "And how can you blame him for losing his heart to our Alessandra?"

I blushed.

"We'll arrange for you to go to Uncle Gianni's," said Papa. "I'm sure he can find a safe place for you."

"It's too risky."

"But what choice is there?"

"There's a group of us—I can't tell you any more than that—but we're west in the mountains. I'll be fine."

"Partisans?" I asked.

Stephano looked at me but didn't respond. Mama grabbed a dishtowel and began to clean.

"Have you heard from Marcello?" Stephano asked Papa.

"He seems to be too busy shining Mussolini's boots to think of his family."

"Antonio, please," said Mama.

"What can I say?" said Papa. "Perhaps Marcello would like to come here and arrest his own brother for desertion, eh?"

"That's enough."

"All right, all right." Papa waved his hands in the air, then rose from his chair, opened a cupboard and brought down a bottle of his best Chianti, which he saved for special occasions. "Tonight we drink to Stephano!"

He stayed for two nights, careful never to leave the house or linger by the windows. None of us could keep our hands off of him as we hovered around him, afraid to let him out of our sight. Mama thanked the Blessed Virgin until she was hoarse while the girls followed Stephano from room to room and Papa peppered him with questions, interrupting now and then to seize him by the shoulders and give him a squeeze. We fed him almost continuously and Mama and I worked to mend his clothes and assemble what supplies we could, even digging up one of the cured hams we'd buried behind the chicken coop, which was now empty. I was so afraid that he would go to the cave and run into Johann that I told him the Germans had found it and searched it regularly, which disappointed him terribly. "They are very thorough," I said, trying to sound convincing.

He slept in the spare bed in my room so that we could talk at night after the lights were out, just as when we were younger. In the darkness I wondered whether to tell him about Johann because I thought if anybody would understand it would be Stephano. But there was no way to explain it, not unless he could meet Johann and see that he wasn't like a *tedesco* at all. So instead I asked him all about the places he'd been and the things he'd seen until I knew he was tired of talking. The hardest part was seeing how he'd changed, all the lightness gone from his movements even though he'd lost so much weight that Mama had to bring in his pants.

"Are you still awake?" he whispered the night before he left.

"I'm awake." I was eager to talk.

"Do you think Papa will be all right? He looks so tired lately."

"He's just been busy, that's all." I didn't want Stephano to worry.

"I hate to see him working so hard."

"It's the only way he knows how to work."

Stephano was silent for several minutes and I wondered if he'd fallen asleep. "I'm still awake if you want to talk some more," I said.

"Sure. What shall we talk about?"

"Are you mad at Marcello?" I asked.

"I feel sorry for him more than anything."

"I'm mad at him. He hardly even writes anymore."

"Maybe he's too ashamed to write."

"Could you forgive him?"

"If he wants to be forgiven."

"I don't think Papa ever could."

"Parents always forgive." Stephano's bed creaked as he turned.

"I miss Renaldo," I said.

"So do I."

"Do you think he's dead?"

"We can't give up hope."

"I think he is," I said. "I shouldn't say it but I do."

"What makes you think so?"

"I have these dreams about him. You and Marcello never appear in my dreams, not the way he does."

"How does he appear?"

"He looks terrible. And he's lost. He's hungry and he can't find his way home."

"It's just a dream."

I listened to Stephano turn again and wondered if he was scared about going to live in the mountains. Where would he sleep and what would he eat? And what if the Germans found him? "I'm going to miss you," I said.

"I'm going to miss you, too. I know it's been hard being left behind with everybody to look after and no one to talk to."

"It hasn't been so bad." I bit my lip to hold back my tears. "You're going to fight with the partisans, aren't you?"

"I can't talk about it."

"I won't tell anybody."

"I know you wouldn't, but it's better not to talk."

"At least promise me you'll be careful."

"I promise."

I listened as his breathing began to deepen. "You still want to be a doctor, don't you?"

"More than anything."

"Good."

"That reminds me. I have something to tell you," he said.

"What?"

"I saved a man's life. He was bleeding to death but I saved him."

"You did? Really?"

"I really did."

"I told you you're going to make a wonderful doctor." I waited for him to say more but he was asleep.

CHAPTER
SEVEN

TWO WEEKS AFTER Stephano left, a German patrol was ambushed by partisans twelve miles from our village. Two Germans were killed and two wounded. That afternoon four truckloads of Germans appeared in the piazza and began rounding up all the men. Then they selected four at random: Leonardo Dubello, Nico Punelli, Rudolfo Anesti and Sergio Bruscanini, Pietro's father. The four were ordered forward and their hands were bound. Villagers began to surge forward until beaten back with rifle butts.

Henecker stood on the edge of the dry fountain in the center of the piazza and announced that these four men would be executed in retaliation for atrocities carried out against German forces. Two Italians for every German. Next time the number would rise to four Italians and after that eight. Johann stood beside Henecker translating, his voice so strained that I didn't think he could finish. That's when I knew that Henecker would win, that Johann would never be able to survive the war, that he was as doomed as any of the four men being taken to their deaths because even if he did live there would be nothing left of him. And if there were nothing left of him then there would be nothing left of me either.

Then I saw Pietro pushing his way through the crowd, tears rolling down his small face. I hurried over to him, grabbing him by the arm just as he made his way to the front.

"No, Pietro, please."

"They can't take my father. I won't let them."

"They'll kill you, too."

"I don't care." He pushed forward again and this time I had to hold him with both hands using all my strength even though I was taller.

"Please let me go."

"No, I won't," I said, trying not to cry myself.

The trucks began to pull away, Johann in one of them. "Papa!" cried Pietro, breaking free from my grasp. As he started after the trucks a German soldier standing nearby leveled his rifle.

"Pietro!" I cried.

He stopped and looked back at me.

"If you're going to get yourself killed then so am I." I stepped out of the crowd.

"Alessandra, no," he begged.

The soldier aimed his rifle at me, then back at Pietro.

"Alessandra go back, *please.*"

"Not without you."

Pietro looked at the trucks, then at me, then at the trucks again. He didn't move as they disappeared down the road.

Later that day Dubello, Punelli, Anesti and Bruscanini were hanged by their necks from the sycamore trees that lined the approach to our village, where their bodies remained for one week with orders that anybody attempting to remove them would be immediately shot. Four Italians for two Germans. By nightfall the same reprisals had taken place in three other surrounding villages.

The next morning Papa hurried off to attend a secret meeting organized by the men to discuss the killings. When a scuffle erupted between royalists and communists twenty minutes into the meeting Papa stormed out. "Nothing but a bunch of braying donkeys," he complained when he returned.

"Will anything be done?" I asked, taking his coat and hanging it by the door.

"Yes, it's been agreed that we are to wring our hands for the next twenty-four hours and if that doesn't work a committee will be selected to vote on the number of rosaries necessary to put San Gianello back in God's good graces." He drank down a ladle full of water from the large copper bucket kept in the kitchen and then headed to the garage. "Donkeys, I tell you. Thank God a few brave souls still call themselves Italians."

I followed him. "Like you."

"And others."

"You're helping the partisans, aren't you?" I asked.

He turned on his heels. "What makes you say such a thing?"

"I want to know."

He picked up a wrench and began to wipe it clean with a cloth. "I'm only a mechanic. An underpaid and overworked mechanic."

"I want to help the partisans too."

"You'll do no such thing. Now if you'll excuse me I've got plenty of work to do." He opened the hood of a German Kübelwagen and leaned over the engine.

"Stephano didn't kill those Germans," I said.

He paused and looked up at me. "I know that."

"How do you know?"

"Because Stephano couldn't kill a tick." Then he gave me a half-smile and returned to work.

That afternoon I carried a basket of baked goods to the Bruscaninis, where Pietro was being closely watched by two uncles who were afraid he would attempt to retrieve his father's body.

"He doesn't want to talk to anybody right now," said one of his uncles, greeting me at the door. I could see Pietro's little brother and sister watching me from the stairs and I thought I heard someone crying.

"Please tell him I'm thinking about him."

"Of course."

"And tell him... tell him I think he's the bravest man I know."

Then I hurried away before I began to cry.

A week later Papa helped cut down the bodies, which smelled so bad that when Mr. Bagiani tried to assist he got sick all over the front of his baggy shirt. The entire village attended the funerals, held under the watchful eye of German soldiers posted around the church. As I looked at the weeping families of the men who had been murdered I felt more angry at God than I ever had before. Where was He when Dubello and Punelli and Anesti and Bruscanini were strung up by their necks? Father Gregorio tried to find a lesson in our suffering but for the first time I found his words empty, even if they were projected with surprising force. A lesson? What teacher instructs his students by breaking their hearts and necks? I looked over at Pietro, who sobbed into his small hands. What lesson did God intend to teach him? What chance did goodness and prayer have in a world where evil had all the momentum?

Then I turned to my mother, whose lips moved in silent prayer. Part of me had always envied her for her certainty. And yet it bothered me too, feeling as if she was privy to something that I was not. How could she be so sure? Had God given her some sort of sign or proof? Why not me? And was her faith really based on love or was it fear that moved her to prayer? I looked at Sergio Bruscanini's wife, Gabriela, who sat twisting a large handkerchief in her lap, her face empty; then at Papa, who appeared preoccupied with his thoughts. He'd never seemed to need God, or at least not the God of the church. Maybe others did but not my father, who'd just as soon rely on the strength of his own two hands. I looked back at Father Gregorio, whose balding and shiny head was now bowed in solemn prayer. Did he have doubts too? And then I felt a shiver down my back as I looked at the flickering altar candles and the soot-covered stained-glass windows and asked myself which I would choose: a world without God or a God without mercy.

I could not answer.

As we left the service I noticed Johann among the Germans standing guard. He looked almost unrecognizable as he stood stiffly with his rifle in his hands and his helmet low over his eyes. He was only twenty feet away and yet he seemed as far as the dimmest star in the night sky. I had to fight the urge to run to him and hug him with all my strength until the color came back into his face. And yet just looking at him made me feel guilty, even sinful for loving a man whose comrades had murdered my own neighbors. Can even love be a sin if it wears the wrong uniform? I tried to catch Johann's eye but he avoided me. *Johann please, just look at me and let me know you are all right.* Without thinking I started toward him through the tense crowd when suddenly Papa took my hand, holding it firmly as the procession walked silently past the cemetery and down the lane before gradually thinning as we headed for our homes.

Life was never the same after that. The piazza was often deserted while the Germans set up several checkpoints, sometimes roughing up the men just for sport and even searching the purses of elderly women.

"They are worse than beasts!" said Aunt Lucia after she was stopped one morning by two soldiers who demanded to see her identity papers and then stole the earrings right off her ears.

I waited and waited to see Johann again, filling my head with dreams of running away with him until the war was over, even though in my heart I knew I could never leave my family. I was at the bakery when I finally saw him through the window. He was patrolling the empty piazza with another soldier, their rifles slung over their shoulders. Even from the distance I could see how miserable he was, his feet barely rising from the ground as he walked. When the school let out I watched him take a deck of cards from his pocket and fan them in his hands as he approached the children. But then an older boy pointed at him and shouted something and the rest of the children ran away in fear. Johann stood frozen for a minute, then put the cards back in his pocket and sat by the fountain, his back to me. The other soldier leaned against a wall at the far end of the piazza smoking a cigarette.

"I'm going over to Pardino's for a moment," I told Aunt Lucia, taking off my apron. "Do you need anything?"

"I need you back in five minutes." Aunt Lucia liked to think of herself as a strict taskmaster even though she was as sweet and soft inside as her *pastaciotti*.

I cut quickly across the piazza, passing within a few feet of Johann. As I approached he looked up.

"I'll be at the cave tomorrow at three," I said without turning my head or slowing my stride. Before he could answer I hurried on to Pardino's.

He was waiting when I arrived, sitting on the ledge with his hands tucked under his thighs and his rifle resting on the ground beside him.

"I've missed you so much," I said, kissing him on the cheek and taking a seat next to him. He was unresponsive.

"What is it?" I asked. He kept his gaze fixed out over the valley. "Please, say something."

He picked up a small rock, turned it in his hand and then threw it high in the air, watching it disappear in the trees. "I was going to shoot Henecker. Just before the men were executed I was going to draw my pistol and shoot him. Yet I didn't."

"I'm glad you didn't." I pulled his head against my shoulder and rubbed my nose in his hair, which smelled of dirt and sweat and apples. (His skin always smelled slightly of apples.)

"How can you say that?"

"Because I don't know what I'd do if anything happened to you. And because it wouldn't have made any difference. Do you think you can stop the war by killing one man?"

"How else does it stop?"

"You're already risking your life. That's enough. What good would you be dead?"

"Do you know why I didn't shoot Henecker?" He turned his head and looked at me closely, his eyes narrowed. "Because I wouldn't have seen you again."

I kissed his forehead.

"But I should have killed him. I didn't but I should have."

"No, you're wrong."

"After my family was killed, after I'd imagined their last moments a thousand times, I reached a point where I stopped feeling anything. One moment the pain was like a wild animal feeding on my insides and the next I couldn't feel a thing."

"That's not living."

"It was better than living." He paused. "But then I met you."

"You make it sound like you wish you hadn't."

"Yes," he said, standing and turning away from me.

"What are you saying?"

"I do wish I'd never met you."

"But why? How can you say that?"

"Because it's unbearable, don't you see?"

"Where have you been?" asked Mama when I got home. She was out by the side of the house pulling laundry from the clothesline, a pin sticking out from the corner of her mouth.

"Just in the orchard."

She frowned as she plucked two pairs of Papa's undershorts from the line and folded them in the air with a series of quick snaps. "It's not safe."

"I wasn't far."

"If I can't see you you're too far." She came closer and put her hand on my cheek. "You've been crying."

"I miss Renaldo," I said, which was true if not the truth.

"You have a heart as big as your father's." She put down the laundry and then gathered up my hair in her hands, arranging it across my shoulder.

"I wish I didn't."

"It's a gift that God only gives to those with the strength to bear it."

"What if God makes a mistake?"

"Only people make mistakes."

After dinner I put the twins to bed, reading them stories by candlelight because the power was out again.

"Are you going to be a soldier too?" Carlotta asked, keeping a firm grip on my dress as I tucked her in.

"Of course not," I said, kissing her forehead and blowing out the candle.

"Good, because we don't like soldiers."

"And why don't you like soldiers?" I asked, standing in the doorway.

"Because they make people sad," said Claudia.

"It's time to get some sleep. And no talking."

"But we're not tired."

"Count to a hundred—slowly."

"*One... two...*"

"Silently."

"I don't want to count."

"Not another peep."

I went to my room and sat in front of my mirror, slowing running my brush through my hair as I studied my reflection. I could still see traces of the girl I once was, the bright round eyes and the narrow ears and the long dark eyebrows I'd inherited from my mother. Yet the child was now almost completely hidden by the features of a young woman, a woman I still hadn't grown quite accustomed to. I traced my fingertips across my forehead and down along the ridge of my nose, then around the side of my mouth and back along my jawline. Not just a woman but a woman whose heart was now shaped to the dimensions of a man. I smiled to myself, remembering how often the young girl dreamed of the day she would fall in love, squirming in her bed at night at the very thought of such exquisite happiness. And to *be loved*. What could be more perfect and wondrous? *Please God, wherever he is out there, let him find me*, I would pray. I leaned into the mirror and mouthed Johann's name, watching my lips as they moved. Yes, he has found you. He has tracked you all the way down to this small village and found you, just as if God had meant it to be.

Now if only you can keep him.

I put down the brush and joined Mama in the kitchen where she was washing the next batch of laundry, humming softly to herself as she worked and pausing now and then to add another few precious drops of olive oil—which was rationed—to a frying pan full of garlic cloves. Through the window I could hear Papa banging away in the garage.

"Have you ever been to Venice?" I asked.

She looked surprised by the question. "Only as close as Verona."

"Would you like to see it?"

"I'd like to see a great many things."

"Why didn't you?"

"When I was young I didn't have the money and then I didn't have the time."

"I want to see Venice. And Rome and Paris and the French Riviera, too."

"Of course you do."

"I will see them. I promise I will."

She pulled one of Papa's work shirts from the wash bucket and lowered it into the rinse bucket. Though most of the women washed their laundry in the communal wash area alongside the shallow river that cut through the village, Mama preferred complete control over sanitary conditions, which required a great many trips by me to the fountain to fill the water buckets.

"You don't believe me?"

"I believe that if you're anything like me, you'll always want more than life can give you." She lifted the shirt and then plunged it back in the water.

"I can't stay here forever. It's not that I don't like it. It's just that…"

Mama raised her eyebrows.

"I'm different than you, that's all." I stirred the garlic cloves.

"I see." She gave Papa's shirt one final dunk, then squeezed out the water before placing it on top of a wicker basket of clean wet clothes. Then she picked up one of the twin's dirty outfits, plunged it into the wash bucket and began to work the fabric between her knuckles.

"I'll always come back."

She didn't respond.

"Do you blame me?"

"You're young. How can I blame you?"

"Didn't you ever want to leave?"

She pulled the outfit from the wash bucket and began to rinse it, working her hand in a circular motion. "I have your father. Rome and Paris, those are just cities. But a man like your father?" She smiled as she gave the outfit one last rinse before squeezing out the water. "One day if you're lucky you'll understand." She placed the outfit on the top of the basket and carried it out to the clothesline.

The next morning I took another basket of food to the Bruscanini's house near the piazza. Pietro answered the door, his younger brother and sister hiding behind his legs.

"I didn't know what to do so I brought some fresh bread."

He silently took the basket, his eyes not leaving mine.

"I don't imagine you're very hungry," I said, feeling self-conscious. "But you should eat."

"Thank you." Then he told his brother and sister to go back inside while he closed the door behind him. We sat together on the front step.

"How's your mother?" I asked.

"She's in bed. Dr. Cardoni said she needs rest."

"If there is anything I can do to help…"

He didn't respond.

"I wish there was something I could think of to say to you."

"I don't want to talk about it."

"Okay. But if you ever do want to talk about it you can talk to me. I just want you to know that."

He started to say something and then stopped himself and wiped his eyes. I could see he was trying not to cry. "Why did you risk your life for me?"

"Because your family needs you."

"But you could have been killed."

"Well, I wasn't." I gave him a smile.

He was quiet for a minute. Then he said, "They would have shot me."

"I know."

He put his small hand on mine. "I'll never forget what you did."

"I probably won't either," I said. Then I kissed him lightly on the cheek.

Two weeks went by before I got to see Johann again. He looked terrible, his face pale and thin and his eyes rimmed with exhaustion.

"You're not eating enough," I said, feeling his ribs. "If you think that starving yourself is going to—"

"You look beautiful," he interrupted. He reached out and ran his fingers through my hair.

"You're not listening."

"Soldiers are always the last to starve." He sat down on a stump near the entrance of the cave. "Did you hear the bombers last night?"

"How could I not?" There had been so many of them that my bed seemed to vibrate with the menacing drone of their engines.

"I wonder what it's like up there?"

"Probably terrifying, at least when they're being shot at."

He nodded slowly. "And when they open the bomb doors over the target, do you suppose they're quiet or do you think they keep talking?"

"Who knows what they do?"

"I was just wondering. It must be a lot to think about."

"Maybe they're too scared to think."

"Yes, I hadn't thought of that."

I sat beside him and placed my hand on his. "I don't want to talk about it. I don't want to talk about anything that has to do with the war."

"Okay."

I stared at his face but he wouldn't look at me. "Don't do this," I said.

"Do what?"

"Disappear on me. I can't stand it when I can't find you."

"I'm right here." He squeezed my hand.

"No, you're not. You're so far away I don't even know where to begin to look."

"What do you want me to say?"

"I want you to tell me again that you love me."

"I love you more than anything." He looked at me, yet his eyes weren't focused.

"But it's not enough, is it?"

"Alessandra—"

"What you feel for me isn't enough. I can see it in your face."

"You don't understand."

"You're right, I don't. I don't understand why you have to…" I couldn't finish.

"What? Why I have to what?"

I hesitated. "Give up. I don't understand why you have to give up."

He let go of my hand. "We've been ordered to the front."

"No."

"We leave in six days."

"But what about your uncle?" I tried to control my voice. "Surely he can have you reassigned?"

"It seems that dear Uncle Heinrich fell out of favor."

"But—"

"He's dead." A strange look came over Johann's face. "At least he was given full honors at his funeral. Who can complain as long as one is given full honors?"

"You can't go. I won't let you." I wrapped my arms around his neck and placed my head against his chest.

"I'll be fine."

"That's what my brother Renaldo said. 'I'll be fine, Alessandra.' And then I never saw him again."

"Then we won't talk about it. We won't talk about anything." He took my face in his hands and kissed away my tears before pulling me down on the rough gray army blanket where we clung to each other until it was time for us to go.

CHAPTER EIGHT

"WHY THE LONG face?" said Papa, cupping my chin in his hand as I sat in the courtyard with one of Stephano's books closed in my lap.

I shrugged.

"You're much too young to be so sad. Now when you get to be my age, well, that's a different story." He put his arm around me and pulled me close. "With a few glasses of wine and a good hard look in the mirror it's possible to perform a nearly perfect swan dive right into the very depths of self-pity!"

"But Papa, you never feel sorry for yourself."

"Only because I feel so sorry for everyone else!" He made a sweeping motion with his free hand.

"So what do you do when you feel sad?"

"I wait for the world to come to a complete stop and make amends. And when I get tired of waiting I get back to work."

"And what if that doesn't help?"

"Then I remind myself that I have the most wonderful daughter in all of Italy." He gave me another squeeze.

"I'm serious."

"So am I."

"Do you think it's more honest to be happy or to be sad?"

"Now there's a question," he said. "My father used to say that unhappiness is just a form of laziness whereas real happiness takes guts and imagination. Your mother, of course, would argue it's all a matter of hygiene."

"But how can a person be genuinely happy when so many horrible things happen in the world?"

"I see that pretty head of yours has been busy." He smiled with a look of pride.

"I want to know what you think."

"Perhaps you'd be more interested in your great-grandfather Massimo's theory. He used to say that if there was one thing the devil hated, it was happy people. He even did a pretty good imitation of the devil. *Argh, I detest the sound of laughter!* And so what better reason to be happy—deliriously happy—than to spite the devil?"

"But you don't believe in the devil."

He raised his index finger in the air. "And that's why I have my own theory."

"What is that?"

"That happiness is good for the digestion. And as I much prefer good digestion, I have every motivation to be happy." He leaned over and kissed me on the temple.

The next morning I brought the twins over to Pietro's house to play with his little sister, Alisa, and his brother, Cristiano. Pietro was out and so I sat with his mother, Gabriela, when I wasn't on the floor playing games with the children. She was silent most of the time, touching her face frequently, but I think she was glad for the company.

"You're the only thing that makes him smile," she said as Pietro came up the walkway.

"How is he?"

"He's so angry. I'm afraid he'll live the rest of his life with hate in his heart."

"I think he has too much else inside him for that."

"Yes," she said, just as Pietro walked in the door. "That's my hope."

Two days later Johann burst into the bakery. "I need to talk to you," he whispered over the counter. Aunt Lucia was in the back, arguing with herself as she greased the baking pans.

"I'll try to meet you after work."

He leaned forward. "I need to talk to you *now*."

I followed him outside where he pulled me into the narrow alleyway. "Your father is suspected."

"Suspected of what?"

"Helping the partisans. Henecker has a list."

I felt my limbs begin to tremble. "No, it can't be. He spends all day in the garage—repairing *German* vehicles. You know that."

"Someone has informed on him."

"But it's not true. You must tell Henecker that it's not true."

"There will be arrests. Tomorrow. Your father must leave at once."

"Leave? But he'll never leave. Where would he go?"

"He has no choice." Johann looked around again. "I must go." Then he turned and hurried off.

I ran home immediately. Papa was in the garage, his legs sticking out from beneath the front of a German halftrack that had several jagged holes running along the side.

"Hand me that wrench, would you, Mouse?"

"I need to talk to you."

"It'll have to wait. I'm behind as it is."

I crouched down beside the front tire, which was almost completely bald. "It can't wait."

He slid out and looked at me closely. "Ah, something is wrong. I always know from your eyes." He sat up and wiped his hands on a rag he kept tucked into his belt. "Let's see what we can do to find that sparkle again."

I began to cry.

His face went pale. "Stephano?"

"No."

"The twins?"

"They're fine. Everybody's fine."

"Then what could spoil such a beautiful face?"

"They suspect you, Papa. The Germans suspect you and they're coming tomorrow to arrest you. Don't ask me how I know but it's true. You must leave. Now."

He slowly rose to his feet, the rag still in his hands. "They suspect me, eh? And what proof do they have?"

"They don't need proof. You have to leave. Please, Papa."

"Leave my home? My family?"

"If you don't leave they'll take you away." I began to cry again. "*Please.*"

He puts his arms on my shoulders. "And how does my little mouse know such things?"

"You just have to believe me."

"I see." Then he waved his arm around the room. "How can they touch me when I seem to be the only capable mechanic in Southern Europe?" He smiled. "No, don't you worry about me. I'm the safest man in Tuscany."

"Your name is on a list. They'll take you and deport you or even worse. I'm begging you, Papa."

"Your German friend has given you this information?"

"Please don't ask me."

He nodded to himself, then tucked the rag back into his belt. "All right, I'll go."

"Really?"

"How could I resist such a face? It's time I visited my old friend Armando anyway. I'm tired of all this work!"

"You'll really go?"

"Until this matter clears up. I should be able to make it to Armando's in a day or two, if the trains are still running. Or maybe I'll walk. God knows, I could use the fresh air. Now, I want you and your mother and the girls to pack only what you need and go to your aunt's house at once."

I spent the evening helping Mama hide our remaining food supplies and any valuables that weren't already hidden. We packed enough for a week, then Papa helped us carry our things to Aunt

Lucia's. He promised to leave for Armando's later that evening once he finished up in the garage.

"Don't take long," I said, as he gave me a hug goodbye.

"Don't worry about me, Mouse." He winked, squeezed me hard and kissed me on the forehead before turning and hurrying off into the dark.

All night I prayed for his safety, wishing I hadn't wasted so many prayers on silly things. Was God tired of listening to me and how could he hear my little thoughts with all the prayers that must be rising to his ears? I imagined the cool night sky thick with prayers, some meek and whispered and others cried from hospital beds and battlefields. How many would simply fall back to earth unanswered? And then in the darkness I suddenly knew that my own prayer had returned like an unopened letter. He hadn't left. Papa would never leave his home and his garage and his tools. Why had I believed him? As soon as it was light enough to see I got up, quietly dressed and hurried out, running the three miles to our house.

Two German trucks were parked in front when I arrived. In the back of one I counted six men from our village, their hands bound. Thank God, Papa was not among them. I ran past several soldiers before they could stop me and through the front gate into our yard, which was littered with clothes and furniture, as though the house had been turned upside-down and shaken.

"Stop!" A soldier ran after me and grabbed me by the arm.

That's when I heard Papa's voice from inside the house. He was shouting at the Germans, calling them all sorts of terrible names. Moments later two soldiers wrestled him out the door, one at each arm. His face fell when he saw me. "Alessandra."

"Let him go," I cried as the soldier holding me began to pull me away. "He's done nothing!"

"Go to your mother," Papa said as they led him across the yard and toward one of the trucks. "Tell her not to worry. I'll be home as soon as this is straightened out."

"Please let him go!"

Then Henecker emerged from the house with Johann right behind him. Johann looked at me, panic on his face. I wanted to scream his name, to tell him to do something. Yet no words would come.

"Go quickly," said Papa, begging me with his eyes.

"I'll find Marcello. He'll help," I said. I tried again to pull away from the soldier holding me but he tightened his grip until my arm hurt.

Suddenly Henecker called out in German in a booming voice. Everyone stopped. I looked at Johann, who mouthed something I couldn't understand.

What is it, Johann?

Then Henecker began to walk slowly toward me, a smile creasing his hard features as he approached. When his face was just inches away he stopped, then carefully pulled a black leather glove from his left hand and placed his rough, bare palm on my cheek. For several moments he turned my head this way and that, examining me, then he gradually traced his fingertips across my cheek.

Johann took a step forward, fists clenched.

Don't, Johann. Please.

I closed my eyes, feeling Henecker's hot breath against my face as I tried to imagine myself safe in our cave, Johann holding me and telling me all about Venice and how something changes inside a person the first time they see the beautiful crowded chaos of the Grand Canal.

Henecker said something in German, but still I kept my eyes closed. Yes, we'd go to Venice together and Paris and London, too. Then I heard Johann's voice. "He wants you to open your eyes."

"Tell him I won't, not until he releases my father."

"Please, just do as he asks."

I hesitated, keeping my eyes squeezed tightly shut. "I can't bear to look at him."

"You must. Quickly."

Gradually I opened them, dropping my head to avoid Henecker's stare. Again he reached out and took my chin, this time firmly raising my head.

"Get your hands off her," said Papa, his voice filling the yard.

Henecker ignored him as he began to run his fingers through my hair.

"I'm okay, Papa," I said, trying to keep the fear out of my voice.

But I knew he couldn't bear to see a German officer caress his daughter. Not Papa. It was beyond anything he could endure. I could almost feel the strength welling up inside of him, strength that was once legendary in our village when Papa was younger. I looked briefly at him, wanting to tell him with my eyes that I could handle it and please not to do anything to anger Henecker. But maybe that's not what I really told him. Maybe without meaning to my eyes cried out for help because he was my father and he'd always helped me before.

"Papa, no!" I cried, but it was too late. With a roar he broke away from the two soldiers holding him and lunged at Henecker, tackling him to the ground.

"Please stop!"

"You filthy pig," Papa yelled as five soldiers struggled to pull him off Henecker, beating him with fists and rifle butts.

"Papa, no, please stop!"

But he kept fighting, months of rage pouring out of him. By the time they managed to subdue him blood ran down from his nose, lip and both eyebrows. Three of the soldiers were bleeding as well as they twisted Papa's hands so high behind his back that I thought they would break.

Henecker rose slowly to his feet, pausing to dust himself off with his free glove. Without even bothering to look at my father he turned toward Johann and uttered a brief command.

"You must go, Alessandra," said Papa, his features now nearly hidden by blood. "Please take her away."

Johann stood frozen as Henecker repeated his command, this time in a louder voice. The soldier who held me from behind tightened his grip when I tried again to pull away.

Henecker spoke a third time, now shouting. Still Johann didn't move.

"You must close your eyes," said Papa, looking directly at me. "You must do as I say and close your eyes and keep them closed as long as you can." The soldier holding me began to pull me away toward the road.

Suddenly Henecker drew his pistol and swung the grip against the side of Johann's head.

"Stop!" I cried. "This is madness!"

Blood ran down from Johann's temple but he remained on his feet, hands clenched at his sides and air rushing through his nostrils.

Henecker shouted again, this time at the top of his lungs.

Now Johann's hand began to move toward his pistol. As his fingers slid around the grip I understood: *He's going to shoot Henecker.* But just as he drew the weapon from its holster Henecker struck again, this time so hard that I heard a cracking sound. Johann looked over at me, a helpless expression on his face, then dropped to his knees, where he wavered for several moments before collapsing to the ground.

"Close your eyes!" said Papa.

"Papa—"

"Please close them, my little mouse. Close them and pray."

Henecker swiveled the pistol toward Papa's head and fired.

The last I saw of Johann he was being carried into one of the German trucks. I couldn't tell if he was still alive but it didn't seem to matter anymore. Nothing mattered because Henecker had won and there was no point left to life anymore. I waited to be bound and taken away or shot on the spot but instead they released me and drove off, leaving me alone in the courtyard with the body of my father. Johann was right: Henecker knew exactly how to draw the greatest amount of pain.

Papa was lying on his back with his head turned to one side, blood pooling on the chalk-white paving stones. I started toward him but when I looked at his face I began to retch, doubling over until I could barely breathe.

What have they done to you, Papa?

When I could finally stand I looked up at the sky, raising my balled fists and wanting to seize God by the collar and pull him down from the heavens until he was covered in the blood of all those he'd forsaken.

Why, why, why?

Then I crouched beside my father's body and took his large hand, which after so many years had become permanently darkened by grease and oil.

"Papa?" I leaned closer. "Papa it's me, Alessandra. It's your little mouse, Papa."

It was him and yet I knew that it wasn't. His body was like a familiar house emptied of all its furnishings, the building vacated and condemned. But where had he gone? I looked back up at the sky, trying to imagine his great big powerful soul ascending. Then I looked over at the garage, half expecting to hear the stuttering of an engine and my father singing to himself as he worked.

I'm sorry, little mouse. I just couldn't leave my home.

I knew you couldn't. I began to cry again.

Remember how I used to carry you into the house when you fell asleep in the rafters?

I remember.

Always light as a feather. And we had some good talks, didn't we? Other people can't stop moving their mouths, but when you and I talk we have something to say, isn't that right?

That's right, Papa.

You'll have to take care of your mother and sisters.

But I can't. Not without you.

Sure you can. They're going to need you, Mouse.

Papa...

I was wrong about your German friend.

It doesn't matter.

You sure he's not Italian?

I'm sure.

You love him, don't you?

I do. I really do, Papa.

Yes, it's all over that beautiful face of yours.

I began to cry again.

I'm going to miss you, Mouse.

I'm going to miss you too. I placed my cheek next to his and gently ran my fingers through his hair, which was sticky with blood.

Tell your mother that I love her—and that I'm sorry about the mess.

I'll tell her.

And promise me you won't try to carry me around with you the rest of your life. I'm much too heavy for that.

I'll never leave you, Papa. Never.

Oh, I won't be far. Besides, you always know where to find me.

I do?

Of course you do! Now do me a favor and hand me that wrench, would you? Renaldo and I have a lot of work to do.

I heard a noise and looked up to see Juliet emerging cautiously from her crawlspace beneath the garage. She sniffed the air and began to whimper as she approached. When she reached my father she licked his face, then curled up beside him and rested her head on his arm. I must have lain down too, or maybe I fainted, because the next thing I knew Pietro was gently shaking me awake.

CHAPTER NINE

HUNDREDS OF PEOPLE came to the funeral, many walking for miles to be there. I remember there was lots of food—more cheese and meat than I had seen in years, all of it dug up from secret hoards. But I don't remember much else of that day or even the next. At first the grief felt so sharp and deafening that I didn't see how I could get through a single hour. The only thing I could think to do was to keep busy helping care for the twins and then when my mother stopped cleaning I took over her work as well, moving as fast as I could through each hour until exhaustion released me into a withered sleep.

One last hope flickered in my heart: Stephano would soon come home. Even with the German Army all around us I kept expecting to find him at the door, knowing he wouldn't be able to stay away when he learned of Papa's death. We heard rumors that he'd been spotted in this village or that, but nothing more.

"He'll come back when it's safe," insisted Mama as we sat at the dinner table with the twins between us.

I stared down at my food, unable to eat. With just the four of us the house felt so empty that I began to think it was haunted. "Yes, I'm sure you're right," I said, wishing I could believe her. But I couldn't, not since Stephano had begun to appear in my dreams alongside Renaldo and Papa, causing me to jolt awake in the middle of the night, my bed sheets soaked through.

We never did hear from him. Only after the war did we learn that he'd been caught and executed by the Germans for sabotaging the rail lines, his body dumped in a mass grave so that we were never able to identify his remains.

But at least God heard one of Mama's prayers, because two months after Papa's funeral we got a letter from Marcello saying he was in America.

"America?" said Mama in amazement as I read the letter to her. "What's he doing in America?"

"He's a prisoner. In a place called Georgia. He says the food is good and that he's even able to earn some money working on a farm."

"Marcello has a job in America? He's a prisoner and he's got a job in America?"

"That's what he says."

"Then he's safe." She clasped her hands together and brought them to her chin. "If he's in America that means he's safe."

"Yes, that's what it means, Mama," I said.

That evening we took the twins for a picnic at Papa's grave to celebrate.

Two months later I was taking my evening walk through the olive grove near our house when I heard my name.

"Alessandra!"

I knew the voice right away, though I couldn't believe it. "Johann?" I slowly turned in a circle. "Where are you?"

"Here." He emerged from behind the old stone wall that bordered the grove.

I ran toward him but stopped just as I reached him, my hand rising to my mouth at the site of his gaunt face and the deep scar than ran down his left temple from where Henecker had struck him with the pistol. His movements were stilted and unsteady and his uniform torn and stained. He held one arm against his chest as he stood staring at me.

"My God, what's happened to you?"

"I've deserted."

"You're hurt."

"Not bad. If you have some food…"

"Yes. Yes of course."

As we stood staring at each other I wanted to hug him and yet I was afraid. There was something in his eyes I'd never seen before, something that frightened me and held me back. I thought of Uncle Roberto and wondered if Johann was in some sort of shock.

"I've prayed every night for you," I said, trying to keep my composure.

He reached out and ran his blackened fingertips across my forehead, brushing aside my hair. "It's like a tidal wave that crushes everything," he said softly. *"Everything."*

"What is?"

"The front. And it's coming, Alessandra. The tidal wave is coming."

"You must hide quickly. Go to the cave and I'll bring you food and clothes."

"I'm sorry about your father. If only I'd— "

"Let's not talk about it now."

"Henecker is dead." A smile came across his lips, which were dried and cracked. "Even he was crushed." Johann raised a hand and closed his fist slowly. "Just like a bug."

I looked around, afraid someone would see us. "We can't stay here. Go to the cave and I'll meet you in an hour." I turned to run back to the house to gather some things.

"Alessandra?"

I stopped.

"It's good to see you." And then in his eyes I saw a flicker of the Johann I remembered and without thinking I ran into his arms.

I spent the first day cleaning and bandaging his wounds as best I could. Most were minor cuts and abrasions but he had a small shrapnel wound in his shoulder that seemed infected.

"It doesn't bother me," he said, never taking his eyes off me as he ate *crostini* that I'd spread with ricotta.

"You need a doctor."

"No, I only need you." He raised his hand and stroked my cheek.

"I'll try to get some iodine."

"But no doctor. It's too dangerous."

"But if it gets worse…"

"Stop worrying." He pulled my face to his and kissed me. "I love you."

"And I love you."

"I'd love you even if you didn't."

"Well I do."

He took my hand and kissed the tips of my fingers one by one. "Do you know what I've realized?"

"What?"

"I've realized that I love you more than I hate all the other things." The skin along the corner of his eyes stretched into a smile. "And it changes everything."

"It's not the most romantic thing I've ever heard."

"But don't you understand? It's why I'm *alive*."

"You've alive because you're lucky. And maybe because I prayed for you every night."

"No, I'm alive because I chose not to die."

For the first few days he just ate and slept. He'd been walking for two weeks, stealing food at night and hiding during the day. "Deserters are shot on sight," he said, his head on my lap. "They leave the bodies on display as a warning."

"You're safe now," I whispered, running my fingers through his thick sandy brown hair, which was matted with dirt and sweat but still smelled faintly of apples. His physical presence brought a warmth back to my heart that I never thought I'd feel again.

He looked up at me. "Did I ever tell you that your face is perfect?"

I couldn't help but smile because I'd never met anybody who changed topics so abruptly, as though every possible subject was always on the table. "I don't believe you did."

"Well, it is. It's not just beautiful but it's perfect, which is different."

"You're being silly."

"But I'm not. Only a few things in life are truly perfect. My sister Anna's hair was perfect. My father's laugh was perfect. The works of Mozart and Tolstoy are perfect. Venice is perfect. And your face is perfect."

"And that's it?" I asked, half teasing.

"No, there's more. I just can't remember the other things right now."

"You need to rest."

"It makes all the difference knowing that at least some things are perfect."

"Yes, I guess maybe it does."

His eyes began to close, then opened again. "I don't dream anymore," he said. "When I sleep I no longer dream."

"Then you're lucky," I said.

"Yes, I think so. But it's not the same." He nestled his head into my lap. "Nothing's the same, is it?"

"No, it isn't."

I came to see him every day, bringing as much food as we could spare. "This is too much," he said when I offered him a small jar of honey we'd been saving. "You must keep it for your family. Things will only get worse."

"We have more," I lied. "You need fattening."

In the beginning he didn't talk much and I didn't ask too many questions, wanting him to rest. But gradually words began to tumble out of him until sometimes he talked so rapidly that I could hardly understand him.

"We couldn't move in daylight without the planes coming," he said early one morning as we lay side by side on our backs on the ledge looking up at the passing clouds, which were thick and doughy, as though ready for baking. "We were like field mice fleeing from hawks."

"How did you get away?"

"We'd begun moving along a road at dusk trying to retreat with as much equipment as we could. Henecker was sitting beside me, drunk on red wine—he was always drunk toward the end—and boasting about how Hitler's secret weapons were laying ruin to London. I'll never forget the look on his face when the first plane came in, screaming just over the treetops. Even the wine couldn't mask his terror. Somehow I managed to jump from the vehicle and into a ditch but Henecker never made it. I don't think he even moved. Four more planes came over and by the time they were gone the convoy was in ruins. Heinrich and Dieter, Franz and Walter; all the men I cared for were dead. There was nothing I could do and so... so I began walking and never stopped."

"You're safe here," I said, kissing his forehead.

He sat up and took my shoulders. "This is the most dangerous time. You must promise me that you'll be careful."

"And you must promise me you won't go wandering around where you might be seen."

But despite my pleas he refused to stay in the cave all day, saying he couldn't breathe without seeing the sky now and then. At his insistence we began to take walks together through the forest, careful to avoid the clearings. Often he was silent, his steps slow and deliberate, as if he was unsure of his footing. But now and then all the life seemed to pour back into him and he became animated as he described all the cities he wanted to visit, creating elaborate itineraries and telling me how we would open offices in London and Paris and New York for our travel company.

"Where will we live?" I asked.

"Wherever you want. Anywhere at all."

"Not Germany."

"No, not Germany."

"Promise you won't leave me home all the time."

He laughed. "You'll come everywhere with me. Don't you see how wonderful it'll be? We'll learn lots of languages and collect books of history and the moment we feel restless we'll get on the next train and there won't be anyone to stop us."

"But what about children?"

"They'll come too. What better way to educate them?" Her took a dried fig from a small bag I'd brought from home and began to chew on it, careful to avoid two teeth that were bothering him and a gap where a third tooth had been pulled by an army medic.

"We'll need money."

"Maybe not so many children."

"At least three."

"At least three." He came up behind me and circled his arms around me, pressing his lips against my neck.

"But what if you're restless and I'm not?"

"Then I'll run round and round our house with our children on my shoulders until I'm too tired to be restless."

"And if that doesn't work?"

"Then I'll carry all of you to the train station."

We continued in silence until we reached the ridgeline where we could look out over a narrow valley that quickly gave way to a series of taller ridges, their steep slopes heavily forested. High overhead we heard the drone of bombers flying north to Germany. I counted two dozen arranged in toy-like formation. As they passed I couldn't help thinking how peaceful they looked, even pretty. Then I looked over at Johann, whose eyes were fixed upward, and I thought of how different they must look to him.

We followed the ridgeline until we reached a large rock field, which we didn't dare cross for fear of being seen. Instead we dropped down into the woods again, pushing through dense undergrowth until we came upon a long slab of granite where we stopped to rest. Above, the trees were filled with birds and the sunlight crisscrossed through the leaves, casting bright patterns on the ground.

"Could you ever really be happy?" I asked.

He didn't respond.

"I want to know."

"Maybe happiness isn't the most important thing. Maybe the important thing is not to cause more unhappiness."

"That doesn't seem like enough."

"I think it's a lot," he said.

"But if you tried?"

"What, to forget?" He bent down to pick up a flower, spinning it slowly between his fingers. "No, I can't forget."

"I can't forget either. But I know that being unhappy won't bring back my father. I know that if he's going to live on in my heart that it should be a place that brings him joy, not grief. Besides, you'll drive yourself mad thinking about all the awful things in the world."

"It seems to me that those who are suffering would prefer to be in the thoughts of their fellow men."

"Then if you can't be happy, what is it you feel when you're with me?"

He took my hand and turned it over, then dropped the flower into my palm. "I feel that I can endure." He gently closed my fist.

"And that's it?"

"That's *everything*."

We made love that afternoon. All the reasons I had for wanting to wait seemed to fall away like autumn leaves from a tree. How could I wait when there might never be another chance, when time itself seemed menacing and spiteful? And I wanted more of him. I wanted as much as I could get so that I'd always have at least a part of him that could never be taken away. I think I also hoped that if we made love—that if he could let go of everything—that it might somehow strengthen him.

I'd spent hours imagining what it would be like. How much of another person can we really grasp with our flesh? Would he travel all the way to my soul, or was there a point beyond which even love and passion couldn't reach? More than anything I wanted to know how close two people could get and whether it would ever be close enough. But of course it has to be, doesn't it?

CHAPTER
TEN

A WEEK LATER we began to hear the war. We'd heard it before. Allied planes seemed to fill the skies, even bombing several neighboring villages for reasons we couldn't understand. But now we began to hear artillery in the distance while more and more German troops passed north through our village; sometimes in small convoys, sometimes in bands of six or a dozen men. They were desperate now, stealing whatever they could carry and smashing windows and furniture in their fury. Alberto Biano and Marco Selvini were shot dead trying to protect their property and we heard of several rapes in nearby villages, which terrified all the women. Most dangerous of all were the roving patrols of SS troops searching for deserters, who were tried and executed on the spot.

"It's too dangerous now," said Johann, insisting that I remain at home until the front passed. He seemed increasingly withdrawn and the stammer had returned to his voice.

"But I can't leave you alone."

"You must. *Please.*"

Finally I agreed, but only if I could return that afternoon with more food and water.

"I need one more thing," he said, stepping toward me and taking my arm firmly. The look in his eyes scared me. "I need a weapon."

"But why? You're safe here."

"If they find me they will kill me. I need at least a chance."

"I don't see what good it would do. As long as you—"

"Please, Alessandra." He spoke in a tone of voice I'd never heard before.

"But—"

"*Please.*"

Later that afternoon I returned with the pistol that Papa had hidden behind a wall in the garage along with a box of shells.

"You are my angel," he said, kissing me before carefully inspecting the weapon. I was surprised and a bit frightened by how confidently his hands worked the metal parts.

"Promise me that you'll surrender as soon as the Americans come."

He didn't reply.

"Promise me, Johann."

"They'll take me away from you. They'll lock me up."

I pressed my palm against his cheek. "As soon as the war is over we can—"

"Years, Alessandra. The war could go on for *years*."

"What choice is there?"

"I'll wait here until the front passes, then hide in the mountains. You could join me. We'll hide together. I'll build us a cabin where no one can find us." He pulled me close. "Just the two of us."

"It's impossible." I drew back from him.

"Why is it impossible?"

"Because we'll be discovered. Because we won't have food. Because in the winter we'll freeze. And if the partisans find us…"

And then the Americans came. The withdrawing Germans were frantic now, fleeing through the woods like animals running from a forest fire. Meanwhile the partisans became more bold, ambushing the Germans wherever they found them, causing savage reprisals. As the hills and valley filled with the sound of sporadic gunfire even the laziest men in San Gianello took up arms, eager to claim some credit for our liberation. Yes, Johann was right, this was the most dangerous time.

Just after dinner I was walking to the garage to make sure it was locked when I heard someone whisper my name. I turned to see Pietro emerge from behind a bush, a large knife tucked in his belt.

"What are you doing here?"

"Bring your family to my house, you'll be safer," he said.

"We're safer here," I said. "And you'd be a lot safer without that knife."

"Then I'll stay here with you."

"You can't stay here, Pietro. Now go run home."

He stared at me, the color of his face changing shades until I wondered if he was holding his breath.

"What is it?" I asked finally.

"In case I die in battle there is something I need to say."

"You are *not* going to die."

"But if I do, well, I couldn't without saying what I want to say."

"Then don't say it and you won't die."

"I love you." He took a step back in surprise. "There, I've said it. I love you Alessandra Mariani and I always have loved you and I always will."

"Pietro, you need to go home. Now go quickly and stay there."

"Could you love me?"

I paused. "No, I'm sorry. You are very sweet but the answer is *no*."

"Maybe someday you'll change your mind."

"I don't think so."

"I'll still love you."

"Okay then. Now you'd better go."

"I feel much better knowing that I've finally told you," he said, smiling ear to ear.

"I'm glad, Pietro. Now *go*."

He quickly kissed me on the cheek before I could stop him, then turned and ran off.

The next morning the house was shaken by explosions as Allied artillery targeted a passing convoy of German vehicles.

"Quickly, to the shelter!" cried Mama, grabbing the girls and pulling up the floorboards in the closet off the kitchen. I climbed in last, then jumped out just as Mama began to pull the planks over our heads.

"What are you doing?"

"I have to do something."

"Alessandra, have you lost your mind? Get back here!"

But I was gone. I dashed out the back door and through the courtyard, stopping to hide behind a bush as a German tank roared by. Then I ran through the orchards and into the woods, running faster the closer I got. I tripped twice, once catching my foot on a tree root and falling so hard that I skinned both knees. But I didn't care. Nothing mattered anymore but making sure that Johann was safe. As I ran I prayed that today would be the day that the war would end, at least for us. And surely the Americans would be kind. There were even rumors that Italian Americans were fighting in our sector. If only I could arrange for Johann's surrender.

Off to my right across the ravine I heard machine-gun fire, this time closer than any I'd heard before. *Just like a tidal wave.* How many would be swept away as it passed over? I ran faster, trying to fight off the panic that rose in my chest. Finally I turned off the path and climbed through the trees toward the boulders above.

I was almost at the entrance when I saw a movement in the woods out of the corner of my eye. As Johann rushed out to meet me I quickly pulled him back inside.

"Someone's out there," I said, trying to catch my breath. My eyes burned with the realization that I'd given away his hiding place. "To the left in the trees. I saw someone. Maybe two people. I only caught a glimpse. Maybe if I talk to them…"

"They must be Germans. Six of them spent the night so close I could hear them talking. They're lost."

"The Americans are just south of the village."

"Yes," he said softy. "It's here." His hand brushed against Papa's pistol, which was tucked in his belt. "But you should never have come. Now quickly crawl as far back in the cave as you can while I take a look."

I tried to stop him but he was already near the entrance, crouched with the pistol drawn. Slowly he peered out until his head and shoulders were in the sunlight.

A single shot rang out, striking the rock face just above him. He scrambled back to where I was hiding. "They think we're partisans. Listen to me, Alessandra. I'm going to identify myself. I'll explain that I was separated from my unit."

"But they may shoot you for desertion."

"Right now they'll only want to save their skins. I can show them through the canyon. They'll need me. Then you can escape."

"You'll be forced to retreat with them—even to fight again. If we just wait for the Americans…"

"There's no choice." He took my face in his hands. "I'll be back. I promise."

"But—"

"Shh." He put his finger to my lips. "You must crawl as far back as you can and lie down and cover yourself with dirt. Don't move until dark, do you understand?"

I nodded.

He helped cover me, working quickly, and hurried back to the entrance. I heard him call out in German. There was silence, then he called out again. More silence, then voices just beyond the entrance.

"They're speaking English," I said, raising my head. "They're Americans!" I started to get up when I heard something strike the ground near where Johann crouched.

A grenade.

Johann snatched it up and flung it back out of the cave. Moments later it exploded, followed immediately by terrible screams. *Please God, no,* I prayed.

"I surrender!" yelled Johann, first in German, then in Italian as he dropped the pistol and emerged into the daylight, hands in the air.

A shot rang out and Johann stumbled back into the cave.

I had to stop the Americans before they threw another grenade. I got up and began to shout as loud as I could. "Don't shoot! We surrender! Please, I'm Italian!" As I neared the entrance several more shots struck the rock above me.

Johann grabbed me.

"No, let me go!" I cried. "They won't shoot a woman." I struggled to break free but he pushed me to the ground.

"You will live, do you understand?" he cried, his eyes on fire. "You will live!" Then he picked up the pistol and ran into the light, screaming at the top of his lungs as he fired again and again.

"Johann, *no!*"

But I couldn't stop him. Nothing could have stopped him.

There was a burst of gunfire followed by several cries. Then silence.

"Johann?" I whispered, crawling forward on my hands and knees. "Johann?"

His body was a dozen yards from the entrance, sprawled on the ground with blood coming from his head. Close by were three other bodies. Americans. The first I'd ever seen.

"Johann!" I ran to him crying. "Johann, no!"

But I knew he would never answer. I knew because all the pain and sadness was gone from his face, his features as smooth and relaxed as a boy's. A boy without any more fears. A boy who could now sleep soundly, his sisters and mother and father safe again, all the far-flung pieces of the world put back together.

As I held him in my arms I realized that it was my own heart I was holding, that the sweet bright blood spilling into the earth was my blood, my life, my dreams. I was alive and dead at the same time, cleaved in two by a blade forged of fate.

Please don't leave me here alone.

And then I went to the Americans one by one, moving as if my own skin was draped upon a ghost. As I looked in their empty faces all I could think of were their mothers kissing them goodnight and praying each evening for their safe return.

When I approached the third American I saw his hand move and he let out a weak cry. I quickly bent down beside him and took his hand and spoke to him gently in Italian. "We didn't mean to hurt you," I said, desperate for him to live. "We didn't mean to hurt anybody."

Suddenly the American opened his eyes and gripped my hand, his face tightening with fear. "It's okay," I whispered, gently stroking his arm. He had a young face, younger even than Johann's, with wide cheeks and freckles. As he squeezed my hand harder I realized he was holding on to me as though I were life itself.

"Hold on," I whispered. "Keep holding on to me."

I don't know how long I sat there on the ground next to the wounded American. Twenty minutes? An hour? I wanted to get help and yet I was afraid that if I let go of the American's hand he would slip away.

Then I heard voices. Soon I could see Pietro and Carlo Manucci and Giacomo Andreone running up the hill, followed by four other men from the village, all armed with an assortment of pistols and rifles.

"What happened?"

"Are you all right?"

"Have you been shot?"

But I had no words for them. I had no words left for anybody. Instead I wanted to go the rest of my life without speaking because from that moment on I knew that words would always fail me. What could I say? That the dead German soldier was my lover? That I'd been hiding him in the cave and that I planned to marry him after the war and that nothing was going to stop us? That he'd tried to surrender but the Americans had attacked first and so Johann had fought back because he saw no other way to protect me and for once in his life he wanted to protect something that he loved?

"I was looking for Stephano," I stammered finally as Pietro held me. "I heard shots and I... I hid in the woods. When I got here..." I gestured toward the bodies, feeling I might faint.

The men nervously aimed their rifles at the surrounding trees until satisfying themselves that the Germans were gone, then walked among the bodies. Andreone crouched beside the GI in my arms. "Let's get this one down to the village."

Manucci bent over Johann. "Wait a minute. I know who this is. It's that young German—the translator. Now what the hell was his name?"

The others leaned over the body. "Johann," said Andreone. "His name was Johann. We used to play *Briscola*. And he did card tricks for the children."

All the men stared down at Johann's body.

"What a pity," said Manucci. "The only good German in the bunch."

"Wasn't he raised in Italy?" said Andreone.

"No, he was a German all right," said Manucci. "But he had a heart just like an Italian."

For years I wondered where God was that day. Are we so easily forgotten? Is God so hungry for our devotion that he forgets to love us back? But then I came to understand that God was there all right. He was busy saving the life of the young GI.

The American hung between dark and light for three days, the smell of death on his skin as Father Gregorio gave him last rites. But the young soldier lived because he refused to die. And so I thought that if God was with this American then that was where I belonged too. And so you see, I married him. But I never deserved him.

There is no more to say but that I'm sorry.

And I'll always love you, Shannon.

PART FOUR

CHAPTER
ONE

And Time, a maniac scattering dust,
And Life, a Fury slinging flame.
– Alfred, Lord Tennyson

January 8, 1945

Dearest Jim,

I had the most awful feeling this morning that something happened to you. It was like a hand on my chest and it wouldn't stop pushing and now there is nothing I can do but pray you are alive. But I tell myself that you must be alive because if you weren't I'm certain I would feel the difference in the world. I'm just not sure I could bear it.

Sue Greeley from down the street (the big brown house with the green shutters) knew the moment her fiancée Thomas was dead. She knew a week before she got the telegram. She told me it was like cold air coming down the back of her neck and so now every night I feel the back of my neck to make sure it's warm.

I try to visit with her almost every day, getting her out or just sitting next to her and holding her hand if that's what she wants. I do my best to be strong but I don't feel strong because every time I look in her eyes it makes me so scared I can hardly sleep at night. And then I wonder why my prayers should mean any more than hers.

Sometimes I think I'll go out of my mind with all this waiting and not knowing and listening to Dad read the paper out loud each morning over breakfast (his contribution to the war effort) and then sitting around the radio each evening, all those gloomy voices crackling in my ears. But then today there was a letter from you and everything inside of me changed as I ran to my room and locked the door and let your sweet wonderful words run all over me, wishing they were your hands.

I want to tell you to be careful and keep your head down and not to be too brave but I know it won't do any good. So I'll just say please come back.

Please.

I love you,

Rebecca

P.S. Tomorrow I promise I'll be brave and I'll be brave the day after that, too. But not today because I can't.

CHAPTER
TWO

FOR SEVERAL MINUTES after I awoke in my hotel room in San Francisco I remained motionless, sleep receding like a tide that left me sprawled in the sand. I spent another minute sitting on the edge of the bed trying to shake off my dreams, then made a small pot of coffee in the machine in the bathroom and drank two cups while sitting in a chair by the window watching the sun pry loose the fog. Then I showered, dressed and walked down to the corner where I caught a cab. Ten minutes later I was standing outside a white two-story building in North Beach.

A handwritten label just beneath the doorbell to the first floor apartment listed two names: Shannon O'Donnell and Brian Sandhurst. I reached for the buzzer, then stopped myself, deciding I'd try to catch her on the street. I walked down to a coffee shop on the corner where I sat for hours, glad for the company of strangers and feeling their need for company too. Shortly after three I watched through the window as a minivan pulled up to Shannon's building and dropped off a young girl bent under a bulging yellow backpack. *The stepdaughter*, I thought, as the girl slipped through the front door. I sat for another hour, then walked around the block, first one direction, then the other, stopping now and then to sit on the curb near the corner.

Just after six I saw her walking up the street, head down and a large purse slung over her shoulder. I was struck by how different she looked, her movements and attire blending seamlessly with the urban backdrop.

"Shannon?"

She looked up and froze. "What are you doing here?"

"You didn't say goodbye."

She started to say something, then hesitated.

"You can't just run away."

"What else could I do?"

"I forgive your father. Not every day but most of them. If I can forgive him so can you."

"You don't understand." She started toward her door and fumbled for her key.

"At least let me talk to you."

"I don't want to talk, Ryan. I don't want to hear anything else." She pulled out the key and put it in the lock. "Maybe you can deal with it but I can't. Not right now. I need to be alone, okay?"

"You don't have to go back to Brian. You don't have to live that life."

"I want to go back to Brian."

"I don't believe you."

"You don't have to believe me."

I reached for her arm. "Don't go."

"Please don't do this, Ryan."

"But I've lost enough."

She stared at me for a moment. "I know you have." She opened her door. "And I'm sorry. I'm *really* sorry." Then she quickly entered her apartment and closed the door behind her.

I stood looking at the door, hoping it might open again, then backed away and started in the direction of my hotel, hiking up and over Russian Hill and then stopping at a bar for a few drinks, which didn't help at all. When I finally fell asleep I dreamed that I was deep inside a cave, unable to find my way out in the darkness.

I watched her leave for work the next morning, careful to keep out of sight. First a white SUV pulled up in front of her building and the young girl appeared, her yellow backpack thumping against her back as she ran to the curb and hopped into the backseat alongside several other children. A few minutes later Shannon emerged and headed down the sidewalk. I started to approach but she seemed to be in a hurry and I didn't want to make her late for work so I watched as she got on a bus, and then I watched the bus disappear down the street. No sign of Brian.

I couldn't think of what else to do with the day so I began to walk, crisscrossing North Beach and Chinatown before following the Embarcadero to Fisherman's Wharf, where I watched mimes and jugglers entertain the tourists. By five I was back on her street. I circled the block twice, then rested against a lamppost on the corner. Nearby a homeless man waved. "What did they do to you?" he asked with a gummy smile.

"They?"

He nodded grimly.

"Hard to say."

"That bad, huh?" He shook his head sadly. "How many of us you figure are left?"

I laughed. "Two seems like plenty to me."

"You think I'm joking with you? Ask yourself this: how come you're the only one who can see me?"

I caught myself looking down the street for witnesses. "This is an absurd conversation."

"We're just getting started!" He let out a throaty laugh, head shooting back. Then he rose slowly to his feet. "I don't like to stay in any one place too long. Word gets around." He started down the block, whistling as he went. "See you back at the ship."

"The ship?" I smiled. "Yes, of course. The *ship*."

"That is, if you make it," he said.

"I'll make it all right." I thought of Lupo, knowing he'd decode all sorts of extraterrestrial implications from the exchange.

An hour later I saw her. This time she was with Brian, shoulder to shoulder and both carrying groceries. I watched them enter their apartment and then I stood across the street, arms crossed against the rolling fog as I stared at the warm yellow light that seeped beneath the drawn curtains. I don't know how long I stood there, mesmerized by a sharpness that went back years. But it wasn't until I watched the windows darken one by one that I told myself it was time to go home. I told myself it was time to forget all about the O'Donnells because they'd taken enough from me and I had nothing left to give.

But I didn't listen.

I rose early the next morning and walked down to the marina to watch the boats and joggers dart through the mist. Gradually the fog began to melt into large chunks that bobbed mournfully on the water before retreating back to sea, hounded by seagulls. When I tired of walking I rented a bike from a tourist stand and rode across the Golden Gate Bridge, stopping mid-span to wonder why it was so much easier to jump from something so beautiful when beauty was a reason to live.

I spent the rest of the day riding through the Marin Headlands, the salty wind drumming against my face as I explored the batteries dug for an invasion that never came. By the time I got back to my hotel it was nearly five. I quickly showered, dressed and tucked Alessandra's journal into my coat pocket before catching a cab back to North Beach. I'd only waited twenty minutes when I saw Shannon get off the bus at the corner.

"Shannon."

She stopped. "Why are you doing this, Ryan?"

"Because I can't forget how it felt to hold you in my arms."

She closed her eyes and bowed her head, pressing her fingertips into the skin just above her dark eyebrows. "It won't work. No matter how much I might want it to work it won't." She looked up at me. "I can't see you anymore, Ryan. I just can't. It's too hard."

"What happened has nothing to do with us."

"It has everything to do with us. And I want my father back. I want to believe in him again even if I have to lie to myself and I can't do that when I look at you. And how can I look at you without seeing things that…" She didn't finish.

"You want to run from the truth, is that it?"

"Why not? My parents did."

"Shannon—"

"I have to go." She began to walk away.

"Go where? Back to a life that seems safe? There is no safety, Shannon. Not for any of us. There is only the raw, messy truth pulsing in our veins and whether we live it and breathe it or spend our lives running from it."

"I'm married. Maybe I don't deserve to be but I am. I have a family. I'm a wife and a stepmother." She walked faster. "They need me."

I followed her. "So what are you going to do, waste your life with some guy you don't truly love? Do you think you can will yourself into loving him because he loves you? Well, it doesn't work. Just ask your mother."

She stopped and turned. "Why are you saying that?"

"How much do you know about your mother's experiences in the war?"

She looked confused. "Why does it matter?"

"Because it's important."

She thought for a moment. "I know that two of my uncles and my grandfather were killed. I know that my grandmother never recovered and I know that Mom went through things she wants to forget."

"And your mother told you that she met your father after he was wounded near her village?"

"She helped care for him and then she volunteered at the hospital in Rome where he was recovering. I always thought it was rather romantic; maybe the only romantic part of their relationship."

"There is more to it than that."

"What are you saying?"

"I'm saying that it's more… complicated."

She stepped closer. "How do you know?"

"She gave me this." I pulled the journal from my coat pocket. "It's the parts of your mother you always knew were missing. She wrote everything down. It's what happened to her and her family and how she met your father. It's where all this started. I don't think she ever intended to tell anybody but now she thinks she's lost you and the only thing she has left is the truth."

Shannon stared down at the journal, then took it in her hands.

We walked three blocks to Washington Square, then sat on a park bench and looked up at the sharp twin spires of the large church that glowed white against the black sky. Shannon placed the notebook on her thighs, hands resting on the top and her back erect. "Tell me what's in here."

"I think it's better if you read it. I could meet you tomorrow. We could go for a walk or have lunch." I started to get up.

"I want to know now. I want to know what you know."

I hesitated, then sat back down and tried to think where to begin. With the pretty young girl in her perch in the garage watching her father work and listening to his stories? Or perhaps the day the Germans arrived? "It's kind of a long story," I said.

"Then we'll just sit here."

"I really think it would be better—"

"Please."

"All right." I paused, then made several starts. Finally the words fell into place. For the next hour I told her the story of Alessandra and Johann, slowing as I approached the end. By the time I finished, tears were running down Shannon's cheeks.

"So she married Dad out of guilt. She married him because she felt sorry for him."

"And because she was young," I said. "And probably because she didn't know what else to do."

"But he killed her lover. How can you marry the man who killed your lover?"

"She never saw who shot Johann. It might have been another soldier. It might have been all of them."

Shannon hugged the journal to her chest. "That's why she volunteered at the Veterans Hospital. She's blamed herself all these years because she gave Johann the weapon; she led the Americans to the cave. He was fighting to protect her." She wiped her eyes. "God, every day she had to look at the photograph of Dad with his buddies and listen to his stories about how much they meant to him. After the war he went to visit each of their families. Mom went too."

"She wanted me to tell you that she loves you. She wanted me to be sure to say that."

Shannon stood up, still clasping the journal to her chest as she rocked side to side. The cool, damp air gathered in tiny droplets on her skin. "Ever since I was a little girl I knew something was wrong with my mother, the way the hours and days seemed to move through her without hitting anything. I always thought it had something to do with me, that I wasn't the kind of girl she wanted or that she wanted a son or that she didn't really want to be a mother at all."

"You're the best part of her life. You always have been."

Shannon turned and looked up at the church. "And Dad never knew that she was at the cave that day?"

"No one ever knew." I stepped forward and put my arms around her.

"And do you think Pietro wrote those letters?" she asked, pressing against me.

"That's my guess."

"But we don't know if they ever secretly met?"

"No, but somehow I doubt it." I held her closer.

"Don't let go," she whispered.

"I don't intend to."

We didn't talk about Alessandra or Mike or the accident the rest of the night. We didn't talk about any of the things that seemed to hover around us, as if the past was a physical weight that could crush you if you weren't careful. Instead we ate dinner at a small Italian restaurant, holding hands under the table and laughing without meaning to because there was something so nice about being together. We stayed until closing, both surprised by all the empty tables, then we walked down Columbus to the waterfront.

"I don't want to go home," she said as we watched the lights of Alcatraz flicker through the mist while a fog horn beat across the bay.

"What about Brian?"

"He left this morning for L.A. on business. Melissa goes to her mother's house on Thursdays."

"Stay with me."

She turned toward the water, the night tussling her hair. "I might not be very good at this."

"We can wait."

"I don't want to wait any longer. I've already been waiting my whole life."

Once we entered my hotel room Shannon turned on a single light by the bed, then took off her shirt and draped it over the lampshade, casting the room in shades of lilac. She began to unbutton my shirt, her lips following her fingers. When she saw my scars she paused and I feared she would pull away but she didn't. Instead she kissed them lightly from one end to the other. She started with my right shoulder, then my stomach, then the faint line that ran along my left shin. When she finished I wrapped my arms around her and pulled her against me, feeling her weight sink into my grasp as I kissed her, my whole body straining toward her as though every other direction was nothing but pain.

"Do you really think you could love me?" she said, rolling on top of me. Sweat gathered on her stomach and with each movement of her hips I felt her drawing closer, both of us working to free each other.

"I really do." I reached up and took her face in my hands, then let my palms trace the lines of her neck and her shoulders and her small breasts and then down to her waist and hips.

"Say it again."

"I really think I could love you."

I started to say more but she put her finger to my lips. "No," she said. "That's enough." Then she bent down and kissed me as I pressed up toward her, feeling an unexpected sense of sorrow because a man can wait years for this moment and then spend years returning to it over and over again until the path is overgrown and one day lost.

But at least it's possible.

I wrapped my arms around her waist and rolled over on top of her, pressing through her as she dug her fingers into the muscles of my back. My limbs shook and the sound of her cries filled my ears as I went farther and farther, my whole being surging toward hers until I couldn't hear anything at all.

CHAPTER
THREE

I KNEW WHEN she began to cry and couldn't stop that she would leave. I tried to get her to talk but she couldn't and so there was nothing to do but hold her, promising myself that I would never let go and then wondering in the darkness if it is only in the arms of another that we can truly fathom our utter aloneness. When I finally fell asleep I dreamed I was a mountaineer resting on the summit of his own life, his oxygen nearly gone but the view more glorious than anything he has ever seen.

When I awoke she was gone.

There was a note on the table.

Dearest Ryan,

How can I begin to explain to you what I feel right now as I watch you sleep, your face so peaceful and lovely? How can I tell you that I would do anything not to hurt you, knowing how much these words will hurt?

When I was a little girl I used to dream that one day I would marry the boy in the bandages with the broken heart. Yes, it's true; you were my secret fantasy. Doesn't every lonely child need one? At first it was because I pitied you and I thought that I could care for

*you and make you happy, or at least not so awfully sad. But then as I
saw your photos each year (how big and handsome you became!) and
I read your cards to my father each Christmas, I began to dream that
you would save me, if only you'd come back. And I knew that you'd
come back one day. The stars told me so.*

*But now that you're here I can't have you no matter how much I
want you. For a moment tonight I thought that I could but I was wrong.
I never could, not without pulling myself apart. I need to get as far
away from the past as I can and I can't get far at all as long as I'm holding on to you. I guess what I'm trying to say is that I'm still my father's
girl and I always will be. I can't bear to lose him more than once.*

I'm sorry.

*I hope that one day you'll forgive me but I think we O'Donnells
have asked for enough forgiveness already. So I will leave quietly because I know of no other way. Please don't ask me to leave you again.
I couldn't bear it.*

Love,

Shannon

I spent three more days in San Francisco hoping she would call. I
walked from morning until night, sometimes hurrying back to the
hotel to check for messages. And then when I knew she wouldn't
call I spent another day gathering the strength to leave. On the fifth
morning I rose and packed my bag and caught a taxi to the airport,
moving from memory.

CHAPTER
FOUR

My Dear Alessandra,

The most ridiculous thing happened yesterday: the short boy who used to climb the tallest trees just for a glimpse of you turned sixty-five. Yes, can you imagine such a pitiful spectacle? In truth, it was a much bigger blow for Mama. (She will surely bury us all.) I think the poor woman has finally given up hope that I will be marrying any time soon, which means that after all these years she will need a new stick to stir her coals. Fortunately for her, San Gianello is full of them.

We had a small party at Giovanni's. (Umberto's old place. The food is better but the prices are criminal.) Alisa's and Cristiano's families were there and the young people danced and dunked each other in the fountain—we finally have water again—while us old goats played cards and pretended not to look at the young women, especially when they were wet. And then I'm afraid that in all my excitement I drank too much wine and fell asleep because the next thing I knew I was being hoisted onto the shoulders of my five nephews and carried home. I pretended to complain but of course I relished every moment, certain that no man ever rode a finer chariot.

I think you would have quite a good laugh if you could see what liberties time has taken with me. I know I never was an inspiring sight—how I once envied your brother Marcello!—but now I'm afraid I've taken on the resemblance of a small, gray elf. My hearing is nearly gone (I suspect Mama has something to do with that) and my knees gave up the ghost years ago. Worst of all I seem to be shrinking by the hour—and much faster than Mama. (The day I find myself once again looking up at her I will immediately board the next train to Rome and throw myself into the Tiber.) But I can't complain. How could I when every day is a gift that you gave me so many years ago? (I told you I'd never forget.)

Ah, my beautiful, sweet Alessandra, if only I could describe the thoughts that swirl inside of me as I gaze out my window at the piazza below, my eyes seeing things that no one else seems to see anymore. It hasn't been the life the young boy in the tree dreamed of (and how he dreamed!), and yet the fewer days I have left the more exquisite each becomes, silent treasures tucked within every lingering moment.

This morning, for example, the sun rose with such a brilliant smile that all of San Gianello glistened with a fresh coat of paint. Mama's heart condition has improved, I've won a fair amount at Briscola this month and my little grandniece Lia has a laugh that runs right up your spine and lights the whole village. (I can hear her now as she bounds up the stairs to visit the old elf and so I must finish quickly.) And just to imagine your lovely eyes upon these very words I write is enough to make me feel sixty again, even fifty-nine when my knees don't hurt. (There are moments when I feel much younger indeed.)

I made one wish on my birthday. It's the same wish I've made every year, and that is that one day you will return to San Gianello and I'll show you the things that have changed and better yet the things that have not. And then when we are too tired to walk any further (which won't take me but a few minutes) we'll sit and watch the clouds play over the most beautiful valley in the world. I don't expect my wish to come true. I never have. But I make it anyway. I imagine the world is full of such wishes, don't you?

Love always and forever,
Your Devoted Servant

CHAPTER
FIVE

———

"HEY MAN, YOU don't look so good," Lupo said as I stopped by his place to pick up the cats.

"Why do people keep telling me that?"

"You want to talk about it?"

"Not really."

"You change your mind you just let me know." He got down on the floor of his cramped bedroom and began playing with the cats. Every inch of wall space was painted with overlapping and highly unorthodox murals—Jesus shooting hoops, Jesus officiating Lupo and Jasmine's wedding, Jesus sharing a Slurpee with the Apostles— while canvasses were stacked in rows against the walls. The air smelled of incense and deodorant and I noticed a pile of girlie magazines by the bed. "Well, I got news," he said.

"What's that?" I tried to summon enthusiasm.

"She finally talked to me."

"Jasmine?"

He nodded proudly. "She said she'd never seen anyone who drank so many Slurpees."

"And?"

"And what?"

"And what else did she say?"

"Give me a break, there were a lot of customers."

"Well, I guess it's a start."

"Hell yes it is! I'm on her radar now."

"Congratulations."

"Thanks."

I picked up the litter box. "I need to get home."

"There's one more thing."

"She's pregnant?"

"HA. HA. HA." Then he paused, his thin eyebrows drawing together. "The thing is, I've been thinking about what we could do with these cats and I've got a solution."

"Do I want to hear this?"

"What I was thinking was that maybe I'd take them."

"You? You hate cats."

"Most cats. Ninety-nine percent of cats. But these cats are different." He picked up Snowball and lifted her above him. "They're more like little dogs."

"And you like little dogs?"

"*Yes!*"

"It's a lot of responsibility."

"Hey, I'm a skunk of Jesus, remember?"

I watched Lupo lower Snowball down to his face and give her a nuzzle. "Okay," I said.

"Really?"

"They're yours—as long as you take good care of them."

"That is *so* great."

CHAPTER
SIX

THAT CHRISTMAS I took Lupo with me to St. Louis to visit
Aunt Margaret. Her French had improved markedly and she spent
hours teaching him phrases as she sat for a portrait in her finest blue
dress with a large yellow scarf tossed recklessly around her neck and
enormous gold hoops making a taffy-pull of her freckled earlobes.

It was Lupo's idea to place her along the banks of the Seine, the
Eiffel Tower in the distance. (I dug up some photos to help him.)
When she saw the painting tears of joy came down her cheeks.

All she could say was, *"I knew it."*

CHAPTER
SEVEN

SOMETIMES I CAN feel Shannon thinking of me. I don't know how but I can. I'm sure she can feel me thinking of her, too. Maybe that's the secret of what keeps the world together, like dark matter that can only be inferred. There's no shortage of love, it's just that a lot of it has no choice but to remain invisible.

It would explain a great many things.

PART FIVE

FOUR YEARS LATER

CHAPTER
ONE

And in the last hours
of dreaming
we shall paint our love
silently
beautifully
and eternally
to the sea

I SPENT AN hour trying to find the road north out of Florence, sweat rolling down my face and onto the map spread out on my lap as I tried to make out the passing clamor of signs. The car I'd rented was so small that it was questionable just who ought to carry whom, but as soon as I'd pulled out onto the packed and narrow roads I was glad for every inch of clearance. Unfortunately, I'd failed to realize that air-conditioning was extra and even at eight in the morning the July heat hugged me like a hot compress. I rolled down the window, then rolled it back up when the outside air seemed even warmer. What a sweaty thing human history must have been.

After two near collisions I was about ready to give up (though precisely how wasn't exactly clear as I'd never find my way back to the rental agency), when a series of one-way turns forced me onto an on-ramp that funneled me onto a fast moving motorway heading north. *Hallelujah.* I gunned the engine to keep pace in the slow lane as cars shot past on my left. Once I was confident that the car could maintain a sufficient speed to avoid being rear-ended without flying apart I began to enjoy the passing scenery, imagining a previous generation fighting for every yard, the heavily defended Apennines looming ahead.

With luck—lots of it—I'd reach San Gianello in two hours.

Lupo and I had landed in Rome six days earlier, fulfilling a promise I'd made on the day he got an acceptance letter to college—and agreed to go. Now a sophomore majoring in art at the University of Georgia, he wanted to spend another day in the Uffizi Gallery (the combination of beautiful art, women and food had whipped him into a state of fervent bliss) and frankly, I preferred to make the trip alone.

I knew that someday I'd visit. Over the years I'd constructed my own visual layout of the piazza and the church and the house as well as the garage with the small window overlooking the valley below. I often thought of the cave, too, wondering whether children still played inside or if it had vanished from local memory, reclaimed by time. But most of all I thought of Alessandra, hoping she had somehow managed to strike a truce with the memory of a day that had turned into years.

She was always much younger in my mind, not an elderly widow interred in the fierce solitude of her Wyoming ranch house but a strong-headed seventeen-year-old who lost her heart to the fury of men. Her sun-beaten face became smooth and supple again, her warm brown eyes grew bright and her arthritic limbs were once more lithe and graceful. And she was always running, her long black hair trailing in the wind as she raced barefoot through the olive groves to warn her lover.

Run, Alessandra.

I often meant to call or write her, each time hesitating for reasons I couldn't shake. Yet I never forgot her story, which I'd come to think of as a sort of chromatic scale of the very best and worst possibilities of life. And sometimes in my dreams it wasn't Shannon that I fell in love with but the young Alessandra. Or maybe I just liked knowing that lovers like her and Johann really existed, if only momentarily before the world destroyed them.

I drove another hour before I saw a sign for the road to San Gianello. I slowed the car, surprised by a sudden feeling of anxiousness, as if by exploring the past I might somehow disturb it. Then I thought of Shannon, wondering how often she still thought of me and whether she'd found enough love to fill all the gaps she'd inherited. I stuck my arm out the window and let the wind stream through my fingers as I remembered the flight home from San Francisco to Atlanta, face to the window because only the clouds seemed to understand, and then the hours spent by the phone, my mouth filling with words I would never speak; or lying awake in bed feeling the memory of her touch against my skin. And then gradually as the months passed I found a way to live without her because that's one thing I knew how to do. But I still loved her, or at least I loved all the possibilities I'd briefly held in my arms, our few days together like delicate fragments of pottery from which an archeologist painstakingly infers a once breathtaking whole. The question I never could answer was whether it was worth finding what you'd most been looking for even if you couldn't have it.

But who gets the choice?

I made a series of tight turns as the road climbed up the broad hillside past freshly tilled fields, the earth carved into large fertile chunks. On the left I came upon the first houses, their yards and windows strung with so many sagging clotheslines that they looked like tattered ships-of-the-line returned from battle. When I passed a dense forest on my right I wondered if the German supply base had been located nearby. Would I be able to pick out Alessandra's house? Would the garage still be standing and would I see the courtyard where her father had been killed?

I drove into the center of town and parked near the piazza, pleased at how undeveloped everything looked—except for the satellite dishes that clung like mushrooms to the red-tiled rooftops. I got out and leaned against the side of the car, filling my lungs with the citrus-laced air as I watched three boys on their bicycles ride past, a small dog following frantically behind. From an open second floor window an elderly woman stared down at me, her narrow features pursed with age. I looked up and smiled but she didn't smile back. From her expression I knew with certainty that she would continue to watch me for as long as I remained in her line of sight, though I couldn't tell whether she was motivated more from suspicion or boredom or perhaps some ancient mixture of the two. I gave her one more smile before locking the car and heading off, aiming for the church at the top of the village where I hoped to orient myself.

I'd only gone a few hundred yards when I saw the first rough chiseling of shrapnel against the side of a house, and above that a row of smaller indentations from rifle or machinegun fire. I'd noticed the same markings in several other towns and wondered how many others still noticed too. As I traced my finger along several of the holes I tried to imagine the desperate Germans withdrawing as the Americans approached, the front rolling like fire. And yet the village seemed unassailably tranquil. Then I thought of the old woman who had stared down at me and wondered what else she had seen and whether there were times when her memory stretched farther than her heart could manage.

I followed a narrow lane past rows of houses, then rejoined the main road as it climbed toward the church. I started in the cemetery, wandering among the darkened stones. Near the far corner I came to a sudden stop: *Antonio Mariani, 1889-1944*. Alessandra's father. I thought of the proud and handsome mechanic carrying his little sleepy mouse back to the house in his great big oil-stained hands. "The world is full of too many talkers, eh, Mouse?" I read the next name: *Stephano Mariani 1923-1944*. And the next: *Marcello Mariani 1919-1952*. And lastly: *Rosetta Mariani 1890-1954*. Her mother. But what about Renaldo? I followed the row to the end but found nothing. Perhaps it was too difficult to ever give up hope.

Before entering the church I climbed a narrow path that rose to a small promontory littered with the ruins of an ancient structure.

Was this where the miracles were believed to have taken place? I looked out over the long valley and tried to picture clouds of dust rising from great convoys of Germans and then Americans. How many other once mighty armies had passed by on their thunderous march to oblivion?

I spent several minutes walking among the piles of stones trying to make out the foundation, then followed another path that led to a much smaller cemetery marked with a low wooden fence. From the uniform white crosses I knew immediately they were American soldiers. I counted eighteen graves in all, reading the names one by one until I found the two I was looking for: Rick Allers and Ben Wallerstein, buried side by side. I thought of the photo above Mike's bed. How did Alessandra live with those young faces all those years? Or did she see it as part of her penance?

Inside the church the still air was damp with the slightly mournful smell I'd come to expect (even anticipate) whenever I entered an Italian church. Three elderly women in black knelt near the front while at the back a young worker stood on a ladder scrubbing the soot from the darkened stained-glass windows. I sat in the last pew and stared up at Jesus on the cross, imagining all the unanswered prayers still crowding the ceiling like flies in a vast spider's web. Had they made any difference?

I closed my eyes, smiling at the smallness of my life, one tiny vibration in a universe sparking with destiny. And yet even in our trembling solitude we sense a secret promise in our hearts, a promise vast and luminous that beckons us onward.

And so we pray.

I opened my eyes and watched the worker climb down from the ladder, surprised to see from his collar that he was the priest, though he looked no older than twenty. He smiled and I smiled back, thinking of Alessandra's stories about Father Gregorio and all the years it took him to find his voice.

"You're American?" he asked, offering his hand. His smooth face was smudged with soot.

"I am."

"Welcome to our church."

"Thank you."

"Is this your first time in San Gianello?"

"Yes, it's a lovely town."

"I think so too." He smiled again.

"Were you raised here?"

"No, Arezzo. I've only been here one month." He gave a wave as the three elderly women approached us. "They haven't had a priest here for three years; we have a shortage these days."

"I imagine you'll be busy," I said.

"Yes, I believe so," he said with a wink as the women encircled him in a flurry of Italian.

After I left the church I headed back down the road to the piazza where small children ran around the fountain and covered their faces with ice cream while their mothers watched from the shaded chairs of a café. I couldn't help noticing how happy everybody looked, as if the whole point of life was to reach this precise moment in this exact place. I tried to imagine the continuity of their lives, surrounded each day by the proud and time-bleached architecture of their forbearers, past and present gracefully blended, and yet I couldn't. I could only envy them.

I walked up to the fountain and dipped my finger in the water, then sat along the edge thinking how glad I was that I'd made the drive from Florence (and hoping that Lupo wasn't getting into too much trouble). Suddenly a young boy in only his underwear approached and started to splash me with great enthusiasm, causing profuse and unintelligible apologies from his mother. I waved her off with a smile, then rose and made my way slowly around the square. I passed a school and a grocery before stopping at a bakery where I purchased a small loaf of *rustica* and a bottle of water. Was it the same bakery? Were these Alessandra's relatives? I briefly caught a pretty young woman's eye and decided that her shy smile was answer enough.

From the piazza I headed south down the main road, hoping I might be able to pick out Alessandra's house from her description. As I walked I carefully examined each building, wondering how many had been destroyed in the war. When I passed an elderly man, age hung on him like a harness he was tired of pulling, I thought to inquire about Alessandra's family but decided not to, fearing the need for explanations. Besides, my Italian was not nearly up to the task.

I'd gone almost a mile when I saw it. I knew right away from the courtyard and the cypress trees and, most of all, the garage, which was larger and taller than the others. The house itself needed paint and several cracks ran along the walls but otherwise it looked well tended, with yellow and blue flowers bursting from large terracotta pots and white wooden boxes. To the east an olive grove stretched toward the wooded mountains that rose above the town.

At first I just stood across the road and stared, surprised by the force of my reaction. I looked up at a small window high on the garage and imagined Alessandra peering out, the world still full of wonder. Then I imagined the sounds of Antonio hammering away and an engine sputtering to life and columns of Germans marching passed, boots pounding the earth in unison, and then Johann pulling up on his motorcycle and knocking on the door, his kind face drawn with the agony of a man who can no longer find himself. How quickly time devours everything, as if our souls were mere plankton intended to nourish some greater force. I looked over at the courtyard, my eyes searching for the spot where Alessandra's father was shot and where she held him in her arms.

But now, only silence.

I began to back away, then changed my mind and opened the small gate, quickly crossing the courtyard. At the front door I hesitated briefly, then knocked, first lightly, then harder. I was about to leave when I heard a voice and the sound of approaching footsteps. A moment later the door opened.

It was Shannon.

Neither of us spoke at first. It was easier to let the silence bound back and forth until nervous smiles came to our faces. She looked noticeably older, time beginning to tug at the corners of her eyes and her mouth. And yet she still looked beautiful.

After a moment she stepped out into the sunlight. "Mom always said you'd come one day. I didn't believe her."

"I don't mean to intrude… I was just in Florence and I thought… I never expected to see you here."

She gave her shoulders a shrug. "I never expected to be here."

More silence, which lingered around our faces before falling to the ground.

"Is your mother here too?" I asked.

"She was. She came here—home—not long after Dad died." Shannon paused. "She passed away four months ago."

"I'm so sorry."

Shannon looked away, one arm resting on the doorsill. "She was diagnosed with breast cancer a year after she moved back. When she got worse I joined her to help out. Guess I finally got my chance to be needed." Shannon brushed a few hairs from her forehead. "And for some reason I haven't left."

I turned and looked over at the garage, wishing I could sit for a minute. "I always meant to call her but I never did."

"She spoke of you often. I think she was more proud of you than she was of me."

I looked up at the house, feeling glad that at least Alessandra had come home. And yet how difficult it must have been. Did the ghosts ever leave her alone or was it their company she had sought?

"Is this yours now?" I asked.

She nodded, leaning against the door frame. "Can you believe it? All those years and I never even knew she owned it. It was rented out."

"It's beautiful."

"Do you want to come in? Better yet, let's sit outside." Without waiting for a reply she slipped past me and headed around the side of the house to a stone courtyard where several wooden chairs and a table overlooked the olive grove. To my surprise a small elderly man sat in a chair beneath a large Ficus tree, a black beret perched on his gray head.

"I'd like you to meet Pietro," Shannon said, watching for my reaction.

Pietro rose very slowly to his feet and shook my hand, both of us exchanging smiles. "*Piacere,*" I said, using one of the few Italian greetings I could confidently pronounce.

"He can't hear much anymore," said Shannon. "Actually, I think he prefers it that way."

"Well, it's nice to meet him."

Pietro kept shaking my hand and smiling. He was considerably shorter than Shannon and missing several teeth but his eyes were light and agile, undefeated by age.

"He lives near the piazza," said Shannon. "He likes to sit here and look at the olive trees and the valley. He comes every day."

"I'm honored," I said, still shaking his hand.

"He wrote the letters," said Shannon, helping Pietro back into his chair. "But that's all it was. Just letters."

Pietro kept smiling, then finally released my hand and eased himself back into his chair.

"But why, even after she got married?"

"Because he's loved her since he was a little boy and he loves her still. He never asked for anything in return. I guess he just had to keep telling her how much he loved her."

"Do you think she loved him?"

"How could she not? But it wasn't romance. I think it was something…" she seemed to search for the right words, "*less complicated.* They went on walks every day and often sat here holding hands or playing cards. It was the sweetest thing I've ever seen. He was with her when she died. We both were."

She gave Pietro a kiss on the cheek and then walked over to the picnic table and sat against the edge. I sat next to her but not too close.

"So you're here on vacation?" she asked.

"Just for a week. I'm staying in Florence. I couldn't resist seeing San Gianello."

"Is it anything like you expected?"

"More than I can believe." I looked again at Pietro, awed by the proud beauty of a heart so freighted with time's fragile cargo.

"That's how I felt."

We both stared at the rows of olive trees that fanned up the slope to the woods. Were they the same trees that Alessandra confided in as a child?

"Are you going to keep the house?" I asked.

"We haven't decided yet—Brian and Melissa flew home to San Francisco last week. He's been commuting back and forth since I moved. It hasn't been easy for him."

I looked over at Pietro again. He sat perfectly still, hands resting on his thighs and eyes just barely opened as he stared straight ahead, a slight smile etched into his heavily lined face. What did he see?

"I should be getting back to Florence soon," I said, looking at my watch.

"But you haven't seen the cave."

"You know where it is?"

"Of course I do." She put her hand on mine. "You can't leave without seeing it." She smiled, then got up and started for the house. "Come on inside and we'll pack something to drink and some flashlights."

"What about Pietro?"

"He's not alone. He never is. We won't be long."

Twenty minutes later we were crossing through the olive grove and toward the woods that ran up the mountain, following the path that Alessandra took to meet her German lover.

I didn't see the entrance at first, not until we left the trail and climbed up through heavy brush and then past several large boulders that pushed out of the hillside.

"There it is," Shannon said, pointing as we reached the small ledge. I stared at the narrow opening, then turned and looked past the clearing at the valley below as I imagined Alessandra and Johann sitting side by side and dreaming of a life that could never be.

"Kind of intense, isn't it?" said Shannon, drawing up alongside me. "The first time Mom brought me here I could feel the hair standing up on the back of my neck." She took my hand. "Come on, it's not haunted."

I followed her into the damp air until we were about ten feet inside the entrance where the ceiling rose to a height of nearly eight feet.

"Johann's buried here," she said.

I looked down at the ground.

"So is Mom, or at least most of her. I scattered the rest of her ashes on the graves of her parents and brother. That's what she wanted." Shannon reached down and took a handful of soil, letting it run through her fingers. Then she aimed a flashlight at the rock face. "Look at this."

I stared at the names carved letter by letter: *Alessandra, Stephano, Marcello, Renaldo.* And then off to one side in smaller, more angular script: *Johann.*

"I feel like I'm intruding," I said.

"I used to feel that way too, but then I decided they probably enjoy visitors." She gave me a wink.

I squatted down next to her and pressed my hands against the rock, then traced each letter of Alessandra's name with my fingertip as I pictured the young girl being initiated into her brothers' secret club, heart pounding at the mysterious thrill of it.

"Mom came here almost every day until she could no longer make the hike. I think she felt closer to them here." Shannon placed her hand on the rock face next to mine. "Sometimes I think she felt them sitting right beside her." She aimed the flashlight at the back of the cave, where the ceiling dropped gradually to the ground. I followed the light until I was forced to my knees and when I could go no further I reached out with my hand and ran it along a narrow seam.

"I can feel it," I said.

"Feel what?"

"The breeze. She said there was always a breeze coming from the back of the cave."

Shannon crawled until she was alongside me, then reached out her hand. "Yes, I feel it too. Where do you suppose it comes from?"

"There must be an opening somewhere—or maybe it's the breath of angels." I gave her a smile, my face just inches from hers, then backed up until I could stand. As I reached the entrance I squinted in the light, trying to imagine the awful scene in the clearing below as Alessandra emerged from the cave, the acrid smell of gunfire still in the air.

Shannon came up alongside of me. "Pietro saw what happened. He was here that day."

"I don't understand."

She sat down on the ledge. "He followed her to the cave. With the Americans coming he'd decided to hide in the olive grove near our house to make sure Mom was okay. When she ran out of the house and into the woods he followed her. He saw what happened."

"Did he tell anyone?"

"No, never. He would have done anything to protect her." She paused, looking straight at me. "She didn't tell us the truth, Ryan. She didn't tell us everything."

"What are you saying?"

Shannon reached into the knapsack she'd brought and pulled out an envelope. "She wanted to take her secret with her but Pietro wouldn't let her because he'd seen what it had done to her over the years." Shannon paused, staring down at the envelope. "He didn't want her carrying it all the way to heaven. So they agreed that she would write me a letter." She handed the envelope to me. "Pietro gave it to me after she died. I thought, well, since you're here... I thought you'd want to read it."

CHAPTER
TWO

My Dearest Shannon,

I've written this letter to you so many times in my mind that I no longer remember where I meant to start, except to say that I love you, and not just from the farthest reaches of my own heart but from the boundless depths of all those who loved me because I've come to believe that love gathers strength like water rushing to the sea (and that may be the greatest hope for all of us). So never forget that should your own strength ever fail, you can always call upon ours because those who have loved you are never farther away than your own beating heart.

All morning I've been watching you through my bedroom window as I write. You're down in the garden and you look so lovely that I think my father must be smiling down at us both with joy. And now as you read these words we are both smiling down at you. I believe we shall smile for a very long time.

But I can't rest yet. Not until I find the words to finish this letter. You see, I've decided (with some convincing by Pietro) that the truth—all of it—is better left with the living, perhaps because only they have the courage to bear it. All these years I thought I was protecting you but I failed. And I failed your father, too. I don't expect your forgiveness. I only ask that you take from me what is good for you and leave the rest behind. It doesn't belong to you.

Now for the last time I must return to the day the Americans arrived in San Gianello because that is where all the mistakes of my life began. Perhaps it will be easier for you to read what follows if you understand that it is not your mother alone who holds this pen but a young and foolish girl as well. (Already I feel her soft hand on mine, a hand much like yours.) Yes, we must tell our story together, this girl and I. We must tell our story so that we may finally leave each other in peace.

Sometimes in my sleep I still feel my legs straining up the path to the cave, never quite fast enough. Run, I tell myself. Run! I was sure that I could arrange for Johann's surrender if only I could get there in time. Then he would be safe until the war ended and we could be together again. What other choice was there? But I knew he would never surrender on his own, not if it meant being taken away from me and confined in a faraway place where he couldn't breathe. And so I had to get to him before the Americans did. I had to.

The woods and canyons were filled with the sound of gunfire. Looking back I could see smoke rising from the valley while on the south side of the village two houses burned. Somehow I'd always imagined the front as a neat line that would roll up like a carpet but now I understood it was more like an earthquake fissuring in every direction. I couldn't even be sure on which side of the front San Gianello now stood.

I made the last turn up the path and crossed the clearing below the cave. I was almost at the entrance when I saw a movement in the woods out of the corner of my eye. As Johann rushed out to meet me I quickly pulled him back inside.

"Someone's out there," I said, trying to catch my breath. My eyes burned with the realization that I'd given away his hiding place. "To the left in the trees. I saw someone. Maybe two people. I only caught a glimpse. Maybe if I talk to them…"

"They must be Germans. Six of them spent the night so close I could hear them talking. They're lost."

"The Americans are just south of the village."

"Yes," he said softy. "It's here." His hand brushed against Papa's pistol, which was tucked in his belt. "But you should never have come. Now quickly crawl as far back in the cave as you can while I take a look."

I tried to stop him but he was already near the entrance, crouched with the pistol drawn. Slowly he peered out until his head and shoulders were in the sunlight.

A single shot rang out, striking the rock face just above him. He scrambled back to where I was hiding. "They think we're partisans. Listen to me, Alessandra. I'm going to identify myself. I'll explain that I was separated from my unit."

"But they may shoot you for desertion."

"Right now they'll only want to save their skins. I can show them through the canyon. They'll need me. Then you can escape."

"You'll be forced to retreat with them—even to fight again. If we just wait for the Americans..."

"There's no choice." He took my face in his hands. "I'll be back. I promise."

"But—"

"Shh." He put his finger to my lips. "You must crawl as far back as you can and lie down and cover yourself with dirt. Don't move until dark, do you understand?"

I nodded.

He helped cover me, working quickly, then hurried back to the entrance. I heard him call out in German. There was silence, and he called out again. More silence, then voices just beyond the entrance.

"They're speaking English," I said, raising my head. "They're Americans!" I started to get up when I heard something strike the ground near where Johann crouched.

A grenade.

Johann snatched it up and flung it back out of the cave. Moments later it exploded, followed immediately by terrible screams. Please God, no, I prayed.

"I surrender!" yelled Johann, first in German, then in Italian as he dropped the pistol and ran into the daylight, hands in the air.

I heard voices shouting in English as I hurried forward until I reached a point where I could look out without being seen. Johann stood with his hands raised while two Americans, one of them bleeding from the side of his face, aimed their rifles at him. A third American lay motionless on the ground.

I dropped to my stomach and crawled out of the cave and around a boulder, fearing they'd search the cave next. Moments later I heard something strike the ground deep inside the cave.

"Alessandra!" cried Johann.

I covered my ears just as another grenade exploded.

As soon as my head stopped hurting from the explosion I peered around the boulder until I could see Johann, who kept screaming my name over and over and trying to reach the cave as the two GIs beat him to the ground with their rifles. The Americans had their backs to me and as Johann rose again to his knees I waved my hand.

Everything changed in his face when he saw me. He might even have smiled but I couldn't tell because he was covered with so much blood. One of the Americans raised his foot and kicked Johann in the stomach, knocking him back to the ground. Then both Americans kicked at his body again and again.

I knew then that they were going to kill him. What possibility was there to find the goodness in their hearts, to explain that Johann was not like other Germans and that he didn't mean to hurt their comrade and that if they killed him they might as well kill me, too? I quickly crawled back into the cave and picked up my father's pistol, then worked my way back to a position behind the boulder.

One of the Americans shouted something in English as he grabbed Johann by the collar and lifted him up to his knees. Slowly Johann raised his hands above his face and pleaded for his life, first in German and then in Italian.

When Johann saw the gun in my hand he began to shake his head no. He started to speak but stopped himself and yet I knew what he meant to tell me: Don't, Alessandra. Please save yourself and that will be enough for the both of us.

One of the Americans shouted again at Johann, then physically forced him to turn around. The Americans slowly leveled their rifles at the back of Johann's head.

I was only twenty feet away when I fired. I hit the first American square in the back. As the second soldier spun around in surprise I fired at him once then twice and then two more times at the first soldier until the pistol would fire no more.

And then silence.

Even before I let the pistol drop from my hand I knew there had been another shot. I heard it just as I was first squeezing the trigger. Or was it right after I shot the first soldier? I wanted to believe it wasn't possible, that I had acted in time. But when I looked at Johann he was crumpled face forward on the ground, blood running from the back of his head.

"Johann!" I ran to him crying. "Johann, no!"

I knew he would never answer. I knew because all the pain and sadness was gone from his face, his features as smooth and relaxed as a boy's. A boy without any more fears. A boy who could now sleep soundly, his sisters and mother and father safe again, all the far flung pieces of the world put back together.

As I held him in my arms I realized that it was my own heart I was holding, that the sweet bright blood spilling into the earth was my blood, my life, my dreams. I was alive and dead at the same time, cleaved in two by a blade forged of fate.

Please don't leave me here alone.

And then I went to the Americans one by one, moving as if my own skin was draped upon a ghost. The two I had shot were dead. You killed them. *As I looked in their empty faces all I could think of was their mothers kissing them goodnight and praying each evening for their safe return.* What have you done?

When I approached the third American I saw his hand move and he let out a weak cry. I quickly bent down beside him and took his hand and spoke to him gently in Italian. "We didn't mean to hurt you," I said, desperate for him to live. "We didn't mean to hurt anybody."

Suddenly the American opened his eyes and gripped my hand, his face tightening with fear. "It's okay," I whispered, gently stroking his arm. He had a young face, younger even than Johann's, with wide cheeks and freckles. As he squeezed my hand harder I realized he was holding on to me as though I were life itself.

"Hold on," I whispered. "Keep holding on to me."

Suddenly I felt a hand on my shoulder. I looked up and saw Pietro. Yes, my very short but very brave protector had followed me into the woods that morning. I knew immediately that he'd seen everything.

"I've killed them," I cried. "I've murdered them."

"No, Alessandra. Listen to me." He gripped me firmly as he spoke. "You and I were hiding in the woods, we heard shots and when we got here, this is what we found. Do you understand?" He turned to the sound of voices coming up the path from our village. "Do you understand, Alessandra?"

I nodded, feeling I might faint as I watched him pick up my father's pistol from the ground and place it beside Johann.

Moments later Carlo Manucci and Giacomo Andreone came running up the hill followed by four other men from the village, all armed with an assortment of pistols and rifles.

"What happened?"

"Are you all right?"

"We were in the woods hiding," said Pietro. "We heard shots. This American is still alive. We must take him to the village quickly."

The men nervously aimed their rifles at the surrounding trees until satisfying themselves that the Germans were gone, then walked among the bodies.

Manucci bent over Johann. "Wait a minute. I know who this is. It's that young German—the translator. Now what the hell was his name?"

The others leaned over the body. "Johann," said Andreone. "His name was Johann. We used to play Briscola. And he did card tricks for the children."

All the men stared down at Johann's body.

"What a pity," said Manucci. "The only good German in the bunch."

"Wasn't he raised in Italy?" said Andreone.

"No, he was a German all right," said Manucci. "But he had the heart of an Italian."

I went back later that night to bury Johann's body, which had been left where he fell because no one knew what to do with him. The mountains were still full of the sound of gunfire and artillery—the Germans had attempted a counteroffensive—but I didn't care. I no longer cared about anything but finding a place to bury my own heart.

It took me nearly an hour to drag his body up the slope and into the cave. He was much lighter than I expected, as if death had robbed him of all it could carry. But still I could barely manage. Once I finally reached the ledge I stopped to rest, then pulled him through the entrance. After I laid him out as gently as I could I began to dig, telling him over and over again how much I loved him.

At first I couldn't bear to cover him with dirt. How could I never look upon his face again? How could I smother the man I loved with cold, dark earth? How could I give him back so soon? Finally, in tears, I covered his face with a piece of cloth I tore from my dress, then slowly placed a handful of dirt upon his chest. After a few minutes I let another handful slide through my fingers, then another and another until I'd covered his entire body with a thin layer of soil. Then I picked up the shovel and began to work faster until my arms shook with exhaustion, feeling with each shovelful the gathering weight of the earth upon my chest as well.

When I finished I dropped to my knees and pressed my lips to the soil before hurrying home through the last hour of darkness.

We cared for the wounded GI in our house for three days, afraid to move him as he struggled for life. We couldn't get any medical supplies because the fighting was too fierce—several times our house was hit by rifle fire—but once the Americans finally secured the area they set up a small hospital nearby where I went to visit him every day, praying that he wouldn't die because somehow I felt that his death would haunt Johann's soul as well. As he began to recover he liked to take my hand and hold it for hours at a time, staring at me with those big green American eyes of his as though I were the one who'd saved him. He didn't remember anything about the day he was wounded but once he could talk he kept asking about his friends until finally I had to tell him that they were dead. He didn't speak for the rest of the day.

Eventually he was sent to a larger hospital in Rome and as he got better he began to write, asking me to visit. I made several trips, volunteering to help care for the wounded and even thinking I might study to become a nurse. And then one day as we sat together in the courtyard of the hospital he asked me to marry him and I said yes because I couldn't say no. I can't explain why I accepted. I felt so numb inside that I had no hopes for my own happiness. But I thought that maybe if I could make someone else happy, that if I could bring some joy to this kind young American soldier, then perhaps in some small way that would make up for what I had done. I was the one who broke his heart so why shouldn't I be the one to try to mend it? And I couldn't stay in San Gianello, not after all that had happened. I wanted to go as far away as I could and here was a man who would take me to a place I'd never even heard of before.

But of course it wasn't far enough. It never is.

There is one last thing I have to tell you and I think it may be the most important thing of all. In the weeks and months after your grandfather died—and I loved him more than anything in life—I heard his voice in my head as clear as if he was standing right next to me. And do you know what he said? He said, "Alessandra, always remember that I fit perfectly in your heart. Don't even think of trying to carry me on your back."

I only ask the same of you.

I love you always,

Mom

CHAPTER
THREE

———

"YOUR PARENTS WOULD still be alive," Shannon said as I handed her back the letter. "If none of this had happened, if things had turned out differently that day, they would still be alive."

"It's all... finished," I said.

"I wish I felt it was finished," she said, folding the letter carefully and placing it back in the envelope. "I can understand why my mother tried to save Johann—but the lies, and marrying my father without loving him, and all those years I never understood her because she wouldn't let me. She wouldn't let anybody understand her."

"Maybe she did the best she could. Maybe they all did."

Shannon's eyes filled with tears. I began to reach for her and then stopped myself. It took everything I had.

We spent another hour sitting together on the ledge, both careful with our words because of where they might lead. I had so many things I wanted to say but I knew there was no right way to say them and never would be; anything but silence would stray from the truth.

"Are you still teaching that writing class?" she asked.

"Actually, I got my credential. I teach English literature at a high school. It's the last thing I would have imagined for myself but the truth is, I love it. Nothing like a good story to remind kids that they're not so different and not so alone after all."

"What about your own writing?"

"I seem to be better at inspiring others."

"But now you have your story." She looked back at the names carved into the rock.

"It's not my story to tell," I said.

"Yes it is, and you're the only one who can tell it."

"What you don't know is that most of my stories end very badly. The fact is, I don't even like to read them."

"Then you'll just have to keep your characters safe."

"I would if I knew how."

She looked at me for a long time, then ran her fingers along the dirt floor. For a moment I thought she was drawing something but before I could make it out she wiped it away.

After a few more minutes I rose to my feet. "We should probably go."

"Yes, you have to drive back." She stood and brushed off her pants.

"Thank you for bringing me here."

"You won't tell anyone where it is?"

"Cross my heart."

She smiled but there was no joy in her face.

We said goodbye at the front gate. The sun was low in the sky, spilling her last colors upon the gathering clouds.

"I hope you enjoy the rest of your vacation," she said.

"I'm sure I will."

She rocked nervously on the balls of her feet. "Maybe I'll see you again sometime."

"Yes, maybe you will."

We passed through the gate and stood by the side of the road.

"I hate goodbyes," she said, her eyes swelling.

"Me, too."

She stepped forward and gave me a hug, backing away before I could get my hands around her.

"Take care of yourself," she said.

Before I could say anything she gave a little wave and turned and walked quickly back toward the house.

"Shannon?"

She stopped.

"Are you happy?"

She turned to face me. "Why are you asking me that?"

"I need to know."

She paused, her hands looking for a place to go. "I'm happy enough."

"What does that mean?"

"It's not a fair question."

"It's the only question."

"No, you're wrong. Life is not that simple."

"But I think it is. I really think it is."

She didn't respond.

"Just tell me that you haven't given up. That's all I need to know. Tell me that and I'll leave."

"Ryan, *please*." She started to say more when from behind her Pietro appeared, shuffling slowly as he made his way along the path that lead from the side courtyard to the front of the house.

"It's time for him to go home," Shannon said. She gave Pietro a smile and then took his hand and helped him across the white paving stones toward the front gate. "I walk him back to his house every day."

"I'll walk him home," I said.

She looked surprised.

"Please, I'd like to."

She looked at Pietro, then back at me. Pietro smiled warmly at both of us.

"Well, I don't see why not." She let go of his hand and I took it. He gave me a wink as he shuffled up next to me, his head not even cresting my shoulders.

"He lives just off the piazza. He knows the way."

"Got it."

"You'll have to walk slowly."

"I promise."

She leaned forward and kissed Pietro on both cheeks, filling his face with color. Then she quickly kissed me before stepping back. I could see she was trying not to cry.

"We'll be off then," I said as Pietro and I began to walk, his feet just barely leaving the ground with each step. We hadn't gone far when Pietro stopped to turn back and wave at Shannon, who stood watching from the gate. And then when she was no longer in sight Pietro stopped once more and looked up at me, his hand squeezing mine. For a moment he looked confused and I wondered if he'd forgotten who I was. But then he gave me a smile and continued on, his hand still gripping mine with a child's trust.

As we walked he began to speak in Italian, first so softly that I thought he was mumbling to himself and then louder until his voice was full of strength. I tried to explain that I didn't understand but he just kept talking, looking up at me now and then to be sure I was listening. Several times I heard Alessandra's name and I found myself nodding as I wondered if he was trying to tell me how he once walked her home down this very road or about the day so many years ago when she saved his life. Or maybe he just wanted to tell me how much he missed her.

It took us nearly forty minutes to reach the piazza. As we approached I noticed the old woman still perched in her second floor window, but this time she smiled and waved and Pietro waved back. "Mama," he explained to me with an embarrassed shrug. When I tried to walk him to the door he stopped me. Then he began to speak again, repeating himself over and over as he grabbed me by both arms and shook me, his lean, gray face now trembling. And then with a force that surprised me he placed both of his small hands on my chest and began to push me back in the direction of the House that Grief Built.

EPILOGUE

—————

November 16, 1945

Dearest Rebecca,

This is my very last letter to you because if I write any more I just may have to open them myself. That's right, my love, I'm coming home.

I keep thinking what it'll be like to get my arms around you again but the truth is I can't even imagine something so fine. After what I've been through I didn't think anything on this earth would ever make me nervous again but I was wrong. I'm already nervous and I've still got another two thousand miles to go. (And I'm counting every single one.) By the time I cross those last few feet I ought to be a sight to behold.

I know you promised that you'd wait for me but deep inside I didn't dare believe it, not more than one letter at a time. And now that the waiting is almost over I find myself wondering how I ever got to be the luckiest man on this earth. All I can say is, it's going to be awfully good to see you again. I've thought about every inch of you so often I'm not sure I can bear to look at you for more than a few minutes at a time without needing to catch my breath. But, by God, I'm going to try.

We had a prayer service today for all the men we've left behind. You've never seen such a beautiful morning, all the clouds circling above like regal swans on a bright blue pond, their shadows skipping over this hungry ocean as the sun warmed our wet faces. (And there were plenty.) There wasn't a man on deck who didn't ask himself why he was spared. I don't think any of us had answers but I know we made a lot of silent covenants. I like to think we'll keep them but only time will tell.

I've done a lot of thinking since I saw you last, but I'm not sure I'm any closer to the understanding I seek and sometimes I think I'm a little further. I know I've changed (and I expect you've changed too), but I hope that the best parts of myself are still intact. I'll leave that for you to decide.

There are so many things I want us to talk about, things that have been piling up inside of me for months now. And yet I fear that all my words are going to fail me for a good while, so if I seem a little quiet I don't want you to think that I'm anywhere but right beside you.

Truth is, I've always been at your side and I always will be. Of all the lessons I have learned these hard years, that is surely the finest. Some might call it grace. Me, I think of it as destiny.

There is one thing I can tell you from all that I have seen and that is that this aching world needs all the joy and laughter that you and I can give it. I think it's time we got started.

Yours forever and always,

Jim